The world is changing quickly for Chris now that he's part of the Immortal Community. With the events of his past finally behind him, he's still having visions and true magic is gradually taking hold in the world. Chris is still new and has no real standing in the Immortal Community, but he is learning that nothing is what he thought.

Old enemies must work together and longtime friends may not be trustworthy. With Juliet, Amanda, and Kirtus by his side, they have to prevent the immortal and witch community from being exposed.

New friendships are made, and longtime alliances are called into question. How will The Called defeat these latest threats, and what does it mean for the world?

THE CALLED

The Calling, Book Two

M.D. Neu

A NineStar Press Publication

Published by NineStar Press
P.O. Box 91792,
Albuquerque, New Mexico, 87199 USA.
www.ninestarpress.com

The Called

Printed in the USA
First Edition
April, 2021

Print ISBN: 978-1-64890-261-1

Also available in eBook, ISBN: 978-1-64890-260-4

WARNING: This book contains sexually explicit content, which may only be suitable for mature readers. Depictions of graphic violence.

For my biggest fan and my harshest critic.

Chapter One

The question of death returned to me as I reflected on recent events. You die and your body no longer functions. I was wrong. You die and your soul leaves, and what's left turns to dust. That wasn't the case.

Everything I thought was no longer my reality.

I sat with a glass of brandy between my hands, focusing on the fire in Juliet's office. The oranges, reds, and yellows of the flames danced around the logs, releasing a warmth that barely penetrated my worried exterior. The crackling of the fire tickled my ears as the scent of burning pine lingered in and out of my consciousness. A knot tugged the back of my neck. What was this new vision? Worse yet, what did it have to do with me? Not to mention Juliet, Kirtus, Gregor, and the other Immortals.

"Chris." Juliet's gentle voice pulled me from my fog of apprehension.

How long had I been like this? A minute? A day? A year? I wasn't sure. I turned from the fire. Kirtus sat next to me on the sofa, his coat removed, replaced by an air of worry. His red hair, green and gray eyes typically so intoxicating, brought me no joy. Gregor's tall solid frame blocked one of Juliet's bookcases, his rugged face a shadow of concern. All of Juliet's tomes and books, several of them personal journals of her long life, sat there taunting me. Would they be able to unravel this new vision? This new mystery? They were next to no help with the witches, or my father. *The monster.* I sipped my brandy, hoping it would take the chill from my soul.

I caught Juliet out of the corner of my eye waiting for me to speak. She was patient as always. She sat with her ivory pant-clad leg crossed and a glass of red in her hand, but deep in her stunning eyes there was unease. Despite her apprehension in moments like this, she appeared so young. Nevertheless, behind that façade of youth was the power of an Immortal who had been around for 1650 years. No one should ever underestimate her.

My eyes narrowed on the red, and my stomach flipped, not from hunger or desire but from this new burden I was meant to carry.

"Would you like a glass?" she offered. Her dark blonde hair, normally combed out, was in a ponytail, making her appear all the younger. I caught a whiff of vanilla and roses, her signature scent. I inhaled deeper, hoping it would soothe me.

I shook my head.

"I realize it's difficult, but please can you tell us the vision again." Juliet's voice was a whisper, but the request rang in my head. How many times would I have to retell this story?

I put the half-full brandy glass on the coffee table, recalling the images to me. "I'm standing in some kind of chamber, but it's not anyplace I've been." I scanned their three faces. "It's not here." My heart pounded louder in my chest. I focused on my breathing a bit more before I continued. "In the center, there is what appears to be a formal table of polished stone with nine ornately carved chairs around it. On the wall..." I kept my eyes closed and focused on the wall. "There's a mural. You're in it, Juliet; so is Sybil, Garrett, Fernando, Rahim, all the members of the Council of Light."

"The council chamber in Egypt." Juliet tapped her finger on the edge of her glass, the noise echoing throughout her office.

The sentence was barely spoken before all the images of my vision flashed back. It was too much, and my eyes flew open. Juliet, Gregor, and Kirtus surveyed me. Considering their strained expressions, they are worried about me. I waved off their unease and shook my head.

"What else?" Gregor's deep voice cool and calm, but the glance he shared with Juliet betrayed his composure. He didn't understand what to do with this information any more than I did.

I pulled the vision to my thoughts and continued, "The wall with the mural began to crack and crumble and I smell smoke. The chamber is on fire..." I focused on Juliet. "The stone table crumbles. The chairs burn and everything is in shambles."

Juliet nodded and sipped her red.

"Something or someone destroyed it, but I didn't see them."

"Who could do such a thing?" Kirtus rubbed his hands together. "Only the Council of Light knows the actual location."

"What else do you see?" Juliet's peaceful aura melted my worry and fear. After a moment my thoughts cleared. Normally I would be upset at her for using her gift on me, but I needed it. Especially after all that had happened these last few weeks. My mother's sacrifice to save me and kill my father still haunted me. My father's death came after we discovered he was in charge of a coven of witches who wanted to destroy the world. It was a battle we had to fight to stop the witches from releasing true magic into our world.

We failed at that. True magic had still seeped into our world before we cut it off.

I had hoped it was all behind us. I wanted things to return to normal, but my gift of being a Seer had other plans. I focused once more on the brandy, wanting a sip but not taking it; my gaze returned to the fire. More of the vision came forward. "As the room fell to ruin and the mural burned, a large carved wooden chair with inlays of gold and decorated with jewels pushed the debris away." I closed my eyes again. "There was a shadow figure sitting in the chair."

"Who is it?" Kirtus asked.

"I'm not sure, but I hear his voice." I pushed my eyes together tighter to help me hear.

"I've stayed out of the way of history, but it's time to return and bring what is right and just back to this world." I took a breath. "That's what he said, but I don't sense malice from him, but I don't know. Sorrow and pain, maybe. Sacrifice?"

"What does he look like?" Juliet called me to focus.

"He's tall and he's wearing some kind of toga with deep crimson and white stripes. I can't really see anything else." My eyes fluttered open.

Everyone was silent. The crackle of the fire might as well have been the rumble of a train going through the room. It was unbearable, and I was about to speak.

Kirtus beat me to it. "Why don't we take a break?"

I shook my head. "It's fine. After the man vanished, I was standing on a grass-covered pasture. In front of me was a hill with a young girl sitting there laughing and clapping her hands. She had long brown hair and her gaze planted on an oversized full moon. It was impossibly big." I sighed. "I'm sorry but that's all." I slouched deeper in the couch, focusing my own gaze on the ceiling and the rich wood inlays and trim. "I have no idea what any of it means." The square patterns offered my brain a relaxing, ordered shape.

"That's okay." Gregor's voice was stronger now as if he realized what needed to be done.

Maybe he did. I couldn't be sure.

"You've given us a lot of information to go through. Add that to the reports of magic both Victor and I have seen. There is a lot happening we still have to address," Gregor continued. "Once we begin to break it down, perhaps more will come to you."

I faced him. "Maybe. I hope so, because right now, it feels like a whole lot of nothing. Especially when you are already dealing with these other problems."

"We're all new to this Seer business." Kirtus's hand rested on my leg.

His touch caused a shiver to rush through my body, and right now, all I wanted to do was take him to me, hold him, and get lost in his arms and warm body.

"Plus, it's not like you haven't been through a whole lot of hell over the last few weeks." Kirtus offered me a grin, the single dimple on his left cheek popping out. It melted away more of my worry.

"Is it possible it's another witch?" Kirtus asked. "Especially if magic is involved."

He must have already known about the reports of magic being seen both in San Jose and up in San Francisco. Either way he didn't seem surprised by this news. Or, he could have an amazing poker face.

I turned toward Juliet, who had left the chair she was sitting in and walked over to her office windows to look out. Her ivory pants and jade-green shirt somehow still looked as crisp as the moment she had glided into my bedroom only a few hours ago.

"I doubt it's a witch, especially given the comment about staying out of histories way and setting things right." Juliet's voice was tight. "The clothing Chris describes is a Roman Senator, I think." She turned to me and the others. "Another Immortal, maybe, one from the fall of Rome."

"That doesn't narrow the list down." Gregor pulled at his goatee. "Especially if we include the Dark." His frown stretched farther across his face. "Perhaps we need to talk to Victor."

"I can ask him," Kirtus offered. "He mentioned he wanted to see me this week." He tried not to grimace.

Was it about the lieutenant position and the posting as his representative to the Council of Light? What he mentioned to me earlier tonight? Was that what he wanted to speak to him about?

"Thank you." Gregor offered a slight bow of his head. "Juliet, is there anyone you know who can help with this?" He walked over to the golden cart with the bottles of alcohol and red on it. He poured himself a glass of red. "What about the witches you know here? What about the local coven? You have a good relationship with them. What about the one who charmed this estate?"

Juliet's lips pulled into a small frown. She crossed over to the cart and poured herself another glass of red.

"I could have gotten you that." Gregor's tone was gentle.

She waved him off before she sipped her drink. "He's a Healer, not a witch, and I'm not sure if he will assist us; we have an unfortunate history." She held her drink in one hand and pulled a book from the shelf. She turned to her desk and walked to her seat, a quiet, far-off look about her.

I peeked over at Kirtus. "We should go." I stood and glanced over to Juliet. "You have a lot on your plate with the reports of magic. I'm sorry I've added to the burden, but with this new vision I figured you needed to know."

"Chris, if you see anything else..." She trailed off.

"Of course."

"Thank you, Chris." Gregor extended his hand. "This new vision and perhaps the magic we've seen may be related."

"I hope not." The pull of Kirtus's body helped me realize he was by my side. "I'll see if I can track down anyone on my end." He glanced over to Juliet. "My network isn't nearly as broad as yours, but you never know."

"I think we'll need all the help we can get," Gregor affirmed.

I spared a worried glance at Juliet. Something was bothering her, and it wasn't just my vision or the reports of magic. I didn't recognize what it was, but I understood my creator well enough to leave her be. She would tell me once she had processed her thoughts and all my vision information.

She met my gaze. "Yes, we'll speak more. Thank you for understanding."

"Of course." I took Kirtus's hand, and we walked out of her office for the second time tonight.

*

Kirtus and I sat at the table in the back of the seafood restaurant. We were at this place on the Santa Cruz pier called Stagnaro Brothers. We had the most amazing view of the lighthouse and the ocean. Outside the rain continued to fall, which was both good and bad. On the positive side the rain kept the fog away, but on the negative side the ocean was more active than normal. Every once in a while the building and the pier shook. Kirtus assured me there was nothing to worry about, emphasizing his lack of concern with a gentle chuckle.

So, I tried to put all my worry away and enjoy our night. There were the fresh scents of the sea and the rain as well as chowders and pastas. I would be lying if I said I wasn't hungry.

The restaurant had a special vampire menu for people of our ilk. The manager, Alfonse, or Al as he went by, was an acquaintance and client of Kirtus's. According to Kirtus, Al had only been an Immortal for barely over a hundred years. When I asked if he was one of the original owners, Kirtus only smirked and shrugged. Regardless our dinner was wonderful. The soup, as promised, was a blood clam chowder highbred that had the most scrumptious mouth feel. They also had a huge selection of bottles of red. But the real selling point of the restaurant had to be the view as my gaze continually shifted to the window.

"So?" Kirtus's eyebrows raised.

I turned from the window to see him beaming at me with a slightly raised right eyebrow. He held a wine glass filled with red.

"This was really nice. Thank you." I forced what I hoped to be a sincere expression.

"It doesn't do you any good to worry."

"I know." I picked up my glass of red and took a deep sip. This red tasted more like oak and had an odd woodsy tang to it. Much to my surprise, the red went perfectly with the chowder. "This place is amazing and the view." I peeked out the window.

"During the summer when there are boats out on the water, it's breathtaking. They have some places to sit upstairs where you can see the boardwalk, but I like this view better."

"I wish the weather was nicer. It would be fantastic to walk down the pier and over to the boardwalk." I took another sip of my drink. "I've never been."

"No." Kirtus's eyes were large, and there was a slight shake to his head as he spoke. "I'm shocked. You mean you've never been to the Santa Cruz Beach Boardwalk in the entire six months you lived here? What kind of monster are you?"

"Oh, har-har. Don't be a dick."

Kirtus's laugh brightened the whole room.

The knot that had been digging into my neck was starting to lose ground.

"Does Juliet realize you talk like that?" Kirtus joked.

Laughter rolled from my lips as a warmth filled my body that I didn't know had been missing. Despite everything I, we'd, been through, it was so nice to relax and be ourselves. "Has it only been six months?"

Kirtus nodded.

We fell into comfortable silence again. I was transfixed by the rain and the ocean outside; the glint of light from the lighthouse hypnotized me. The conversation with Victor prior to my vision played in my head. How much both he and Juliet risked so Kirtus and I could be together, to share moments like this. How much danger did our relationship put us in? A Light vampire and a Dark vampire in a relationship was something the Immortal community was not pleased with. Why? Our relationship surely couldn't have been the first; there must have been other Dark and Light Immortals who got together. Luckily, everyone had been focused on the witches and the trouble they were causing to give us much of a thought, but now. Who knew?

"Do you know what Victor wants to meet with you about?" I asked after a moment's pause. I wanted to tell him about the offer to come, but this news wasn't mine to share and telling him was not my place. I hated it. However, if he knew and he told me, then I was not withholding anything or having to lie to him.

"No." Kirtus turned from the window, he had been as transfixed as I had. "Probably something to do with magic and what happened." His expression soured. "Or his and Sahin's taxes. They are always trying to work some tax angle."

I chuckled. I imagined Victor and Sahin trying to get Kirtus to bend, if not fully break, some tax rules.

I changed subject. "Have you been told that true magic had somehow seeped into our world?" I asked, trying to figure out how much he knew. I was hoping he would be more informed than me.

"Sadly." He rested his hands on top of the table. "I was in downtown San Jose at one of my clients in the KQED building, and we spotted a lightning spirit."

"A what?"

"I don't know; that was the best name I came up with. I had to convince her the energy was ball lighting, rare but not magic."

"That couldn't have been easy."

"Nope, especially when I swear the lightning spirit—thing—stopped and stared right at me. It hovered there for a few seconds and watched me." He shuddered. "Creepy as hell."

I sipped my drink. The faded taste and scent of oak tickled my nose and my throat. I wasn't used to the muted flavors of bottled blood after having fresh for the last few weeks.

"Anyway, after that happened I stopped by Victor's and reported the incident. He told me there had been a few other reports but nothing as overt. I guess." Kirtus continued to watch me. "I don't think it's anything to worry about."

"We don't know."

"No, we don't, but like I mentioned earlier, whatever this new situation is we've got this. We'll face it together."

"I hope so."

"Hey." Kirtus reached out and took my hand. "We can do this." He squeezed my hand, offering me his reassurance. "What do you think after we finish here, we walk up to the candy shop; they have this *red* taffy you'll love."

I gulped down his wonderful sandalwood scent, allowing the aroma to wash over me. Every part of my body tingled. "That sounds nice."

"Good." Kirtus finished the rest of his glass of red.

I turned to mine. "I've gotten spoiled." I tapped my glass.

"It's annoying how Victor is right about how fresh is best."

"How does any of this even work?"

Kirtus blinked several times, his jaw working.

"The bottles and—" I lowered my voice. "—and the feeding."

"The bottles are enchanted with Immortal blood. Juliet will teach you. I was lucky to have both Victor and Juliet train me in that regard. As for the other, that is something up to Juliet, but I promise you it's not what you see in the movies..." He paused and glanced around the dining room. "But it's part of our dark nature." His head shook. "That's why a lot of the Light have staff and Keepers. So, they don't have to hunt and risk going into Bloodlust."

"You mean what happened with Ben, and my test is based in reality." That night returned to me. Watching Juliet feed from Ben, feeling a need so deep within me I was sure it was embedded in my DNA, not to mention my groin. I wanted to be in the middle of the experience, but I had managed to keep my cool, despite how hard it was. Both figuratively and physically.

Kirtus leaned back.

"Fuck." I shuddered at the memory of the darkness.

"Remember, you are in charge and you hold all the power in those cases. You can make feeding as pleasant as you'd like." He frowned. "I get it's not what you want to hear, but Juliet will show you and teach you the right way."

I finished the last of my red.

"Feeding doesn't have to be awful," Kirtus added. "But it doesn't have to involve sex either."

Our server returned with our check.

"My treat." Kirtus took the bill from the server.

"Okay, I get next time."

"You got it." Kirtus pulled out his wallet and handed the server cash with the bill. "Tell Al we had a great meal and I'll see him next week at the office."

"Will do," the male server said with a polite nod.

"Keep the change," Kirtus added with an ease of charm.

"Thanks." The server headed off.

"Shall we go?" Kirtus stood and grabbed his jacket. "Plus, it looks like it stopped raining." He pointed out the window.

"Sure." I joined him, standing. "I can't wait to try this taffy you spoke so highly of."

Kirtus beamed and waited for me to pass as we headed out of the restaurant and into the cool damp air. I was momentarily blinded by the bright lights on all the rides across the pier and the water at the boardwalk. I drew in a deep breath to allow the scents of ocean mist and rain to chase away the last of the knot in my neck.

Chapter Two

I rolled over in bed and stretched out; there was nothing. As I shook off the edges of sleep, hints of sandalwood filled my sense. A content sigh escaped my lips. It was so nice to be here in Kirtus's house knowing he was somewhere nearby. His flannel sheets and down comforter brought me to a whole new level of relaxation.

The door to the bedroom opened so quietly I wouldn't have heard it if I weren't already awake. My eyes flittered opened and there at the door was Kirtus. He was dressed in his blue checkered flannel PJ bottoms, and he carried in a tray. I sniffed, smelling the fresh fruit and the red he was bringing in.

"You're not supposed to be awake." He pouted.

"Sorry. I reached out, and you were gone."

He crossed the distance from the door to the bed and sat the tray down. There were two glassed filled with red and two bowls full of sliced bananas, berries, and apples.

"Breakfast in bed." I shifted more to the head of the bed and sat up.

"Well don't get used to it." He winked at me and climbed into bed next to me.

"This is nice." I picked up the glass of red and took a sip. "Thank you."

"I figured we both needed a nice break from the world."

I glanced around the bedroom. Despite his home being in Morgan Hill and not nearly as grand as Juliet's, he kept his place comfortable, and there were always hints of sandalwood which made the space feel all the more homey. The bed was a king and not overly soft, which was wonderful. Across from where we lay a chest of drawers with a TV mounted on top. On either side of the bed were nightstands with lamps framed by windows with the curtains pulled shut. A door next to the TV led to the bathroom. On the opposite side was a door leading down a hall to the rest of the house.

On the last wall were several photos taken around what I assumed must be all the different places Kirtus had traveled. A closed door leading to the walk-in closet was flanked by his photos.

"I really like this room."

Kirtus gave me a queer look. "Thank you?"

I laughed. "I'm serious. I really like the space. It's homey. Comfortable. Nice."

"You mean you'd give up living in the hills in a vast estate to live in a simple country hovel like this."

"Har-har. I've only lived in apartments, well, as an adult, so this is special." I took another sip of my red and put the glass down on the tray between us. I picked out a banana from my bowl and popped it into my mouth. After I choked the piece of fruit down—thankfully eating human food was getting a lot easier to do, so it wasn't too bad—I sighed. "How do most Immortals live? I mean Victor and Juliet clearly live in a world that would make even the one percent jealous."

Kirtus finished chewing his scoop full of fruit. He glanced around his bedroom before answering. "I think the older you are the more you acquire..." He raised his eyebrows. "For example, I have this house, and a cabin up in Truckee. The cabin is nothing fancy, mind you, but I enjoy it. I also have investments and my financial consulting business, but that's all. I'm by no means rich, especially for living here in the Bay Area, but I manage to travel a lot, which I enjoy, and I have special places and memberships I take advantage of."

"What about Sahin or Gregor?"

Kirtus laughed. "Ugh, Sahin is a nightmare and lives way outside his means. I only have this information because I do his financials, and I'd appreciate you not saying anything."

"Don't worry. I won't."

"Victor had to financially rescue Sahin a few times years ago, mind you, and he learned, but his debt ratio is still too high. I keep telling him that, but he won't listen. His only assets are a club in downtown San Jose, which does surprisingly well, and a small place in Campbell. From what I've heard, his condo is nothing special."

"So there is a possibility for there to be poor Immortals?" I asked. I wanted to find out more about Sahin and Gregor, but I didn't want to pry too much.

"Well, in some cases poverty is possible for Immortals. Your financial security depends on who's Called you and I guess where you live. Sadly, like many things Immortals have a unique privilege that humans don't." He shifted on the bed and met my gaze. "Gregor has a nice place in San Francisco and I'm pretty sure he has two other homes, but I'm not sure where. I don't do his taxes, unfortunately." Kirtus reached out and lifted my chin. "Why all this concern about money and being poor?"

I found my heart was beating fast and my mouth was a desert. "I... Well, you know my family didn't have much and I didn't have much and now here I am in a world I know next to nothing about, living like a king, but on someone else's dime."

Kirtus took my hand. "Listen. Juliet will never let anything happen to you. If I'm honest, you hit the Immortal jackpot. You have nothing to worry about."

His touch and his dimple made the edges of my lips rise up, forcing me to relax. "She really is a wonderful person."

He beamed, turned, and grasped for his phone on his nightstand. He picked up the phone, unlocked the screen, and began typing. By the time he put his phone down, my cell buzzed. My eyes narrowed and I tilted my head. "What did you do?"

"Check your phone."

I rolled to my side and picked up my phone, unlocking the screen and seeing the message. "I have a meeting invite from you for next week?"

"I'll come to the foundation and we'll go over your current financials. I'll set you up with investing accounts, and we'll talk long term financial strategies including real- estate."

"Seriously."

"Yep, and I'll give you the family rate." He laughed.

"Gee, thanks."

"Let's finish breakfast, and maybe I'll let you scrub my back in the shower."

I didn't need any more motivation. I finished off the glass of red in one gulp and managed even to eat over half of the fruit in my bowl, which I deemed pretty darn good. The mix of fruit still had no flavor, but I did enjoy the creamy nature of the banana and I liked the chew of the apple and berries. What made the meal all the better was the sexy naked reward joining me in the shower.

*

"Dinner over at the coast, breakfast in bed, a wonderful hot shower with a sexy redhead, and now...what?" I asked from the passenger seat of his car.

"I thought about taking you to the cabin in Truckee, but 80 is a nightmare with all the people going to the mountains to ski."

"Plus, it's a little too close to my old home."

"There's that as well."

We continued heading up 101 toward San Jose. We were still early enough, so the weekend traffic wasn't too bad. I had no idea how lousy traffic was until I moved here and had to drive around. People were insane. They drove like they wanted to die. No one paid attention to what they were doing and traffic... Ugh.

"So...where?"

"I figured we'd go to the Pruneyard, walk around, check out this cool bookstore, and kind of enjoy the day."

"Seriously?"

He glanced at me, the edges of his mouth dropping from his face.

"Oh no...that sounds really nice." I took his free hand. "I haven't done anything normal in a while."

"If you don't want to..."

"God. No. That sounds brilliant."

"Good."

The idea of hanging out and walking around and being normal; I couldn't think of the last time I had done that. The last time had to be with Cindy before I came to San Jose. Sure, there were events and things I did with Juliet and Amanda, but that was always either at her house or in Los Altos, and as nice as these outings were, they never felt normal to me, like what actual people do on the weekend.

I had assumed the Pruneyard was a mall, but it wasn't. The complex housed three towers that looked like they would be more comfortable in downtown San Jose than here. At the front of the development, a series of two-story buildings housed a bunch of retail. There were things like a hotel, restaurants, a movie theater, clothing stores, and the bookstore Kirtus had mentioned.

"This is kind of quirky."

"Yep, it's different especially for this part of town, but...you'll appreciate...how normal and every day the shops and restaurants are."

I laughed.

We found parking and made our way to the shops and restaurants. I took in all the scents and all the people. This place wasn't slammed like Stanford Shopping Center had been at Christmas, but there were lots of folks out and about enjoying the late morning and brisk winter day. As promised we hit the bookstore, which I enjoyed, I got to nose around and check out all the books they had. The store didn't have any LGBT books or even a section dedicated to books of that genre, but what did you expect from a small book retailer? They couldn't have everything. Still I managed to find a couple of books to read, which made me happy.

Kirtus and I walked over to the Coffee Society. I found us seats, and Kirtus disappeared inside to get himself a coffee. I didn't need anything, and sadly these kinds of drinks tasted like hot air to me now, which was a shame 'cause I really would have enjoyed a nice hot cocoa.

He returned in short order and placed a cup in front of me.

"What's this?"

"Figured it best to get us both something."

"Oh right." I hadn't considered that. I picked my drink up and sniffed. "Tea?"

He grinned. "Hot chocolate."

I frowned. "Bummer." I picked up my hot cocoa and took a sip... Yep, air. I put it down and caught a whiff of the ocean. I inhaled a bit more and my frown deepened.

"Oh look. How sweet." Sahin's voice rang out.

Kirtus sipped his drink and put it down. "Sahin. How nice."

Sahin appeared in a pair of tight dark jeans and a muted brown long-sleeve shirt with hints of his white undershirt showing. Over the shirt he wore a brown suede jacket. His appearance annoyed me with how good he looked—not as good as Kirtus in his black jeans, polished black shoes, and light blue V-neck cashmere sweater, but still.

"What are you boys up to?" Sahin pulled out a chair and sat down at our table. "Especially, here in my neck of the woods. Mighty...brave." A flicker of malice raced in his eyes.

I crossed my arms over my chest and tried not to sneer at him.

"My plan is to show Chris around." Kirtus appeared unruffled. However, the lines in between his eyebrows betrayed him.

With all the people around, I didn't figure either Kirtus or Sahin wanted to make a public scene. Which was good, I supposed.

"How charming." Sahin picked up Kirtus's drink and finished it off with a long, steady gulp. "Well, I'm off to pick up my tailoring. Don't overstay your welcome." He dropped the empty cup on the table and winked at me. "Always lovely to see you, Chris. Enjoy your day." He strolled off without so much as a peek over his shoulder.

"What the hell is Sahin's problem?" I shook my head.

"I should have known better." Kirtus sat the cup upright. "I forgot today was Sunday and this is one of his haunts." He leaned back in his chair. "Sorry."

"You have nothing to be sorry about. He's the ass." I leaned forward and took his hand, not giving two shits at who observed us. "This can't be only because you're who you are."

"Sahin's been out to get me for years." Kirtus sighed, keeping his voice soft. "When he checked me for my ability, he saw my power. He downplayed it to Victor, but Victor remained interested in the ability. He didn't know anyone like this, and even with as much as Sahin tried to downplay my gifts, Victor agreed to sponsor me. Sahin wasn't happy. Well, none of the Dark were. They didn't want to have someone tainted like me among them."

"He's jealous of you?"

Kirtus rubbed his forehead. "Maybe. Who knows with Sahin, but I think what did it was maybe ten or fifteen years later as I assisted Victor with... Well, I helped Victor with a situation involving Juliet."

"What?"

"Never mind. Forget I said that... Anyway once Victor and Juliet witnessed the strength of my gift, Victor got pissed and summoned Sahin to the Bay Area. Originally Sahin had the territory under Betty's charge now."

"Who?"

"Betty, she's one of Victor's lieutenants. She's a piece of work. You think Sahin's bad." Kirtus shook his head. "When Sahin arrived in San Jose, I don't know what all transpired between the two of them but after Sahin and Victor met, things changed. Sahin lost all the territory he controlled and returned to San Jose permanently to work by Victor's side. He hasn't left since. Sahin managed to spin the change as a promotion and a great honor, but a few of us knew better. Since that happened, he's done everything short of trying to have me killed."

"Jesus."

"So...um...yeah, Sahin." Kirtus shrugged.

"I had no idea."

"Don't worry about it, just...you know, don't go blabbing. What happened isn't a state secret or anything. I would prefer to not drudge up any of that with the others, especially Sahin or Victor."

"I get it." I glanced around as our location grew busier. "Why don't we get out of here?"

"Sounds good to me." Kirtus snatched up the cup Sahin had drained. "Plus, I don't want to run into Sahin or one of his buddies, and I'm sure by now he's sent out the Bastard Signal."

I chuckled at the image and grabbed my books so we could make our way to the car.

Chapter Three

The engine of the Fusion came to a halt. I pulled my phone from the center console and opened the door. I buttoned my suit jacket as I stepped out of the car.

I glanced around the parking lot seeing few cars, but I didn't give the sight much thought as I strolled through the large double doors of the foundation. Amanda stood ready to greet me at the reception desk, her hair and nails perfect as ever. Today she wore a peach skirt suit with a white blouse. Seeing her looking so good was hard to believe as a few weeks ago she had been on death's door. The attack on the estate had cost the lives of Adam and Mia and severely wounded Amanda, but Juliet had saved her with her blood and some forced bedrest. Amanda had been lucky, and I was glad of it.

"Did you enjoy your sleepover with Kirtus?" Amanda winked at me.

Amanda's playful personality made it hard to remember how deadly a Keeper she could be. Her dangerous nature had to do with the fact that even though she was human, her link to Juliet kept her alive. I assumed she was close to two hundred years old so far, but probably older.

"Hopefully he didn't need to have a special shower," she continued.

"Amanda!"

Her laugh played off the walls of the lobby, and the stress and worry melted from my shoulders and neck.

"What?"

"I should have never told you about that." I glanced around the lobby and didn't notice anyone else. Granted it was still early, but usually Rachel would be at the reception station by now and all the lights were off except for a few in the lobby. "Where is everyone?"

"Today's Martin Luther King Day. You should read the handbook with the list of foundation holidays." She glided over to the desk, pulled out a binder, and handed it to me.

"Oh. How'd you know I was here?"

Amanda waggled her eyebrows. "Kirtus."

"Ugh."

"What? It's not like I asked him any details about your weekend together. Or, if you guys played hide the sausage."

My skin burned with embarrassment. Amanda loved to make me blush. You would swear teasing me was sport for her. "Poor Kirtus, he would be humiliated if he found out I told you about any of this."

"Oh come on. He's less of a prude than you think." She continued to watch me with her devil-may-care smile. "The things I could tell you about him."

"Oh my God."

Amanda laughed again.

"Anyway, how is Juliet?"

"She's been locked up in her office at the house." Her tone shifted to a more serious and business manner. "She asked me to bring you to her."

"Ah, crap." I sighed and peered out the double glass doors. "I should call her and tell her we're here and gonna be a bit."

Amanda smirked and pointed up the stairs. "Nope. She's here. She wanted to get caught up on some foundation work and figured today would be quiet, so you two can talk all you want."

"So, she knew I would be here?"

"I don't think so, but you know her. She may have."

We headed upstairs to her office.

"Have there been any more magical reports?" I asked at the halfway landing of the staircase. The space opened into a two-story lobby with stairs filling up a good chunk of the lobby, but without the Christmas tree the space was a big sad void.

"Not that I've heard."

I peeked over at the giant painting of France with a star south of Paris designating where Juliet's family supposedly came from. As far as the public and the staff knew, Juliet's family was old world money and Juliet's grandparents had founded the Lumière d'espoir Foundation after they arrived in the United States and the Bay Area. It's an impressive family history, bogus as hell, but still fascinating.

"Good." I continued the rest of the way up the flight of stairs.

"I doubt the quiet will last, but we can hope." Amanda took my arm. "Have you had any more visions?"

I shook my head. "Nope."

We made the rest of the way in silence and stopped at Juliet's office door. On this floor were the executive offices, with the exception of mine, the board conference room, two other meeting rooms, and the restrooms. The privacy and limited space of this level worked for a variety of reasons, least of all for Immortal business.

"I'm going to run to the ladies'. I'll be in my office later if you two need anything. I have some work to catch up on as well."

I glanced at my smartphone to ensure the device was turned on.

"Oh, before I forget, you and Juliet have been at a conference. I'll send you all the details so you'll know what you're supposed to know."

I huffed. "I don't understand how you manage all the deceptions. I'm worried I'm going to screw up one day."

"What you have to understand is people don't care. They are so focused on their own stories they don't have time to worry about you and yours. Plus, you and Juliet are, in fact, scheduled for a nonprofit conference in Denver, and as far as they are concerned you attended. So, it's not technically a lie." She gave me another wink.

There was no use questioning her. In my short time as an Immortal and knowing Juliet and Amanda, there would be no point. Still, I didn't like all the lying, and at some point, I might have to attend one of these conferences I'd supposedly been to. And like Amanda said, most people didn't care much about these types of things, especially since no one had ever asked me about them.

Amanda pointed to the door. "I'll talk to you later."

I knocked.

"Come in." Juliet's voice sang out.

I strolled in. Juliet's office displayed the quintessential executive director's office. There were photos of her meeting different community leaders. Her at a few high-profile Silicon Valley events. An article by the *Silicon Valley Business Journal* about her hung framed on the wall. All very impressive. By the large picture window, with a view of Los Altos's First Street, a large glass conference table sat. Like her conference table at home, the table sat eight people. Juliet mainly used her office conference table for staff meetings or meetings with donors or grantees. On top of it, a vase sat filled with fresh white roses. Just like at home, the scent of roses and vanilla filled my nose as the aroma wafted over me.

Juliet busied herself at the conference table with her laptop. I didn't remember if I'd ever seen her sit at her actual desk when here. Standing, she crossed over to me and greeted me with a peck on the cheek. "Did you enjoy your weekend with Kirtus?"

"I did. Thank you." My face and neck heated up. "Juliet, I want to thank you for all you've done to allow Kirtus and I to be together. What you and Victor have done means a lot especially considering our relationship is so new."

She beamed at me. "Yes, well, Victor has a way of making everything come across like a hardship but, trust me, he doesn't agree to do anything that doesn't help him in one form or another." She skimmed the conference table. "I'm sure he's up to something, and Kirtus and you will help him to achieve whatever this new goal of his is."

"Still, I appreciate it."

"Come, let's sit and talk. I've been going over the details of your vision and mapping out where the recent magic sightings have been."

I took my seat as Juliet tapped a few buttons on her computer, and the overhead projector kicked on, reflecting a map of the Bay Area—well, mostly the South Bay—with red dots marking locations. One was Westfield Valley Fair where the witches were going to try to expose the Immortals to the humans, which, if my vision would have played out, would have led to the death of the Immortals and destroyed Los Altos, and who knows how much more. The second was the old domed theaters in San Jose that served as the witches' base of operation, and the last one on the other side of the valley I wasn't sure about.

"That is the location where Victor found Daniel's body."

"Oh." I frowned, remembering what had happened to Victor's Keeper, Daniel, and how they had dumped his body along a road heading toward James Lick Observatory. Daniel's remains being left for the animals was not a memory I enjoyed, especially since I took responsibility for his death. If I controlled my powers better, maybe we'd have found him in time. But even Victor assured me nothing more could have been done, which was nice, but his assurance didn't make me feel less guilty.

I pushed the images of Daniel away and studied the map. "Everything is radiating from where the witches where."

"Except the location got sealed by your mother."

"True, but she told us the rift may not have been fully sealed."

Juliet typed, and some additional markings appeared on the map. They were in blue.

"What are those?"

"Those are locations that should have had magic sightings but didn't, assuming the pattern and timing of sightings we have is correct. Lake Cunningham Park, Moffett Field, the County Building, Japantown, and the new courthouse."

"Nothing happened there?"

Juliet's head motioned in the negative.

"So, we really don't have any clue about how, where, and when these incidents are going to occur?"

"Not yet, but we will." Juliet typed again and the image faded away.

"Now what?"

"I called William—"

"Who?"

"William Marshal." She moved her laptop to the side. "He's the Healer for the Muwekma Ohlone Nation here in the Bay Area. Sadly, they are a small nation." Juliet shook her head. "William's ancestors initially charmed the land I bought in exchange for my assistance in keeping their nation together and healthy from the plagues the Spanish brought here." Her voice softened. "I tried, but there wasn't much for me to offer."

"Oh wow." I only knew bits and pieces of Native American culture and history. Basically, I understood how poorly they were treated and how we took everything from them, and that was all.

She sighed. "Anyway, we talked about what was going on, and I asked if he or any other members of the Ohlone Nation had heard or seen anything."

I stayed quiet, unsure what more to add.

"We've had a basic agreement with each other, and I've only met William twice. Once as a boy with his grandfather, then about a month ago when he came and strengthened the charms on my property and here at the foundation."

"You think he'll help?"

"Yes. He's a man of his word, and despite what little help I was able to offer him and his people, I still honor my promise today, and he knows it. Unfortunately, most of my assistance these days comes through the foundation."

I motioned my agreement. I had seen some line items on the budget that now made sense.

"Anyway, he also has strong connections to the Mohawk People here, and they may possess ways to stop true magic we don't." She took my hand. "Plus, William is interested in learning more about you. He's aware of what you have done and of your power."

I licked my lips, to refresh them and keep them from cracking. "How does he know about that?"

Juliet chuckled. "He's a powerful Healer, but more than that, he's a well-connected retired lawyer. I doubt there is much William isn't apprised of when it comes to these matters. Even if he wasn't a Healer, William would be a good person to have on your side."

"The Native Americans are familiar with Immortals?" My voice elevated even higher for me; I cleared my throat, returning my voice to normal. "Who we are and what we do?"

"We are not public knowledge among the Nations, but some know. Just like some non-Nation members know."

That made me feel better. The idea lots of humans knowing about us didn't sit well with me. If there was one thing I remembered from school, it was how badly humans had treated and still treated anything they didn't understand. Even with the additional information Juliet gave me about the other creatures such as werewolves and how they were hunted down into extinction was too much for my simple mind to comprehend.

"Why is he interested in my abilities?"

"I'm not sure. I didn't ask," Juliet admitted. "My guess is this kind of power is even more uncommon among Native American Healers, and since the Ohlone are such a small nation, I doubt they have ever witnessed such a thing."

"I see." I didn't like the idea of becoming a novelty for people to study and poke at, even for a good cause. I still had a bitter taste from when the Council of Light tested me and how badly that all turned out.

Juliet took my hand again, giving it a squeeze. She didn't say anything. She didn't need to; we were bonded and she sensed my emotions. I found the idea both annoying and, at this moment, kind of nice.

"You understand when we fought the witches in Salem all those years ago." She paused and clicked her nails. "I had to do some things I wasn't proud of. Both Sybil and I killed close to a hundred or so witches, but even at that time I grasped they weren't all bad witches, I understood some of them were innocent caught up in the hysteria, but we told ourselves we were doing what we had to; not only to stay alive but to protect the world." She released my hand and leaned back in her chair. "We went against everything the Council of Light stood for. I went against everything I stood for." She shook her head. "I failed the light."

I gulped.

"I won't fail you or the light again. I would never let anyone harm you, to study you. Not even to keep magic at bay. That's not who I am—"

"Don't the needs of the many outweigh the needs of the one?" I appreciated the sentiment, but I wasn't so sure I could make such a statement. We had to kill my father, and I had to watch my mother sacrifice herself to protect everyone.

"This is different. None of us would let you or any Immortal be studied or sacrificed in such a way. But, as to what happened when we battled the witches this time, everyone was ready to give their lives. We all made that choice. No one made it for us."

I supposed I understood. "But William would like to learn more about me?" My chest grew tight at the prospect of being examined.

"I think so, and I would ask if this is the case you agree, but I won't force you."

For the first time since she had told me William showed interest in me, I breathed again and my heart beat at a regular pace once more. "I don't see why not, and maybe he can help me to learn to control my abilities better. I don't want to go through testing like I had to do with the council, especially if we're going to stop what is happening."

"Maybe between all of us, including William and the coven I've reached out to, we'll be able to stop what is happening with true magic and figure out what your vision means."

"That would be nice."

Chapter Four

Two wine bottles sat before me on the highly reflective wooden dining table in Juliet's home. The typically grand dining room with its gold flatware, bone china, and crystal stemware were all put away tonight. The centerpiece, however, overflowed with roses, orchids, small branches, and greenery all arranged in an intricate pattern perfectly centered under the brightly lit candelabrum.

In the hearth a warm fire filled the room with comfort and a wonderful earthy scent. The light from the candelabrum and the fireplace bounced off the rich walnut paneling, making the room feel all the cozier. I loved this room, especially like this. This room held such good memories for me.

Our hours at the foundation melted away the day, and by the time night had broken, we found ourselves home in the dining room. Not only were there empty bottles of red before me, but also a tray with two pitchers of orange juice, several small sandwiches, homemade chocolate chips cookies, and a big bowl of potato chips.

God in heaven, I missed chocolate chip cookies and potato chips. A slight sigh slipped from my mouth.

Clearly Nadira and Mason had been busy today, especially with the cooking bit. I really missed eating food, but we still had to make a show of it, which wasn't too bad. Still, eating lacked enjoyment for me.

Juliet tapped the bottles and called my focus back to the task before me.

I raked a hand over the side of my face. "Let me get this straight. You want me to help fill each of these bottles with blood?"

"Yes. However, before we begin each bottle needs several drops of your blood," Juliet instructed. "We will have Amanda and Ben fill up one bottle apiece. After we fill them and seal them, they will be stored for later consumption."

"But that's only two bottles. How often can they donate blood?"

"The average adult human can safely donate about two units of blood in one sitting, or in our case, one bottle." Juliet crossed over to the sideboard and picked up another tray, bringing it over to the table and setting the tray down. The polished tray remained covered.

"Okay, but how often can they donate?"

"In an emergency, about once a month." She faced me. "However, we do a quarterly blood drive at the foundation, and I ask the household staff to participate, but today, it'll only be Amanda and Ben."

So that explained how she got her blood. I peeked around the room. I wondered if the new house staff would agree, but even with my limited interaction with them, they all seemed pretty easy-going and nice. "That seems like a lot of blood, and blood seems like something people would miss."

"Not really." She pointed. "The foundation pays for the blood drive, and I only keep about a quarter of what is donated. Manipulating the numbers isn't hard."

I shook my head.

"You'll learn, especially since you will be running the blood drive in a few weeks—"

"I'll what?"

"Other duties as assigned." She patted my cheek.

"Won't it be odd when you and I don't donate blood?"

"Sadly, I'm anemic and, of course, you, as a gay man, are not allowed to give blood. That is why we both feel so strongly that those who can give, do."

I chuckled. "You really do have this whole blood thing sorted out, don't you?"

Juliet ignored my question and pulled off the cloth from the tray. "To make the blood last, we mix a drop of our blood with a full bottle of theirs. This will allow the blood to keep."

"That doesn't seem too hard." Part of me instantly regretted those words, but how could I screw this up? A few drops of my blood mixed with their blood; easy. Sure, there might be a mess, but given the rest of the tools laid out on the table, I didn't see how to mess up the process. Humans have been drawing blood for years. All the equipment looked like something you would see at any doctor's office.

I froze, the reality hitting me.

"Juliet, I've never drawn blood before."

The edges of her lips tugged up "Only a moment ago, you didn't think the task too difficult."

I crossed my arms over my chest. "I...well..." I didn't know what to say.

"Are you ready for us?" Amanda glided in. Next to her, Ben offered a nervous wave, which I judged as odd considering how friendly he typically was.

"There you are," Juliet beamed. "We were just talking about you."

"Hi, Juliet. Hi, Chris." Ben's freckles and hazel eyes always charmed a reaction out of me, whether I liked it or not. He looked like such a baby, but the reality told a different story. Ben's age hit at least thirty years above mine. At one point, he mentioned his birthday as some time in 1960, but honestly the month and day never stuck in my mind.

"Hey there." I continued what I believed to be a warm, welcoming aura.

"Why don't you two take a seat while I get Chris all set up?"

Amanda and Ben sat next to their respective bottle as Juliet called me over to view the equipment.

"Don't worry. I'm not going to let you draw their blood, but you are going to watch. Later this week I'll be setting you up with a phlebotomist who will train you and work with you so you don't end up accidently killing someone. You will need to learn this still for survival sake. We'll also go out hunting, but I want you to learn this way first. Okay?"

I gulped. My legs became noodles, and I wanted to sit down.

Juliet patted my shoulder. "Trust me, you'll be fine."

I reached up and gripped her hand a second, enjoying the moment of comfort and closeness.

She pulled on her sterile gloves. "You kids today." She snapped on the second glove, checking them. "You have no idea how easy you have it. In my day, this was akin to bleeding out a pig." Juliet peeked at me, her brows furrowed. "Oh, don't make faces."

Amanda and Ben both laughed.

I didn't find any of this funny, but I agreed this would be better than having to hunt and feed. Anything that didn't cause harm made me a happy boy. I did wonder if this made me some kind of vampire equivalent to a vegetarian or vegan. I had to bite back my chuckle at the idea. Any mirth I had vanished the moment I focused on the tray with all the tools.

I pulled my head away and glanced over at Amanda and Ben. "I suppose you are both used to this?" My lips pinched as my gaze narrowed on them.

Amanda flipped her hair over her shoulder.

"Actually, I hate needles," Ben responded. Both his legs bounced back and forth, and he didn't seem as chatty as usual. "So...um...I'll have to be charmed."

"And that is going to be on you." Juliet pointed over to Ben but didn't touch anything with her gloves on. "But first, time for your blood." She extended her hand to me.

I gave her my hand, not sure what to expect. With her free hand, she picked up this plastic tube from the gold tray. The tube thing was shaped like a large pen. She held the pen to my finger and tapped the top. The pinch was quick and the pain minimal, but the noise caused me to jump. "What the hell."

"It's a diabetic testing pen." She held my finger over the first bottle and pinched my finger as several drops of my blood fell into the bottle. She moved my hand to the second bottle, took another one of my fingers, and repeated the process over the other bottle. This time I didn't jump.

"How will this work for the blood drive? Don't they use plastic bags with chemicals in them?"

"Yes, some of the bags will have those chemicals, the ones going to the blood bank, those will be labeled accordingly." Juliet squeezed my finger harder, I assumed to milk out a few more drops of my blood. "The ones for us will have our blood in them instead. Once the drive is over, our supply will come home, and you will get to fill the bottles."

"And the process is a lot of fun." Amanda's tone and the way she flipped her hair over her shoulder indicated these activities would be anything but fun.

Finished with my finger, Juliet released me as the second pinprick began to heal. I shook out my hand, not that the movement helped with the healing process, but mentally it made me feel better.

"So, we have two different blood drawing kits, one for Ben and one for Amanda. Safety is key as is making sure nothing gets contaminated. We don't want either of them to get sick."

I agreed through pursed lips.

As familiar as the equipment was to me, there were some differences. Instead of glass test tubes, there were two long rubber tubes

I assumed would be connected to the wine bottles for filling. Amanda had her bottle already set up.

"I'll be honest." Amanda tested the connections to make sure the tubbing was secure. "This is my least favorite thing to do."

"The procedure's all clinical," Ben added. "I miss the personal touch." He waggled his eyebrows at me. Ben was a mystery. He flirted, not only with me but with everyone, in a way I found the idea flattering, but I had someone. I didn't want him to get the wrong idea, so I ignored the advance.

"Yes, well, I appreciate you both agreeing to do this, especially to help Chris learn." Juliet pulled over the equipment and checked the needle thing. She also changed out her gloves.

"Soon enough, this will be your new job once you get procedures all down." Amanda winked.

"What?"

Juliet took Amanda's arm and put the rubber band around it right above the elbow. "Once you learn the ins and outs of drawing blood, and get enough practice, this task will be yours. You'll not only be in charge of drawing blood from the staff should we need it but ensuring our blood supply is accounted for and alternated." She shrugged for me to come over. "Watch what I'm doing."

Juliet took an alcohol wipe, cleaned the area near where Amanda's arm bent, and tossed the wipe on the tray. After that, Juliet took the needle, and with one quick steady movement, she had Amanda pricked and the connector tub thing hooked up. She taped the tube in place, and before I processed what happened, the end of the rubber tube was connected and secured in placed. Juliet released the rubber band from Amanda's arm and gave her a rubber ball to squeeze.

"Easy." She took off her gloves and put them on the tray next to the used alcohol wipe.

I gave a quick peek to Ben who faced the direction of the goodies on the sidebar. His legs were still moving, and it appeared as if some of the color had drained from his face.

"Okay, let's get Ben all set up." Juliet pointed to all the fresh equipment on the tray. Unlike with Amanda, I had to connect all the tubing and make sure the equipment was secured to the wine bottle. Juliet walked me through each of the pieces of equipment and had me do everything up to the point where she had to stick the needle in Ben.

Surprisingly I only almost dropped the wine bottle and the tray of equipment once. Each. "You need to charm him."

I didn't have a ton of experience with forcing my will on people, but every opportunity I had to practice I would take. Part of me enjoyed the power, perhaps more than I should, but I did need to learn and practice these new skills, so I didn't worry too much.

"Um...sure...but why? The process won't take long, will it?"

"Unlike when you donate blood, we are taking more, and the process lasts longer. Unfortunately, the blood drawing can also be uncomfortable. Using our abilities is better for everyone, including Ben; if he's relaxed, then he won't be thinking about what is happening and he won't be as anxious, making the process better for him."

I gestured my agreement and walked over to Ben. "Hey there." Ben's bright demeanor shifted to nothing like what he usually wore. I heard his heart beating faster and watched the sweat on his brow. "You really don't like this, do you?"

He forced a laugh. "No. Normally Terrie gets Feeders. It's a lot easier but..."

I made a mental note to ask about Feeders later; that was a new term to me.

"Well, let's see what we can do." I shook out my hands and forced myself to shift into my true vampire form. My fangs grew longer and bit slightly into my lips. My forehead ached as the hard ridges of my brow took shape. The more I shifted, the less my transformation hurt. This time wasn't like the first time when my head wanted to explode, but changing still didn't tickle. Once I transformed, I appreciated how much my senses increased. Nadira and John talked in John's office at the back of the house about the schedule for the next day. In the garage, Lecomas worked on one of the cars. He sure loved tinkering with Juliet's cars. I suppose it kept him busy when he wasn't making repairs around the house or assisting John with other domestic work. And Mason was outside cleaning the pool while listening to some song unfamiliar to me.

I had to concentrate.

I took another breath. The scent of buttered popcorn tickled my nose: Amanda's blood, I recognized that smell with ease. I focused my gaze on Ben's hazel eyes, pushing everyone else out of my consciousness. "Ben, I need you to relax for me." I made sure his eyes never left mine, and I concentrated only on him. Everything around me vanished; I focused on his heart beating as our heart rates became one. We had a connection between us, and if I listened hard enough, the whispers in his mind rang out. I gulped a lung full of air. I needed to avoid getting lost in his mind; I had a job to do.

After he took a breath, I sensed the muscles in his body release, but his heart still beat faster, and as deep as his respiration seemed, it was still too shallow and shaky for my liking. He would need to be a lot more relaxed than this. I wanted to peek at Juliet, but I needed to keep my attention on Ben.

"What is something you enjoy?" I asked, taking Ben's free hand in mine. I rested them on his leg as I kneeled in front of him.

"Um... I like movies and video games."

I tried to not laugh.

"I also enjoy working out." he added.

If I didn't know better, I would swear Ben was still in high school, and his youthful appearance didn't really help matters. I pictured him walking around campus, in a team jacket; running maybe, or swimming. He had the body for it. I pushed the image from my mind only for that image to be replaced by the memories of the test Juliet had put me through with Ben. Her letting me think Ben was underage. How she had fed off him and proceeded to make him orgasm while I watched, suffering through my own personal enjoyment of the scene. I hated her at that moment, and I hated myself for allowing the feeding to happen, but that had been the purpose of the test, and thanks to my feelings, I had passed. That test still hadn't felt good.

"Chris." Juliet's voice echoed in my mind. "You need to keep control." She must have been monitoring my emotions. I took stock of myself and noted my heart beat faster and the tentacles of anger and lust pushed their way to my mind. I forced all those images from my brain. And inhaled again. Before I refocused, Ben spoke.

"I didn't mind that night." Ben's voice was low and calm. Kind of hollow.

As much as I read him, he must have been in tuned to me and my thoughts as well. The images rushed to my mind, but this time they were from Ben; his lust and desire from that night filled my mind. It had excited him. Ben enjoyed being observed and enjoyed both men and women; the images were part of my consciousness and showed he wasn't attracted to the sex, but to the person. Even though he enjoyed sex, a lot of sex... I pushed to clear the images from my mind and returned my focus to keeping Ben calm.

"Have him squeeze the ball in his other hand," Juliet instructed me.

Happy for the instruction from Juliet, I noted the smell of sweet apples filling the space around me. "Ben, I need you to squeeze the ball in your left hand."

"Okay." His voice still distant. "Oh, that reminds me—"

"Ben," I tried to stop him.

"If you want to feel me now, you can. I really don't mind, but you already know that." Ben's voice vacant but also filled with desire. Desire for me to touch him and for Amanda and Juliet to watch us. He moved his and my hands to his lap where his growing excitement pressed against his pants. He tried to get my hand to massage him.

"No," I yelped. "Ben, enough. Stop. You will focus only on your breathing." My voice a growl at this point and I noted a slight flash of fear in Ben. I didn't want to scare him, but I needed to get control of the situation.

"Ben, take another breath for me." I used my most commanding voice. I did this as much for him as I did for me, but I needed to keep myself calm for the both of us. The one positive: neither of us focused on Juliet or Ben's blood being drawn. My only hint at the process now: Ben's blood smelled like apples which grew stronger.

Good thing I ate earlier.

His chest rose and fell, and I allowed mine to do the same.

"Ben." I relaxed my tone. "I want you to keep breathing nice and slow. You're going to move your hand back on the table."

He sighed. "Fine."

I licked my lips and removed my hand from his. I wanted to peek over to Juliet for guidance, but Ben's gaze needed to be my priority.

"Ben, when we're done here, you're only going to remember us talking about movies and video games. You're not going to remember your blood being drawn or anything else."

"But I don't mind. Please leave me with some good memories. Maybe you and I having sex, or what about an image of you naked? Please."

"I don't think so." I kept my words level as I leaned in closer to focus on Ben's eyes. "Now, tell me, what's your favorite video game?"

"I guess it's *Assassin's Creed*. It's older, but I like older things." His manner shifted, and the warmth of his hand touched my inner thigh.

"Ben, please keep your hands on the table."

He returned his free hand to the table.

After a moment, his heart rate steadied as did his breathing. As much as I had difficulty keeping him firmly under my control, he was at least calm and not worried about the needle or what happened with his blood. Instead of trying to engage Ben in any more conversation, we continued to focus on what we were doing. Breathing might have been a bit of an easy path to take, but this path I controlled. We sat in silence, allowing the air in and out of our lungs. Like being in a yoga class I took once. Every couple of minutes I would repeat my instructions and I would take a breath with him.

"Okay, we are done." Juliet's voice broke through my concentration.

My head motioned in the affirmative, indicating to Juliet I understood, and I spoke to Ben. "Ben, you're going to close your eyes and quietly count to five. When you reach five, you will be at ease and open your eyes. Okay?"

"Okay."

"Great. Start counting."

By the time Ben counted to five, the needle was disconnected, the bottle full, and he had a small bandage where the needle had been. Amanda drank a glass of orange juice with a big shit-eating grin on her face. I really wasn't excited about the ribbing she was going to give me.

"Well, that was fun." Ben took a cookie from the tray. "I had no idea you knew so much about video games." He bit into the cookie and chewed.

"Oh, you know." I moped at the bowl of chips and the cookies. Why did they have to be two of my favorite things? So not fair.

"Anything with a joystick or knobs, Chris is all over." Amanda sipped her drink.

My face and neck were instantly on fire. I shot Amanda a look.

"Oh, big scary vampire."

At that moment, I recognized I was still shifted, so I cleared my throat and returned to my human face. "Better?" My normal voice returned.

"I don't know. I think you look good both ways. Both you and Juliet do." Ben's shoulders loosened. He was clearly relaxed and appeared to be back to his old self.

"That's kind of you," Juliet handed him a glass of juice. "Take it easy the rest of the day. Both of you." She shot a raised eyebrow look at Amanda who held up her glass in acknowledgment.

Ben moved his arm around. "Thanks for keeping my mind occupied. I appreciate it. I hope I didn't give you too much of a hard time."

I closed my eyes and shook my head as Amanda chuckled.

*

"This is where you stock the red?" I had never been in the wine cellar before, and I found myself all giddy. Matching stone made up the back wall which also held a niche. Inside the niche on the upper half were small wooden wine racks. There were several bottles of wine; however, the empty spaces outnumbered the filled ones. On the lower section, a closed cabinet with a lock held more bottles that appeared to be where the red was kept. Each of the sidewalls had a similar design. In the middle of the room under twin chandlers, a large wooden table had a few small wine rack that appeared to be easily moved if Juliet ever hosted a wine tasting here. The space was certainly large enough.

Despite the chill to the room, the space was well lit and comfortable. I ran my hand over the stonework. "Wow."

"I'm glad you like it. I don't come down here nearly as often as I'd like." She laughed. "I like the idea you had. Maybe I should host a wine tasting for the foundation."

I pinched my lips together.

"Sorry, I'll stay out of your mind," she said. "But it's a great idea. The Party Helpers would, of course, cater the event; we'd bring in our largest donors. We would easily raise fifty thousand dollars." She patted my shoulder. "Well done."

I crossed my arms over my chest.

She chuckled. "No more. I promise."

I wasn't sure if she would or wouldn't keep her promise, but I appreciated the comment.

I tapped the wood table. "A wine tasting would be cool. Especially since I didn't even realize this was here." I walked over to the cases holding the blood and tugged at the door. "How do you keep John or any of the other staff from pulling the wrong bottles?"

"Amanda, John, and I are the only ones with keys to these cabinets." She placed the two new bottles on the wood table, pulled out her key, and opened up the locked cabinet on the left wall. Inside, at the top, there were drawers. She slid open a drawer and pulled out a clipboard. "We keep them labeled, like the wine bottles." She put the clipboard on the table, peeled off one label, and affixed it to one of the bottles, and she repeated the process with the second bottle. "I'll ask John to make up wine labels for the bottles that are sealed with your blood. For these two we'll use mine. You can change the labels later."

I picked up the bottle to inspect it. There were custom labels. The bottle had Juliet's family name, de Exter, on the bottom of the label with the year. Above the name a family crest. Everything shone in gold except for the label which was red. How fitting. The label was simple and classy; however, the family crest was not and I had a better look at the artwork. A mullet with gold crescent on top and a star between the crescent stood out. The mullet rested on top of a shield, and the shield had three more gold crescents in a diagonal going from left to right. There were also red and blue flourishes coming from the mullet, and the colors on the shield were in red and blue. The crest was pretty. I had to ask, "Is this really your family crest?"

Juliet's lips curled up. "The crest is real enough. I've had it for several hundred years."

I supposed that counted. I put the bottle down. "Ben...today..." I shook my head.

"Ben is...Ben; that is why I asked him to help us." Juliet marked the clipboard, leaving it on the table as she put the new bottles away and locked the cabinet. "Not everyone is going to be easy to control like Cindy or Fredrick."

Oh, poor Fredrick. That day at his shop, when Juliet altered his memory, I thought he was going to freak out, but she controlled him and we proceeded to buy and order more clothes, making his sales for the day double or triple. Still, guilt about messing with him plagued me. He was a nice man and an amazing tailor and didn't need to experience that...did he?

"Some people will fight you"—Juliet's voice pulled me from my memories—"and push against your will especially if they are scared. I figured dealing with a flirty Ben was easier then dealing with someone who may try and hurt you."

"You realized something like this might happen?"

"Ben is attracted to both of us..." She paused. "His tastes are open. The idea of part of his desires and emotions seeping into you was possible."

"I don't think I did very well." I picked up the clipboard, seeing the different dates and the quantities of bottles.

"But you did." Juliet took the clipboard from me and returned it to the table. "I only had to intervene slightly, and you never lost control of Ben or compromised your morals. I'm very proud."

The edges of my lips pulled up. "Thank you."

Juliet reached into her pocket and took out a key. "This is for you." She handed me the key. "The key is to the wine cellar and the locked cabinets. As you learn to restock, you will need to update not only the clipboard but the computer upstairs in John's office. John is moving us over to digital to keep track of all our wines. Once all the information has been entered into the computer system, he will install a panel with a tablet so we can scan the bottles in and out. He'll also network us all together so we don't have to only use his office computer." She snapped her fingers and went to the cabinet, unlocking it and opening the drawer. Once it was opened, she pulled out another roll of labels. "I almost forgot the barcode labels."

She checked the number on the clipboard and the number on the barcode label. With a satisfied nod, she put the clipboard away again. "I have to admit it will be nice to have better inventory control. Victor has an amazing setup, one I'm jealous of, but he had Daniel to manage his supply." She stopped. "I hope he finds another that will be as good as Daniel."

"I wish Daniel's death never happened."

"I know you do." She took my hand; her comforting aroma of roses and vanilla washed over me. "Come on, let's get out of here. I think we had enough training for one day. How about a movie?"

Now that sounded like fun.

*

"How was your wine lesson and movie?" Kirtus nudged my shoulder as we walked along the sidewalk at Santana Row. The night had been beautiful, and I couldn't hold back my joy when he had called and asked if I wanted to meet him here after work.

"It was good." My relaxed response eased out. "We watched an old Disney movie, *The North Avenue Irregulars*. I had never heard of the movie, but I enjoyed the humor and its light-hearted nature."

"I remember that movie. I watched it when it came out. I love the scene when they all meet for the first meeting." He laughed. "Oh the look on Cloris Leachman's face, I thought she was going to kill...oh man...what's the actor's name..."

"You mean the Reverend?"

"Yep."

"I don't know."

"He was in *The Good Wife*?"

I raised my eyebrows.

"You are no help."

"Sorry."

Kirtus chuckled again. "I'll remember." He pulled me over toward the Sur la Table. "Come on, I want to check out their cooking stuff."

"Why?"

"Hey. I cook." Kirtus crossed his big arms over his chest.

"Yes, yes you do...Your Majesty." I bowed deeply before him. When I stood up, I got a quick flash of Kirtus in a meeting room with others around him. He wore a gold crown and held a dagger in his hands dripping blood. I shook my head and stepped back.

"Hey, you okay?" Kirtus took my arm.

"I just... There was a flash... You wore a gold crown and held a dagger in your hand; the dagger dripped with blood." I kept my tone hushed, so no one would hear us speak.

We moved over out of the way and sat on one of the benches. People passed us, not giving either of us a second glance.

"Are you okay?"

I waved off the question, unsure how to answer.

"The vision appeared so real. Like, you were doing what needed to be done. You were leading the Immortals. I can't... I can't explain it any better."

Kirtus leaned in the chair.

"What?"

"Nothing," Kirtus had deep lines running across his forehead, and the edges of his lips dropped. I wondered if maybe Victor had talked to him about the lieutenant position and if he was trying to figure out a way to tell me. Maybe that's what the flash indicated.

"What is it?" I rested my hand on his leg, not caring who noticed.

"For you to see me like that..." He bit at his thumbnail. "I don't know."

"Hey. Come on. You would make an amazing leader. You are one of the most honest and hardworking people around. Not to mention you are kind-hearted which is an amazing quality to have. Anyone would be lucky to have you as their boss."

"I suppose, but this whole idea's an odd feeling. And you saw me with a bloody dagger."

"Well, I'm sure whoever the victim was deserved it, assuming that is even what this vision meant. Who knows?" I didn't want to say any more because I wasn't sure what Victor had or hadn't told him so I pulled him up from the bench. "Let's check out your cooking store. Who knows, maybe we can put some of your mad cooking skills to work, perhaps have Amanda be judge."

His gaze met mine, but I didn't see the twinkle in his eyes, and if I'm being honest there was something oddly familiar to all of this.

Chapter Five

The bass vibrated through my body and the space pulsated with more bodies in the club than I believed would be legal, but I remembered Sahin owned the club and more than likely didn't care about such things. Still, on the plus side, the club was beautiful. The lack of lighting added to the mood and the excitement. A stage filled almost an inter wall, built for a band to perform; however, a DJ currently occupied the space doing her thing tonight.

Through all the dancing bodies, along the back wall, were booths with tables filled with people drinking and partying. In the middle of the club, like an island surrounded by a sea of bodies, sat a bar. The bar ran the length of the interior of the building. I counted at least five bartenders who were all smiling and mixing drinks and chatting people up. On the opposite wall, a circled staircase led to a second level with private boxes on three of the four walls, which I assumed housed the VIP section, especially since there were two men standing next to the steps heading up to that section. An additional circled staircase went up another level to what might be an upstairs VIP patio. To the rear of the VIP section, closer to the stage, appeared to be a private office where, I assumed, Sahin watched his club.

The walls and ceiling had enough neon and flashing lights to cause anyone a seizure, but I will admit all the flashing light added to the atmosphere and excitement. As if the décor and style didn't scream Sahin, my olfactory senses were assaulted. No, assaulted wasn't the right word. The club didn't smell bad; it just screamed Sahin, by the ocean and the salt. I focused on the club, and my gut told me this place was probably modeled off something from either New York or maybe Europe. As such, I doubted Sahin had any problems getting only the best DJs and bands to play here.

"What do you think?" Juliet asked as we stood at the top of the steps before we walked all the way into the club. She wore a sapphire club dress with boots that gave her at least two more inches of height. Her hair and makeup were as ready to party as the rest of her.

She looks freaking amazing.

"Now that I've seen the club, I can't imagine Sahin having anything else."

"I figured you might enjoy it, especially since you've been doing such a good job with the phlebotomist."

"Thanks." I'd only been working with the woman a couple days, but I had to admit, drawing blood wasn't as hard as I supposed it would be, and I wasn't nearly as squeamish as I assumed I would be either. All in all, I was rather proud of learning my new skill.

"Look what we have here." Even over the loud music, I heard the snark in Sahin's voice. The overwhelming scent of ocean mist gave him away long before his voice did.

Both Juliet and I turned to meet our host.

Sahin extended his hand and took Juliet's hand. Decked out in a black pin-striped suit, with white shirt open at the collar and a blood-red pocket square, Sahin shined. "It's such a pleasure to have you here; your presence isn't nearly often enough. Come, let's go upstairs. I have someone special I would love for you to taste." He led Juliet and me to the VIP stairs. With a wave of his hand, the two guards moved, and we proceeded up.

I caught their scents; oranges and lilac, along with a slight pull in the rearmost part of my mind; they were both vampires and both people I hadn't met.

"What do you think of my little bar?" Sahin said over his shoulder to me.

"It's nice, but somehow I expected more." Especially given what Kirtus had told me, but I left that part off, even though I wanted to drive my point home. I still wasn't thrilled with how he had treated Kirtus.

Sahin's eyes narrowed slightly, but he laughed. His laughter rang shallow, but I deserved nothing more, as I was being a bit of an ass. "And I'm sure all the clubs in Nevada are so much..." He waved his free hand around.

Juliet gave me the side eye and a slight shake of her head. "Sahin, the Night Stalker is truly lovely. How long do you plan on keeping this iteration going?" Juliet asked as we continued up the stairs.

"About a year, maybe more. After that, we'll shut down, re-brand, and re-open. Taxes and finance is the one thing I give Kirtus credit for;

he does have an amazing head for numbers and business." Sahin led us through the various VIP boxes smiling and greeting people. He acted as if he was holding court. An image of Sahin kissing babies crossed my mind. A walk that should have taken three minutes max ended up taking us an hour. He made sure Juliet was seen and introduced to everyone. Much to my surprise he even managed a few introductions for me. I had to give it to him; Sahin understood how to work the crowd and made a fairly good host.

By the time we arrived at his private perch, the music had dulled to a low roar. "When I re-opened the club two years ago, I installed noise-canceling speakers in this area. The speakers cuts enough of the bass and the music to make the music enjoyable."

"It's superb and extremely smart." Juliet was sincere in her compliment.

Sahin offered her a slight bow of his head, then motioned to one of his guards who I recognized from my short visit in Victor's penthouse a few months ago for my trial. A shudder ran down my spine, his scent now lost to me, as ocean mist and salt were all I smelled, thanks to Sahin.

"Are you cold?" Sahin eyed me. "I can increase the temperature if you'd like."

"No. I'm fine."

He faced Juliet. "What brings you both to my slice of heaven? Are you looking for Feeders, or did you want to hunt tonight?"

I hadn't had a chance to ask Juliet about Feeders, but with Sahin's opening, I had to. "I'm sorry, Feeders?"

"Seriously?" Sahin shook his head and his eyes rose; his features came close to sympathetic expression.

Juliet ignored him. "*Feeder* is a term we use for people who we pay to allow us to feed off them. I don't tend to use them, but it's an option."

"And I have the best selection in town. Hell, in the whole Bay Area," Sahin added. "Or you can, of course, hunt the club if you like. Some people enjoy that more; hunting keeps their skills up." He motioned. "Whatever you prefer."

I didn't know what to say.

"Tonight, we are going to hunt, even though I abhor the term. Chris needs to practice."

"Oh, so I get to watch the baby vamp go on his first hunt. This night won't disappoint after all."

I struggled to keep my eyes from rolling, but I managed.

"In that case, I shall let you have at it." A pleased grin took up residence on Sahin's face. "The club is yours, but please watch yourself. None of the regulars are here tonight, and for my staff I have a 'family eats last' policy." He walked to the open edge and glanced out at the sea of bodies. "I'll have my staff set up a private VIP booth for you on the third floor, where you can take your guests." He peeked at Juliet. "And I'll give you the family discount."

"You are more than fair. Please charge my account."

"Done the moment you walked into the club." Sahin gestured toward the doors.

"How efficient." Juliet took my hand, and we walked out of Sahin's private box. Upon our exit, the music slammed into my ears. We made our way into the ocean of bodies and crossed over to the bar. Juliet promptly ordered us two drinks. "I want you to relax tonight. Find someone who you think you might enjoy. You'll have to pick through the colognes and perfumes, and, of course, ignore Sahin's scent, but your sense of smell is strong so I'm sure you can manage."

"Actually all I've noticed is Sahin's aroma." I sniffed the air, pushing the smell of ocean to the rear of my mind. A sea of aromas from pine to chocolate to mint assaulted my nose, forcing me to hold off a sneeze, but after wiggling my nose a bit the sensation went away.

"From what I understand, we are able to filter out artificial scents and home in on what is natural," Juliet commented before taking a sip of her cocktail, bouncing to the music and appearing much younger than she acted or appeared to me.

I peeked around at all the dancing bodies, now conscious of their rhythmic motions, reminding me of how I never went to clubs with Cindy, especially clubs like this. A hand rested on my arm.

"Remember, you can take it as far as you'd like. If you want to have physical relations, you can. But you don't have to. That is the reason for the VIP lounge on the third floor. Don't feel pressure to do anything though. Like with Ben, you'll be in control. I will only be there if you need me. But, when you feed, I'll be there to ensure nothing happens. Once finished, we can either stay and enjoy the night or leave. The choice is up to you, but tonight you must do this."

Sounds fun.

A slight tug in my brain called my attention, the pull similar to a bright flash of lightning. I gulped, but said nothing. This jerk didn't feel like the start of a vision—that would have been more intense. My logical brain told me Juliet tried to calm me down, but I didn't feel calm. I didn't enjoy the idea of using someone in this way, but I understood. Realizing this is how a good percentage of both Light and Dark Vampires feed didn't help, and the idea made me appreciate how lucky I was to be Juliet's Called, to have her as my teacher. Kirtus had been right; I had hit the creator jackpot. I stared at the drink I held before taking a deep swallow, not even sure what the flavors were, but I put the empty glass down and faced Juliet.

"I'm really lousy at talking to people. Even before I met you..." I shook my head.

Juliet sipped more of her drink. "Listen to me. You look amazing; the dark jeans, the light blue sweater, and the black shoes show off all your best features. There isn't a man or woman in here who wouldn't mind making your acquaintance."

I laughed. "You have to say that."

"I don't have to say anything." She rolled her drink in her hands. "That is the benefit of being me." She finished off her drink and took my hand. "Come on, let's go and dance. That'll help you relax."

"Ugh." I moaned as Juliet pulled me to the dance floor. I tried not to focus on the goal of the night but instead let the music move me. I wasn't a bad dancer, but I wasn't the best either. Still, I enjoyed dancing. Not surprising, Juliet's movements were perfection; her sapphire club dress hugged every one of her curves, and as she moved the glints of colored lights played off her dress, making her sparkle.

The more the music played and the more we danced, the more I relaxed. Not long after we started dancing and I started enjoying myself, I noticed two sets of eyes on me. I sniffed the air and smelled caramel apples. I was transported back to the fair as a child, memories rushing back to me. An enjoyable memory. My stomach released a small rumble; I had found my mark. All other scents including ocean mist began to vanish, even Juliet's roses and vanilla, which tended to always be around me, fell into the background.

With only a look from me, Juliet slowed her dancing and moved off, which enabled me to work my way over to the two girls watching me. A hard tug at the back of my brain forced a dip in the smile I hoped I presented. I pinched the bridge of my nose, pushing the pain away. I gulped the sweet scent of the girls. Happily, I zeroed in on them, so feeding off them wouldn't feel like I would be cheating on Kirtus.

Perhaps that caused the tug in my brain, the *yuck* feeling I had over doing this.

"Relax, Chris. You'll be fine." Juliet's gentle tone sent a calming wave into my mind. I didn't know where she went off to, but I was reassured she would be there for me. I moved in with what I hoped to be a light, bright aura, masking anything ominous.

The two girls, both in their early twenties, had brown hair. One clearly white and the other a mix of Latina and Asian, but I couldn't be sure and the ethnicity didn't matter to me. The mixed woman who smelled like caramel apples garnered all my attention. I had my target. The other girl kind of smelled like wet animal, which struck me as strange, but the foul odor made my choice all the easier, and I blocked the white lady's scent from my mind.

The ladies were both dressed in nightclub attire and gave off the impression of being alone, which improved my odds for a successful training. I made eye contact with the mixed girl and proceeded to dance my way closer to her. Once I joined the two of them, the white girl nudged her friend and kind of moved off a bit to give us room. We proceeded to dance. After several of my, what I hoped, best moves, I glanced at my quarry. "Hi."

"Hi, yourself."

"You're a really good dancer." Even to my ears the cheese level hovered around 100 percent. I was acting like such a tool.

She laughed. "So are you."

The music made me feel like we were both shouting, but on the plus side no one payed us any attention.

"You know the owner?" the girl asked.

"What?"

She pointed up to Sahin, who watched us like we were the only two people in the club.

"Oh, him, kind of." I turned away from him, trying to ignore him. "He's friends with my um...my..." I didn't know how to talk about Juliet.

"Your girlfriend," she said with a bit of a frown.

I laughed. "No. Juliet is not my girlfriend..." *She's my trainer here to teach me how to feed off you so I don't kill you.* I didn't say this last bit, despite the thought being true.

"Lucky me." The girl beamed at me.

I forced a laugh.

"Hey, can I buy you a drink?" the girl offered.

I laughed even harder this time. "Isn't that my line?"

"I don't like waiting for guys to make their move. Come on." She took my hand and led me to the bar.

Us getting comfortable with each other didn't take long before Samantha, as she introduced herself, and I chatted like old friends. She was twenty-four and recently began working for Adobe here in downtown for their marketing department. Her friend and roommate, Ashley, the one whose scent of mutt made my nose squinch, was twenty-six, worked over at Santana Row, not sure doing what; I tried to focus only on Sammy as her friends called her. Chatting her up wasn't hard because I told her the truth. I told her I was twenty-eight and I worked for a foundation in Los Altos which is where I met Juliet. We worked together. All in all pretty easy.

The more comfortable I got, the more ill at ease I became for what I planned. I took a sip of my new drink, which to my surprise had a hint of a fruity tang to it that must have been the alcohol. And as if on cue, Juliet bounced over to us, wrapped around this kind of cute Asian guy.

"There you are, Chris. I told De all about you." Her voice giggly, I scarcely recognize her. "How we worked together, he assumed we were a couple. Isn't that a hoot?" She twirled her hair and danced from one foot to the other. "I suggested we go up to the VIP lounge." Juliet pointed to herself. "I know the owner."

I tried not to die laughing as Juliet spoke, her tone every bit the age she appeared to be, if not younger.

"I'm game." De wrapped an arm around Juliet.

Sammy glanced around the club, trying to find Ashley. I found Ashley quick enough and pointed her out to Sammy. Ashley had found a random guy in the corner to make out with.

Juliet laughed. "Oh, she looks all up in that guy over there."

Any unease Sammy had vanished as she needled her arm through mine, and we made our way up the two different flight of stairs. The VIP lounge was much quieter and with a small buffet of food off to the side and a bar. Over in the corner, a piano played by itself.

"I've never been up here," Sammy said. "It's amazing."

"Ah, baby, this ain't nothing," De's tone full of an overinflated ego and confidence that didn't match his stature, and I wasn't so sure he could back up any of his bluster. "You should see the clubs in Vegas or the City. This...nah." He walked over to the buffet, grabbed some cheese cubes, and popped them in his mouth. Juliet draped herself off him and allowed him to lead the way.

"It's really nice," I said. "Did you want a drink or something to eat?" A server as if from nowhere appeared with a tray of drinks. I pulled a glass of champagne and grabbed one for Sammy. "Champagne?"

"Thank you." She took a sip. "This is delicious."

All I tasted was fizzy bubbles, but didn't contradict her; it would have been rude. We moved over to the private booth that had been set up for Juliet. The Reserved for Juliet de Exter sign helped. I have to give credit to Sahin. This part of his club had the right mix of class and elegance, each booth private enough so when you walked by you couldn't see anything going on, but I'm sure someone kept tabs on everyone. Despite Sahin being an ass, I doubted he would be reckless enough to allow anyone to get hurt here, which made me feel better.

We made ourselves comfortable in this private room...booth thing, and Juliet tugged at my mind and I understood what she wanted me to do. I finished off my drink and offered to get Sammy another one.

She shook her head and touched my hand. "I'm happy we got to meet tonight."

Another tug at my brain, this time a bit harder, and I pinched my noise again.

"You okay?" Sammy asked.

"I'm fine." I waved off any concern. "I'm happy we met as well." I wasn't 100 percent sure what Juliet and De were doing, but given that last tug, I figured they were doing a heck of a lot more than what I failed at doing with Sammy. I needed to relax and remember to stay in control. This had to be one of the best experiences for Sammy possible. I inhaled her amazing scent of caramel apples and focused on her deep brown eyes. I needed to change forms for this to work, but I wasn't sure the best way to do transform.

"Trust your instincts." Juliet's voice in my head reassured me. "Remember what you did with Cindy and Ben. You'll be fine."

I gazed deeper into Sammy's eyes, and I forced myself to change. Sammy let out a gasp, and at once panic coursed through her veins. Her heart about jumped from her chest, but she didn't scream. I counted the lack of a shriek as a win and continued. "Relax. Breathe, Sammy," I commanded and she obeyed. Her heart rate instantly lowered and every part of her eased. Some of this had to be the alcohol, which would make sense. I would have to remember for the future.

As a neck man I would feed from there, but I wanted to ensure her comfort during the feeding. "Sammy, you and I are going to make out, and we're going to have a great time, okay?"

"But your face." She licked her lips. "What are you?" she whispered.

"I'm Chris, the guy you met at the Night Stalker tonight. We came up here, listened to the piano, had some amazing drinks, ate a little, and got to know each other a lot better."

She nodded. "You're not going to hurt me, are you?"

"No, of course not." I leaned closer and sniffed her caramel apple scent. I needed to taste her. I pulled away and met her eyes again. "You're going to have an amazing time tonight. You understand?"

"Yes, I understand."

"What happened here tonight?" I asked. I needed to ensure what I told her would stick.

"I met you, Chris. And you brought me up to the VIP lounge and we talked, drank, and had something to eat as we listened to the piano play. We made out." Her voice rang out hollow and empty, but she appeared to fully understand.

"Excellent," I said. "Sammy, may I kiss you?"

"I'd like that." Her voice remained empty.

I leaned into Sammy's neck, and the moment my fangs pierced her soft supple neck, the apple caramel taste washed over my tongue. Delicious. A sweet moan of delight came from Sammy. I paid attention to her pulse and her respiration. More moaning on her part, which I took as a good sign. I focused on my task, trying not to get lost in the moment, not at all easy. I now understood how vampires got lost in blood lust, but not me. Not now, and not ever.

The flavors filled all my senses. As I took another swallow, a bolt of pain bashed into my brain. I didn't know what had happened as I tumbled to the floor. Something hit me, but I didn't recognize what. There were yells and some screams. My eyes focused and my senses returned. Sammy sat still in the booth, but De and Juliet were by the twisted wood, wires, and pedals of the former piano. A bright blue light rushed around the room and blasted into me again. Out the door the energy ball went and headed down into the club.

"Juliet." I picked myself up and rushed over to Juliet. De lay passed out, but he didn't look any worse for wear if the still throbbing bulge in his pants held any indication. "Juliet!" I shouted and pulled her up.

She shook her head. "What happened?"

"Magic, has to be." I held her shaking body. "A blue ball of lighting, but something before—"

"The club," Juliet interrupted and shook herself free of me.

"What about Sammy and De?"

"Go check the main level. I'll take care of them."

I didn't question and hurried out the door. Halfway down the stairs, the music was replaced by yelling and screaming. I ensured I appeared human again as I hit the second-floor landing; people were on the floor, and tables were overturned. Sahin and his men met me.

"Upstairs?" Sahin asked, his black suit jacket gone and his white shirt sadly not long for this world given the state of everything happening around us.

"Juliet's got it."

We moved to the first floor. The blue ball lightning bounced around, not only hitting people, knocking them off their feet, but crashing into the bar and tables. I suspected there would be more injuries from people rushing out of the bar than from the blue energy ball. Sahin signaled to the two people who came with us. They tried to move in, but the energy blasted around and hit both of them, knocking them to the opposite side of the dance floor. Everyone freaked out, including the vampires on staff who were getting tossed around like toys. The energy made its way toward me again and hit me square in the chest before I moved. I flew into a railing and landed ass up on the other side.

As I pulled myself up, three people stood in the middle of the dance floor, two women and a man. The lightning bolt, or whatever you wanted to call this thing, separated into three, blasting into each of them.

"What the hell?" Sahin yelled as he helped me up.

"Who are they?"

"No idea."

The three people collapsed on the dance floor, and the ball of energy repaired itself. As more people rushed out of the club's main entrance, two women fought their way in. They were older for sure and didn't appear to be EMTs or police. They grabbed each other's hands, and their mouths began to move. As their chant began, Sahin and I took the opportunity to get the three people who were passed out, or dead, on the club's dance floor out of the way. As the women continued their chant, a woman's voice in my head told me to hurry.

"We have to make this quick," I shouted to Sahin as I reached the woman, who appeared to be Sammy's friend, Ashley. I hurriedly glanced at the guy next to her. He was the guy she had been making out with earlier. They both had that funky wet smell about them. I stepped back, appalled, before I blocked the repellent smell from my mind.

I pulled Ashley and the guy next to her by the collar…

"Hurry!" the female voice in my brain yelled at me.

"I am," I shouted and tugged at both my rescuees harder to get them away from the blue energy ball.

Sahin's eyes narrowed on me as he picked up the other woman. His dress shirt ripped and now spotted with a few drops of blood; I wasn't sure whose.

The blue ball of energy vibrated. It froze in the middle of the bar. I pulled Ashely and her male friend faster, trying to get them to cover 'cause whatever was going to happen was going to be loud and big.

"Take cover now," the woman's voice shouted, and I wiped at the dripping wet sensation around my nose and upper lip, no doubt blood from my bleeding nose.

I knocked over a table and pushed all three of us behind it. This protection would be the best I would be able to do. I peeked at the two women again by the entrance. The more they chanted, the more the energy ball vibrated. The two women lifted their hands, and with one motion the blue ball of energy vibrated itself into an explosion, sending out a shock wave of energy that blasted into the table I used for cover. The table cracked, and splinters of plastic or wood flew in all directions. I did my best to cover my two charges until danger passed.

I don't know which was more deafening: the buzzing from the blue energy ball blowing up or the complete silence.

After peeking around to ensure we were safe, I stood. Ashley and her boy were unconscious. I caught sight of Sahin, who stood next to the bar using his own table as a shield. He managed to get farther away from me, no surprise; he was close to the stairs going to the second floor. He must have seen me take shelter and did the same. We shared a quick gaze as Juliet made her way down the stairs, her eyes fixed on the two women now talking to each other.

*

Dealing with the police and the EMTs was easier than I thought it would be, which bothered me to no end. People were hurt, no one too seriously, but still, someone might have died. Yet thanks to our gifts, we were able to down play tonight's events as if they were nothing. Situations like this should not have been that easy to brush over, but thanks to our vampire tricks it was. Sahin was clearly a masterful liar, and with Juliet and the other vampires there I witnessed first-hand how these types of occurrences had been underreported or not reported at all. I wasn't sure if I should be impressed or worried with the skill they showed in dealing with the emergency services. After explaining this accident as an electrical malfunction as part of the nightclub's light show, everyone seemed content. What helped the situation the most was that no one had ended up seriously injured, even the three who were unconscious. Juliet and Sahin took care of what they assumed they saw before the EMTs cleared them to leave.

Way too easy. I mean it's good and all, but what if someone died? I really wasn't sure how I felt about this.

Despite the ease of dealing with the emergency services, we still waited a couple of hours to ensure there were no additional problems, giving me time to think about what happened and why the ball of energy had attacked those people. I didn't see Sammy or De again. I had no doubt Juliet had no trouble changing their memories, and I wondered if I should have tried to say good night.

My throbbing headache, aching chest, and spine reminded me I should stay out of the way and let the pros deal with the situation.

As I did my best to focus on my own wounds, I found myself in Sahin's second-floor VIP lounge rolling an untouched drink in my hands. No one spoke. Juliet stood at my side, and the two African American women who I still hadn't been introduced to were off in the corner talking. All the while Sahin spoke with the media and the police, spinning the story so they would be kept unaware to the actual happenings of the night.

"What about Sammy and De?" I had to ask.

"They're fine." Juliet's voice was completely flat. "They went home with the three that—"

"You shouldn't have let them go," the older of the two women scolded.

"They were attacked by magic, and we have no idea what'll happen to them, or how that energy will affect them in the future," the younger of the two women stated.

"We'll keep an eye on them." Juliet's eyes never left the two women.

"Fear not, Juliet, leader of the Light. We are now allies, are we not?" the older woman declared.

"Witches," I whispered.

"How clever. I wasn't so sure earlier; you need to listen when elders speak, boy," the older woman admonished.

"The voice was you."

She bowed her head.

Juliet's eyes narrowed a bit more.

"Patty, don't be rude," the younger of the two witches rebuked through pursed lips. "This is my sister, Patricia, and I'm Deb."

"Nice to meet you." I stood and walked over to greet them.

Deb took my hand, and with a glance to Patty so did she. They both had similar dark features, but Deb's head was shaved clean and she reminded me of one of the warrior women from *Black Panther*. Patty, on the other hand, had her dark hair slicked back and pulled into a bun on the top of her head.

"How did you know about the energy ball?" Juliet asked.

"We didn't. We were at Cream's getting ice cream." Deb rested her hands on her hips. "Patty picked up on the charge; we followed it and ended up here, where we heard the screams."

"We're in January, and you were getting ice cream?" Juliet questioned, disbelief dripping from each word.

Juliet never spoke this sharply with people. Regardless of how well they were acquainted, for her to act this way confused me. Still, so far, the witches were polite and helpful, if not a bit standoffish.

"We saved you and the rest of the people here, and you dare to question our motives?" Patty stood up. "I would have expected more from the leader of the Council of Light, especially given all that has happened."

Patty was right. My gaze narrowed on her. I would have never expected this from Juliet. Victor, sure, but Juliet, no. She must be flustered or upset at what had happened.

Juliet softened. "My apologies." She sank deep into the sofa. "With all that has happened and now this, if you are not responsible, then who?" She began to massage her temples.

"Well, I took care of the media and made sure all the cattle were safe and sound." Sahin's voice rang out as he strolled into his private office area, two of his people in tow. He had a black jacket on which covered any dirt or grime on his shirt. Even his pocket square was perfectly in place. "Does someone care to fill me in on what happened in my club?"

"Shouldn't we wait for Victor?" Juliet asked.

"Victor is out of town on business." Sahin's voice matched the exact tone he had with the police earlier. "I will call him in the morning and fill him in."

"We were discussing with your leader—"

"Leader? Who, Juliet?" Sahin scowled. "I'm not of the Light. I'm Dark, and it's best you two learn the difference."

"I smelled the stench of darkness on you; your vile nature permeates this entire building." Patty glanced around the space, a scowl over her lips.

"Who do you think you—"

"We're the ones who saved you, you ungrateful leech."

"Leech!"

"Enough." Juliet's voice rang out. "Please." Her tone softened, and I sensed her pushing her soothing nature around the room. Her calm was followed by soft hints of rose and vanilla.

"You undoubtedly caused this with your careless nature." Patty voice shifted in tone, and she fired off a steely gaze at Sahin.

"How dare you."

Both Patty and Deb crossed the room. The energy shifted as the lights flickered. Ozone hung heavy in the air, and the hair on my arms stood up—so much for Juliet's ability. Sahin's men both shifted and snarled at the women. I shifted how I sat so I was farther away as I had no intention of getting in the middle of this. I had already been attacked by a blue ball of light energy, and I didn't want to be in the middle of an Immortal and witch fight. Not again.

"Everyone, please," Juliet commanded. Her voice echoed in my mind, and my body relaxed and all anger and worry pushed away. "It's been a long night, for us all." She stood and stepped between the two groups. "The attack was not our doing, as I'm sure you had nothing to do with this attack."

Patty gave a firm nod.

"We've been investigating the magic since the New Year and the Black Coven," Deb offered. Her voice had grown softer as if all the fight had drained from her.

"So you have nothing to offer." Sahin signaled toward his people, and they shifted to their human form.

"We saved your club and the people here. There is no telling what the magic would have done."

Sahin waved off the comment.

Ass.

"We need to get a handle on this." Juliet's calm voice bounced around the room again, and a new energy wave pushed through the room; even the scent of the ocean gave way to a heavy scent of roses and vanilla. "I've reached out to William Marshall for a meeting."

"So the rumors are true." Deb's voice raised an octave, and her eyes opened wider. "You've contacted the Muwekma Ohlone Nation and us. This must be more of a concern than you originally led us to believe."

Juliet clicked her fingernails.

"Wonderful." Sahin shook his head. "More rabble."

"Sahin, please," Juliet chided.

"The Tribes around here are not going to help us." His voice was almost a full-on chuckle by now. "They keep to themselves and their numbers are too small to be of use. The human federal government doesn't even recognize them as their own nation, and you think they're going to assist us? Why would they? We are nothing more than legend and myths to them." He laughed. "Imagine letting them in on our secret?"

"Some of them are already aware of us and have been for longer than any of our people have been on this continent." Juliet frowned. "You would do well to remember they were here first and have a greater understanding of the world than given credit for."

"Please," Sahin grumbled.

"Do you have any other ideas?" I asked, tired of Sahin's lack of respect for everyone in the room and for those not in the room.

"Oh, look whose balls showed up to the party," Sahin sneered. "I wondered if they were here or if Juliet...or maybe that Lighter, Kirtus...kept them in a safe for you."

"You're such an ass." I stood then took a step towards him.

Much to my surprise, Sahin took a step back, his movement barely a small step but enough to be noticed.

Better back off.

Patty and Deb shared a quick amused smirk.

Juliet cleared her throat. "I suggest we call an end to this evening. Sahin, please inform Victor I'll be calling him. Patricia and Deborah, thank you for your help tonight. Patricia, I would like to invite you, as coven leader, to the meeting I have planned with William. I think now is the time for the four of us to sit down and figure out what is happening in our shared community."

Patty dug into her pocket and pulled out a card. "Here's how you can reach me."

"Thank you." Juliet took the card as she crossed over to me and took my arm. "It's been a long night."

I was ready for this night to be over.

Chapter Six

I remember when I first arrived at Juliet's mansion. I had this desire to sit out on my bedroom balcony and have breakfast or even lunch and enjoy the view of the mountains and the trees, taking in the aroma of damp pine and chamomile tea. That was my fantasy. Today, I can't focus enough to even hear the birds. I still reeled from last night's event. What had happened at the club? Was that how magic had been rearing its ugliness in our reality? I tried to clear my mind and focus on my first attempt at feeding off a stranger.

I put my tablet down and massaged my temples. Once I opened my eyes again I glanced out at the green lush gardens and the trees. I forced myself to inhale deeply and be present. The cool damp air was a welcomed sensation on my face. The pine in the air made my nose tingle, and for a brief second everything subsided. The calm didn't last as I remembered the tug in my brain before the magic attack. I remembered the pain in my temples and how none of that had been anything like what I experienced with Juliet.

"My visions." I stood up, grabbed the tablet, and went to my room.

No suit jacket covered me today as I made my way downstairs. The silence of the space greeted me like a pounding drum. Typically, I enjoyed Saturday mornings in the house. The staff had the weekends off unless Juliet had a party or something big that required additional support. On days like this the house seemed truly ours...well, Juliet's. I still kinda had the personal opinion of being a guest; however, as Juliet's Immortal child, the line blurred even more for me.

With respect to the staff, I didn't see them often but benefited off all their hard work. I liked how John, the estate Manager, worked with Nadira, the cook and cleaning lady; Lecomas, our handyman; and Mason, who acted as kind of the jack-of-all trades. They were a good group. I still missed Mia and Adam, and what happened to them sent a shudder down my spine. I wasn't much of a prayer, but I did pray Mia and Adam were at peace and didn't suffer, but given the state we found their bodies I doubted if peace was even possible when they died. I also prayed nothing happened to the new staff as they all had gone through enough in their lives. Especially Mason.

I suppose Juliet was fond of finding strays and lostlings. How else could I classify myself, other than a lostling Juliet took in? This idea of myself held up with the house staff as well.

At Juliet's office door the scent of roses and vanilla wrapped around me like a warm blanket. I took stock of myself, cleared my mind, and knocked.

"Good morning, Chris," Juliet called out.

I opened the door. "I'm not disturbing you, am I?"

Amanda sat at the conference table with her laptop out and a cup of coffee in her hand. Juliet appeared to nibble on a small bit of fruit salad.

"Not at all." Juliet pushed the fruit to the side.

"Morning," Amanda greeted me with her chipper tone, her appearance amazing of course. She wore jeans with a black top and pastel pink blazer, perfect as I had come to expect. "Would you like some fruit, maybe a salad? Oh, how about some chips?"

I hadn't really eaten food, well, real food that didn't contain blood since the fruit with Kirtus. I understood vampires over the years had to adapt to eating light meals to help blend in and keep up the facade with humans. The ruse only made sense. I would need to practice. "Um...how about some fruit?"

Amanda stood. "I'll be back in two ticks."

"You don't have to..."

She took my arm. "Chris, it's fine. I offered." She patted my arm and headed out the door in the direction of the kitchen.

"I didn't mean..."

Juliet waved off my comment and pointed to the seat next to Amanda. "What's up?"

"Last night, when you were in my mind guiding me, I think I had a vision or maybe some kind of warning." I sat and leaned in, resting my arms on the table. "I thought the push to be all you, but..."

"No..." Juliet shook her head. "You were pushing me out to focus. I had to use all my will to reach you when I did." She sighed. "I had no idea."

"Me either."

"So, what happened?"

"Well, a couple of times I had this pull at my brain and sharp pain in my temples. The pain went away pretty fast. Still, that mental jerking happened two or three more times, I think, and at one point I saw a bright flash of light."

"What you describe sounds like a vision, a warning. Like an early alarm."

I shrugged.

"Good, we'll explore it more." She flipped open a note pad and scribbled a few notes down. "I'll see if we can repeat that sensation again. This ability is new and there are no rules, so we're going to have to learn together."

"But how will I know? Everything is new to me."

Juliet tapped the pen to her chin. "Honestly, I'm not sure. Was there anything else that happened last night you considered strange?"

I remembered the smell from Ashley and the two others who were attacked by the energy ball, and my nose crinkled at the reminder of the odor. "Well, Ashley and the two other people had this odd funny wet animal smell." I shuddered.

"Oh, that happens." Juliet crinkled her nose. "Not all humans will smell appealing to us. I observed the aroma as well, but I can make a note, though I doubt their scent is anything major." She jotted down the additional details.

I leaned back; a bit of my smile tugged at my lips. "Does Sahin watching me count as something strange?"

Juliet's bright laugh continued to raise the edges to my lips as I relaxed.

"No, Sahin is...Sahin. Be grateful there were people around or you might have seen more of him than anyone should have to."

"Oh gross." I frowned.

"He can be a bit much." Juliet sighed. "That's never happened to me, of course, but I've heard the stories, mostly from new Called."

"I guess for him he was well behaved." I massaged my neck, still sore from last night.

"Last night." She dusted off some invisible lint from her pants. "We were in his house, so to speak, and even though we paid handsomely for the evening, he's a proper host." Her gaze met mine. "When he wants to be."

Being a vampire and being part of this community offered a lot, but still had a lot for me to learn.

The door cracked open and Amanda returned. Moments later I forced myself to choke down the fruit. Juliet had told me all those months ago about how fresh fruit and vegetables were easier for our bodies to digest. I wanted to say I enjoyed my apples, strawberries, and bananas because I used to enjoy them quite a bit, but not today.

I glared down at my fork with a chunk of banana and strawberry on it. Why couldn't I have a blood milkshake or red smoothy? Now that sounded good. The fruit sat there mocking me.

Ugh.

"How's the fruit?" Amanda asked.

"Great."

Both Juliet and Amanda laughed.

"Eating is difficult." Juliet examined me. "The sooner you learn to eat the better off you'll be. You'll want to incorporate more than fruit as well. There is nothing worse than having to explain to a host or hostess why you aren't eating. It also shows poor breeding." She chuckled more to herself than with us. "Marcel would beat me if I didn't clear my plate in my youth. He said no Called of his would be sniffed out as Immortal for not eating." She shook her head.

"I'm sorry."

Her eyes softened on me. "You have nothing to apologize for."

"I can't believe he would beat you."

Her gaze became measured, and I noted the subtle changes of her shoulders tightening and the edges of her lips dipping. "Beatings were commonplace during my youth. We didn't know better. A different world."

"That kind of treatment is barbaric." Amanda had no problem allowing the scowl on her face to match the bite of her tone.

And I agreed. After witnessing the cruelty of my father in such a short time, the idea of being raised by the kind of monster who abused a child was beyond me. It didn't matter if that type of behavior was acceptable or not for the time period.

"Yes. Growing up wasn't easy," Juliet confirmed. "As difficult as he may have been, he was still a good mentor." She instinctively waved our protest off before we even raised one. "I learned both how I would mentor someone and how I would not train them." She pointed to my half-eaten bowl of fruit. "Which is why I'm starting you off on fruit and veg instead of lamb and heavy cheeses as I had to learn from."

I couldn't hold back my look of disgust. Even before becoming Immortal I didn't like lamb and now even more so.

After our lunch together, I offered to leave and let Juliet and Amanda return to the work I had interrupted earlier. Having nothing to do at the moment was odd. I strolled around the house and practiced finding objects. This task was part of the training we came up with from when I first learned I was a Seer. The training wasn't nearly as much fun as when Amanda and I had practiced. Still, I focused on an object to see where it was. I picked objects at random, and when I found what was missing, I moved on to the next. The practice reminded me of an Easter egg hunt, without the money or chocolate.

Oh, a chocolate blood shake made my stomach rumble. I licked my lips. Later, I promised myself, and tried to find the keys to Juliet's 1964 metallic-blue Mustang convertible with its pristine white interior. Maybe I'd buy something similar on my own. That might be nice. I focused on the keys and realized they were in Juliet's office and I didn't want to bug her and Amanda again.

When I had enough of going from the first floor to the second floor, to the basement, to the wine cellar, to the pool house, I found a nice quiet place in the living room. I sat on the sofa and took a pillow and rested it behind my head. I wanted to focus on locating people. Last time I did this, my vision of Kirtus provided more of him than I wanted to see at the time, followed by getting the snot kicked out of me by my father. The experience didn't make for a fun time.

I can do this.

Today, I figured I would try again and focus on people that, with luck, would not cause me embarrassment or physical pain.

I closed my eyes and focused on Gregor. I called up his ebony scent and his short blond hair. I focused on every physical feature he had. His broad shoulders, his deep solid voice, and his goatee. He lived in San Francisco, so I concentrated there as well. Given the weekend and it being in the middle of the afternoon, I hoped I wouldn't find him in a compromising situation. It took a moment or two, but soon enough the fog cleared and I observed him walking down the street with another guy, the other man fair-skinned and tall. I believed him to be Stephen, Gregor's Keeper. They both had duffle bags. Gregor pulled on a door. Instantly I spotted all the cardio machines and people passing him in workout gear.

A gym.

"Color me surprised." I chuckled. I made a quick mental note of the time and figured I'd check with Gregor about his workout schedule later; plus, it would give me an opportunity to chat with Stephen too. I had only met him once, so another excuse to talk would be nice.

My legs were shaking, and my fingers tapped as I tried to think of someone else to check on. The problem being I didn't know many Immortals. Sybil, one of the Council of Light, but she lived somewhere in Europe; I wasn't exactly sure where. Rei, one of Juliet's top governors, was another consideration but he lived in Canada somewhere, Edmonton maybe; I wasn't sure about that either. I had a similar issue with Maria, another of Juliet's top governors. I figured she lived in Mexico, but where?

I sighed.

"Victor." I weighed the pros and cons of what Victor might be doing. A wild card for sure, but Juliet trusted him, and I was better acquainted with him than any of the others, so I figured he would be a good call. Trying to find him would be a risk, but one I wanted to take, especially since we hadn't seen hide nor hair of him in a while. Resting my head and shutting my eyes, I focused on Victor. His black well-groomed beard, his olive skill and dark eyes. He had an odd mix of sweet almonds and amber around him. I wasn't sure where to focus for a location, so I concentrated on him.

All the ticking of the clocks gave me a focal point as I continued to control my respiration and my heart rate. With each inhale and exhale, I focused my mind on his scent and strong jaw line. The fog lifted and I found Victor, his face transformed, and he snarled. Blood ran from his forehead. As the picture grew clearer he struggled to hold something. Someone. His mouth moved, and if I had to guess, he was yelling. I didn't identify what he said, but every fiber of my being told me he was angry. I tried to focus more on what happened around him. With the tick of the clock, he ripped the head off the man he held and tossed it to the ground.

My eyes flew open and I wanted to throw up. The air couldn't fill my lungs rapidly enough. I jumped from the couch, the pillow following me, and I tossed the pillow as if the stuffing and fabric had bitten me or, worse, was the severed head. "Oh God, Victor killed a man." I closed my eyes and tried to unsee what I saw, but the image burned into my sight even with my eyes open. Victor and the dismembered head were everywhere. I forced myself to gulp down air.

This reminded me of my first vision where I witnessed heads on stakes. An awful image I wanted gone. I rested my hands on my knees, bent over, trying to breathe.

"Chris." Juliet's voice called me out of my panic.

I followed the voice and found both Amanda and her standing there. Amanda rubbed my back to help calm me as I stood there.

"Victor. I just saw Victor," I forced out as I took a shaky gulp of air, able to breathe again.

"What happened? Is he okay?" Juliet's voice cracked with a mix of dread and horror.

"He ripped the head off some guy." I groaned through my pursed lips. I closed my eyes several times as tears slipped out and down my cheeks, dropping to the floor.

"Oh God." Amanda stopped rubbing my back.

Juliet crossed the distance between us and rested a hand on my arm. "Sit down. Tell me what happened."

I inhaled a few more times as I returned to the couch. Amanda next to me, already armed with a glass of red. I took the glass in my shaky hand and sipped.

"I was practicing locating people. I focused on Gregor first; he was at the gym."

Juliet rubbed my shoulder.

I sipped the red again.

"I ran through the list of other Immortals and figured I would try to find Victor, since I knew him best."

"And you did?"

I focused on my glass of red, unable to meet her gaze.

"Oh, Chris." Juliet pulled me a bit closer to her. "That had to be awful. I'm sorry you had to see that."

"You and me both." I finished off the red and put the glass on the coffee table. "Why would he do that? How could he?"

"Listen to me." Juliet's voice calm and pleasant, she used her ability on me, and I allowed it. The scent of roses and vanilla snaked its way around me and into my nose. "There are a lot of Immortals in the Dark who don't always agree with Victor. Since we don't understand the circumstance, I don't want to rush to any conclusion." She rested her hand on my leg. "Right now, I'm more concerned about you. We can worry about Victor later."

I massaged the sides of my head. "Okay."

"Why don't you try to focus on your friend Cindy?" Juliet beamed at me. "Would you like that? See what she is up to?"

I rubbed a hand over my face. "Yeah, anything to not see what I witnessed."

"Good."

Amanda handed me the pillow I had tossed. I rested the cushion behind my head and closed my eyes, and after taking several moments to focus, I pushed the image of Victor away and trained my thoughts on Cindy. Her brown hair and simple but pleasant features. The more I put my attention on her, the more I relaxed. I zoomed in on Reno and on how her blood tasted like chocolate-covered strawberries. Within seconds I witnessed her laughing, grasping for something...popcorn... She had to be at a movie. Movies were the only time she ever ate popcorn. I tried to see who sat with her, but the image wouldn't come to me. I pinched my eyes tighter. I wanted to see who made her laugh so much. Her giggling and having fun warmed my heart. I tried again to get a clearer picture, and noted she sat with a guy. An Asian American with broad shoulders and high cheekbones, his dark black hair perfectly styled. Cute to anyone's eyes. He had pouty lips and an adorable smile, making him appear extremely kissable.

"She's on a date." My face warmed and my cheeks rose. A happy warmth filled me. She was on a date, she had to be, because Cindy only did her hair and makeup when she was trying to impress a guy. "And he's beautiful...well, cute...good-looking...whatever."

My spying on Cindy and her date began to cross the line to creepy. Reluctantly I opened my eyes.

"How do you feel?" Amanda inspected her fingernails.

"Better." I frowned. "But now I'm curious as to who this cute Asian guy is, and I want to ensure he's good enough for her."

Juliet chuckled "Good." She patted my leg.

Chapter Seven

"Look, I don't want to bother you with this." I kept my tone as level as possible. "We're supposed to be finishing all the financial paperwork you put together this week." I shook my head, still unable to stop thinking about Victor and what I had witnessed in my vision. Yes, focusing on Cindy and seeing her happy was a nice break and the vision kept me from a full-blown freak-out, but still what I saw Victor do... A cold shudder ran down my spine, and I shivered.

Kirtus massaged my leg. I realized he had been quiet for too long. "What is it?"

He removed his hand and rubbed his chin. "Remember the vision flash thing you had at Santana Row the other night? Plus, with what happened at the club and now this." He sighed. "Before Victor left, he offered me a position as one of his lieutenants. I would be a liaison between the Dark and the Light Immortals. The new post would elevate my status not only in Victor's territory but all over."

"You think my visions have something to do with this new position?"

Kirtus raised his hands.

I pinched the bridge of my nose. This was nuts. "I should have never tried to focus on Victor. What a stupid idea."

Kirtus took my hand. "No, you need to practice, and you need to build up your mental fortitude so you can deal with images you may not like." The edges of his lips pulled up at the corners. He tried to smile. "Given what happened at Sahin's club, I doubt you will only see happy things."

I adjusted my position on his sofa. Kirtus's home held so much comfort for me. The warmth from the fire as it crackled away filled the room with a cozy orange glow. The scent of sandalwood encompassed every part of the room, and I turned to face him, his red hair catching in the orange glow of the fire. His dueling green and gray eyes sparkled for my attention. I wanted to kiss him, but instead of leaning in, words broke from my lips. "Are you acquainted with the two witches from the club? Was what happened with the energy ball similar to your experience?"

Kirtus frowned and leaned back.

I didn't realize how close we were to each other, and I spoiled the moment. He wanted me to kiss him, or to kiss me, but my mind hovered around other matters.

"No. The energy ball sat there, didn't attack me or anyone." He sat back.

All of this was insane. All my hopes for normalcy slipped like sand through an hourglass.

"As for Patty and Deb, I only know them by reputation." He leaned deeper into the sofa. "I've never had the pleasure of meeting them."

"Bummer."

"If it helps, what I've learned of them has been positive. As far as witches go, they keep tight control on their coven and they keep to themselves." He let out a small chuckle. "San Jose and Silicon Valley are kind of an important part of the world. No one wants to mess that up."

"I suppose."

"Anyway, if I know Victor, he'll task me with working with the witches too."

His words were sharper than I had expected. "You don't want the post as a lieutenant?"

"I don't know." He huffed. "Victor always has ulterior motives with everything he does. Everything he does is like a chest game. I'm unable to pinpoint what angle is he playing, and it's got me worried. Plus, Sahin won't be happy; this promotion or whatever will mean he and I are equals. Or I might even out rank him...ugh."

"What happened in the past isn't your fault; that's on Sahin." I shifted on the couch, seeing his face easier. "And the title would keep people from treating you like crap, not to mention the position would make things a lot easier for us." I hated dancing this line of a lie with him and pretending this information was all new to me.

"Sure, the change might, but this new whatever also might make things difficult." He ran a hand through his hair. "You saw how Victor deals with people when he's not happy with them. Plus, there are a lot of his people unfamiliar to me, and taking on this post means I would have to deal with them, and I'm not too popular."

"Screw them. I said it before and I'll say it again. I think you'll make an excellent leader or lieutenant."

"Thanks. The posting would be a big jump in my standing. I'm pretty sure I could handle the work; it's just..."

"Hey, you got this." I put on what I hoped to be a teasing expression. "Maybe Victor will give you a gold crown to wear."

He marked my comment with a chuckle, but no mirth accompanied the joyous sounds.

The bloody dagger from my vision popped into my memory. "You don't think he would ever hurt you?" The minute the words left my mouth, I regretted saying them. I had seen how Victor treated Sahin when he was pissed at him, and I had observed how easy Victor had killed the witches at the battle. Not to mention the man in my vision.

Kirtus reminded silent.

I fumbled with my shirtsleeves a moment before asking him a question. "This guy Victor killed, in my vision, if I describe him, do you think you might recognize him?"

"Maybe."

I studied my hands for a moment before closing my eyes. The man's face appeared before I took another breath. "Um..." I pushed the blood aside and focused on what surrounded me. "He's got a roundish face, light olive skin color—maybe Italian—dark hair too." I squeezed my eyes tighter. "Brown eyes." I shook my head. "He looks kind of heavy." I opened my eyes.

Kirtus bit at his lower lip.

He was worried and I understood, but I had no power at the moment to do anything. "What I saw wasn't much help, is it?"

"Sorry. It's not Betty or Masko for sure, but..."

I rested my head on his shoulder. "Don't worry. I'll figure out who was in my vision."

"Well, if it helps, the person you witnessed is no one I've seen around here. So, at least it's no one in Victor's main territory."

"I suppose that's a good thing."

We fell quiet, and I focused on the fire again, watching the flames dance around. I pushed the image of the man aside and concentrated on being here with Kirtus and enjoying this quiet time. The scent of burning oak and cedar played around me as I relaxed and let everything go. I spared a glance at the file folder on the coffee table. All the effort he went through, us meeting this week to go over my finances, and there all his work sat in a blue file folder.

And not a very large file.

I wasn't sure how much time passed before Kirtus took my hand. "Come on." His voice gentle. "Let's go to bed."

"What about all your paperwork?" I pointed to the file.

"I think we can use the rest."

"Rest?"

Kirtus gave me a mischievous grin as he pulled me up and we headed to the master bedroom.

Chapter Eight

I had no idea how much work went into a blood drive and not any normal blood drive but an Immortal blood drive. I understood why Juliet had tasked me with the event. Thank goodness for Amanda; she helped me out and ensured I didn't screw anything up. Juliet, on the other hand, busied herself with foundation business and only made a few appearances to thank the staff and some of the folks from the downtown Los Altos area who came out.

I glanced up at the sky, happy to see some sun today. Given the rain earlier in the week, the break in the weather was welcome, but with the sun came cooler temperatures. I was pleased I hadn't canceled the large tent for the parking lot because we would be able to bring in heaters to keep everyone warm and out of sun allowing us to keep the blood flowing.

I strolled into the tent and spotted everyone lying on these recliner type chairs, balls in one hand squishing away, and bags being filled. I guessed there were about twenty people in here at the moment. I imagined all the blood we were collecting and how we were going to skim off the top.

Amazing, creepy, and disappointing.

I gulped for air and coughed, not because something caught in my throat but for of all the various scents. I had forgotten to try to breathe through my mouth. Now I smelled everyone's blood, and this mix of scents, this awful mix of scents, almost became unbearable. I crinkled my nose. Chocolate, raspberries, peanut butter, lemon, curry, sage, and even a wet dog smell...ick.

"Hello, Christopher. I wouldn't take you as so easily upset by the site of needles and blood." Fredrick's French accent tickled my ear. He leaned back, his free arm resting comfortably across his chest.

I forced out a laugh. "Thank you for being here, Fredrick. No, something stuck in my throat." I coughed to act as if to clear out my throat to strengthen my lie.

Fredrick adjusted how he sat in the chair, careful not to disturb the arm connected to the tube stuck in his soft flesh. "I don't understand this government not letting you donate blood." He waved his hand around, trying to show his annoyance but coming off more humorous than anything. "Juliet I understand, the poor thing, but you, because of who you choose to spend time with, the rule is ridiculous. I would trust your blood any time. No questions asked. When will the government and the Red Cross change that stupid rule? It's not as if they don't test the blood."

If they did, I wouldn't have an excuse anymore. But I agreed. The mandate needed to change. "I don't know. I'm just glad I'm still able to help."

"I am glad for it," Fredrick responded. "We need more people like you in this world. For what it's worth, I think you did a good job with all of this, especially for your first time." He leaned forward and his cheeks rose more. "Except I think we need better snacks." His large laugh echoed all around the tent, causing others to chuckle.

"Better snacks, I will make a note for next time." My cheeks were a bit sore from smiling. "Anyway, I had to return to see you."

"You, like today's blue sky, are welcome any time."

"That is kind of you." I nodded and moved on. "Oh, and I'll see if I can get you better treats." I wondered if when I whammied him I accidently overdid my persuasion. I would have to check with Juliet. I continued my tour of the tent, waving and chatting with a few more folks. The more I walked around under the tent, the more all the scents assaulted my nose. I needed a break and hurried out of the tent and stepped into the sun. I moved away from the blood mobile and tent. I inhaled deep, needing a cleansing breath. There were still hints of blood in the air, but not as overpowering. I never thought the smell of blood would bother me, but clearly that much blood did.

"You see Fredrick?" Amanda asked, adjusting her sunglasses.

I scanned the space, finding him on a bed hooked up to a machine. "He seems overly happy to be here."

"Nah, that's just him. He's a good person. He and his staff are here for every blood drive." She checked her phone. "Did he tell you about the awful snacks?"

I chuckled and glanced over my shoulder back at Fredrick.

"It's tradition." She grinned.

I gasped again and cleared my throat this time for real.

"How you doing?" Amanda dusted off a piece of lint from her skirt suit. "Juliet says all the scents can be a bit much."

I considered this. "You know what it's like? All these smells are like walking into a perfume store." I squished my nose. "Separately they all smell fine, but when you get all those various scents together, it's too much and not in a good way."

"Well, the event is only for a few more hours."

"Until next quarter when we get to do this again."

Amanda winked at me as a grin blossomed on her face.

I moved closer to her and lowered my voice so only she heard. "Any news about Victor?"

"According to Sahin, he should return next week." She patted my arm. "But don't worry."

"I never imagined anything like that would happen."

Her eyebrow raised.

"You know what I mean."

"You have to understand." Amanda's gentle voice found my ears. "And I don't mean this in a negative way, more a statement of fact—you and the others are predators, and you all have a violent streak. This nature is part of who you are. Some like you, Juliet, and Kirtus do a better job controlling the violence, but a man like Victor..." She shook her head.

She was right, of course. I'd seen Victor in action. His actions were to help us, to help everyone, but what I witnessed in my vision had a brutality unseen by me before. Still, I didn't see the circumstance; it may have been warranted, but who knew?

"Ah, little one." A deep tone of the voice disapproved. "So squeamish, you will need to outgrow your delicate nature."

I recognized the voice at once, the voice from my council and moon vision. The man alleging he had stayed out of the way of history or whatever. I glanced around, looking for him, but saw nothing. Even Amanda had vanished. No noise, no smells, nothing except for the buildings and the cars. All the people and animals were gone.

"Who are you? What do you want?" I shouted.

"In due time," the voice answered. "But right now, I'm here about you. Tell me, little one, what are you afraid of?"

"What?" I rushed over to the tent. No one. "Nothing."

"Really. Interesting." The voice dripped with placation. "You will do him no good if you are weak. I didn't plan all this time for you to end up a weak little boy." More silence as I rushed about looking for people. Everywhere I considered nothing. No one.

"Fuck!"

This had to be another vision, which meant I still stood with Amanda or rushed around like a damn fool. Either way, he was here. I sensed him; his age weighed heavy around me. He was old. Accent. Powerful. "I'm not a weak little boy."

"We shall see."

My vision blurred. Now I hung over a pit. I peeked down, and below me a mix of what assumed were dead bodies. No. They were moving. Most were half-starved, some grasped for me, and others gazed up at me with lifeless eyes and jaws snapping toward me. The sweet putrid smell of rot and death hit me in the face. I wanted to gag. I had to remember this was a vision, nothing more. I needed to take control. Nothing here could harm me.

I hope.

I struggled to force myself free, but I didn't budge. "Okay, think." I pictured another location. Somewhere else. Somewhere pleasant.

I found myself in a grassy field. There were trees and flowers. A bright sunny day and I tasted the grass on my lips. "You want to test me, or talk to me, come to me here." My voice filled all the open space. I massaged my wrists as I waited. Who was this mystery person? They might be anyone. I learned not to trust just the voice. I needed to see them.

A disembodied laughter erupted all around.

My left leg tickled, and something scurried over my feet. When I glanced down through the grass, all around me beetles and spiders inched their way up my leg. I tried to step back, and when I put my foot down, a sickening crunch filled my ears. "No," I yelped. "This isn't real." I swatted at the creatures, making their way up my legs; the more I swatted away the more appeared. I tried to move. I tried to run, but the more I moved the more they were everywhere. "No," I called out. My heart pounded in my chest and what I hoped were beads of sweat in my hair and my forehead ran down my face. I shook my head, and I closed my eyes before I witnessed what fell out.

"There, there, little one." The voice mocked me. "The scary images are gone."

I opened up my eyes, no longer in my spider- and bug-infested garden but in a hall with white marble walls and what had to be a hand-carved throne in the middle. The room filled with white light, but where it came from I didn't see.

"This throne belongs to him and you'll need to stand with him. You are the only true Seer since her death. If they do not accept him, they will be destroyed. The two will be joined or perish. Only the pure will stand. The rest will kneel," the voice declared.

I walked over to the throne to search for features that stood out, but there were no carvings or anything special, other than looking like a throne. The room was plain, all white, no doors. Clearly I viewed what this voice wanted me to see.

"Remember, little one, Kirtus is your better, so treat him as such."

"What? What are you talking about? Do you even know him?"

"I've waited too long for this moment," the voice barked. "He is important, and his purpose is for bigger things. Help him accept this, I don't care how, but this new purpose must come to be. Use your abilities to help him. The Immortals need him."

My eyes quivered open, and I stared at a ceiling, my brain pushing at the edges of my skull. I tried to raise my hands to my ears, but they were met with resistance. My head rested on something soft. My heart pounded, and I needed to rub my temples, something to help the pain go away.

"Don't move," Juliet's voice commanded.

"My temples. My head," I moaned.

Cool warmth rested on my forehead, and two hands massaged the side of my head. "What happened?"

"When we were talking, you acted strange like I wasn't there anymore." Amanda's soft voice pushed its way through the dissipating pain. "You took off and searched through the tent."

I tried to find her, but so much haze covered everything. I tried to focus in the direction of the voice. I shifted. I was on a couch. My office.

"You freaked people out."

"Fuck." I frowned. "Sorry." I reached up, my hands free, and rubbed my forehead.

The hands massaging my temples stopped.

"Once you collapsed, me and a few others brought you here, and I got Juliet."

"Was I talking?" I sat up. My heart no longer pounded; however, droplets of sweat ran down my face and off my chin. I made several glances around to see if there were any dead things or creepy-crawlies about. Creepy-crawlies, why did it always have to be bugs and spiders?

"Not a word." Juliet ran a damp towel over my face. The warmth from her soul touched mine, and the scent of roses and vanilla calmed me even further.

"I'm glad you didn't." Amanda patted my hand. "Your actions are a lot easier to explain when you don't speak."

"What did you tell everyone?"

"That you passed out and you hadn't eaten," Juliet said.

I rubbed my forehead.

"What did you see?" Juliet got up, walked over to the desk, poured me a glass of red, and brought the drink to me.

I took a sip and every part of me relaxed. I glanced down, and for the first time my hands had a slight shake to them. I shook them out and forced myself to relax, then spoke. "I think this vision was some kind of test at first. He, or whomever, wanted to test me, find out what scares me."

"And did they?" Juliet asked.

I peeked down to my legs, a shudder running down my spine. "Scaring me isn't hard. Spiders and bugs. Anything creepy-crawly will do the trick."

Amanda shrugged.

By the time I finished telling them the rest of my vision, I had finished off another glass of red and felt more like myself.

Juliet tapped her lip.

"There was one more thing."

Juliet and Amanda leaned in closer.

"He said Kirtus is my better, and I need to treat him accordingly." I shook my head. "Do you think this has to do with his new post in the Dark?"

"I'm not sure," Juliet said. "Maybe." She faced me. "What does your gut say?"

"That all this is something more, and Kirtus is more important than we appreciate."

"Maybe he's meant to unite the Immortals?" Amanda suggested.

"Perhaps." Juliet leaned deeper in her chair. "Technically he lies outside both the Light and the Dark, but I don't see how either group would follow him. The council..." She shook her head.

"The voice said they would join or perish."

Juliet clicked her fingernails. "I'll have to speak with the Council of Light and Victor about this, see what they have to say." She pinched the bridge of her nose. "Don't share what you observed with anyone until I have a chance to speak with the others. I don't know how I'm going to even begin the conversation with them, but clearly someone or something is making a play for power and using you. I do not know how or why."

I hated mysteries; they made my brain hurt. Literally. I rubbed my temples, not liking what any of this meant.

Chapter Nine

The drive from Los Altos Hills to the east hills of San Jose didn't take nearly as long as I figured the drive would or hoped. Given the events of the morning and afternoon with the blood drive, I had a lot on my mind. Plus, the vision I'd had of Victor weighed on my mind. Still, Juliet had set up this meeting with the Healer William Marshall a week ago, and it was too important to reschedule, especially if we were able to shed some light on the trouble we'd been having with the magic attacks and, of course, what I'd seen.

A sigh escaped my lips as the scenery changed. We went from trees and nicely trimmed yards, through suburban sprawl, to an increasing downtown with high-rise structures rising from the ground like metal and stone trees. Victor's tower, The Heights, rested at the center of the forest of towers. It was utterly in contrast to one of the older stone buildings that had a big cupola at the top of it; this building almost hiding in The Heights shadow. I would need to ask Amanda about the stone building later, as the design seemed unique for the area and offered its own gravitas to the city. Despite that, Victor's building seemed like a beacon of the Dark Immortals foothold in San Jose. The hairs on my arms stood on end as a shudder ran down my spine at the idea of Victor. The farther east we headed on the 280, the older and less urban the area became. Once we crossed the 101 and the freeway we were on magically turned into the 680, we were ensconced in an older suburban area.

I found my voice. "I haven't been to this part of San Jose."

Juliet peeked at me through the rearview mirror. "The area we're going to is called Alum Rock. There is a park up here that has hot springs. In the twenties and thirties, the area used to be the place to go. Now...well, the park is still nice for hiking, biking, and all that, but the green space isn't the same; there is no longer a resort feel."

I ran a hand through my hair.

"William lives over here in the hills." Amanda pointed out the window to the homes dotting the range of mountains. "The foothills are a nice area," she added from the passenger seat.

I had been relegated to the back seat of the Tesla, which didn't bother me, the ride was comfortable enough, and the separation gave me an opportunity to check out this new area and not have to engage in conversation if I didn't want to.

We exited the freeway and continued up Alum Rock Avenue, passing a cemetery and strip malls with various ethnic restaurants and places of business. The mix of businesses surprised me. They had everything from Indian to Asian and Mexican restaurants and shops. The selection here was kind of cool to see. I wasn't used to that in Reno.

"We're coming up on my favorite bakery in all of Santa Clara County." Amanda chuckled. "In all probability the entire Bay Area," she added. "Peter's Bakery." She gestured to the right out the window at the now closed bakery. "They're amazing."

I frowned. "And you couldn't have thought to share this with me before I turned...just like La Fondue in Saratoga."

Amanda snickered.

"Don't let her teasing bother you. She's been doing this to me for years," Juliet complained, but her tone hinted at amusement. "At least you have a point of reference for some of these things. Amanda teased me once with a Kouign-Amann from this bakery in Los Gatos." She pointed back at Amanda. "I still have no clue. The pastry looked and smelled good."

"Their Kouign-Amann isn't as good as the bakery in Salt Lake City, but..."

I huffed.

The car silent again as we drove up the road and the houses went from bungalows to midcentury to Spanish style. Again, an interesting mix of designs. The houses got larger as the road narrowed. Some of these homes were as impressive as Juliet's, but they didn't have a lot of land and were close to their neighbors. I leaned back as the car slowed down and turned as the road wound the more we climbed into the foothills. In what seemed to take hours, we arrived at a single-story house clearly built in the sixties or seventies. The home appeared well kept, however, from the outside view nothing impressive. As Juliet parked, I noted two other cars in the driveway, an older Prius and a Jeep Grand Cherokee.

"Who's supposed to be here?" I grabbed my suit jacket and tugged it on after I stepped out of the car.

"Patty and Deborah. I also asked Gregor to meet us here."

I nodded.

I pulled at my shirtsleeves and sniffed the air; nothing remarkable about the fragrance struck me. I did notice the hints of freshly cut grass, which reminded me of growing up and playing in the yard as a kid. I took another sniff. This place definitely didn't belong to an Immortal, according to my sense of smell. We moved to the door and Juliet knocked. She glanced at me, offering me a reassuring bow of her head.

I adjusted the collar of my jacket and fussed a bit more with it as we waited. With a soft click the door opened, and framed in the middle stood a man of medium build and advanced years with dark hair, tanned skin, and dark brown eyes. He wore khakis and a long-sleeve light blue dress shirt. He appeared more of a grandfather type than a Healer. William came across more like a high school or college instructor, not what I expected, and I wasn't sure how that made me feel. Was I expecting a stereotype? My neck grew warm.

"Not what you were expecting." His voice was deep and strong and his eyes accessed me.

"I... um..." I stumbled over my words. I hated being caught staring.

"It's lovely to see you." Juliet's kind and polished tone made up for my lack of class. "Thank you for hosting us tonight."

"Please come in." William stepped to the side, allowing us entry.

As we moved around him, his home offered an updated interior. Thick plank hardwood floors placed vertically led your eye deeper into the house. On the walls a comfortable light brown paint balanced the bright pops of color from the otherwise simple decorations. Cozy.

Juliet beamed and walked in, both her and Amanda's heels clicking on the hardwood. "William, may I present Christopher Raymond." Juliet gestured to me. She glanced to Amanda. "And you remember Amanda."

"Welcome to my home." William took my hand.

"A pleasure to meet you, sir," I managed to choke out.

"William is fine." He showed us through the house. We passed a comfortable dining room with an oak table, a china hutch, and a sideboard. The room maybe held six people, but the space still came across like a wonderful spot to have dinner. To our right, as we continued deeper into the home we saw a newly remodeled kitchen with lots of cabinets and an incredible island with a built-in cooktop. We cut to the left and into a large living room with large picture windows.

"Wow." I noted the view of the valley. My mouth dropped open. The sight of the valley was like a chest filled with jewels sparkling in the light of the moon. You could easily make out downtown San Jose, and I noticed the lights from the airport. I bet you could see all the way up the peninsula if you were out on the patio. There didn't appear to be much of a backyard. Still, with a view like that, who cared?

"You don't get views like this on your side of town, do you?" William shared my glance out the windows. He turned to the group. "I think everyone knows one another."

I hadn't noticed the others, and I found it difficult to pull my eyes from the view of the city below.

As I turned from the window, Patty and Deb were both standing, same with Gregor. Definitely an interesting mix of people. Juliet, Amanda, Gregor, and I were all dressed in suits and appeared as though we were going to a business dinner. Patty and Deb were both in jeans, sneakers, and nice tops complementing their skin tones. And to be honest, they appeared the most comfortable. I adjusted my collar. William bridged both styles with his more business-casual dress.

"So nice to see you Patty, Deb." Juliet offered each woman her hand.

I caught a sniff of ebony and found Gregor next to me. "Evening, Chris." He held a glass of white wine.

"I like your Jeep," I mentioned.

Gregor laughed. "I drove the Prius."

"The Jeep is mine." Deb sounded pleased. "I call her Burgy, because of her color."

I chuckled.

"What do you call your Prius?" Deb asked Gregor.

"Nothing," he responded much too sharply.

I bit back my laugh at his horrible attempt at avoiding the question. Now I had to find out what he called his pretty blue Prius. Seeing him and being part of the banter helped me relax. After everyone made their pleasantries, offers of wine were made, and soon enough, we were all sitting. I took a seat on the sofa with its back to the wall to continue my viewing of the valley below. Impressed, I wondered what living here would be like. Also, I imagined the parties one might have here. They had to be extraordinary.

"Shall we begin?" William called us all together from the lone club chair he sat in. Based on the placement, his chair seemed more like his own throne.

Juliet relayed the story as Gregor, Patty, and I filled in bits and pieces as we brought William up to speed. The man sat quietly as we talked; he made mental notes of everything we discussed, but he didn't interject. Once we finished, he bowed his head as if in meditation, and no one spoke.

William raised his head, worry written across his expression. "There is much happening in our valley, and sadly the rift created by your father and closed by your mother has altered our reality."

"What?" I asked as everyone sat quiet.

"Much like all of you, I, too, have seen these magic spikes." He adjusted deeper into his seat. "It was good your mother closed the breach, but the small amount of magic which escaped has already affected our world and we cannot change that; however, we must adapt to the magic and minimize its effects."

"Which is what we've been doing," Patty confirmed.

"Good." William rested his right foot on top of his left knee.

"Can we siphon the magic off?" Juliet asked. "In Salem, once we dispatched the witches, the magic eventually dried up."

"Magic, like energy, cannot be destroyed; it can only change." William pushed the strands of hair falling over his shoulder behind his ear.

"Well, can we change the magic into something that won't attack people or cause trouble?" Gregor leaned forward, resting his hands on his legs.

William fell silent.

Everyone glanced around at one another, and before Juliet spoke again William turned to me.

"From what I've seen and heard of your power, it is impressive." William focused on me and everyone else in the room vanished. "I've hidden three objects here in my home. One is a gold coin my grandfather received from Juliet in 1906 when he was a boy right after the earthquake. The next is a black-and-white photo of my mother and father in front of a black 1940 Ford Coupe. They took the photo in 1943 when they were dating, and it's outside of Alum Rock Park. The last item is my diploma from Santa Clara University. Bring me these three items."

"You're kidding," I scolded as the room came into focus.

"Bring me these three items," William repeated, crossing his arms over his chest.

"William, what does this have to do—"

William held up a hand to Juliet. "I've heard a great deal about his gifts, and I need to see them for myself. He will find the items for me, and I will consider assisting you further. If he is unable to find them, then there is nothing more I can do, and we are done here. I will still honor our agreement but nothing more. You are talking about witchcraft and magic, both of which go against everything I believe. My people, we do not play with such matters. For me to even entertain such a conversation here, in my home, my personal loss could be more than any of you imagine." He leaned forward. "If he can't, or won't, do this, then neither I nor those whom I'm acquainted with will engage in a fool's errand and risk greater trouble with our Native Nations."

"This is ridiculous." Patty stood up. "Come on, we're leaving; this has been a series of bad ideas. We'll do what we need to do to protect our people but the rest..." She motioned to Deb.

"Fine," I acquiesced. "Please stay. Please sit." I glanced up at Patty. Me being the cause of this already shaky alliance failing was not an option. I faced William. "I'll do it. Finding these items shouldn't be too hard."

Deb took Patty's hand and pulled her into the seat.

"We can't do this alone," Deb reminded the room. "You comprehend that, right?"

Patty sat with a huff.

Juliet offered me a slight tilt of her head.

Gregor leaned forward, his gaze narrowed in on me.

"You got this." Amanda gave me a firm bow of her head. She even offered me a hint of a grin for encouragement. Of everyone here, she understood how much I practiced this skill, and she was right. I could do this. I hated the idea of being treated like a show pony.

I centered myself and closed my eyes. I focused on the first item, the gold coin. William doubtlessly picked the coin as there was a tie to Juliet, so I concentrated on both the coin and Juliet's scent. As with all my visions, the haze cleared, and I noted the coin: on a counter in a bathroom. I scrutinized the space and saw a walk-in shower and large double vanity with wall length mirror. An open door led to a closet behind. Next to the bathtub separated by a half wall, a toilet. Clearly the master bathroom. I opened my eyes and stood.

I left the living room and marched down the hall we had passed when we entered the house. There were three closed doors on my right and at the end of the hall a single closed door. This was a test, so I didn't bother knocking. I opened up the door at the end of the hall and strolled in. Several feet walked behind me. They were all following.

Of course.

The bedroom was nothing special, a king-size bed, nightstands with lamps. The room also had carpet and a chest of drawers with a TV on top. I noted the door to the bathroom and walked in. On the counter right where I expected the gold coin to be, it shined at me. I picked up the gold coin, turned it over in my hands a few times. I found William watching and headed over to him and gave him the coin.

"Nice coin." I examined the coin in my hand. Instead of walking out to the living room, I sat on the bed. I hated having all these eyes on me, but there wasn't much of a choice. If they were talking, I did my best to block them all out. I had two more items to find, and I wanted to be done with this as fast as possible.

I closed my eyes again and focused on the picture. I had no clue what a black 1940 Ford Coupe looked like and I'd never been to Alum Rock Park, so this was going to be a whole lot of guesswork on my part. I called up images of park entrances and people dressed in 1940s-era clothing. I figured the car wouldn't be impressive even though the vehicle manufactured date preceded the US involvement in the war, but they had been helping their allies so... Of course, the idea of war made me think perhaps William's father served in the military, so I narrowed my focus. The fog lasted much longer this time as movements and reverberations materialized in every direction. And I got a whiff of wet grass, or perhaps a wheaty smell. Since the aroma wasn't part of my task, I pushed the scent to the side.

Gradually an image came to me. A man and a woman stood smiling; they were both in military uniforms from the looks of their outfits. As I zoomed in on the image, they were in fact standing in front of a car outside what I considered to be a park. I glanced around again, and this time, William opened a book, slipped the photo into the novel, closed the book, and returned the book to its spot on the bookcase. I focused on the book's title, *Introduction to Trible Legal Studies: Fourth Edition.* I glanced around, taking in the surroundings.

An office.

I tilted my head up and down and opened my eyes.

I had this. All eyes were on me as I stood up. I moved out of the bedroom. I opened the first door on my left a linen closet. I walked further down the hall and stopped.

I rested my hand on the doorknob.

"Nope." I walked down the hall, past the living room and the entry hall. I passed through the kitchen. A small eat-in dining area with double French doors leading to a backyard. I continued on, beyond the kitchen a family room. I peeked over my shoulder at William and shook my head. In the family room, I moved to the door next to the fireplace and opened it. The office. I sauntered to the bookshelf, scanned all the books. He liked books as much a Juliet did. I found the one I needed. I pulled the legal book down and flipped to the correct page, pulling out the photo. I studied the photo and grinned. After my inspection, I handed the picture to William. "Good-looking parents."

"Is this necessary?" Gregor grumbled. "He'll find the next item as well. We all know it."

"Do we?" Patty asked.

"Yes, without a doubt." Amanda examined her nails. She played at being bored, which I appreciated.

I walked through the family room to the kitchen table and sat at one of the wood chairs with a blue cushion on top to improve the padding but failing. I closed my eyes. I hated being tested, but I did my best to have fun with the hunt. I had the opportunity to snoop around this amazing home and prove, yet again, I'm not some fraud. I settled into the chair, planting my feet on the tile floor, and rested my hands on my leg. I sniffed a few more times, trying to focus on William's scent. I hadn't tried this before, but for the diploma I would need to try something different. This last item was all about William, so his scent, I hoped, would be the best place to start.

I hadn't thought about what William smelled like, so I had to pick my way through the scents around me. I easily ignored both Amanda's mix of florals and Juliet's roses and vanilla. Next, I found Gregor's smell of ebony. Four more scents remained. I focused on Deb and Patty. The memory of what they smelled like from the night at the club slipped my mind, and I didn't remember what they smelled like when we walked in, but I needed to focus. I inhaled again and forced myself to see them in my mind. Once I had their images I sniffed, trying to put a name to what I smelled. "Cucumber and watermelon," I said.

I pushed those scents away as well and focused on the last two. One was wildflowers and the other... I crinkled my nose; it smelled like wet grass or wheat, something earthy. I instinctively recognized the earthy scent wasn't William, so I focused on the wild flowers. With the scent firmly planted in my mind, I focused on an image of a diploma. I was surprised at how promptly the image came to mind.

I opened my eyes and headed off to the hall with the bedrooms. At the first door, I opened it and walked in. I headed straight to the nicely framed diploma on the wall. I pointed with two figures. "There. Your diploma." My chest puffed up with pride and my head held high. I had completed his tasks. "Piece of cake."

I glanced around the room, and this time no one followed.

"What the hell." I walked to the hallway. No one had followed me. What were they expecting me to do, bring the diploma to them? "Fine." I went into the room and took the framed diploma off the wall and marched into the kitchen. The wood frame nearly dropped from my hands. There I sat at the table and everyone hovered around me. I must still be in the vision.

"Well done, little one," the male voice praised. This time when I turned around, I stood face-to-face with an older man who appeared to be in his sixties. He had amazingly crystal-clear blue eyes and salt-and-pepper hair. His body soft and rounded, he had a handsome face with defined cheekbones and what once had been a strong jawline. I even made out his broad shoulders.

"Who are you?"

"Oh, I think you know who I am, even if you don't want to admit it yet," he responded. "You passed the Healer's test. I'm impressed, but I never doubted you." He pointed to the group. "Unlike the others."

"What do you want?" My heart pounded and my stomach dropped.

"Help to bring him to power where he belongs." The man's tone pleaded. "There are great things in store for Kirtus, and you have to ensure he does them."

"What can I do?"

"When the time is right, you'll understand what to do. Don't forget what I've shown you. The others need to stand in line or perish; this foolishness has gone on long enough," the man reminded. He straightened his shoulders and raised a hand. "Oh look, we have a visitor."

I turned around to see what he referenced. William stood there.

"Chris, you need to return. Now." William stepped forward with an outstretched hand.

"You don't belong here, old man," the blue-eyed man said.

"I never thought I would live to see you. You've been alive in visions and stories from my father and grandfather even farther back." William motioned for me to come to him. "Chris, you must come back."

"Relax, Healer. My grandson is in no danger from me."

William's eyes narrowed.

"You, on the other hand." He laughed and waved his hand. "Bye-bye, William Armija."

William vanished before my eyes, and I stepped away from the blue-eyed man. "What happened to him? What? Who are you?"

"I'm a friend. I'm here to set things right. And the Healer is fine, for the most part." He shook his head, and he transformed in front of me. His canine fangs grew, and heavy animalistic ridges appeared on his forehead, forcing his whole face into a scowl. "I'm like you, a bit older, but still the same."

"You're Immortal." I found myself extending more of my mind to him.

He chuckled. "Now, go and finish your test. I'll be interested to hear what they all have to say about this, especially my little Juliet." He flicked me in the forehead, causing me to blink.

I opened my eyes to gasps. William sat in a chair; both Deb and Patty were trying to bring him around. In my hands I held William's diploma. Gregor took the framed item from me and put it down on the table, not bothering to ask me how the diploma had appeared out of nothing.

"Are you okay?" Juliet reached for my collar to loosen my tie and undo my top button.

"I saw him."

"Who?" Gregor asked.

"The man. He's Immortal."

"Not possible." Amanda's tone questioned. "Is it?"

"He's coming to." Deb ran a hand over William's forehead. "Patty, get a glass of water."

"Thank Christ." Patty rushed over to the sink, found a glass, and filled it with water.

"Chris, what exactly did you see?"

I inhaled deeply several times; I needed a glass of red right about now. I pulled my thoughts together and told Juliet and the others my vision. "Who is he? How can an Immortal enter my visions? And why did he call me his grandson?"

"If they have the power of telepathy, anything is possible." Patty stood in front of William. "How common is telepathy among Immortals?" She held the glass of water in her hands.

"Not very," Gregor stated.

"I've never met anyone with his gift," Amanda added. She stood next to me and Juliet.

"The man was Marcel." William motioned for the water and took a sip. "He knows my last name."

"William Marshall?" Gregor's eyes narrowed in confusion. "We're all familiar with your last name."

"Armija." William took another sip of water. "My great-grandfather changed our name long ago to be more *American*." William frowned.

"But I..." Juliet shook her head.

"You never mentioned anything, Juliet," William affirmed. "Your discretion is part of why my family has always assisted you. You have honor and are a good being. But that isn't important now. Marcel stood before me, and Marcel is able to reach Chris now."

Juliet shook her head. "Impossible. Marcel vanished in 1165 in Frankfurt. He was almost two thousand years old. There is no way he can be alive today."

"Impossible or not, the vision is correct," William insisted. "I saw him with my own eyes."

Juliet stood. "How can you possibly know anything about my creator?" Her words struck hard, as if they were full of venom. I had never seen Juliet like this. "You and your people have never seen him, let alone met him. He never came to this continent."

"That you're aware of." William kept his inflections calm and his words succinct.

"Enough!" Juliet stood. "This is insane. That man, or person, or whatever, has to be someone else."

"Then who?" I peered between Juliet and William.

"Do you think me or my people would deal with an Immortal we hadn't researched?" William insisted and stood to meet her. "Yes, you have been fair with us, but my ancestors, who you were supposed to help, learned the truth in the Spirt World with the help of the Hummingbird and Eagle. You may be a creature of this world, but naturally they were not so certain." He stood his ground.

Juliet's eyes narrowed and the energy in the room shifted, as if a thunderstorm was going to break out any second. "Still, you would have no idea what he looks—"

"Crystal-blue eyes, black hair, about five foot eight inches tall. I told you we know him," William added. He glanced around the room as if he sensed what I sensed.

"Not possible."

"Did he smell like wheat?" I asked.

Juliet turned on me, and her face transformed enough to scare the hell out of me and cause everyone to step back except for Gregor. He stepped toward her and rested a hand on her shoulder. "Juliet, this isn't helping. We should leave. See what more we can learn. We will figure this out."

She tilted her head, and without a word she marched to the door. Amanda's lips pulled down and her eyes dropped. Still, she helped me up and we moved to catch up to Juliet. Gregor, Patty, Deb, and William continued to speak, but we were out the front door and in the car before I even registered what had happened.

*

The next morning, the house sat silent. I wasn't sure what was going on, but with everything happening I figured I should check in on Juliet. After getting ready, I made my way down to her office. The door hung open, but she wasn't there. I sighed.

I walked to the kitchen and made my way out to the garage.

"Good morning, Mr. Raymond. Heading to the office?" Lecomas's words announced his presence before I noticed him wiping his hand on a rag.

"I..." I wasn't sure what my plan was, but Juliet's Grand Cherokee was missing, and I glanced to the blue Fusion I typically drove. I thought of Kirtus. I really wanted to talk to someone, and going into the office right now was the last thing I wanted to do. I pulled out my phone and texted Kirtus.

Can I swing by?

I sent the message. I didn't wait for him to reply. What was the worst he could do, catch me on fire again? I snorted.

"Can I take out the Fusion?"

Lecomas nodded and went to the counter and grabbed the keys, crossed the garage, and handed them to me. "Absolutely."

"Thank you." I pocketed the keys.

"Have a good day." Lecomas waved and headed into the kitchen.

My phone buzzed with a message from Kirtus.

Sure. I'm at home this morning, no meetings until this afternoon.

I tapped out a quick response and hopped into the car.

I called into the office to inform them I had an offsite meeting and would be in later. I tapped my hands along to the music. That was one of the nice things about my position; I didn't always have to show up at the office first thing in the morning. The drive to Kirtus's home didn't take as long as I assumed. Once I got past downtown San Jose, traffic opened up. What really helped was my driving against the traffic flow.

I pulled up to Kirtus's home and stopped. Studying his home, I shut down the car. I took a deep breath. I wasn't as flustered as when I left the house, but being here and being able to talk to Kirtus relaxed me even more.

"Okay, so what's going on?" Kirtus questioned as we sat on the sofa in his living room. "It's not every day you text me and stop by, especially on a school day."

"Har-har." I took a moment to inhale his wonderful sandalwood scent. Contented, I proceeded to fill him in on what had happened the night before. I tried to keep the anger out of my voice as I spoke about Juliet, but I'm sure my displeasure slipped into my tone as I spoke. I didn't understand the way she'd acted and continued to act.

Once I finished Kirtus rubbed his chin. "I get it. Finding out your creator is alive and responsible for all this—this is a big shock and has to be hard, assuming your vision is correct—"

"You can't..."

Kirtus held up his hand. "I'm not doubting you. Honestly."

I sighed.

"Look, I've come to trust your visions and you. You say Marcel was there. I believe you."

"Thank you."

He picked up my hand and kissed it. "See, this is a problem with vampires like Juliet and Victor. They think they have all the information.

I mean they, well, we, know a lot, but with the position Victor is offering me, I want to listen to people; I want to keep learning. There is so much we don't understand, even about one another, and I want to help bridge the gap. There is a lot I won't be able to do, but there will be a lot I can do. I'm going to be open and there for people to come talk to. I don't understand why Juliet and Victor have this lone wolf mentality. It's frustrating. I want to do better, and I think as one of Victor's lieutenants, I'll be able to."

I beamed over at him. "See, you are already sounding like a leader... I knew you had a talent for leadership in you."

"I hope so." Kirtus continued to hold my hand. "I'm sorry Juliet's locked you out of this. Maybe she needs some time to process."

I raked a hand through my hair. "Well, I hope she sorts herself and all this out soon."

Chapter Ten

The following morning, I walked down the hall and tapped on Juliet's office door. No answer. I sniffed the air. She was in there, but still no response. I knocked again.

"Juliet." I kept my intonation gentle.

Nothing.

Amanda walked over to me and rested her hand on mine, stopping me from knocking again. "I've tried."

"What do we do?"

"Give her time."

My gaze dropped to the floor, and I rested a hand on the door.

*

I didn't bother her for two more days. I spent the morning down in the wine cellar working on the new bottles of red from the blood drive, a much longer process than I had hoped. Amanda helped me and did her best to keep my spirits up. We had music playing, which also kept an upbeat atmosphere, but I continued to find my gaze drifting up in the direction of Juliet's office. I couldn't help but worry.

We were finishing up, and I grabbed the last bottle. "Do you mind?"

Amanda didn't say anything as she locked the cabinet door, and I headed upstairs.

I passed John's office and the kitchen and made my way down the hall to Juliet's office. The door opened and I peeked in.

"She went out." Lecomas stepped off the ladder.

Several of Juliet's books were on her conference table in neat stacks. Lecomas worked on her bookshelves.

"What happened?"

"Ms. Juliet said she had one of her fits and fell into the shelves." Lecomas exhaled. "I guess the seizures where bad, but at least she wasn't hurt. Just need to fix the shelves for her. I'll have to make them stronger, so if she uses them for support again they won't collapse."

I nodded and glanced at the bottle. "She didn't say when she would be home?"

"No, sorry," he responded.

"Thanks, Lecomas."

"Have a good evening." He left the office with his ladder and tools.

Amanda leaned against the wall a ways down the hall, her arms crossed, watching me.

"Did you know?"

She sighed. "No."

I took the bottle to the wine cellar; there was no point now.

*

I had to remind myself I'd only been part of this Immortal world for seven months. I still didn't know a lot. One of the many things still weighing on my mind, especially since Juliet left William's home so abruptly, these people were still new to me. Yes, I was connected to Juliet and by extension Amanda and the others, but what had happened at William's home bothered me. Could that man really be Marcel, Juliet's creator? Was his continued life even possible? If he still lived, how old would he be? Were there other Immortals out there everyone assumed were dead, but weren't? How powerful would they be? What would that mean for the rest of us and the humans if some super-powered vampire walked the Earth still? Would there even be a way to kill them?

Ugh.

If I were to believe William and my own eyes, then yes Marcel was alive. But could my sight be trusted? I wasn't so sure because the female Dark Witch from several months ago ended up being my father using my fears against me and almost killed everyone. Could I trust my eyes this time? Could I trust my vision? And what about William and the Muwekma Ohlone Nation? Sure, he was a Healer and clearly entered my vision, but did that prove he or his people had the ability to witness the past and treat the information as fact when it came to Marcel?

Plus, what the hell did I know about Native American culture or magic to begin with? It's not like I had any point of reference. The only references I had were in TV shows, movies, and the occasional book.

All useless.

I bit my lip as a frown tugged at the edges of my mouth. I glanced over to my cell phone. Not a word from Kirtus all day. "I wish he was here."

Juliet's reaction, Native American Healers, visions, magic...ugh. Me a college dropout from Reno, Nevada, who had worked for a nonprofit a year ago. My biggest life goal, at the time, finding a boyfriend, ensuring I caught the latest Marvel movie in the theater, and maybe, just maybe, having my dick sucked on occasion. And not necessarily in that order.

"Grr." I banged my hands on the steering wheel of the Ford Fusion Energi I drove. The Fusion was the vehicle Juliet offered me until I bought my own car. My shoulders and stomach were less clenched driving this car versus the 1964 Mustang or the 1955 Thunderbird. At least I understood this type of car since the Energi was similar to what Kirtus drove, which was a nice plus.

I glared at my cell. There better be a damn good reason for him not responding to me. I needed to call him when I got home. It would be nice to hear his voice. And give him shit for not talking to me all day. "Bastard."

I loosened my grip on the steering wheel and continued down Foothill Expressway. I gasped, trying to relax. I came to a stop and picked up my cell phone, found my play list, and hit Play, all before the light changed. I peeked around the car as music filled the air. Considering the age of the vehicle, it still showed like a new car. Everything still sparkled from the deep blue of the exterior to the dark interior seats. I had enjoyed driving this car—a frown tugged at my lips—until today.

"I need to buy a new car. My own car. I have all the paperwork from Kirtus, so there isn't any reason not to get one." I sighed with a shake of my head before I checked my blind spot as I turned up El Monte Road on my way home.

"Frack. I need to go see Fredrick." I banged the steering wheel again. "Later."

With everything going on, was now the best time for me to ponder my independence? Shouldn't I learn everything I could from Juliet and this new world? Clearly, I still didn't understand a lot, and being here, being part of this, was the first time I felt like I belonged. Not to mention I'd been spoiled by the creature comforts living with Juliet had provided.

As I focused on the soothing music of Scott Williams playing through the car's speakers, my breathing came easier. I loved the calming effects the music of the dulcimer hammer had on me. By the time I reached the driveway, my heart wasn't pounding in my head. And, by the time I parked in front of the garage, the tension in my neck vanished. I sat there for a moment with my eyes closed, enjoying the peace as I waited for the current song to end.

Wanting to talk to Kirtus and the nip in the air added to my haste at grabbing my jacket from the coat hook in the backseat and getting inside the house. I shrugged on my jacket and glanced up at the large two-story brick façade of the Tudor mansion. The hand-carved doors and the charming casements always impressed me, but not nearly as much as the always-present scent of roses and vanilla. I breathed in deep.

A light shone from the garage. I would have to make sure I got Lecomas the keys, or he would be after me. I pulled them from my pocket to ensure I didn't forget to give them to him. I'd once made the mistake of taking the keys with me and leaving them in my bedroom. He was not a happy camper the next day. How was I supposed to know he had made an appointment for the car to be serviced that day? And, why didn't he use the extra keys?

I chuckled as I made my way to the front doors.

As I went to reach for the doors, they were pulled from my grip as they opened. Amanda and Juliet were standing there with their jackets on.

"We need to leave." Juliet rushed past me.

Amanda pulled the door shut.

"What?" My gaze met Amanda's. "What's happening?"

Amanda remained quiet, which was never a good sign, and nudged her head toward Juliet.

Juliet stopped and turned to me, her face neutral, her eyes finding mine. When she spoke, her voice rang kind but strained. "I'm sorry for the way I acted at William's. As you can imagine, I found the news shocking... I apologize."

And?

I didn't move. I've been waiting six days to hear this and find out what happened with her. She had dodged me and Amanda the entire time, no matter the effort I put forth. She never showed up at the foundation, leaving me to handle a majority of the work. Thanks to Amanda, I found out she had spoken with the Council of Light, but as with events a few months ago, I was kept in the dark.

I crossed my arms over my chest, not moving.

Juliet closed her eyes and sighed. "I've been trying to corroborate any of what both you and William said all week, and I can't." Her gaze dropped.

I wanted to reach out and place my hand on her arm and give it a squeeze, but I was still pissed.

"Sybil and the rest of the Council of Light are concerned your vision is being corrupted again, as am I. However..." She frowned and met my gaze. "They believe, more so than I, what you witnessed may be possible."

My mouth dropped open. "But no Immortals lived past two thousand years, which would mean Marcel..." I trailed off.

"If Marcel had lived to his expectancy, he would have still died six hundred years ago."

"Jesus." I raked a hand through my hair.

"The problem is, Immortals, like some animals, roam off when they believe their life is coming to an end." Amanda spoke. "Unlike animals, Immortal bodies are never found, and even if Juliet or any other Immortal went to search for him—"

"We will talk more of this later." Juliet raised a hand. "Please, Chris. I'm sorry. But right now, we have to go. I heard from Victor and he has *invited* us to his penthouse downtown."

The tension in my neck returned with a sharp pain and a thunderous roar all through my head.

"Well, hell..." I put the keys to the car into Juliet's hand. I agreed everything else needed to wait. This news of Victor's return held precedent, especially with what I had witnessed. "This is one heck of a fluke," I muttered as I made my way to the car, this time climbing in behind Amanda.

"Coincidence doesn't even begin to cover what is happening here." Amanda eyes narrowed as her lips pinched together. She offered me a slight shake of her head.

The engine roared to life as I closed my car door. I caught another glance at Amanda and Juliet. Neither of them was happy about any of what was going on. At least we were all in agreement on this one thing.

Chapter Eleven

"How is it Victor's building is taller than any other building in downtown San Jose?" I asked as we pulled into the guest parking of The Heights.

"Victor used his charms not only on the city planner but with the Federal Aviation Administration person to get the clearance." Juliet shook her head. "That man doesn't care about anyone else but himself." Her attitude sharp as she spoke, but the bombardment of her attack was not directed at Amanda or me, perhaps the universe.

"There's a height limit for buildings here, thanks to the airport," Amanda added. "I think the reason no one challenged the construction, even after the process, was because the building was far enough off the flight path, and the building only ended up sixty feet over the height limit."

"Which ensures he will have the tallest building in Silicon Valley indefinitely or until they change the rules," Juliet added.

"Well the structure is still an amazing building." I glanced around at the marble pillars and the high-gloss lobby floor.

Amanda fussed with her hair in the reflection of the elevator doors but managed a nod.

Juliet pushed the buzzer for the penthouse's private elevator and peeked over at the camera.

Once the elevator arrived, Juliet stepped to the side. As I passed her, I got an overwhelming hit of vanilla and roses. Either I was more attuned with her tonight or her stress had manifested in a stronger scent. She pushed the PH button, and we lifted off to the penthouse. At the top, the elevator dinged, and the doors opened. Nothing had changed since we were here last. The foyer had glossy white marble floors contrasted by a single black wall with a red painting in a brushed nickel frame. I half expected Victor to change out the painting to something less juvenile, but having no idea what he paid for the work, I doubted that to be an option. I still didn't care for the piece. However, I did appreciate the high-gloss table and crystal bowl under it. The contrast of the white, black, and red was spectacular. Still nothing compared to the floor-to-ceiling windows framed in black, which made the city below appear like a painting.

Sahin moved from leaning against the wall to standing in front of us. He greeted us in a dark gray suit with bright red tie. I hated how he always presented so handsomely.

"Everyone's out on the patio." He pointed with a huff.

"So good to see you." Juliet's overly polite and upbeat tone countered his cantankerous greeting. "How's your club?"

I whispered to Amanda, "Weren't we going to be talk to Victor alone about my vision and what's going on? Who else does he need here?"

"Not sure," Amanda whispered.

If Juliet or Sahin heard us, they were polite enough to ignore our conversation as theirs continued.

"My club would have been open sooner if I wasn't relegated to being Victor's lacky." Sahin marched us forward to the outside balcony. "I hope Victor finds a Keeper soon," he complained and pulled open the doors for us.

Outside on the balcony, the cool night air rushed in, as did the scents of sweet almonds and amber. There were whiffs of other scents, but Victor's scent stood out, and I'd be lying if his scent didn't make me feel welcome and provide a nice contrast to Juliet's. I found myself inhaling again as I peered around at the group of six people. Three I recognized: Sahin, Victor, and Kirtus. The rest were new to me. I scanned the group. These people must be part of Victor's organization.

"Welcome." Victor's Spanish accent, heavier than I remembered, accosted my ears. He crossed over to us and greeted Juliet with an openhearted handshake.

"Victor." Her tone polite if not slightly strained, she managed her typical bright-eyed relaxed appearance. However, her eyes focused on the others and not Victor. "You look well."

"Thank you." He moved on to Amanda and me. He greeted each of us before he turned to the others in attendance. "Juliet, Amanda, and Chris, please allow me to introduce you to my lieutenants." He pointed to the tall Hispanic man; he was huge and reminded me of a giant. Not anyone I would want to run into in a dark ally. "This is Masko Nez. He oversees my holdings in the southwest, Utah, Colorado, and Wyoming."

Masko walked over to us with his sparkling eyes and his lips pulled up in greeting. "An honor to meet you, Juliet." He stretched out for her hand and beamed. He turned to Amanda and me. "I've heard a lot about both of you, and it's a pleasure to meet you."

I caught a sniff of sage, but I wasn't sure if the scent belonged to him or his cologne. Meeting a Dark who seemed so much like...well, like a normal person caught me off guard in a good way. He appeared every bit as charming as anyone on the Light, some of them more so. Such a nice surprise.

"Oh, for fuck sake, stop sucking up to the Light," this woman who presented herself like my fifth-grade teacher snapped, her voice harsh and sharp. The visceral and vocabulary didn't match her small frame or how impeccably dressed she was. Her eyes narrowed on me.

Her gaze sent a chill all the way to my soul. I never believed people were pure evil until tonight and meeting her. No kindness about her, no redemption, and my body and mind repulsed the more time I spent around her. Recoiling from her wasn't an option at the moment. My feet remained planted and I held my expression as neutrally as possible.

"That would be Betty." Victor frowned in her direction. "She handles much of the northwest and western front of Canada." He waved a hand in her direction. "And she is charming as always."

Wow. Kirtus hadn't exaggerated when he'd mentioned her. She was... I shuddered. She got Sahin's territory. Given what I'd observed, I doubted he would ever get his region back unless she died. I enjoyed the visual more than I should have.

"Don't forget Alaska." She glanced at her nails, seemingly unimpressed with any of us at this point. She didn't move toward our group but stood firmly in place with a glass in her hand.

"Of course not." Victor waved her off.

A dark man with equally dark eyes crossed over to us. He stood next to Kirtus, who remained stationary. Before he spoke I caught a hint of spiced mango—wonderful. It's crazy to say this, but I loved how he smelt. The man opened his mouth into a bright white grin, the contrast of skin and teeth brilliant. He moved closer, and seeing firsthand how dark his eyes were—stunning.

"I'm Joaquín de León." He welcomed all of us. "If you every wish to come to Belize, contact me. I have a beautiful home on the ocean. If you like to dive, Belize is the place to go and we have amazing *clubs* there."

Victor bowed his head in approval. "Joaquín oversees much of Mexico, Guatemala, and, as he mentioned, Belize."

"Enough of all the happy horseshit. Can we please get onto why you called us here and why you have him here?" Betty growled, pointing to Kirtus before she finished off whatever she drank. "I have business to attend to, and this trip was not at a convenient time."

At least she wasn't drinking from a person right there on the balcony, but I had no doubt she would if she were allowed. She may even do worse if Victor let her. I made a mental note to check online tomorrow to see if any children or babies had gone missing. Another shudder went down my spine. I still found it hard to believe Masko or Joaquín were of the Dark, but Betty's dark nature made up for the lack of seeing that quality in the others. She was even worse than Sahin. How could Victor work with her?

"I called you all here as I'm in charge, and you will answer my call without question," Victor chided her, then faced the rest of us. "Now, I don't want to keep anyone longer than needed as I'm sure we all have other more pressing engagements to attend to." His eyes narrowed on Betty. "However, I have no idea what that may be."

Her lips curled into a dark sneer.

Yep, I'm sure there were going to be children missing in the news tomorrow.

"I've been meeting with the other Dark Immortal leaders from around the world, in Frankfurt." Victor walked over to Betty, took her glass, and refilled it from the crystal decanter on the teak patio table. "I apologize for being away for so long. However, as Juliet can attest, these high-level meetings can be arduous especially when I had to explain what happened here over the holiday. I had to make assurances to them all we have things well in hand." He poured three more glasses.

"About that." Juliet's voice was polite with a slight edge.

He handed Betty her glass. "Sahin has kept me up to date. The other members of the Dark don't have the details." He poured a glass of white wine and picked up one glass of red and the wine. "Additionally, I had to take care of a personal matter." He crossed to Juliet and handed her the glass of red, passing Amanda the glass of wine.

"You've been dealing with the Dark this whole time?" Joaquín asked.

"Yes." Victor moved to the table and picked up the two remaining glasses of red.

"And why isn't Pedro here?" Sahin crossed his arms over his chest.

Victor ignored Sahin for the moment and strolled over to hand me a glass of red. "Cheers." He toasted Juliet, Amanda, and me.

"I thought the summons included all of us?" Masko asked from his spot next to Kirtus, who still stood quiet and hadn't moved from his location.

"I have Pedro dealing with other matters; however, his support for what is to come has been assured." Victor's voice dodged; not weak, but no swagger either. If his voice held something more, I didn't see it, but still something nagged at the back of my brain.

"What is so fucking important you called the rest of us here?" Betty sipped her red. "They have these wonderful inventions called Skype, Zoom, and Facetime. Might I suggest—"

"My dear, sweet, Ms. Martin," Victor warned, shutting her up. "If not for your loyalty, your tongue would have gotten you killed long ago."

"Pfft. You enjoyed my tongue the last time I was here." She wiggled her tongue, licking her glass and sipping her red.

I practically spit out my drink but managed to cover my gagging as a cough. The idea of Victor and Betty...was more than my stomach could handle.

Victor shook his head. "I wanted you all here as I've decided, and the Dark leaders have agreed, that Kirtus—" He pointed to Kirtus. "—will become my top lieutenant and our liaison to the Council of Light."

"Fuck that." Betty slammed her glass down onto the table. A crack grabbed my attention, but neither the glass nor the table broke.

"What?" Joaquín said.

"Congratulations." Masko took Kirtus's hand as they shook. "I can't think of a better man."

"The Council of Light is honored to have such a man as Kirtus Lancaster to liaison with." The push of acceptance and welcoming warmed my whole body, which I had no doubt reflected in my face. I had little doubt the change was Juliet's doing.

"It's...it's absolutely an honor and responsibility," Kirtus managed to say.

"What the hell do we need this tool for? We've been doing fine without anything like this." Betty shook her head. "A complete waste. We should be—"

Victor cut her off again. "Because, Betty, my dear"—each of his words dripped with warning—"unless you have some power I'm ignorant of, to counter magic, we need him and we need to work with the Light. As I recall, you were nowhere near here for the battle. Despite my call for assistance."

For the first time, Betty shrank.

Victor gave her a wide birth, but she had reached the end of the rope.

Victor continued, focusing on Betty. "Now, unless you want the post?"

"Not fucking likely."

"Unbelievable." Sahin shook his head side to side. "This is what you've been up to? You've been setting things in place so Kirtus and Chris can continue to screw without having to worry about any interference from the Dark Community. Unbelievable. And Pedro agreed to this shit. He hates Kirtus." His eyes narrowed on Kirtus before turning on me. "You gotta have one hell of an ass and cock to match." He pointed at Kirtus. "And you. If you think this is going to change—"

"Enough." Victor's voice tore through the air and ended all comment or protest. "Nothing and no one will bother Kirtus. I neither need nor request your approval in this matter. Kirtus's station in our community has changed as has his position in my territory and the territory of most of the other Dark leaders. All of you will follow my instructions and consider this matter settled." He motioned to Kirtus. "Whom he chooses to spend his time with is none of your concern, Sahin."

"Well, I'm not reporting to this dick." Sahin puffed up his chest and leveled his shoulders.

Victor moved so suddenly he held Sahin before I blinked. "You will report to whomever I tell you to." Victor's hands were around Sahin's neck, and Victor lifted Sahin off the patio.

I peeked at Juliet and Amanda. Amanda remained quiet, and Juliet only offered me a slight shake of her head. I got the message loud and clear; we're not to say or do anything. This was a matter between Sahin and Victor. Being witness to this event made my stomach turn, and despite Sahin being an ass, I still ached for his embarrassment.

"Now make yourself useful." Victor deliberately lowered Sahin. "Get everyone fresh drinks so we can honor my new chief lieutenant properly." He dropped Sahin to the patio.

Sahin's face burned red.

"Oh, Sahin, next time you decide to voice an opinion, I'll have you serving at all my events in nothing more than a white bow tie." Victor sneered. "I realize how much you enjoy showing off and flexing your...authority."

Sahin glowered, and with shaky hands he did as instructed.

"Does anyone else have any protests? Betty?" Victor glared at her.

"No, Victor." Betty's voice became meek, matching what I would expect from someone of her stature. "Congratulations." She rested her hands on her hips as she scrutinized Kirtus. "I look forward to working with you, and of course, if there is anything I can do...well, you can count on me."

"Good." Victor's welcoming presence returned to his face.

Once Sahin had refreshed everyone's drinks, Victor raised his glass. "Kirtus Lancaster, my chief lieutenant, welcome. Serve us well and you'll be rewarded for your efforts. Congratulations."

We all raised our glass to Kirtus.

"Congratulations." I found the word easy to say and the smile at Kirtus natural. He returned my grin with his own. I had no delusions this would be difficult for him, but Victor had made his intentions clear and the others fell in line pretty quick. Even Sahin managed to raise his glass.

"There will be an official ceremony in a few weeks, which Sahin will put together." Victor raised an eyebrow at Sahin.

"As you wish, Victor." Sahin managed to keep his words barely above a whisper. "If you'd like to use my club."

"No, I want something classy. I'm sure you'll sort out the details...and won't disappoint me." Victor turned to Juliet. "How do you manage these things?"

"I have help." Juliet kept her tone polite but measured.

Victor nodded as a glint of sadness filled his eyes.

*

"Why weren't we invited?" I glanced over to Amanda as we stood out on the patio.

"I don't know." Amanda's expression was tight, and she clicked her nails. She wasn't happy about not being included in the meeting either.

"Given all that has happened, it's best for Juliet and Victor to speak privately." Kirtus rolled his glass in his hands.

After the toast and more awkward chitchat, Victor dismissed his lieutenant and asked to speak with Juliet privately, leaving Kirtus, Amanda, and me out on the patio, which wasn't too bad. Masko and Joaquín made their goodbyes and mentioned they were looking forward to the ceremony in a few weeks, while Betty and Sahin vanished away together in a cloak of whispers.

"So, Chief Lieutenant, what does the title even mean? Is that why I haven't heard from you today?" I bumped into Kirtus's shoulder, blowing him a kiss.

Kirtus ran a hand through his hair.

Both Amanda and I faced him.

"What's wrong?" Amanda asked.

I grasped for his hand.

"This position," Kirtus articulated. "You and me. There will be a lot to it. There may be things that I will not be able to share with you."

I understood, probably better than he realized.

Kirtus continued. "I had to meet with Victor today, all day, and I'm sure it's only the start." He closed his eyes and lowered his head.

"Hey." I squeezed his hand. "It'll be fine. Victor is...well...Victor, but still, he's a fair man."

"In all my years, I've never heard of a Dark Conclave." Kirtus's head dipped, and his eyes closed. "I'm sure they have had to have them in the past, but if they did, they had them and I stayed away, but..." He raised his head and met my gaze. "I'm going to be in the middle of all this now, and Victor mentioned the Dark are trying to consolidate and pull together more like the Light, but...something's up."

"I'm the one who's supposed to say that." I forced a warm expression to my face as I tried to lighten the mood.

"You know what I mean."

"Well, I haven't heard anything," Amanda said. "But with all the...stuff...happening with everyone on our end."

I leaned closer to her. "Isn't all of this a good thing?" I asked. "They, the Dark, working together and creating ties, a consolidation of power might be good for everyone."

"Assuming we can work with who ends up with all the power," Kirtus said. "A Dark Conclave like this wouldn't be like what the Light have. There would be a lot of fighting and..." His head dropped.

"Yes, this is a big deal and the ramifications are huge." Amanda kept her phrasing soft as she could. "This is new for everyone. And I think the Dark meet more often than you think. They have a loose structure already. I remember hearing from Juliet how they met a few years ago."

"Maybe, but what about your vision?" Kirtus asked. "That guy you saw."

"I think the vision had to do with ensuring you succeed," I said. "He seemed really interested in you. Given what happened with Sahin and that Betty person, I can see why I've been having the visions and I can understand his worry."

"There are a lot of people who aren't going to be happy," Amanda added. "Even members of the Light—Taqi, Fernando, and An, they are going to prove to be difficult to come around."

"I haven't even met any of the other Dark Leaders." Kirtus sighed. "How am I going to be expected to work with them, if I don't even know them?" he bemoaned. "And I doubt anything going on with the Light will be like what I'm sure Victor had to do."

"You don't think he…" I slid my finger along my neck.

"Who knows." Kirtus adjusted his collar. "I doubt he would have to resort to such measures. Victor is strong, but he's not stupid. He wouldn't move on any of the other Dark leaders, not right now, not when he needs something."

The door to the patio opened. "Thank you for waiting," Juliet offered. "We can go." She pointed to the foyer. "Victor said he would see you tomorrow as well, Kirtus."

Kirtus pursed his lips, giving the space the onceover.

I wasn't sure if he had been holding his breath this entire time.

"Is everything okay?" Amanda asked.

"This position of Kirtus's is going to take some finesse, but it'll be fine." Juliet held the door open for us.

"Do you mind if I go with Kirtus?" I asked before thinking to ask him, but I didn't want to be with Juliet tonight. With everything going on here and at home, all I wanted to do was cuddle next Kirtus. "Do you want the company?"

"Your company is always welcome." Kirtus took my hand.

Juliet beamed. "See you at the office tomorrow?"

"Have fun, you two." Amanda winked as they walked out.

We waited for them to leave us on the patio. "I'm not going to be good company tonight." Kirtus frowned and walked over to the edge of the patio, glancing out at the city, a king studying his lands.

I leaned into him, resting my head on his shoulder. Catching sight of the shorter, older stone building with the cupola on top somehow peeking up at us, its lights somehow brighter. "Come on, let's get out of here, and I'll see what I can do to change your mood when we get to your place."

Kirtus chuckled.

Chapter Twelve

Last night with Kirtus turned out to be everything I needed, well, sort of. He had a lot on his mind and didn't want to talk, so we sat and spent quiet time together, enjoying our time with each other. No noise. No TV. No talking. Nothing. Waking up nestled in next to him in the morning was amazing; however, having to leave him to head to the office sucked. Sadly, traffic didn't make my drive any better. Getting from Morgan Hill to downtown Los Altos was akin to playing a video game that involved making your way through the seventh level of Hell. Only this time death and destruction are real and everyone had five-thousand-pound vehicles able to kill. How people managed this on a daily basis...no way I wanted to do this every day.

My day at the office was quiet and luckily uneventful. I enjoyed having a normal workday again. I even managed to make it over to Fredrick's shop to get fitted for my tux and to pick out some new clothes. We chatted about *mundane* lives, and he wanted to ensure I felt better. I assured him everything with me was fine, that my illness had been caused because of the stress and not only had I skipped breakfast but lunch. Once I reassured him I wouldn't make the same mistake again, he seemed happy and our conversation moved on. As we talked about clothes and my tuxedo, I asked him to set up my own account and he obliged, which released the unknown knot in my stomach I had been holding. One more step for me becoming my own Immortal.

By the end of the day, I had the proverbial song in my heart and dance in my step. A good day overall. The road up into Alum Rock wasn't too difficult, which was nice. I pulled into the driveway of William's home and put the car in park. I wasn't sure I wanted to do this alone, but I didn't want to ask Juliet given what happened last time, even though she would have come and been gracious. Why do that to her? Also, I needed to try to see where and how I fit into this Immortal world I now inhabited.

Once out of the car, I made my way to the door and knocked. Moments passed before William appeared and opened the door, allowing me entry. A nice fresh scent of wild flowers greeted me as I walked in. I found his scent relaxing and nice, something different. William appeared dressed similarly to what he had on the last we were all here: khaki pants and a buttoned-down long-sleeved green shirt.

"Welcome." He gestured to the living room.

"Thank you for having me."

"Considering our last meeting being cut short…" He walked ahead of me. "Now that I have a better understanding of your gifts, I can see how I can help you."

"How we can help each other," I corrected. I didn't want this to be a one-way deal. I liked William. He came across like a good man, and I wanted to see what I could do to help him as well.

Assuming there is anything.

He wrung his hands, glancing around the comfortable living room. "I don't keep any…"

"I call it red." I took a guess at what he was about to say.

Williams offered a slight chuckle. "I don't keep any *red* in the house, but would you like water, or I have wine?"

"Water would be nice."

"Please have a seat." He walked off. I made my way to the windows and enjoyed the sky as the sun continued to set. The sky shifted from yellows and oranges to reds and purples.

I caught William's scent. "This view is amazing. As is your home. When did you remodel?"

"A few years ago."

"I wouldn't have expected…" I took the offered water and frowned.

"We don't all live on a reservation or in teepees." William pointed to the couch. "And not all of us run casinos either." He sat in his club chair. "When I worked full-time, I was a lawyer. Now I take on special cases every so often, mainly for my Nation."

I sat. "I'm sorry. I didn't mean…"

He waved off my apology. "I understand. I'm sure not all Immortals feed on the innocent and corrupt people." He sipped his wine. "And I'm sure you don't sleep in a coffin."

I laughed and shook my head.

"People get offended too easily these days. I detected no maliciousness, and it's only you and I here; we can talk like people. If you have questions, I'll answer them as long as you promise to do the same."

"Sounds fair."

He took another sip from his glass and put it on the coffee table. "You don't strike me as old. I understand you are a new Immortal, but that could mean anything. You might be older than me."

"No." I shook my head. "I'm twenty-eight. My twenty-ninth birthday is in August."

"You are new to this."

An understatement if I had ever heard one.

"Amazing. Do you have any more questions for me?" William asked and reached for his wine, taking another sip.

"Are you married? What about kids?"

His mouth twitched, and he peered to the floor. He raised his head, watching me. "My wife Susan passed five years ago." He cleared his throat.

Memories flashed in his eyes. At least that was what I believed. He didn't say, and I wasn't going to pry.

"We have two children and I have five grandchildren." The pride he radiated extended all the way to his face.

Clearly, he was proud to be a grandfather.

"Wow." I sipped my water. At least this tasted as I expected, like nothing, and water was easy to drink and easy to pee out. So a win both ways.

"Your family?" he asked.

"I assumed you had heard all about that."

"Only the rumors."

I put a pin in the "rumors" because I wanted to know more about that. I frowned at the memories. "I was an only child. I assumed my parents were both dead, but that was a lie my father created so he could absorb my mother's power and mine." My neck grew warm, and I clasped my hands together to keep them from trembling as I spoke. "My dad was a full witch, and my mother was a quarter witch. Of course, all this information hidden from me until..." I gulped another mouthful of water.

"I apologize." William leaned forward. "I shouldn't have asked."

"I can't believe he would do that. I thought he loved her. I thought he loved us." A tremble caught my voice, but I didn't want to stop. "I mean he was a great dad when I was kid. To find out my childhood was all BS..." My heart pounded and my hands were in tight balls. "How could anyone do that to their family?"

William leaned in his chair, quiet and sympathetic. All the wrinkles of age and wisdom appeared on his face. His expression didn't help me relax, but curiosity had me and I wanted to see if he would say anything. I really wanted him to have some words of wisdom for me. He seemed like a good man, and I had no doubt he was a better father than mine. I supposed any father that didn't try to kill their son made the good father list in my book. I glanced down at my water glass and forced myself to sip some more. Instead I gulped the last of the water down and set my glass on the coffee table harder than I wanted.

"Sorry," I mumbled and wiped my hands on my suit pants.

He shook his head. "Sometimes people are fucking assholes." William's words showed his annoyance, but not at me, at people in general. "I'm sorry your father was one of them."

I laughed. I couldn't believe what he said, and his annoyance made me laugh. He hit the nail on the head, but his comment wasn't what I had expected. Once I stopped laughing, I glanced over at him, meeting his gaze. "You and me both."

"At least you have your good memories of him. Hold on to those."

My head dropped, but I forced it back up wanting to stay positive. "I try."

"Good." William adjusted in his chair.

"If I may," I began, "you mentioned rumors. Rumors about me?"

William nodded. "When the events started to happen around the holidays last year, I did some digging around. I talked to Patricia and Deborah. When Juliet called me about the wards on her house and her business, I understood something changed. That something was you. Finding out information on you wasn't hard, especially when you know who to ask and where to look."

His abilities made sense. People like William were probably able to find out things about the Immortal community and the witch community that no one else could.

"Did you want to try and see if I can help you control your powers? Crossing into your mind is far too easy. I think we should try to build up some defenses for you first. Unless you would like to talk more?" He examined me. "Up to you."

"I'm here so you can study my gifts. Learn more about them. Right?"

"Can't we do both?" Williams leaned forward. "I've not seen powers like yours ever, and I don't make it a point to spend time with Immortals or witches; however, you have piqued my curiosity, and I would be remiss to turn down such an opportunity. Even among my people we have stories about people with your gifts. So you are a true treat."

"As long as you don't take me to a lab to dissect me or lock me up in a cage." My heart sank a bit even though I tried to keep my remarks upbeat. "I'm pretty good with whatever, and learning how to protect my brain and my psyche would be a good thing. I don't like people having free access to me like that." I glanced out the window. "Do you think you can help?"

"We can try." He sat in his chair and studied me again.

After several moments of him watching me and us not talking, I broke the uneasiness. "What do we need to do?"

"Sorry, I picked at your mind."

"I didn't feel anything."

"And that is another thing we should try and address." He rubbed his hands together.

"Okay...how?"

"I suggest a wall," he responded. "It's cliché but accurate. I would also suggest creating a mental vault for all those things you don't want anyone to take advantage of. Like your fear of insects."

I shuddered. "I understand this all conceptually, but how do you build a wall in your mind or even a vault and keep the barrier up all the time, and what about when you sleep? Are such things even possible?"

"Asks a vampire to a Muwekma Ohlone Healer."

If logic hovered in the air I missed it, but I understood his point. "Okay." So, I sat deeper in the sofa and closed my eyes. I focused on a wall. I caught hints of wildflowers but pushed the aroma to the side.

"I think that is wise." William's hand rested on my shoulder.

I jumped and a yelp escaped my lips. "How did you get here?"

"You have an open mind." He took his hand off my shoulder. He pointed. "No wall. No defenses, but you were able to smell my scent."

"Wildflowers." I sighed.

"Interesting. Can you smell everyone?"

"Yep." I sniffed at the air as if to reaffirm my assertion.

"Use that. I think smell is important. If you can eliminate, not push away, the scent from your mind, it might help you defend against intruders. We will need to explore this more, but first the wall."

I tried to picture a wall again. But what kind of wall? Something strong, something not even a tank could get through. I focused on concrete blocks and steel plating. The combination seemed like a good mix, so I put my wall together; each level built in a staggering line with steel plates bolted and glued in place.

"Don't place the wall; see it built," William instructed.

I focused on every detail, the mortar, the blocks, the steel reinforcements, the bolts, and the steel plates. He wanted me to picture every detail, so I did. I continued to focus on my wall, and by the time it reached over my head, I ran my hand along the wall to feel the smooth texture of the steel. I examined the bolt work; happy with it, I moved to the seams where the steel plates met. I wasn't happy; like a vulnerability hit me in the face, so I envisioned them welded together. The aroma of steel and metal melting together drifted to my nose. The wall shifted and changed, and soon all the seams were welded and ground smooth. I walked along the wall, running my hand along the metal.

The wall pleased me and seemed to be what I needed.

Cold and solid. Nothing could get through.

"What do you think?" I turned, not seeing William. "William," I called and nothing. Alone. Or what I assumed to be alone. I opened my eyes, and William sat in his chair, his eyes closed. "William," I called out. I considered getting up and tapping his leg, but instead I snapped my fingers. "William." This time much louder.

His eyes flickered opened and he sat up. "Your wall stopped me." He struggled with his breath after each word. "Once you put the wall together, I couldn't get through. How long have I been like this?"

"I don't know, a minute or two."

He peeked over my shoulder at the clock on the wall. "Chris, it's been an hour and a half."

"What?"

"Impressive, well done." He nodded.

"How is that even possible?"

"Time is a concept, but not the constant we believe it to be."

"Say what now?"

"Nothing." He waved off my question. "You have a wall built. Use it. Even if you don't always need the structure for defense, pull the wall up when you feel threatened. I think the barrier will help you. The more you focus on the wall, the easier it will become for you." He massaged his temples.

"Okay. Did you want some more water or something?" I got up.

"That would be nice. It's in the kitchen." He pointed.

I got up and grabbed both our glasses, making my way to the kitchen. Once there, I took advantage of watching the view for a moment as I focused on my wall. I called up all the details again and remembered how smooth the wall was under my fingers. I filled his wine glass with water and topped off my glass. I made my way into the living room.

William rested his head on the back of his chair.

"Are you sure you're all right?"

"I'm fine. Just needed the rest." He took the glass of water I offered him and had a few sips.

"Amazing."

"Practice and it should become second nature." He cleared his throat and leaned forward.

I took my seat again and sipped my water. Playing with my wall filled me with relief and safety I could remain in my mind and work on my defenses indefinitely.

"You ready to try and remove me from your mind?" he asked.

"You sure you want to do that?"

"I don't see why not." He finished his water, cracked his neck, and shook out his hands. His warm-up looked like he was getting ready to play football. Maybe wrestle, or something.

"Okay." I closed my eyes, imagined the wall I had created. For practice, I washed the structure from my mind and focused on the scent of wildflowers. I drew the scent in as deeply as my lungs would allow. The image of William grew even more solid in my mind. I touched him. Once I had the full sense of him instead of pushing him from my mind, I... *Boom.* I pictured the image and the smell blowing up into a million pieces until they vanished completely. Glass shattered a cry of pain followed. I jolted out of my seat as my eyes flew open. The living room windows were blown out, and I surveyed William.

He sat there, blood dripping from his nose, and he shook. His eyes were closed, and his body trembled.

"Oh God." I jumped from the sofa and ran over to him. I took his hand. "William." His heart still beat, fast but slowing down. "William." He stopped shaking and his eyes fluttered open.

"Water," he moaned.

I grabbed his glass and ran to the kitchen, filled it up with water. On the kitchen counter were a few napkins. I grabbed them and rushed to his side. I dabbed at the blood dripping from his nose with one napkin keeping the others clean should they be needed.

He reached up, took the napkin, and held it to his nose as he sat forward.

In my hand, I held the water. After a few beats, he took it and had a sip. He dabbed at his nose again.

His heart rate returned to normal. However, the windows in his living room were gone, and the curtains were billowing as the cool night air made its way into the house.

"Crap." I didn't know what to do.

"That." He set the bloody napkin on the coffee table. "That was...the power."

"I'm sorry. I figured blowing up the image and the scent were the best way. I didn't think."

He patted my hand. "I'm fine, but maybe we've done enough for tonight." He peered at where the windows once were. "Plus, I'm not sure my living room can take much more."

"Your windows. I'll pay to have them fixed."

"Yes, yes, you will," he agreed. "Acts of the supernatural are not covered under my homeowner's insurance." He chuckled while massaging his temples.

I grabbed my phone, not sure who to call, and texted Amanda. She would know what to do.

*

"I'm so sorry," I reiterated to William. We had moved into the family room to give Amanda and the glass repair company space to work. I had been fussing over William, trying to get him to drink, and I even offered to make him something to eat, but he declined.

"I'm fine."

"But what I did? Your house. Ugh." I raked my hands over my face and into my hair. "I'm sorry."

"Please stop. It's not like you meant to. I'll be fine and the windows are getting fixed." William glanced in the direction of the living room. "How did they get here so fast anyway?"

The magic of Amanda and this power, like all magic, came with a cost that I would have to pay. A big chunk of change I had no doubt, but the new windows would be worth it.

Amanda glided into the room and took a seat. "Well, they are getting the windows all sorted; they should be done shortly. We're lucky the windows are a standard size, so the cost won't be nearly as much as it might have been."

I raked a hand through my hair, my neck and cheeks still warm.

"It must have been quite a shock to have your windows blow out. Micro bursts can happen, but wow." Amanda glanced around the rest of the room. "I'm happy there was no additional damage."

William appeared puzzled. After a moment a grin blossomed across his lips. "Well, I'm glad Chris was here to help."

"Yeah, help." I frowned.

"In the future, maybe blow them away or wave them gone," William suggested. "Don't blow them up."

My gaze dropped. That was a good suggestion.

The glass guys needed about three hours to fix the windows and get all the debris cleaned up. Amanda was gracious enough to point them in my direction when it came time for the payment. I pulled out my wallet and handed over my credit card. I didn't even want to see the total, the cost unimportant at this point. By the time all was said and done, I checked my phone to see eleven thirty-eight flash at me. Once both Amanda and I were satisfied William and his house would be all right, we made our excuses and headed out to the front.

Once the door clicked, Amanda took my arm and led us to my car. "You blew out his windows with your mind?"

"No. Well, sort of...I don't know."

She crossed her arms over her chest.

"We were practicing. I built up my mental fortifications, wall and stuff like that. William had me focus on removing people from my mind. Like witches, or ancient Immortals who shouldn't be there. Well, you heard him. I blew him up and..." I shook my head. "I thought I killed him."

"Wow! No wonder Sahin fears you."

"Can we get out of here?" I peeked around the neighborhood, but no one watched us. "I'm tired and I want to go home."

"Sure." She gave me a hug and walked over to her car.

She got into her car and started the motor. She waved. I slipped into the driver's seat and spared another peek at William's house. I still had a lot to learn, but practice was going to be the only way to discover what all my talents were. In the end William was okay and everything had been repaired. I wished destroying William's windows hadn't happened in the first place.

My biggest concern, to be honest, was, would I be able to fend off both a mental and physical attack?

Chapter Thirteen

I sniffed the air. Everything smelled wrong. No roses. No vanilla. Nothing. No movement, no other scents, the air perfectly still. The windows hadn't been harmed, the door still intact, and everything appeared to be in order. I closed my eyes and listened—not a single chirp of crickets or other night creatures. I shuddered. My eyes opened and I studied the windows again. They were dark. Where was everyone? Rocks from the driveway crunched under my feet as I stepped forward. The crackling popped like fireworks and echoed in my ears.

I froze.

Not good. My heart thundered like a drum; the hairs on my arms stood on end. I needed to shift. I brought forth my true self. I expelled the air from my lungs and allowed myself to transform. My head ached where the ridges grew and deepened my brow. My tongue ran over the tips of my extended teeth.

The transformation complete.

Power coursed through my body; every part of me tingled. I stopped and closed my eyes and focused on my mental wall. The image appeared and I ran my hand over the solid barrier firm under my touch. The cold smoothness of my mental barricade comforted me.

I took another moment to reach out with my mind. Was anyone else here—Marcel, a witch, anyone with mental powers that had the ability to me harm?

Nothing.

Ready.

At the door I reached out with my mind again, my eyes shut to focus. Something happened here and I wasn't privy to those events. The energy was all wrong. With the door in front of me, I rested my hand on the handle. I pictured the handle. Who had opened this door last? I spotted Juliet and several others. None of them speaking. My gaze went from Juliet to the others. Who were they? They were all dressed in black or dark colors. The more I fixated on them, the less clear my surroundings became. The knob on the door opened with ease. The foyer dark, on my left down the hall to Juliet's office were soft footsteps moving away.

I sniffed the air again.

"Nothing," I whispered. My heart banged in my chest, even though I tried to calm it. I pushed my heartbeat as far from my consciousness as possible. I needed to concentrate on two things: what happened here and my mental defense. I couldn't spare thoughts for anything else.

To my right, a presence. Someone stood waiting for me.

I turned in time to stop the object coming for my head. I pulled a bat from the person, swung with all my force, and crashed the club into their stomach. With an additional swing, I bashed the bat down on their head with a wet crunch, knocking them to the floor.

"One," Juliet announced in my head.

I listened for a heartbeat; they still had one. I didn't want to kill them, just disable them until I found out what was going on.

"This isn't funny." My voice echoed through the hall. I let the bat go. Not the best move on my part, but I can respond quicker with the use of both my hands. At least I hoped.

No response. I inhaled deeply again, but as with the outside, nothing. The house stood devoid of scent, and even with my enhanced sight I only saw about a foot in front of me.

How did they get the house so dark?

I moved past the still form on the floor to the sitting room. I had no idea how many more people were here and without the ability to smell them... I shook my head. I continued to focus on the use of my second sight, or whatever to sense the danger. I frowned. The anger in my gut grew. I hated games and being tested.

Despite realizing there was no point, I still grasped for the light switch.

Nothing.

"You cut all the power to the house." I spoke to no one, at least I assumed no one. "Fuck." My bag of tricks for my mental ability had grown, with the addition of the mental wall and the ability to blast people out of my mind, but no one was in my head...at least that I sensed. Even Juliet's voice echoed in the real world, not my mind.

To my right something fell and hit the floor, another distraction like the footsteps before. I waited for the person in front of me to come in for the attack. Something swung at me, but I stepped so they only hit air. I spun to the side, stepped up behind them, pulled the object out of their hands, another bat, and hit them in the back. They crumpled to the ground.

"Two." Juliet's voice rang out.

My eyes closed again as I tried to reach out and locate the others. I needed to know who and how many people I faced. Before moving on I made sure my mental barrier was in place. Calming my heart, I focused and again tried to reach out with my mind. At first, only fog, but it cleared. In the dining room, a woman waited for me. I sensed someone at the top of the stairs in the foyer and one more person—

"Shit!" I ducked, but the wood cracking registered before my brain acknowledged the pain. Flashes of light filled my sight, and a thunderous roar echoed in my head. I crashed to a knee, barely able to catch my breath. I sensed the next attack coming; this time I blocked with my left arm. The pain erupted into my shoulder and neck and down into my fingers, but I stood ready for discomfort, or as ready as anyone else with my level of training; this was nothing like the movies. I grabbed the wooden object and snapped it in half. I grabbed the person; they were shorter than me and male. They had no scent, but I picked up on their fear, their heart pounding in their chest. I growled as I tossed them across the room. A glorious yelp of pain sang out.

"Yes!" I sneered.

Green apples filled my senses and overcame me. Side-stepping, I transformed to my human form. "Oh God!" I ran over to the form splayed out on the floor.

"Ben!" I pushed his wonderfully scented blood from my mind despite the quiver in my stomach.

"Ben." I moved a hand over his face.

"Hiya, Chris." Ben's voice was barely a whisper and uncharacteristically weak.

Something moved along my leg, circled my groin, then moved to my side. Hot pressure. My mind slow to process the pain. I peered down and, in my side, a dagger with Ben's hand connected to it. "What the..."

Ben pushed me off him, and I collapsed to the floor, pain searing through my body, all but paralyzing me. My mental wall also crumbled in my mind.

Fuck.

"Enough." Juliet's word echoed through the house, and the lights flickered on, the sudden brightness blinding me for a moment.

Ben wiped the blood from the side of his face. Amanda rushed in and knelt next to me, wrapping her hand around the dagger. "This is gonna hurt." She slid the dagger out as a towel instantly covered the wound.

I tried to move, but pain shot from the gash in my side.

"Silver dagger," Amanda whispered. "The wound is going to hurt for a bit, but you'll be fine."

"Bastard."

Ben leaned next to me, his warm breath on my cheek. "Sorry, man, but you got me good. Be glad I didn't spear your sausage. Trust me, the thought did cross my mind." He stuck out his arm. "Here, drink my blood; it'll help."

I turned my head away from him.

"Don't be stubborn." Ben pushed his arm closer to me.

"Fresh blood will help," Amanda added as she held the towel to my side.

"I'll be fine." I tried to keep my voice calm, but the shaking and how fast my heart beat said differently.

Two more sets of hands helped me to my feet. On my left Juliet and on my right Gregor. They moved me to the couch.

I peeked at Ben, Terrie already tending to his head wound, and he sat on the floor where I found him, blood still ran from his temple where he must have hit his head. The sweet green apple smell teased me more than anything he did.

"Where's Kirtus?" I scanned the room.

"He's still in the foyer." Juliet brushed the hair from my forehead. "You hit him hard."

"Oh." My lips pinched together at my annoyance.

Juliet put a glass of red to my lips and I greedily drank. With each drop sliding down my throat, life returned to my aching body.

"If you won't drink from Ben..." Amanda rolled up the sleeve of her mint-green blouse. "At least drink from me."

After I finished the glass of red, Amanda thrust her arm to my mouth, and I bit down. The taste of buttered popcorn filled my mouth, and I eagerly drank more. The ache in my side was replaced by a stitching of the wound as my healing began to close the gash. I would be sore for a day or two, but at least the wound would be gone. A familiar pressure in my mind signaled me to stop, so I pulled away from Amanda's arm after biting my tongue and licking the wound to heal the bite I had created.

"Better?" Gregor asked.

I nodded and sat up. Kirtus appeared in the archway, rubbing his head. His sweatshirt had a tear in it, but his jeans didn't look any worse for wear.

"I'm sorry." I reached up for his hand as he crossed over to me.

Instead of a sore face, he greeted me with a laugh. "I've been through worse."

"I'm sorry, everyone." I tried to meet all their eyes.

Juliet rubbed my arm. "Don't be. This was my test, and overall, you did well. Of course, considering what happened at William's house last night, we took some extra precautions."

"Like no scents and no one trying to get into my head."

She smirked and lifted her shoulders slightly.

I peeked over at Ben again. "I didn't realize you would be using Ben and Amanda. I would have been more careful."

"That's the point," Gregor declared. "Vampires don't play fair and will use their Keepers to protect them. Or anyone else they can utilize to their benefit."

"Which is why we can kick ass." Ben plopped down in one of the armchairs.

"Did you manage to locate us all?" Terrie sat on the arm of the chair Ben rested in. He leaned in and rested his head against her.

"Someone waited at the top of the stairs. Either you or Amanda were in the dining room. I'm guessing Juliet hid down the hall by her office, with Kirtus, Gregor, and Ben in the foyer, living room, and sitting room." I massaged my temples. "But I didn't sense Ben till too late."

Juliet tapped her lips. "It may be harder for you to sense humans as you've only focused on Immortals and other supernatural beings at this point. You will need to expand your reach."

"Okay." My head ached from using my ability and my body was beat up, so I hoped I would remember. I glanced for a piece of paper and pen but didn't see any.

Amanda checked my wound again.

I peeked down and witnessed firsthand Ben's handiwork. Instead of a bleeding gash where he had stabbed me with his knife, there was only a red mark. The healing cut still burned from the silver, but at least the bleeding had stopped. "All of you were hard to sense, and I think my figuring everything out took too much time over all. I should have been faster. Not to mention the mental strain. Trying to keep the wall up, sense you all, and fight..." The banging of my temples halted my remarks.

"Maybe." Juliet clicked her nails together. "You are going to need to work on building up both your mental strength and your physical stamina."

Amanda, satisfied with my wounds healing, lowered my shirt and crossed the room. Taking a seat on the second sofa, she checked her arm and pulled down her sleeve.

"But this was still a good practice," Juliet commended. "We'll have to do more practicing." She went over to the gold cart and poured several glasses of red. Gregor had already picked up the chair and side table I had tossed Ben into.

"Maybe not in your house." Gregor showed the broken lamp.

Juliet pursed her lips. "I didn't like that lamp anyway." She sipped her drink and proceeded to offer drinks to everyone. "Still, you're right. We'll have to find a place."

"There's a gym in town," Amanda remarked.

"I have an outbuilding on my property we can set up and use." Kirtus tasted his red. "The building used to be a barn, but now I use it as storage and a workshop. At least there nothing will get broken, and there is a lot of open space."

"Are you sure? You don't mind?" I took the glass of red and drank. The warm mix of flavors made their way over my tongue. The red soothed my head and my side.

"Using the space will give me a reason to fix it up. At one point I used the barn for horses but..." He shook his head.

"I miss having horses." Juliet had a wistful tone to her voice. "I turned the old carriage house into a guest house. John lives there now." She sighed. "Such a different time."

"Cars are so much faster and don't make nearly as much of a mess, especially in the city." Gregor drank his red. "Still there is nothing as majestic as a beautiful steed and a ride in the country."

There were several nods from those experienced in such things. I had a fleeting image of what this world would be like in a few hundred years and if I would miss this time period as much as the others seemed to miss the horse and buggy era.

*

The warm flavor of fruit punch filled my mouth. I eagerly gulped the blood down, every part of me alive with energy. The burn in my side from Ben's silver dagger vanished. I noticed my arousal. God, I needed to come but I didn't want to stop the feeding. Once the blood stopped flowing, I pushed the body away. At that moment screams of terror pulled my attention as someone pushed past me.

My eyes focused as I took in the scene around me. We were in an arena. There were people running, stepping over one another, pushing others to the ground. Confusion overtook my desire to feed. Where was I? What was happening? I scanned more of the building. So many people, thousands. And us. We were feeding out in the open. I peeked down to the arena floor and witnessed hockey players hitting people with their sticks. They were no match. Terrie pushed one of the players to the ground, ripped off his mask, and tore into his throat. People ran in every direction, and the sweet smell of death and blood was everywhere.

What's happening?

I needed to find...I needed to find Juliet. I didn't see her. I searched for Gregor or Kirtus. I recognized the short red hair and silly Disney sweatshirt at once. He leaned over a body. "Kirtus," I yelled and rushed over to him. "Kirtus!" I grabbed his shoulder.

He turned to me and growled. Kirtus had transformed into every bit the monster we all could be.

"What's your problem?" he snarled as drops of red life dripped from his mouth.

I stepped from him. "What's happening?" My heart pounded in my chest.

"We're feeding." He wiped the blood from his mouth. "Now, unless you want to fuck, leave me to it." He turned to the young guy he fed from.

I took another step back and nearly tripped over the body of the woman I had drained. I tried to reach out with my mind to find Juliet. The floor shook, and I grabbed onto the arena chair. Next to me, Juliet landed, blood running down her chin and covering her cream-colored blouse, the blood and cream a sickening contrast.

"You've already had your fill." She licked her lips.

"What are we doing? The cameras?" I pointed to the jumbo screen broadcasting this whole nightmare. "The people?"

"This is the final reckoning." Voice crisp and clear, Sahin appeared next to me. "We are taking our rightful place as masters of this world."

"No," I said.

"We had to strike before more of the others woke. The world will soon be in chaos, and we are the only ones who can save us all." Juliet sneered. "All our power is at stake, and we have to keep those who would see our end in check." She jumped over the row of seats and immediately found a woman holding a child, screaming. The woman froze in fear. Juliet ripped the child, maybe four or five, from the woman. That woman. I recognized her. I had seen her before; white with brown hair, maybe twenty-six or twenty-seven. No. This was Ashley, the woman at the club when I had met and fed off Samantha. How did she have a child? I flinched as Juliet sank her fangs into the screaming little girl as the woman tried to pull her child to her.

Sahin laughed and vanished. I tried to find him, but he was gone. I peeked to the big jumbo monitor over the ice arena, the camera clearly abandoned as the image was lopsided. The screen flickered, but I noted some of what appeared on the screen. *The San Jose Sharks welcome the Anaheim Ducks.* The date flashed out, but before I caught the whole thing the lights blinked out. Still, I saw *March.*

A scream pulled my attention as Juliet now fed off the mother, the child discarded on the ground with the overturned popcorn bin and spilled soda. All around me, blood and chaos. Light and Dark Immortals attacking any human they got their hands on. The attack was a mad house. A complete slaughter and I didn't want to imagine what happened outside the building.

A sudden thump on my head and the arena vanished into a fog.

"No," a man called out. He clutched a woman to his chest. Rocking back and forth. Tears streaming down his checks. "You can't..." He sobbed. Marcel.

This place was new to me. Where were we? "In a vision," I said. "This is a vision." I tried to focus on Marcel and the woman he sobbed over. She had black hair and fair skin, but that was all I made out.

"Sorry, little one, you aren't meant to see this." Marcel rested a hand on my shoulder.

"What's happening?"

"A warning," Marcel declared as the room fogged over. "The Light and Dark are dangerously close to an end. They need a ruler. They need a leader. Betrayal is everywhere."

"What are you talking about? The Light and Dark are fine. They are working together."

"But the new voices in the world will push them; you need to stop these Newlings. You have seen what will happen."

"They would never do what I witnessed. Not Juliet. Not even Sahin. Victor wouldn't allow it."

"And what would happen if there was no Juliet or no Victor?"

Silence.

"Now go, little one, and wake up." He touched my forehead and my eyes snapped open.

"What the hell?" I glanced around my bedroom. I focused on my mental wall, not that the structure would help now. I didn't have enough time to react or to think. Marcel had still gotten in, but he wasn't in complete control. The image of him with the woman. The light of day crept above the horizon, breaking up the night sky. And as if to remind me of what I had witnessed, an uncomfortable throbbing ache of my crotch begged for attention. "Seriously?"

*

"Juliet, I'm telling you. What I'm experiencing now is like the visions I've had before. These events will come to pass if we don't do something to stop it." I rubbed my aching head. I'd had a serious headache since I had woken up.

"Immortals would never expose themselves in such a way."

"Maybe not, but why would Marcel show these events to me?" I rubbed my throbbing temples. "What if we exposed ourselves to keep something worse from happening? Is that possible?"

Juliet leaned in her chair, eyes narrowing, but not saying anything.

"Fine, but all that badness I saw is going to happen in March, and it's going to happen here. At the arena in downtown San Jose."

"The Shark Tank." Juliet shook her head.

"Whatever. I think the sign said SAP Center."

Juliet sat quietly for several minutes before speaking. "Did you try to block him? Did you push him out of your mind?" She leaned in. "Is it possible we were under some kind of spell or curse?"

"No." I shook my head. "I didn't have time. Everything was a mess." I rubbed my forehead. "In the vision you callously said, 'We had to strike before more of the others awaken. The world will soon be in chaos, and we are the only ones who can save us all.' You, Sahin, Terrie, and Kirtus all seemed..." I shook my head. "You all were so cruel..." I snapped my fingers. "Like Betty. You all acted like Victor's lieutenant, Betty."

Again, Juliet fell silent.

"And what about what else Marcel said? How I wasn't supposed to see him holding a dark-haired woman. He wept and yelled as he held her."

"Marcel would never show compassion to a human. Granted, he wouldn't go out of his way to harm them, but I've never seen him cry, not for anyone."

"I had the feeling this happened long before you were around. I didn't recognize the clothes; I couldn't even tell you what they looked like."

Juliet got up, walked over to her bookcase, and pulled down one of her journals. "I made a list of everyone important to Marcel—Immortal and human. I even included descriptions or drawings. The list is nowhere near complete, but we can check it and see."

"If we find someone? Will you talk to the Council of Light?"

She adjusted the sleeves for her burgundy cashmere sweater. "I will try. Right now..." She shook her head.

"What? They still don't believe you or me?" My neck grew tight and began to warm.

Juliet put the tome down, resting both hands on top and leaning over the book. "With everything happening, they are not pleased, and I'm finding it harder and harder to work with them."

"But you're the head of the council."

Juliet bit her bottom lip. "For now that's true."

Chapter Fourteen

I glanced out the car window, looking up and down Main Street. With a view like this, how anything was wrong in the world was beyond me. The weather crisp and clear, life in Los Altos continued without so much as a hiccup. Sadly, this wasn't ideal. There were issues and issues of plenty still going on, but in this moment all the worry vanished.

I opened the car door, picked up my cell, and got out. Once out of the car I zipped up my jacket, closed the door, and made my way up the sidewalk to Fredrick's shop, Los Altos Beaux Vêtements. I enjoyed my trips to Fredrick's shop; always peaceful. In my human life, I would never have come to a store like this. However, after comparing the costs and taking into account the quality of his work, there wasn't a huge difference in price. In addition, visiting Fredrick's shop saved me from having to go to the mall or even a department store, which was another huge benefit.

The handle to the shop chilled my touch as I opened the door. A soft chime called out. The shop greeted visitors with a clean, well-organized, and brightly lit appearance. Spotlights focused on the men's and women's mannequins dressed in styled clothing that would look great on anyone. On the side wall, brilliantly colored bolts of fabric hung. Near the back, on the opposite side, different styles of men's leather shoes reflected the display lights across from them a larger selection of women's shoes filled the space with bright colors and lots of different styles. There were many more options then the men's shoes had. As with my previous visits, a few customers talked to one of the two sales associates. They were chatting and smiling as they lingered. As typical, no one rushed.

I walked past the shelves of men's dress shirts and ties. A bright purple tie caught my eye, and I stopped to take the color and the tie in. I picked it up and held it to my neck. I nodded my approval and kept it with me as I made my way to the counter.

"Chris." Fredrick's slight French accent tickled my ears.

I glanced over to the door leading to the rear of the shop. "Fredrick. Hi." I waved.

"You ready to try on your tux?"

Every part of me tingled with excitement. I had been anticipating what he would create for me since I had come in and commissioned him to create my formal outfit.

"I very much enjoyed creating this piece. I hope you like it." He pointed to my hand. "I had a feeling you would appreciate the color. The tie is new."

"Yep, I guess ties won't kill me after all." I chuckled.

"Let's get you set up in a dressing room."

"Perfect." We made our way to the other side of the shop, and Fredrick opened a changing room door for me.

"Please disrobe, and I'll get the tuxedo."

I closed the door and took off my jacket. When I had come in for my fitting and to talk materials, I had mentioned I wanted to go with something classic and timeless. This, of course, was for more than one reason, cost being lower on the list—mainly I didn't want to have to buy a new tux every couple of years. That seemed wasteful. So, we found a design that had the evergreen look I wanted.

A tap on the door found me down to my socks and underwear. I carefully opened the door, just enough for him to hand me the garment bag. Once the door closed, I unzipped the bag and pulled out the jacket and pants. If I weren't already immune to the quality of Fredrick's work, I would have stood there staring at the pieces. They were amazing. I pulled on the pants and grabbed the shirt, slipped it on, only buttoning a few of the buttons since Fredrick would be playing with the shirt and the pants to make any final adjustments.

"Ah, little one, don't you look impressive," Marcel's voice mocked in my head. I turned to the mirror and the image shifted. My reflection was no longer there, replaced by Marcel. "No time to play—"

"Not today." I pulled up my mental wall. I needed to block him out of my mind. But instead of the wall coming to life, pieces filled in, then vanished, then froze, like a computer when you got the spinning wheel of doom or the blue screen of death. My mental defence wasn't coming together. "No."

"Is everything okay?" Fredrick's voice called from somewhere close but also far away.

"I'm fine." My voice and tone struggled.

"Remember we can fix anything."

My head lowered and rose in the affirmative before I frowned, realizing he couldn't see me. "Yep, thanks." I couldn't focus on Fredrick. I needed to get my wall up.

"Oh how cute, you're trying to lock me out." Marcel's tone dripped with mockery. "Chris, we need to—"

"Get out." I tried to push him out, but nothing worked.

"Chris!" Fredrick called.

I closed my eyes and focused on Marcel, his wheaty scent and his appearance. Instead of fighting him, I welcomed him, got his image in my head along with the rest of him. I took in his wheaty scent and relaxed.

"Finally." He dusted off his sleeves. "Good boy."

I drew in as much air as my lungs would allow and glared right at him "BOOM!" I yelled and pushed with everything I had in me; the shock wave burst through him and blasted him into a million bits and pieces. He vanished from my mind, his face contorted and pale. I had a fleeting worry I might have hurt him, but I didn't think that possible. At the same time as my mental push, everything around me shook with a loud crack and a few raised voices echoed about. With Marcel gone I pulled up my mental wall, and without him bothering me, the structure came up with ease. Once I had the wall in place, banging on my changing room door now caught my attention.

I hastily opened the door.

"Wow, that... We haven't had one of those in a while." Fredrick tugged at his jacket to create a breeze for himself.

"What?"

"The earthquake. I doubt it was very big but still a good jolt."

"Oh crap." I gasped. "Is everyone okay?"

Fredrick scanned his shop. "Oh yes."

"I'd never experienced one before." I glanced around the immediate area, my statement the truth. "Sorry if I worried you."

"I thought maybe you froze," Fredrick responded. "It can happen, especially if you've never experienced one before."

My head motioned my agreement as I began fanning my face. "The earthquake was a shocker for sure. You sure everything is okay?"

"Let me get you some tea." He rushed off.

I took the opportunity to glance around the store; nothing broken, and everyone seemed to be fine. Their heartbeats were quickened and their voices raised, but nothing and no one worse for wear. I peeked outside the picture windows, and nothing out of place or out of sorts caught my eye. "Good," I said, then focused inward. I checked my mental wall; my hand ran along the surface. Not only did I focus on the feel, but this time I focused on the scent of the wall, the metallic smell of metal, the slight burn smell of the welding, and the dusty chalky smell of the concrete. Marcel had been able to keep me from forming my barrier; I would need to work on that a lot more. The addition of the scents from the wall, I thought would help make my mental structure more real to me and hopefully make the wall stronger and harder to penetrate. I released the wall in my mind, and I closed my eyes as I called to it. This time not only did I run my hand along the blockade, but I also sniffed it. Once satisfied, I opened my eyes. Fredrick stood watching me.

"Breathing exercise to calm my nerves." I took the tea he offered. "Thank you for the tea. This will help."

"You're welcome." He pulled me over to the mirror and the platform to stand on. "I bet the quake was close by, but not too big."

I sipped more of the tea. The warmth did make me feel better. I enjoyed the scent of orange spice. *Nice.*

He took the tea from my hands and placed the cup on the table next to the mirrors. "Now let's see about the fit of this tuxedo. Get our minds off that rumble."

"Sounds good." I made sure to keep my wall intact. I didn't want any more interruptions from Marcel. Not today.

Chapter Fifteen

I stepped out of the Tesla and pulled at the ends of my tuxedo sleeves, amazed at the work Fredrick put into his creations. My black formal wear was magnificent, and like all of Fredrick's work the fit was impeccable. He even managed to enhance the appearance of certain parts of my body, which although not necessary was still appreciated. What he managed in two weeks' time was nothing short of a miracle. If you asked me, he had the best ability of any of us; he made anyone look good.

I caught my reflection in the mirror. I went from smiling to frowning. I still felt bad about the incident at his shop. Luckily, no one had been hurt, and even more so no one outside of the shop or the immediate area had witnessed anything. I was going to need to be more careful when I banished intruders from my mind. At least I hadn't heard or seen anything more of Marcel.

Speaking of walls, I pulled all my mental protections together, including the mental vault for my personal thoughts I'd been trying to create, not wanting to take any chances tonight.

A slight cough to my right called my attention. I glanced over at the valet. I stood at the car with the door open the keys in my hand. Tonight, I drove, which for some reason made me feel all the more sexy. Stepping away from the Tesla in my tux was a nice feeling. "There is a suitcase in the trunk." I motioned to the valet. "Please ensure the bag gets to room 2006." I slipped the young man not only the keys to the car but a twenty-dollar bill.

He grasped the money and my hand. "It would be my pleasure." He glanced over to Juliet. "If you need the car, the valet desk is open twenty-four hours." He handed me the stub for the car.

"Thank you." I adjusted the gold-and-sapphire cufflinks before pulling on my jacket. I stepped over to the passenger side of the car where Juliet waited.

"You look amazing." Juliet beamed as she stepped to the side of the car, draping her black wrap around her shoulders. She stood in black heels and a black velvet and sapphire-jeweled cocktail dress cut right below the knees. Her blonde hair held a slight curl cascading over her right shoulder and shined silky smooth. Nothing out of place, not even her small black clutch. Sparkling on her wrist, a sapphire and diamond bracelet, if I knew her, cost more than the car we drove tonight.

"Not nearly as amazing as you." I offered her my arm as we headed through the Fairmont's double doors. "You sure you don't mind driving yourself home tonight after the ceremony?"

Juliet chuckled. "I've been driving long before you were alive. I'll be fine." She tightened around my arm. "Tonight is about Kirtus. Plus, the two of you deserve to enjoy the evening. Especially after the incident in town."

I bit back my frown. I didn't want to talk about what happened at Fredrick's shop and the potential disaster I could have caused. I took a deep breath. What lay ahead was...unknown. "I can't believe Victor is having this *event* here at the Fairmont."

Juliet patted my arm. "Of course he is. I'm surprised he didn't try to get the Glasshouse or rent out the Museum of Modern Art." She adjusted her purse. "He does enjoy making statements."

"Oh, I remember." The image of Sahin hanging over the balcony of his penthouse begging for his life flashed to mind. I shuddered.

"You all right? You cold?"

"No, Mom, I'm fine."

"You should have brought the trench coat."

"And what about you?" I glanced over at her. She didn't have a coat, only her wrap.

"I don't need a coat." Juliet winked up at me.

We made our way to the escalators and down the hall to one of the ballrooms. Outside the doors stood a bruiser of a man in a black tux and an equally formidable woman opposite him in a blood-red evening dress holding a tablet.

Juliet nodded to them. She opened her clutch and pulled out an ivory invitation. "Juliet de Exter and Christopher Raymond." She offered no more and handed over the invitation.

The man peeked at the ivory notice, then glanced to his female counterpart.

The woman tapped on her tablet as she scrutinized the device for a moment. "Good evening, Juliet. Chris." She opened the door to the ballroom.

My mouth dropped. Everything I imagined the space would be had been delivered. The banquet room had been completely done up in red velvet draping and antique freestanding chandeliers. Uplights were everywhere, and all the tables and decorations were cast in a blood-red glow. A stage had been placed at the front of the room, flanked by red-rose-filled vases as tall as any of us standing. No music and no other lighting other than what the chandeliers provided filled the space. The room looked so much like a movie set it blew me away. Around the room were cocktail tables, and along the four different walls were small buffets with nothing but bottles of red. A low hum of conversation filled the space, and I picked up hints of sweet almonds and amber marking this space as belonging to Victor.

"No food?"

Juliet shook her head. "Not tonight; there will only be Immortals here."

That explained why Amanda wasn't invited.

"But the people who work here?"

"LARPing." Masko's warm sage scent came from off to the right of us.

I turned to face him. His outfit was similar to my black tuxedo, but his clothes appeared to be more of a costume than modern formal attire; he wore a crushed green velvet vest, and the ends of his cream-colored cuffs had ruffles. His black dinner jacket had been tailored to be midlength, and it was pinched at the waist creating a perfect silhouette. And his dark hair perfectly slicked back. "Lar-whating?"

"LARPing." Juliet repeated. "Live action role play. We are here under the pretense of the San Jose Vampire LARPing Society."

I found it difficult to keep the amusement out of my voice. "Let me guess, Victor happens to be the head."

Masko laughed. "Ding-ding, we have a winner."

My lips pinched together as I smirked. "Explains a lot." I gestured over to Masko's outfit.

"What better way to hide in plain sight." He ran a hand over his velvet vest. "We have various bottles of blood, so help yourselves." He pointed in the direction of the buffet tables adorned in more red with crushed velvet accents, more red roses, and smaller flickering chandelier lights. The table somewhat pretty if not a tad over the top even for my wild expectations.

I loved this space. When I pictured vampires, this was what I imagined. The only part of this that bothered me, the jealousy that we were at a Dark vampire event and not a Light event.

Ah well.

"I'm fine." I glanced at Juliet. "Would you like something?"

"Not right now. We should go and pay our respects to our host." She motioned to Victor.

I would have burst out laughing if I didn't know any better. Like the others in the room, Victor wore stereotypical vampire garb, a lot of black and red crushed velvet, but what put the outfit over the top, for me, the cloak and the cane he had next to him. The man appeared on a stage sitting in a throne, not a cheap fake throne that looked like something someone had made in their garage either. Victor's throne clearly something out of a medieval castle I had no doubt. The chair screamed ancient. I had a fleeting thought that maybe it was his, or perhaps his human families, from Spain, or wherever he was originally from. Unsurprisingly there were people standing in all manner of costumes, in line to greet him. Behind him on his left Kirtus. He stood in a modern tuxedo. The thumping of my heart increased. He wore a brown cummerbund instead of black, which struck me as odd.

"Ah, that's sweet." Juliet patted my arm.

"What?"

"Kirtus is wearing a tie and cummerbund that matches your eyes."

My cheeks instantly burned as I bit back my awkwardness. We moved through the small group of Immortals, most of whom ignored us, which didn't bother me. I got a closer look at how everyone dressed in various forms of formalwear, or what humans assumed vampires wore when they went out. The combinations were cool, but considering who we were around, my palms were sweaty and my heart beat faster.

"Relax," Juliet whispered to me, and she pushed her ability my way.

I lowered my mental wall and allowed her calming nature to wash over me, and her aura instantly made me feel better. I tried to look for faces I recognized. I managed to discover Joaquín but not Betty or Sahin, which I thought odd. I found the sneer of Cynthia as she watched both Juliet and me as we waited to greet Victor. Clearly, she still held a grudge against Juliet and me for the death of her Called, Malcom, but that wasn't our fault. The events at Christmas had been caused by Tom, my father, and his evil coven of witches. I suppose that didn't make the situation any better for her, and I had a feeling Juliet would react the same way if that had been Amanda or my death.

"Juliet. Chris. Welcome." Victor got up from his throne to greet us. Several Immortals stopped to watch our interaction.

"You honored us with the invite." Juliet offered her hand.

"Nonsense." Victor took her hand and gently kissed it. "Tonight wouldn't be a proper party without a few members of the Light invited." He grinned and stepped to me. "Ah, Chris, what am I going to do with you? What do I have to offer you to get you to blur the lines and come to my camp? I can use you. I really can." He shook my hand. "And the benefits." He eyed me up and down.

I laughed. This wasn't the first time Victor had propositioned me, and I had a feeling this offer wouldn't be the last.

"So coy." Victor released my hand. "Kirtus, come greet our guests."

Kirtus walked from behind the throne and greeted Juliet with a polite shake of her hand. When he stepped to me, my heart jumped from my chest and I wanted to do nothing more than give him a kiss, but that would be later, along with doing a lot more. Instead, I offered my hand, and we shook. "Thank you both for being here."

"We wouldn't have missed the event for anything." Juliet's voice swelled with pride and grace.

"It's exciting..." My voice cracked, and I cleared my throat before continuing. "I've learned about LARPing." My tone returned to normal.

Victor sighed with no hint of malice. "A masquerade to keep the status quo." He glanced over at his cane, cape, and top hat. "Still, the *accoutrement* can be fun."

"We haven't seen Sahin nor Betty." Juliet's tone was casual, but considering she mentioned the topic I recognized this as a breach of protocol. "Is everything okay?"

Victor's lips pinched together. "Sahin is more than likely off sulking, and Betty is out consoling him, I'm sure. They will be here for the ceremony if they both wish to stay in my good graces." Victor stood taller and beamed. "However, we do have Sahin to thank for this evening's event. I'm pleased."

"Everything is absolutely lovely," Juliet flattered.

"Well, I hope you enjoy. Now, please excuse me. I have hosting duties to continue." Victor motioned to the table off to the side of the stage, where chandeliers flickered on opposite ends, more tall, freestanding vases with roses. Next to the table stood a man and a woman dressed in serving tuxedos who held trays with crystal glasses filled with red. The man had a mixture of boredom and partial amusement on his face. The woman looked more interested in what happened around her. I imagined what they had seen in their duties here and wondered if we were the largest group of freaks they had seen.

"If they only knew," I whispered as we walked to what appeared to be an empty table. Instead there were envelopes and a few small boxes.

Juliet unclipped her black clutch and pulled out a cream-colored envelopment sealed with her blue wax signet of a dragon perched on rocks. She placed the envelope on the table.

"What's that for?"

"A token of our friendship to the host."

I contemplated the words for a moment.

"You mean a bribe."

Juliet laughed. "No, well, yes... I suppose. The offering is a Dark custom to bring something of value to your host. In the olden days the gift would be a virgin or something like that..."

"What?"

"Now the present is typically cash."

"But I—"

"I have us covered and traditionally we are not expected to provide tribute, but I do so out of respect for Victor and Kirtus." She leaned into me and her voice dropped. "By following their traditions, the others here have less of a reason to hate us, since we are playing by their rules."

I licked my dry lips as we moved over to the servers, and we each picked up a glass of red.

Being here seemed so strange as so few people spoke to Juliet or me. I had grown used to being ignored, but to brush off Juliet like this bothered me. They knew her, or knew of her, yet they ignored her. What the hell? Joaquín and Masko did their best to come by and chat. They even went as far as to make introductions to some of the other Dark leaders. Unlike the Light, the Dark were indeed fractured. I met a female Dark leader for the states of Texas and Oklahoma, who was not under Victor's thumb, as she put it. We met the rest of the Dark leaders from Canada, and the southeast of the US and the central northeast of the US. Another person we met was a quiet man, whom they called Gypsy for some reason, from the northern part of Africa, who I found out planned to try to take over parts of the Middle East. The area he wanted was controlled by another Dark Immortal who went by Fred, a short form of his name I couldn't even try to pronounce if I wanted to; he also attended tonight. They proceeded to sneer at each other. Or ignore each other. I doubt they differentiated between the two.

Juliet told me they were both here to seek support from Victor, which I found interesting.

A lovely woman who I learned oversaw Japan, Korea, and a few other regions introduced herself. Juliet warned me not to be swayed by her sweet personality and quiet demeanor; this woman was a constant thorn in the side of both An and Yoi, who would often call on the other Light Council Members for assistance when dealing with her. Especially Garrett since her territory overlapped his as well.

Despite the whirlwind of names and introductions, I continually got struck by the fact this wasn't even all of the Dark leaders. And I had no idea how many more there were. The guests tonight were the Dark Victor had either good relationships with or trusted enough to have them in his territory for such an occasion. After about an hour I wanted this night to be over. By the time Victor stood and began addressing the group, my focus was lost on Kirtus and going up to our room and enjoy our weekend together.

"Welcome." Victor's voice boomed over the crowd. "Tonight we're here in celebration. To welcome Kirtus Lancaster into my circle of lieutenants." He paused and the obligatory applause filled the room. "However, not only will Kirtus be one of my lieutenants, he will be my chief lieutenant, answerable only to me. He will speak for me in my absence and assist me in my dealings with the Light."

To my surprise, more applause. Still, I wasn't sure if that had more to do with those in attendance not wanting to deal with the Light or if they were happy for Kirtus. I supposed the reason for the applause didn't matter.

"I would like to thank my distinguished guests tonight, Juliet de Exter, leader of the Council of Light and her Called, the young and talented Christopher Raymond, without whom the recent dealings with the out-of-control coven would have been much worse for all of us."

After a moment of silence, once Victor clapped, everyone joined in. Definitely not as jubilant as earlier. Still the gesture was polite. Juliet offered a gracious bow of her head, and I contributed my burning checks and neck. Why did Victor have to make this kind of fuss?

"Now, Kirtus, if you'll come forward." Victor motioned to Kirtus. "Give me—"

"Enough of this bullshit!" Sahin yelled from the rear of the room. Betty flanked him. "Victor Rey, you are liar and a traitor to our kind."

The room broke into murmurs as people moved to the side, forming a direct path from Sahin and Betty to Victor and Kirtus.

"You ungrateful—"

"I said enough," Sahin bellowed, his typical handsome face already transformed.

I scanned the room for the human servers. The guy had perked up at this new development. He stood watching with a stupid grin on his face. This must have been the best show he had ever seen. The woman stood not too far from her counterpart and glanced at the door to the serving area. I had a feeling she was trying to sort out how long to let this go on, or if this display was all part of the game. Thank God neither had a cell phone to record this.

"How long did you think we would allow you to sell us out to the Light?" Sahin pointed to Juliet and me. "Appointing this *lund k laddu* as your chief lieutenant. Killing Pedro because he refused to accept this travesty. After all his years of dedicated service to you. To the Dark."

I gasped. The man in my vision had been an Immortal. Victor had killed one of his own.

"Pedro was a fool. Like you're being now." Victor, to my surprise, was calm and his voice level. "The world has changed, and Pedro, sadly, was too stupid to see these changes." Victor turned to Betty. "You better watch who you align yourself with, Betty, my dear."

"Oh, I have." Betty's tone bit at the air. "I couldn't understand why Pedro didn't make the meeting you called. Him not being there struck me as odd especially since we didn't hear from him, and now I understand why. You've failed us and are bending over for this Light bitch and her Called."

I wanted to speak, but Juliet took my arm in warning. This was not our fight. We were simply witnessing what was to come.

Victor glanced at us with a tilted head and a wry smile. He turned and glared at Sahin and Betty. "What would you two brilliant minds do? Hmm."

He picked up his cane, stepping from the stage and moving toward them. "Tell me what would you have done to keep the witches from destroying us? Would you have run and hid in the face of the recent magic attacks? Again, tell me, what is your grand plan for our continued existence?"

Sahin's chest puffed up. "Face whatever comes like a true Dark. We don't need the Light, never have. Plus, our alliance with the Light has done nothing. Now you want to work with more witches and a Native American Shaman. Why? We are Dark; we are at the top of the food chain. We should enslave the humans and put them in their rightful place: blood farms. They're nothing but cattle."

There were several nods from the crowd. Clearly not all the Dark Immortals felt the way Victor did, but even they had to admit the Light would never stand for such a thing... I froze. My vision of Juliet, Sahin, Kirtus, and the other Immortals feeding off humans at the hockey game. Was this how we spiraled out of control? Was this how we lost ourselves? Was this what led us to the moment of murder and mayhem? I hadn't seen Victor in my vision. "No," I whispered.

Juliet held my arm tight and peeked up at me, her eyes pleading with me to stay quiet.

"As I recall, Sahin—" Victor's polished tone and warm expression didn't leave his face. "—you whimpered at my feet when you had the opportunity to confront Chris. Now that is strength. An Immortal of your age and ability whimpering terrified of a *Newling*." Victor glanced around. "I believe... Ah yes, Cynthia can attest to your cowardice."

Cynthia stepped forward. "I can. Sahin had the opportunity to enact justice on the member of the Light, Chris Raymond, and chose to do nothing. Like a coward. He's a fraud."

There were more gasps and glares at Sahin. The people who only moments ago had appeared to be in Sahin's corner settled into what I hoped to be Victor's court. Even Betty had a hint of worry that hadn't been there before.

"You short-sighted fool." Victor's voice still filled with mirth. "The humans would destroy us, and the Light would never allow such a thing. You've never learned that important lesson." His voice grew soft. "I've failed to teach you, and for that I'm sorry."

"Enough!" Sahin demanded. "You taught me all I needed. It is you who has forgotten yourself. Your teaching." His voice boomed.

"Sahin, enough." Joaquín's voice bellowed. "I don't agree with the killing of Pedro; however, Victor has always done what is best for the

Dark, not only in his territory but around the world. Look at those who are here to witness this event. They wouldn't be here if Victor wasn't worthy. You are on a ledge. Please do not step off."

"You will not disrespect our leader like this." Kirtus stationed himself next to Joaquín. "Not in his house, not in his city. You ungrateful weasel." Kirtus's voice was strong and sure.

"You disgusting *lund fakeer*," Sahin snapped. "You're only saying that because with the position you can continue to fuck your little Light boy toy." Sahin pointed at me with a snarl.

The air in the hall came alive. Kirtus used his power.

Mine was not the only gaze glancing around the banquet hall, as the flames on the candles flickered and even a few of the petals from the roses dropped to the floor or the tables their vases sat on.

How soon before other Immortals called forth their abilities? Betty's ability was a mystery I wasn't sure I wanted to uncover; the same for Joaquín and Masko. An undercurrent of calm weaved out from us through the crowd. I peeked down at Juliet and her eyes were closed. She called her own power, trying to keep level heads so this didn't become a blood bath in the heart of downtown San Jose.

Both Joaquín and Masko took up stations behind both Victor and Kirtus, who were standing shoulder to shoulder.

Sahin laughed, catching everyone off guard. "You take me for a fool. I have no wish to fight you here and now. But I'm issuing this challenge." His voice became quiet and level with hints of menace dripping through his tone. "I will take control of your territory and lead the Dark you have forsaken; you have three days to prepare. You and me, Hicks Road, you know the location. Bring whatever witnesses you want, but understand this, Victor Rey: by the light of the full moon, you will be no more." Sahin turned on his heels, and with Betty by his side, they marched out of the hall.

The door slammed behind them, and all eyes were on Victor and his lieutenants. The clap of his hands caused me to jump. "Well, that is unfortunate." The mirth never left his voice.

What was he playing at? None of this bothered him. Were these events some kind of joke to him? Was he playing the part for the two humans watching us? What was going on?

"Sadly, Sahin has grown a bit too ambitious for his own good." Victor sighed. "As you've all heard he has issued a challenge, and I have no choice but to answer the challenge. A shame. Ah well, it's time for some new blood in my ranks." He strolled to his throne and took his seat. "In a few days I will need not only one new lieutenant but three." Victor snapped his finger, and the server who had watched the whole exchange rushed over. Victor took a glass and handed one to each of his lieutenants. "I welcome Kirtus Lancaster." He raised his glass, and everyone made sure to do the same.

"To Kirtus," the room echoed.

*

The night had been too much for me. Learning Victor had killed one of his own lieutenants in order for Kirtus to hold this new position, which by extension would allow us to be together. The idea of Sahin openly challenged Victor in front of all those Dark leaders. Insanity and my mind jumped to my vision and how Victor hadn't been present. I closed my eyes and rubbed my temples, trying to stop the pounding in my head.

I checked my mental walls, everything in place. Good.

Here we were in the suite Kirtus had booked for us for his "special" night, and I freaked out over what happened with Sahin and what this all meant with respect to my vision. Not to mention Marcel lurking about. "Ugh."

"You okay?" Kirtus whispered in my ear as he pulled off my black tux jacket.

"This whole thing with Sahin."

"Don't," Kirtus instructed.

I opened my eyes and met his gaze.

"Sahin has been a pain in the ass for years. I told you what he did. This has been long overdue." Kirtus kissed my forehead. "Please don't let this ruin our night or our weekend. Victor's not worried. I'm not worried." He lifted my chin. "And Juliet wasn't worried."

I sighed. Everything he brought up rang true. Still, I wanted to tell him I wasn't okay. I wanted him to realize I was as far from okay as one could be, but the voice in the back of my head reminded me this was his night and I wanted to make tonight special for him. To make him feel as good as he always made me feel. "You're right." I put on what I hoped was my most appealing façade. "I'm fine."

Kirtus smirked at me. "Yes, yes you are." He pulled at the buttons of my shirt. "Damn, I wanted to rip your clothes off the minute you walked in. I assumed everyone would see my pants come alive. Luckily I controlled myself, but now I don't have to." His voice purred.

When I didn't move, he stopped.

"You're not okay, are you?" He sighed. "Tonight was supposed to be a celebration, and the whole thing ended in a shit show."

His frown stung my soul. I sniffed his scent, leaning in and gently kissing his warm, full lips. He returned my kiss.

I needed to put everything else to the side and focus on him.

On us.

"I wanted tonight to be special for us." His words were warm on my cheek. "Tonight's party was, in a way, like prom night for me. Me being crowned prom king, and you were my sexy-as-hell date. Who I couldn't wait to rip his clothes off." He pointed around the suite. "That's why I did all this."

My heart lightened with his admission. Even though my prom had been less than perfect, the night had still been a good night and I had enjoyed it. What did he have? I'm sure he'd never had a celebration like this. I ran my hand along his cheek. To hell with all the drama and other crap. Tonight was for Kirtus. Whatever was to happen with Victor, Sahin, and the rest of the Dark, for that matter, I had no control over. Just like I could do nothing about the vision I'd had. Witches, Healers, Immortals, all of it needed to fuck off for tonight.

Before I thought anymore about tonight, I found myself on my knees in front of Kirtus, pulling down his pants and stripping him of his sexy light blue trunk underwear. I wasn't greeted by his typical overly excited prick, but what found me was still magnificent. I eagerly took him into my mouth. A gasp of pleasure escaped his lips.

"We...don't...have to do this," he protested between gasps.

I wanted to, if not for me, then for him. I met his protest and engorging cock with a slow, methodical gulp and a playful flick of my tongue, ensuring I circled the tip the way he enjoyed. We needed this closeness tonight. I think I needed our contact more than he did.

This was real.

We were real.

I continued to work him as I got us to the bed and pushed him back, dropping him to the softness of the bed, allowing the duvet to engulf us with me on top of him.

An excited chuckle escaped his mouth. His wry grin caused the fabric of my tuxedo pants and underwear to grow much too tight for my own comfort. Damn these tailored pants. I focused all my attention on Kirtus and making him feel as good as he always made me feel.

"Check...the duffel bag." He moaned.

I sucked him a bit harder before I got to my feet. I scanned the bedroom for the duffel bag, finding it next to the desk, and moved over to it. One of the benefits of being an Immortal, I didn't need to turn on the lights. My night vision was perfect.

I found the lube and the condoms and realized what Kirtus wanted. If intercourse would make him happy and bring pleasure to him, then I would do anything he asked.

"You really came prepared." I held one item per hand.

He ogled me up and down, stopping on my crotch. "Figured if you were interested, I wouldn't mind letting you..." He trailed off.

I returned to the bed and put the items next to me. Time for the rest of his clothes to be gone. Once naked, he got higher up on the bed, clearly making himself comfortable.

The ends of my lips pulled up in lust as my dick pushed against its constraints with excitement. These darn clothes of mine needed to be gone as well. Inhaling deep, I caught a whiff of his sandalwood scent, which drove me crazy, and I instantly wanted him. Typically, I enjoyed receiving more than giving, but that didn't mean I didn't enjoy this position. In fact, my abilities in this regard were something I felt quite adept at. I didn't pay attention to where I tossed my clothes. They would either be on the chair where I hoped to find them, or on the floor; it didn't matter.

The electricity from our naked bodies and the touch of his bare skin to mine was all I needed. Our lips met as my hand massaged his balls. The more I played with him, the tighter and firmer everything got. By the time I slid a lubed finger into him, I figured the slightest movement would thrust him over the edge. I worked him more as soft moans escaped his lips.

"Is this okay?"

"God, yes." He gasped.

My heart skipped a beat; I wanted to laugh with joy. I loved making him feel good, his pleasure more important than any other feelings right now. I experienced nothing as wonderful as making the person you were with feel like they were the one and only. Everything you were doing brought them pleasure.

After unrolling the condom and ensuring my dick was sufficiently slicked up, I carefully found my way into him. Kirtus let out a whimper, and from the top of my head to the bottom on my toes, his moan caused me to tingle. We were one. One body. One soul. In this moment there was nothing I wouldn't do for him. I pushed the night's events farther from my mind and focused on bringing Kirtus as much pleasure as possible.

Our mouths found each other, and our tongues danced. Tasting him on my lips brought feelings of home and peace to me. I tried to lose myself in those feelings. Love, togetherness, being with this beautiful man, was where I wanted my mind and body to go.

The more I tried to focus on our togetherness, the more images of Victor and Sahin fighting, or Victor killing his lieutenant Pedro came to my mind. My anxiety kept creeping into our moment. A moment meant for Kirtus and me. How I managed to stay erect was beyond me. Perhaps the primal part of my body controlled me. I didn't know. The more I pushed our bodies together and the more I tried to focus solely on Kirtus, the more I recognized tonight was only going to be about him. My worry and my fears were stealing this moment from me.

"Oh, God," he whispered into my neck. "Don't...oh man... I'm going."

His body shuddered as my hand stayed wrapped around him, moving in time with my hips. At the very least I would ensure he felt amazing. His body convulsed under me and I pushed harder, riding the wave of his orgasm hoping beyond hope somehow my body would respond in kind.

He collapsed on the bed with one final groan.

I found his mouth and kissed him long and deep. All this for him. And, as if on cue, my own body, knowing it had performed its task, deflated. My heart rate eased and my breathing returned to normal. I pulled myself out of him and made my way to the bathroom, disposing of the condom, washing my hands, and pulling a washcloth under the warm water so it wouldn't be cold on him.

When I returned Kirtus still panted and I gently cleaned up his body, still tender under my touch.

On my return to the bed for the second time, after disposing of the washcloth in the bathroom, I found him and pulled him close to me, kissing his forehead.

"You didn't finish," he whispered.

"Tonight's not about me. It's about you."

"But making you happy makes me happy." His hand found my limp dick and warm balls.

"I wanted to do this for you. I'm fine." I kissed him again to reassure him. My lack of orgasm didn't matter to me. I was relaxed and ready to rest.

He sighed.

I turned and faced him. "When I'm with you, I'm happy. Coming when we're together isn't what makes me happy. Yes, I would have loved to climax with you, but..." I squeezed him tighter.

"That shit with Sahin tonight–"

"And learning about Pedro." The words dropped from my mouth.

"Chris, Pedro was worse than Betty and Sahin combined. Victor doubtlessly saved hundreds of lives by doing what he did."

"I know," I whispered into his neck. "I do, but you didn't have to see his death. I did."

Kirtus wrapped his arms around me. He had stopped trying to make things happen that weren't going to happen tonight. "And for that, I'm sorry."

I leaned back, resting a hand behind my head.

"I still wish you would let me satisfy you."

I chuckled. "Not right now. Maybe later. Right now, I want to snuggle up next to the man I love and fall asleep in his arms." I turned on my side and draped an arm over his chest.

Kirtus leaned in next to me, and I drew in his earthy sandalwood scent. If anything got my motor running, it would be his scent, but I was grateful nothing happened.

"Thank you for this," Kirtus whispered. He relaxed almost on the brink of sleep as was I. "We have the room all weekend," he added.

"Plenty of time for you to make tonight up to me."

"Plenty of time for us to enjoy ourselves again and again." The sleepy, mischievous, satisfied tone of Kirtus's voice managed a jolt of energy from my ear all the way to the tip of my penis.

I nuzzled the side of his head and closed my eyes, looking forward to the morning and the rest of our weekend together.

Chapter Sixteen

"Little one, I need you to hear me. See what I'm showing you." The deep voice bounced off in the corner of my mind. Behind the wall, but still there. He tried to get through.

I didn't want to respond. I believed him to be Marcel, or pretending to be Marcel; either way, that had to be impossible. I pushed at the voice, not wanting to be pulled into whatever drama he wanted to put me in.

"Little one!" the voice demanded.

I held my eyes shut tighter and focused on my wall, remembering the smells associated with it and how the hard steel chilled my fingertips.

"*Christopher*!" he yelled, and the whole wall rattled. My mental structure held, but if he did that again, who knew?

"*What!*" I yelled as my eyes snapped open. "I don't want to do this. I want you out of my head."

I sensed Marcel holding up his hands in surrender. "You think I enjoy this, little one? If Juliet was a Seer, I wouldn't be here, but her mind is a castle built of granite and she has no talent of foresight. Even that Healer William's mind is locked too tight for me to reach. And if I reached him...he might... No, I doubt he would want to understand even though he should... Regardless, I doubt he would help me. You are my only chance, despite you blasting me out of your mind and your mental barriers. You have no idea how much energy this is taking. Please don't fight me." His voice changed. "I need your help."

"What do you want?" I growled. I allowed a small section of my wall to drop, but I kept that section within reach in case I needed it. We were in an empty void of fog, nothing around, and fear crawled up from every corner of my being with what I might see.

"See what will come to be," Marcel warned.

"Ah, crap." A tugging in my brain and a sickness in my stomach pushed me to an edge I didn't want to reach. Sweat pooled on my brow and my hands shook. Nothing good came into focus. The fog transformed into smoke; my lungs burned with the heaviness of ash. I waved my hands in front of me to clear the air, but the motion had no effect. Despite my best efforts, I wanted to see what happened, and I found myself moving forward. At first I walked on pavement, but as I glanced around, I actually walked on nothing. Air. Maybe. Below me, San Jose—buildings were on fire. From this height I made out flashing lights from emergency vehicles. Off to my left an explosion. The Shark Tank. The area I had visited earlier. I squinted and waved my hands in front of me, trying to see more. Another explosion, this time at Victor's building, The Heights. Instead of a glass and steel building, only fire and smoke remained. Even the older stone skyscraper wasn't intact the oversized copula or what remained of it lay on the street below. Fighting spilled into the streets. A riot, but more than that.

Police were shooting at people. No, not people, Immortals. But the Immortals weren't paying attention. They were fighting one another.

"I need to see closer."

I moved lower as I continued to walk. Sahin and Betty were there. Terrie's head dropped from her body as a silver sword gleamed in the moonlight. Ben yelled and shot the gun he held. The bullets ripped apart the man with the sword. I gasped. I recognized him. The Immortal was that man Fred. I shook my head and closed my eyes.

When my eyes opened, I appeared in another location, not downtown. I remembered this place, the outdoor shopping center. What's the name? "Santana Row," I whispered. Everything destroyed, there were cars overturned, and someone tried to build a barricade with some of the cars to block off the entry points. There were bodies tossed about, some missing heads and some bleeding out. I pushed my way through the scene until I found a small group of Immortals and humans. Gregor spoke with them. Some of the humans cried or appeared to be in shock; a few had weapons from whatever they gathered. There were two police officers, listening and checking their weapons as Gregor spoke.

A male police officer glanced beyond Gregor and pointed his gun, firing several rapid shots.

I turned to see four Immortals standing there glaring down at them.

"What is this?" I turned to Marcel.

He stood next to me. He appeared so old to me at this moment. I'd not seen him look this bad, and I wondered if that had to do with my blasting him out of my mind.

"War." Marcel stepped next to me. "The war between the Light and the Dark. The humans now caught in the middle. Some will help the

Light, but most will fight both groups of Immortals. Only the One can stop this and unite them, but they have to see the truth, or this will come to pass."

"This is impossible. Victor and Juliet would never—"

"They are gone."

"What?" I took a shaky step and glanced around. I didn't see Juliet or Victor. They might have been in another location. They may have been anywhere. I found myself in the middle of madness and chaos. "I don't believe you."

"And why should you? But here we are." He rested a hand on my shoulder. "This is the truth; you could not see these events if the vision wasn't a possible future."

"How do you know?"

"I've been around a long time, longer than I should, and I've grown to learn a great deal. You, just like the One, are special."

"You mean Kirtus." I shook my head, not understanding any of this. "He's been installed as Victor's chief lieutenant—"

"You think that's what this is about?" Marcel pinched the bridge of his nose. "Yes, why wouldn't you? You don't know any better." He shook his head. "No. Kirtus is to unite both the Light and Dark. He is the true heir to the throne. He can bring peace and join what's been shattered so long ago."

A lot of the royal history was lost on me, but I remembered from Juliet's books the queen was killed along with her Called before her council split into the Light and the Dark. But she had no additional heir; no one from her blood line remained. How could Kirtus be her heir?

"The queen had a young sister before she turned. Everyone believed her family perished in a fire, but the child survived," Marcel stated. "The girl was found by scavengers and lived with another family never knowing who she was. The child grew up and had children. Kirtus, is the last of her blood line."

"Too convenient. This is ridiculous. You want something, but I don't understand what that something is...yet." The smoke around me thickened—not smoke but fog. "Wait. What's going to happen?"

"Why do you care, little one, if you don't believe me?" Marcel's hand lifted from my shoulder.

The pit of my stomach dropped. Did I believe him? Was he right? Was I wrong? I didn't know, but what if? "How do I stop this?" I asked.

Even if this was all bullshit, we had to find a way to stop these events from happening, just in case.

"There is betrayal at play. The magic that seeped into this world has caused more harm than any understand. The Dark and Light will be betrayed; the children of the moon will return on the upcoming full moon. Stop them; save the leader of the Dark." Marcel had vanished, but his voice came through. "Friends are now foes—" The voice faded. "—and enemies are enemies no longer."

My eyes burst open. There were hints of light from the heavy drapes the soft breathes of Kirtus next to me. My heart pounded, and a chill ran through my body as I lay in a bed of ice. Much colder than I should be especially with Kirtus next to me, I trembled.

"You okay?" Kirtus nuzzled my neck and ear. His hand glided down my chest and stomach until he found his less-than-interested target.

What do I tell him? The truth. Did I have a choice? "I had a vision... Well, I think what I saw was a vision. Marcel came to me again."

Any drowsiness or romance Kirtus may have had were gone, and he sat up and stared at me. The bed sheets dropped, falling around him to reveal his chest and partial leg. His eyes were wide, and he bit at his lips. The typical scent of sandalwood was faint, and there were additional hints of wheat or some grassy earthy smell, reminding me Marcel had been there.

I raked a hand over my face and grounded myself in my seat. I shook my head and relayed my vision and conversation with Marcel to Kirtus.

By the time we were making our way out of the elevator through the lobby to check out, Kirtus and I had agreed we were going to head over to Victor's.

"What did Juliet say?" Kirtus asked as we walked. He looked amazing this morning in his black jeans, black dress shoes, a bright blue long-sleeve shirt, and a lightweight black leather jacket. The blue made everything pop, and I really wished we were upstairs in bed, instead of dealing with all this shit.

"She and Amanda will meet us there." I slipped the phone into my pocket.

He stopped and took my hand. "Look, do me a favor; don't say anything about this link to the queen. Not yet..." He shook his head. "I can't even, right now."

The back of my brain pulled as my neck tensed. I didn't want to lie to anyone, but everything swirled up in the air so there was no point in saying anything right now.

"So much for our weekend." There was an edge with hints of disappointment in Kirtus's tone.

I understood his disappointment, but with everything happening there would be other weekends.

We walked up to the reception desk, met by the overly cheery guest relations person. His name tag read Tomas.

"How can I help you?" Tomas asked in a bright tone.

I realized this was awful, but right now I wanted to rip that perfect, perky white smile off his face.

"Checking out of 2006, please." Kirtus managed a polite warm tone.

Relief washed over me as Kirtus spoke. No way would I have been able to mask my frustration, especially with my facial reactions reflecting my annoyance and disappointment.

"I see you weren't scheduled to check out until tomorrow. Is everything all right?" Tomas typed away on his keyboard as he viewed the monitor in front of him.

"Unfortunately, we have to cut our stay short; work seems to not be able to live without me." Kirtus managed a chuckle.

"I hate when that happens." Tomas typed. "Let me see if I can waive the charge for tonight."

"No, that's fine. I'll pay for the night." Kirtus held up his hand.

"Are you sure? I'm happy to ask my manager."

"It's fine. I appreciate the offer." Kirtus waved Tomas off.

"Let me get your package. I can—"

"Package?" Kirtus asked.

"What package?" My eyes perked up as did my ears.

"My computer shows a package has been left for you." Tomas tapped on his keyboard. "I'll be back in two ticks." He walked off.

"Did you order something?" I asked Kirtus.

"No."

"Maybe Victor or Juliet?"

"Maybe."

Tomas returned holding something wrapped in brown paper. A book. The size and shape made that clear.

"Oh, right." Kirtus snapped one of his fingers. "I forgot I asked for this to be brought over."

"What?" I had no idea what was happening here at the moment. What had I missed?

Kirtus winked and picked up the book, handing it to me. "Thank you for all the help, Tomas."

"My pleasure, Mr. Lancaster." Tomas printed a few documents for Kirtus to sign, and we were on our way.

I didn't talk or ask anything about the package until we were in Kirtus's blue Ford Fusion driving the few blocks to Victor's building.

"You knew about this book?" I held the book up, the parcel clearly the size and shape of one of Juliet's tomes at the house.

"Nope." Kirtus stopped at a stoplight.

"Okay?"

"Someone wanted us to have that book, and if it's important enough for them to leave at the hotel the morning after you have a vision, and the morning after Victor gets challenged by Sahin, then this book is important."

I nodded, it was the only reaction that I could think of.

Chapter Seventeen

I finished off my glass of red and peeked around Victor's office, my gaze returning to the book sitting in the middle of his desk. The book rested on the brown paper it had arrived in. The brown binding appeared to be leather, at least I hoped, because honestly, I couldn't be too sure. An additional strap of leather kept the tome closed. If the idea of the book weren't creepy as hell, I would say this was cool. An aroma of earth surrounded the book; the fragrance wasn't mold or mildew, but that same earthy wheat scent I had come to associate with Marcel.

"And you've never seen this book before?" Victor waved a hand at the book, as he addressed Juliet and not me, his casual attire something I wasn't used to. Jeans, a brown polo shirt, and basic brown shoes were his outfit of choice today. Still pulled together but not in his typical fashionable way.

"No, but..." She ran a hand over the leather binding. She also had the appearance of a hastily put-together outfit: jeans and a jade sweater. Her nails on her free hand clicked together, beckoning back to the chirp of a bird or something equally as loud. "It's like one of mine, and the book's scent is familiar."

"That book is one of Marcel's?" I pulled at the sleeves of my own lightweight powder-blue cashmere sweater. I had planned for a weekend of enjoying time with Kirtus and maybe some walking around the shops in downtown. At least I didn't look out of place. I really needed to focus, but this whole thing tied my stomach in knots, and I doubted I could spell my name if someone asked me.

"Perhaps." Juliet's lips as tight as when her dark blonde hair was pulled into a ponytail. Her gaze stayed focused on the book. Several times she sniffed at the air. I even noted a slight tremble in her shoulders.

Juliet slipped the leather band out of the loop and opened the book. She flipped through some of the pages. "The writing...the script is Marcel's hand, but how? I assumed I had all his books." Her eyes focused on me.

I chewed at my bottom lip before I responded. "I didn't believe him. Everything he showed me, Terrie and Ben. You and Victor gone. Gregor with the humans. San Jose was a war zone. This building burning. I observed the destruction and death not only from the street but from above the city. There were fires and explosions everywhere. The sickly sweet scent of burning flesh and blood mixed with ash and fumes of burning cars. The attack, all of it, came from everywhere." A shudder ran down my spine as the scent rushed to the front of my memory.

I had kept my word and didn't say anything about Kirtus's potential link to the queen, even though I should have.

"And what about this challenge from Sahin?" Amanda asked. I had forgotten she was there, and I startled slightly from her voice off to the left of me. I peeked over at her. Of everyone Amanda was the most put together. Her darker hair and nails were perfection, and she wore a minty-green skirt suit, with a white blouse. Impeccable as always.

"That piss ant." Victor laughed. "He has ambition. I groomed him to be a leader and a fighter, but I hoped he would challenge the leader of Texas or the leader of the rest of Canada..." He trailed off.

"To increase your area of influence." Juliet's manner was more conversational than confrontational.

"Obviously." Victor agreed, showing no offense at the question. "I've always maintained the Dark needed to take a page from the Light and consolidate power. If we had regions like the Light..." He nodded his head. "We are too fractured, and maybe having a more unified chain of command would be beneficial to us all. I'm still pushing for this change. Surprisingly, Ponleak and Elena are for these modifications. Makes sense as they control big areas, so I suppose I shouldn't be too surprised by their support... Still."

My gaze shifted over to Kirtus. I raised my eyebrows and tilted my head toward Victor. He shook his head. Fine. I wouldn't say anything, but I would need to tell Juliet later. I couldn't keep this secret from her, the news too important, and Victor had a point. What good did having a community do with everyone so fractured? The Immortal community was small. Why not have the leadership combined?

"I never thought Sahin..." Victor frowned.

"But you realized something was going on." Kirtus sank deeper into the cushions of his seat. His black leather jacket had been taken off and rested behind him on the back of his chair.

"Not until yesterday morning before the ceremony, but I ensured Cynthia would be there, luckily. She's still angry with Sahin and the whole lack of action he took with respect to young Mr. Raymond here." He gestured my way. "I assumed the note came from you, Juliet."

"Me?" Her eyes opened wide, and both Amanda and I faced her. "How would I know?"

Victor pointed at me.

"No. Sorry, I had no idea about any of that." I stopped and considered my vision. I hadn't seen Victor in any of them, and I hadn't put Victor's absence together until this morning. Well, put together in the sense Marcel had told me.

"Then who?" Amanda put the glass of water down.

"Marcel?" Kirtus messaged his temples.

"Or someone who wants us to believe they are Marcel, or at the very least thinks they are talking for Marcel." Juliet sighed and closed the book. "What are you going to do about Sahin?"

Victor waved off the comment. "Kill him, I'm afraid."

"What?" My voice a lot louder than it should be especially when everyone was already focused on me.

"Chris, killing Sahin gives me no pleasure, but he has challenged me. Not only did he offer up the challenge, but he did so in a public place. I have no choice. With luck, his death will be quick, and the other leaders who stick around to witness the challenge will fall in line and see not only how deadly I can be, but what a strong leader I make." He huffed. "With the additional openings in my ranks, I may be able to acquire additional territory with promises of expanding their territories."

"All this is about politics." I crossed my arms.

"But if someone interfered with the challenge and manipulated Sahin to make him challenge you, isn't that enough to save him? Wouldn't a questionable killing hurt your standing because of exploitation?" Juliet asked, which made me feel better. "I can talk to Patricia and Deborah. I can see if William has heard of anything."

"Marcel mentioned betrayal. What if that has something to do with this, has to do with everything I've seen? The whole mess? Or what about those moon children things?" I asked.

"Werewolves." Kirtus shook his head.

"What?"

"Moon children are what we call werewolves, but there aren't any. They were destroyed long ago."

"Are we sure?" Amanda asked.

"More damage has been caused by the magic coming into our world than we comprehend." I met the gazes of those around me. "That's what the voice said at the end."

"Maybe true magic has returned them," Amanda added.

I raked a hand through my hair. Why not now, when everything was possible? I had a fleeting image about dragons. If those showed up, that might be cool.

"It doesn't matter." Victor's voice winced with pain. "None of this matters. I've been challenged, and I have to answer for this fucking mess. Perhaps if this happened in private, but with the Dark leaders—" He shook his head. "I can't back down and the only outcome is Sahin's death."

"Or yours." Juliet frowned.

"Have you so little faith in me?" Victor's gaze met Juliet, and he appeared hurt. "I've survived more challenges than I care to remember. How do you think my territory got to the size it is today?"

"I'm worried about the duplicity surrounding the fight." Juliet pulled at her ponytail. "What if whomever left you the note is also in league with Sahin? What if this is a setup, as Chris says?"

"We need to be there." My voice didn't betray me and came out strong. No way was I going to sit by and let this challenge happen even if Sahin had been a class A ass.

"Chris, you are new to this world," Victor began. "For you to be there would be inappropriate."

"Not if we were there in an official capacity," Amanda chimed in. "I may not get everything about Dark politics, but both Chris and Juliet were present for the challenge which Juliet, as leader of the Light and head of this territory, would allow us to be at the challenge as a representative to ensure nothing happened to endanger the Light community or anyone else."

"But you cannot interfere." Victor pointed at me. "None of you."

I understood. I didn't want to interfere. Well, I did, but I wasn't going to get in the middle of these two Immortals while they fought. I didn't have a death wish.

"If we attend and you are victorious, I could request you stay Sahin's execution if we witness anything that goes against tradition." Juliet clicked her nails.

No comment crossed Victor's lips, to my surprise. He glanced at Kirtus.

"With all the Dark leaders in attendance and Juliet there as a witness, this may be all we need to ensure a fair fight, but with Sahin who knows." Kirtus raised his brows and shoulders at the same time, unsure what additional advice to offer.

"So be it." Victor rose, crossed to his wet bar, and poured himself a glass of red. "Would anyone like a glass?" He held up the bottle in offering.

Chapter Eighteen

Most of the time Juliet's office was warm and welcoming, even on days like this. The rain tapped on the window before bouncing off the ground outside. Her typical scent of vanilla and roses had an underscore of wet dampness even inside the house. I peeked over to the fire, watching the oranges, yellows, and reds dance around the burning walnut. An actual wood-burning fireplace was still a novelty to me; I enjoyed sitting and watching the fire, getting whiffs of the earthy walnut smells. A sigh escaped my lips as I turned to the book before me.

Amanda confirmed for me that the leather was indeed animal and not any other kind of tanned hide. Juliet grinned when I asked, at least she didn't outright laugh at me. Considering everything happening, I didn't find my question silly. Clearly, I was in error. Much like how quickly the wood burned, Juliet's mood shifted once I told her Marcel had mentioned Kirtus was the queen's heir. After that revelation, she put me to task on the book.

Marcel's book. The tome was from him, I had no doubt, like I accepted what he showed me, what I saw, would come to pass if we didn't stop it. Even if I didn't want to believe everything I saw, my vision was a truth I couldn't escape or run from.

None of us could.

Turning the page, I glanced over at Juliet's reference book. Marcel's book wasn't written in English, but some ancient language—I forgot the name Juliet told me—so her reference book acted as a way for me to translate Marcel's book. I would type my translations into the laptop, allowing Juliet to fill in whatever I missed, or correct what I had wrong. Translating was a long, painful process. I asked for an easier way, if the translating was something Gabe might help with. He had been helping with tracing my family tree. He was a freaking genius when it came to all this, but Juliet said she wanted to keep this in the family. At least until after she spoke with the council, which thankfully happened as I worked on translating, or trying to translate. I wondered if this book duty was punishment for me not telling her the whole truth earlier.

I closed my eyes and played with my mental wall, calling the barrier into focus, the industrial scents dancing around my nose. My barricade became more and more familiar to me, which made the process of summoning easier. I considered adding turrets to the wall for the sake of style, but the images came across as dumb. The turrets however, gave me an idea for my mental vault which I hadn't worked anymore on.

The door opened, and instead of Juliet, Amanda glided in. I tried not to frown. I wanted my visitor to be Juliet so we could talk. Still, Amanda was a welcome sight.

Amanda crossed over to the table, still dressed in her minty-green skirt suit from our earlier meeting with Victor. I had opted to change the minute we got home into sweats and a sweatshirt, especially since being relegated to research duty.

"How goes the translations?" Amanda stopped at Juliet's gold-and-glass mobile wet bar. She poured two glasses, one with red for me and one with hot water for tea—jasmine, if my nose worked—for her. She brought the refreshments over and handed me my glass. She pulled out a chair next to me sitting. "Drink." She pointed and put her tea down.

I took the glass and had a sip. The blood had hints of mixed nuts. Not bad.

As I took another sip, she pulled the book over in front of her.

"What are you—"

"I'm helping." Amanda flipped through a couple of pages of the book. "Despite you not telling us about Kirtus being the potential heir to the immortal throne." She paused. "Plus, you're going to take forever, and I've been translating for Juliet longer than you've been alive. I'll translate and you type. That'll make the process go much faster."

"Was she mad?"

Amanda stirred her tea. "No. Well...no. More surprised and worried. It made sense for you not to bring up the information on the queen and a potential heir with Victor there, but he's going to have to find out at some point." She sipped her tea. "Especially if your assertion about Kirtus is real."

"It is."

She glanced over her tea at me.

I took another sip of the red, savoring the nutty goodness, which I found odd, but I didn't mind especially as my stomach had been grumbling earlier. "Thanks." My gratitude wasn't only for the drink but also for believing me. I set the glass down, moved over a bit more, and focused on my laptop.

"Is Juliet still on the video chat with the council?"

"Yep." Amanda frowned down at the book.

"That bad?"

"Oh yeah." Amanda's voice was hard, and all her expressions were tight.

I opted to not say anything else and gestured in her direction to signal my readiness. Once Amanda dictated, I began typing away. I wasn't the fastest typist, but I managed to keep up with her. The process moved a lot faster now with Amanda's help. Where I had to use Juliet's reference book for practically every word, Amanda glanced at the reference tome only when she wanted to ensure her translating.

The only way time passed was by the crackling logs in the fire; I had to get up twice to add fresh logs. The other indications were by the pounding of the rain as it beat against the window before lessening to a point where I barely made the sound out.

"Well now." Amanda tapped the page and shifted the book for me to see. "This is interesting."

"What?" I peeked down at the book, which was ridiculous. I barely recognized the scribbles as writing let alone able to read the words; however, I did notice a list of what appeared to be names with dates next to them. A date of what might be births and a date of what I assumed were deaths. Also, on the sheet a column with notes and another row with numbers, but the highest number in line appeared to be five with the occasional six if my roman numerals were right.

"This is information we can verify." Amanda pulled out her cell phone from her suit pocket. She snapped a couple of pictures before tapping away on her phone. "I'm sending this list to Gabe."

"But Juliet wanted to keep this—"

Amanda shut me down with a raised eyebrow. "This is a family tree. One that confirmed what you said about the queen having a sister. These images may prove Kirtus is her long-lost heir."

"So you believe me?"

"That's what this list will decide." Amanda scanned her smartphone. "Which is why I sent the information to Gabe; his resources are far better in Salt Lake City than anything we have here. Gotta love the Mormons,"

Amanda teased. "And yes, I believe you. I never doubted you...well, not anymore." A wry grin greeted me as she put the phone away.

"Aren't you worried about the information getting out?"

"There is one thing Gabe is known for, and that is his complete discretion. He has built his reputation and business on being a neutral third party. That is why both the Light and the Dark trust him."

"Isn't he part of the Light?"

"No." She shook her head. "Gabe renounced both the Light and the Dark long ago. I'm not even sure if Victor or Juliet know if he's Light or Dark. Regardless, his neutrality has served him well. Both groups respect him and seek him out when they need assistance with Immortal law or in our case lineage."

"Still, this is huge news. These details are valuable to someone."

"Everything we do is a risk, but I don't see an alternative."

"Should you have asked Juliet?

"She trusts my judgment."

The door of the office cracked as Juliet burst through. She grumbled to herself in what, at first, I assumed to be French, but I learned otherwise; the words sounded older, but her phases weren't Latin. I stood up. "What's wrong?"

She froze as if learning for the first time Amanda and I were present.

As if on cue, the wind picked up outside and a branch hit the glass, startling me. My eyes focused on how dark it had gotten, and a prick at the base of my neck rushed through my body. Within seconds, we were amidst a downpour again.

"The council?" Amanda scowled.

Juliet exhaled before licking her lips. Her eyes closed as she tried to compose herself before speaking. "The council, in its combined wisdom, has chosen not to get involved in Dark Immortal affairs even if there are signs of outside interference."

"What about my vision? Didn't they..." Thunder snapped outside. I glanced at the window again and frowned. "They still don't believe me. Even after everything."

"They believe your vision is possible, just like they believe your foresight is a possible manipulation like before."

"But I'm able to detect that now. Plus, I've been working on my mental wall..." The rest of my sentence was barely a whisper as my heart sank. Why didn't they trust me? Hadn't I proven myself? "I'm able to banish people from my mind." I glanced at the floor.

"True or not, the council finds the situation easier to believe if someone is manipulating you and your visions for some yet-to-be-stated goal." Juliet's voice shook as she spoke. "Because you are so young, they believe your ability is underdeveloped and you require years of practice before..." She moved to her bar and poured herself a drink. Her hands trembled to the point of only being able to fill the glass halfway. "What you've seen is hard to believe, I will admit, even for me, the idea of Marcel being alive. That Kirtus may be the rightful heir of the queen." She sipped her drink. "Chris, why is Marcel hiding? Why won't he come forward? If I could talk to him..."

I shook my head. "He said your mind is too strong; he can't reach you or William." The image of the dying dark-haired woman popped into my mind. "But maybe the blockage William suffers from has something to do with the woman who died in his arms. Something he's trying to hide."

"He's afraid if he steps forward we'll figure out what he's actually doing." Amanda tapped the book.

"Possibly, but I'm his Called. His only Called. He can trust me." Juliet frowned and her shoulders dropped. For a moment, she appeared hurt.

"You're also the head of the Council for Light, and you hold great reasonability." I crossed my arms and gently squeezed myself. "I think he knows you better than anyone and can't risk whatever is happening until he knows for sure. Or has a way to stop Armageddon or knows we can stop it on our own."

"Gods, Marcel, always playing angles and controlling people." Juliet glanced at both Amanda and me. "I'm sorry if I've been bitchy lately. I hold him responsible for the Dark Ages and his game playing. If he would have..." She faced the ceiling and sighed. With another deep swallow of air, she walked over to the book and picked it up. "A family history?"

Amanda peeked at her phone. "I've taken a few photos and sent them to Gabe. I figured we would need undeniable proof."

Juliet's lips pulled tight and her gaze narrowed. The muscles in her neck twitched. She fought a frown; of that I had no doubt. "You're right of course. As much as I wanted to keep this quiet, we'll need Gabe and his resources to confirm if this lineage is accurate."

"And when he confirms what I've said?" I asked. "Will that make Kirtus the king of all the Immortals?"

Both Amanda and Juliet grew quiet, silent for much longer than I wanted them to be. Amanda glanced over at Juliet, both of us now waiting for some kind of response.

"The validation would give him a claim, assuming he wants to rule, but to reunite all the Immortals... Maybe that causes the war you observed." Juliet's voice wavered. I had to struggle to hear her. I met her gaze and didn't see any anger, only uncertainty and even undertones of fear. "It's possible by us doing this right now we are getting everyone closer to your vision, instead of stopping those events. It wouldn't surprise me if Marcel wanted to create some chaos. So he, or someone close to him, could seize power."

"And that's why the Council of Light won't get involved. They're scared." I rubbed the back of my neck. "Aren't they? They're afraid."

Juliet's head dropped. "Yes."

"That's stupid. How can—"

"Chris, you don't know. None of us do. What you've suggested may rip us and this world apart."

"Or unite everyone."

Juliet turned quiet again.

"You made those arguments, didn't you, Juliet?" Amanda's voice calm. "And they still wouldn't hear them..." She leaned closer. "They threatened a vote of no confidence on you, didn't they?"

"Fuck." I collapsed into my chair. "How could this be any worse? What's the point? We proceed and you lose your position, or we start a war that kills everyone, or who the hell knows what is going to happen. Even doing nothing can be the wrong move."

"Which is why we are going to proceed forward, not with the council, but we will still do what we believe is right. I'm still in charge of one of the largest and most powerful territories on the planet, and that comes with a lot of sway I may need to use." Juliet clicked her nails. "I'm going to invite Deb, Patty, and William here tomorrow night to see if we can figure any of this out. The council thinks this is a problem in the New World; they won't be affected by any of the changes, even Sybil, with everything we've been through. We don't always agree, but I had hoped..." Juliet sighed. "All we can do is move forward with the knowledge we have and hope our good intentions are not leading us on the road to hell."

Outside Juliet's office, the rain picked up, beating at the window. The wind howled as a tree branch scratched at the glass again. If I believed in bad omens, this would have sent a shiver down my spine. It did anyway.

*

"Do you realize how crazy this sounds?" Kirtus paced my bedroom, scanning from the bed to the patio door. He ran a hand through his beautiful red hair. Tonight he had his contacts in, so both his eyes showed green. I missed his gray eye.

"Crazy or not everything we've seen is possible." I touched his arm. "We found a family tree and are having Gabe examine and verify the information."

He rubbed a heavy hand over his face. "I'm not interested in being a leader. I can't do any more. No one will want me. You think they barely tolerate me now. Wait till this hits." His gaze met mine. "Chris, I barely want this position with Victor, but I have it, and have to make the changes work."

"And you'll make this ruler thing work. I have faith in you."

"Faith or not, no one is going to accept me. Not the Council of Light and sure as hell not the Dark leaders."

"You don't know." I reached out to his face, trying to hold him, so our eyes met. "Look, we'll figure out something that will work." I tried to pull him over to me, but he released my hand and walked to the window. "At least we have an idea of what the worst is that can happen."

"Oh sure." Kirtus glanced over his shoulder at me. "Total chaos, blood on the streets, vampires killing vampires, and humans killing who remains. Sounds peachy."

I got up, crossed over to him, and wrapped my arms around him, holding him tight. "If there is one thing I've learned about my visions, they are fluid. Look what happened and what I saw before Christmas. Those images were all awful. My sight's a warning; the visions are possibility of events that may come to pass if we do nothing. We stopped the Christmas massacre then. We can stop this apocalypse as well."

"Except in this version of your happy ending, I'm in charge of all the vampires in the world…" His voice trailed off. "I can't sit on a throne and dictate to people; that's not me."

I kissed his neck.

"How do I even get my head wrapped around that?"

"At least you have people who are here to help support you. I doubt Juliet, Amanda, and Victor would leave you out in the cold. We'll all support you."

He huffed.

We stood there, and I continued to hold him in my arms. Nothing more to say. If him being king was meant to be, it was meant to be. I supposed the biggest wildcard now was how everyone would react when the reports were verified.

*

I tugged at my tie. After spending the last day and a half in sweats and sweatshirt, the tie was slightly stifling, despite my having grown fond of them. A wave of calm crept into my psyche, which I had no intentions of complaining about. I figured Juliet was up to her old tricks, and I agreed tonight, of all nights, we needed the calm. I wasn't so much worried about Patty, Deb, or William. My concern lay with what happened outside our control, and I figured worry wouldn't do any of us any good tonight. So, the calming was there to help keep me and maybe the others focused. It didn't help that Kirtus wasn't going to join us tonight. He and Victor had other plans.

Much like Juliet's office, the living room had a big fire going strong in the fireplace, but instead of the subdued lighting, which allowed for the warm glow from the fire to light the room, we were engulfed in the artificial warmth of lights. With having human guests in the house tonight, Juliet had asked John, Mason, and Nadira to stay on, ensuring her guests would be comfortable. Nadira had created some wonderful-smelling mini quiche or croquette things that appeared amazing, along with a fruit, cheese, and nut display. There were crusted baguettes and even a chilled dish of caviar and assorted fixings.

John and Mason acted as our servers for the night, and I loved seeing them in their uniforms, which had to be tailored by Fredrick. No one, other than him, had the ability to get the fit as good.

Mason poured me another glass of red. I grinned up at him. "Looking sharp."

"Thank you, Mr. Raymond," he whispered and moved off to the other guests.

I reclined into the sofa and sipped my red as Juliet brought our guests current on all the happenings.

William rested his foot on his knee, his uniform tonight similar to what he had worn when I first met him. The exception was his khakis, which had been swapped out for dress slacks, complementing a nice light green button-down shirt. He had arrived wearing a leather overcoat, but that had been taken and hung. "So your council will be no help?" While he talked, I sensed him picking away at my mental wall.

I had been working on my wall every chance I got and continually made sure the defenses were up. I didn't want any more surprises.

"Good." William's gaze scanned me up and down.

"What?" I glanced between him and Juliet.

He turned to Juliet without another word.

"Not at this time. However, I'm hopeful they will come around." Juliet had her hostess face on. She used several of the same neutral expressions as when I had first met her all those months ago. I peeked over my shoulder in the direction of the dining room where all those months ago my life had changed. Those events now seemed ages ago. A time long since gone.

"Fools." Deb scoffed, playing with the sleeves of her turquoise blouse. She wore a pair of black, simple, but stylish dress pants. "Well, we've been in contact with our fellow coven leaders, and they are all watching for any signs of true magic. Luckily, the phenomena has been limited to California with some slippage into Reno, Nevada."

"But nothing like here." Patty stirred her tea, resting the spoon on the side of the saucer when finished. She had on a lavender sweater and a pair of black jeans and black boots. She was so stylish in her outfit, especially with how the lavender played off her tawny beige skin tone and shaved head.

"And yes, we've been able to keep the reports of magic all quiet," Deb added before anyone had an opportunity to ask.

"Well, that's good." I rested my hands on my legs.

"What about the people who were attacked at Sahin's club?" Gregor rested his jacket over the back of his chair as he sat down. He had just arrived, but somehow didn't seem to have missed a beat. Juliet wasn't sure she wanted to include Gregor in the meeting, but inviting him to keep him in the loop made sense, especially since he was her second-in-command.

"They've completely fallen off the radar." Amanda sipped at her wine. "I've talked to everyone and there is nothing. After the incident at the club, they were fine, no side effects, and now...poof"—she gestured with her hands— "gone."

"How is that possible?" William frowned. "People don't vanish into thin air."

"I'm sure they didn't vanish into nothing, but we can't find them at the moment. There is nothing at their homes or their places of work. For all intents and purposes, they vanished." Juliet flashed her hands for emphasis.

"You should have done more." Patty tsked and shook her head.

"We couldn't lock them up, so unfortunately they're gone. That happens a lot. People move around. We can't follow them indefinitely, especially since they were fine." Amanda sighed. "There are other things happening as well that need our attention."

"I have my people out looking for them," Gregor added. "I'm confident we'll find them."

"Sloppy." Deb crossed her arms in front of her. "They should have been watched nonstop."

"I don't want to belabor the subject." Juliet ended the conversation. "What is done is done. We'll find them and continue to ensure their safety." She waved a dismissive hand. "We have more pressing concerns. The challenge Sahin has made of Victor, Kirtus's potential blood line, and the possibility Marcel may still walk the earth."

"Manipulating things from the shadows." Deb raised an eyebrow. "As your people so often do."

My hands balled into a fist, but I held my tongue.

"The question at hand is, what do we do if Sahin wins the challenge?" William called our attention to the matter at hand, his scholarly tone forcing us to focus. "That will hold ramifications for all of us. Regardless of our neutrality or not."

"I'm not worried about Sahin." Gregor took the glass of red John handed him. "Victor is many things but not a fool and not to be underestimated in a fight." He rubbed his left shoulder, more out of a memory from the way he continued speaking. "What concerns me is Chris's vision."

"In the event Sahin wins the battle, what will the Light do? Can they stop the death of Victor? Offer him some kind of protection? Sanctuary?" Patty asked.

"No." Juliet clicked her fingernails. "I will have to find a way to work with Sahin, but there will be nothing I can do for Victor, not without causing...a war." She frowned.

William laughed. "Noninterference all the way around." He pointed at Deb. "Your coven will do the same as will I." He faced me. "I agree with Gregor; I'm more worried about the vision Chris had. A true Seer's vision should not be ignored as your council has elected to do. I believed they were wiser."

"Chris, would you mind..." Patty's request softly met my ears. "Can you share your vision with us?" She pointed between William and herself.

"I've already told you everything."

"No, like we did before." William leaned in. "When you were at my home."

"I..." My gaze fell to the floor. "I don't know how to do that."

Deb huffed, but the warmth of a hand on my knee gave me hope, the hand belonging to Patty. "Time for you to learn." She pulled an ottoman over and sat in front of me. "William and I will help guide you to the vision, and we'll see if there's anything you missed."

"The choice is yours," Juliet reassured me. "But I trust them."

I gulped down my nerves.

William scooted his chair closer to me.

I glanced between the two of them. "I can't really control my visions either."

"You'll learn." William's wrinkled face smoothed slightly, comforting me. "Now lean back and close your eyes."

I did as instructed and closed my eyes, allowing the warmth and the softness of the chair to absorb me. I ran a hand along my barricade.

"Focus on your breathing and the sound of..." Distracted by shuffling, I forced the noises from my mind. "Do you want to guide him, or should I?"

"I have entered his vision before. Why don't I go with him and you guide us both?" William's gruff voice bounced around in my head, beyond my wall.

"Good." Patty's voice softened. "Focus on my voice."

I nodded again.

"Keep your eyes closed and breathe," Patty instructed. "You'll need to lower your mental defenses. I can feel you pushing against us."

My eyes remaining closed, I swiped the wall away but still kept my defense close at hand should I need to call the wall back. I saw nothing, the typical blackness of my mind.

"Chris, breathe and try and relax."

I focused more on her voice, my eyes shutting. I leaned my head against the couch and inhaled deeply. Vanilla, roses, sandalwood, watermelon, and wildflowers all washed over me; the aroma wasn't an awful scent but comforting.

"Now focus on the fight at the SAP Center."

I didn't want to see that again, but if witnessing that horror show helped us, I needed to do it. The darkness faded and the fog of my visions filtered in. With each tick of the clock, the fog morphed into smoke, and I tasted the death and the burn in my mouth as the choking air continued to my lungs. My heart picked up speed like a runaway locomotive making a beeline straight for my brain.

"Relax," William's voice gently persuaded. "We're here. You're safe."

The scent of wildflowers danced around me. I turned, finding him next to me.

"Did you see *The Shining*?"

"What?"

"The movie, based on the book—"

"Yes, yes, but why is that story important?"

William's warm hand rested on my shoulder. At least that was what my senses told me, but I wasn't sure. "What they say is true. These are like pictures in a book; they can't hurt you."

"Oh." I pondered the idea for a second and my brows furrowed. "Wait. Didn't they end up hurting them and killing the father?"

"Chris, this is Patty." Her voice echoed in my brain. "Do me a favor, sweetness; keep breathing, and try to ease the tension in your body."

I forced my lungs to take in as much air as they would allow. Wildflowers tickled my nose.

Pictures in a book. Right.

"You okay?" William reached out.

"Yep, let's do this."

We walked, and like before Gregor, Juliet, and Kirtus were all attacking people and feeding off them. This crappy vision was not something I wanted to relive, but here we were. The whole time William stood with me as we walked, but unlike the last time these events unfolded like pictures in a book—well, more like a movie—and I watched. The smell of blood and death assaulted everything around me, but I didn't allow the odor to affect me this time. These images were a cheesy B movie to be turned off with a click of my mind. At least that was what I tried to remind myself as I continued to ignore my urge to freak the hell out.

William's hand rested again on my shoulder, or maybe it had never left. "There is nothing more to learn here. This is a vision of what may come to pass, but what we see here is not new."

Happy to hear that, I wanted to move on.

"Let's focus on what's happening outside." Patty's voice echoed in my head.

I closed my eyes in the vision and concentrated on the other images, the ones with everyone fighting and me walking on clouds in the sky. When I opened my eyes, we were there, and like before much of San Jose burned. Overturned cars, fires, the distinct blare of emergency vehicles. But unlike the last time, William stood next to me, his scent of wildflowers, which helped me to focus.

He spoke in a whisper, and I wasn't sure what I heard. The words weren't English, and he wasn't really speaking. The sounds seemed more like a song...no, a chant.

"What are you doing?"

"Despite what I view being a vision, I'm saying a prayer for all the lost souls." He continued his chant.

"You don't think we can stop what's to come?"

"Perhaps, but why tempt fate?"

I couldn't argue the point, so I continued to walk. We observed Gregor helping the people at Santana Row, before the Dark showed up, but nothing more. The fog thickened as the dense wisps returned.

"Nothing more." William shook his head. "Unfortunate."

"No, there's something else." I tried to pin down what I saw. "The vision of Marcel." I closed my eyes again and focused on that image; that seemed important, and I didn't want us to miss anything. The fog cleared, and this time I watched myself watch Marcel and the woman he held in his arms. "Look." I pointed.

William moved closer. "She's human."

I continued to glance around the Council of Light chamber, trying to see anything that might be new. Instead of a single table, a throne and on either side sat tables with chairs behind. On the stone wall a mural of a woman with deep auburn hair flowing past her shoulders; behind her were several other faces, one the woman Marcel held. "William. She's there." I pointed toward the mural.

"This place is foreign to me." William glanced around the space.

"We have to be in the royal chamber, before the Council of Light took the location over." I stepped closer to the mural and studied the woman with dark hair. I had never seen her outside of this vision, but I wanted to remember her face. I ran a hand along the wall and came to the queen. She was lovely. The events leading to her death were a shame.

I turned to Marcel.

Marcel wept and yelled as he held the lifeless woman in his arms. I took a few steps forward, and my eyes snapped open. "She was part of the queen's council," I relayed to everyone in the living room. "That's what Marcel didn't want me to see."

William gently opened his eyes. "What Chris says is correct. The woman was in the mural. He held her in his arms, a human...dead..."

"A human as part of the queen's council?" Amanda shook her head. "A Keeper? Maybe she was the queen's Keeper or Marcel's, for that matter."

I considered the queen and shook my head. "No. She wasn't a Keeper. I'm 100 percent sure about that."

Juliet sat deeper in her chair.

"Can we prove that?" Gregor asked.

"Wouldn't there be records?" Amanda leaned forward.

"Many questions." William tapped his lips. "But the only Immortal blood I sensed was Marcel's."

"No..." Juliet shook her head. "Marcel didn't have Keepers...well... I don't know." She clicked her fingernails several times.

"Could this woman have been a witch?" Gregor asked.

"There are rumors the witches may have had a seat at the queen's council, but..." Juliet's voice quiet, and again she trailed off.

"I doubt any witch would hold such a post, even during the queen's time." Deb crossed her arms over his chest.

"That was thousands of years ago." Patty peeked over her shoulder at her sister. "We don't know."

"There would have been a record," Deb countered. "Plus, can you imagine witches and vampires working together in that manner?"

"We're doing it now," I reminded Deb.

"Still, Marcel's hatred for witches was no secret." Juliet countered my optimism. "He didn't trust them and grew rather fond of killing them, well before he convinced the humans to do his dirty work for him."

"What about Marcel being on the queen's council?" Gregor stood at the fireplace, leaning against the bricks.

"No." Juliet sighed. "Despite how old he may be now, even at his age he would have never been old enough. From the records we have, the vampire royal court only had senior vampires serving the queen. They had to be at least a thousand years old."

"This is all interesting, but how does this help us now?" Amanda asked.

"Perhaps, if we stand united and refuse to recognize Sahin or Victor, if they kill the other, that may hold some weight?" Patty suggested.

"Doubtful. The Dark will see our refusal as a challenge to their autonomy." Gregor rubbed his temples. "And that action may cause a war."

"The winner could exile the loser?" William suggested.

"To where...the moon?" Amanda's tone bit at the air.

Juliet shot her a look.

"My apologies," Amanda offered.

"You are assuming Victor loses," Deb questioned.

"In all my visions, he wasn't there, and in the one where the city was under attack, Juliet wasn't around either. And the part in the SAP Center appeared to be a different time apart from the actual attack."

"I agree; they didn't feel like they were happening at the same time," William confirmed.

"Maybe whatever we are going to try won't work and causes Juliet's...absence." Patty frowned at her own suggestion.

"I think Juliet is right—" I froze.

All eyes were on me.

"The betrayal, what about the betrayal?" I couldn't move my mind past that detail. "Marcel mentioned some kind of treachery. What if we stop that from happening?"

"We have no idea who is betraying whom," Deb said.

"Let's assume Sahin is going to cheat or someone is going to interfere with the fight," Gregor said with raised hands.

"Okay," I agreed.

"We understand Juliet will be there, as will Chris, but the rest of us should hang back and ensure there is nothing going awry."

"To what end?" William asked.

"Sahin can't win a fair fight, from what I've heard and seen. He is being overly confident, a quality shared with Victor; he's acting as if he's already won or going to win, so maybe he's got something planned. He's going to cheat. Somehow."

"Agreed." Juliet bobbed her head in the affirmative. "So a small group in and around the area. We won't tell Victor or Sahin. We'll keep an eye on everything." She nodded. "That's all we've got."

"It's worth a shot," Patty agreed.

"So, we plan on being there in case Sahin, or Marcel, or the Council of Light, or the other Dark leaders, try and rig the fight." William massaged his right temple.

Gregor inhaled before releasing a heavy sigh.

Both Patty and Deb shared a concerned glance.

Amanda frowned down at the floor.

My stomach sat in knots as a throbbing creeped its way up the spine of my neck and into the top of my head.

Juliet bit her lips. "This isn't a great plan, by any stretch of the imagination."

There were nods of agreement all around.

Chapter Nineteen

I wished I could say tonight was a dark and stormy night. That would be fantastic, with thunder rattling the car windows and lightning casting the scenery in an eerie white glow when it streaked through the night sky. Sadly, that wasn't the case. A full moon lit our February night and not a cloud in the sky. The night wasn't even cold—well, not Reno cold, which was what I was used to for this time of year. I barely needed my black jacket, but I wore it anyway.

After our meeting, I spoke privately with Patty and William about my mental defenses, specifically my mental vault, while they enjoyed the hors d'oeuvre provided by Juliet. They both suggested that for the time being I solely focus on my mental barrier and leave the vault for latter, after I perfected my mental wall.

"What a great night," I commented as I continued to watch out the window, the lights of buildings and houses passing us by.

"Beautiful." Juliet kept her eyes focused on the road.

"I talked to Kirtus today; he doesn't seem worried about tonight." I sighed. "In fact, he seems kind of glad."

"I doubt he will miss Sahin." Juliet paused as her grip tightened on the steering wheel of the Ford. "Such a waste."

"Yes, but with Sahin gone, and Kirtus in a greater position of power, this will force the Light and the Dark closer." Amanda adjusted how she sat. "I never had issues with Sahin, but he's no friend of Kirtus's and barely tolerated any of the Light." She leaned forward from the back seat for us to hear her better. "Who knows? Maybe this will help."

"If only I saw the future more clearly." I closed my eyes and focused again, but there wasn't much of a point. My temples still ached from trying all afternoon. "I've tried to focus on the challenge, but all I get is a whole lot of fog and nothing else." I rubbed the side of my head.

"You've only had this ability for less than six months." Amanda patted my shoulder.

"My powers took me almost twenty years to fully control, and I'm still improving on them every day." Juliet tapped the side of her head to emphasize the point. "These gifts are not something one can master in a few weeks."

"But—"

"Years, Chris, years and years," Juliet chided. "And I still get queasy, especially when I'm tired or I've overexerted myself."

Instead of pushing the subject, I changed tactics. "What's the deal with this location? Why's Hick's Road so important?"

Amanda laughed. "You mean to tell me, in all your research into the area for witches and local history, you never came across the legend of Hick's Road?"

"No. Should I?" I shifted in the passenger seat to more easily see Amanda in the back.

"I assumed everyone in San Jose heard the legend." She grinned at me.

"I'm not from here."

"Oh, right." Amanda tapped the side of her head and pretended to act surprised by my admission.

I shook my head. "So..."

"Oh, the locals think the area is haunted, or a crazy cult of albinos live out here and attack people..." Amanda raised her hands and wiggled her fingers in a mocking jester. "And eat them."

"Ugh. Seriously?" I huffed. "Some people are so stupid, especially when it comes to some dumb urban legend."

"Sadly, the legend's been around for a long time..." Juliet chimed in.

"Before people understood such things," Amanda added. "Mostly, now people think there is a cult of Satan worshippers up here. They chase cars and so forth." Amanda glanced out the window. "There's an old mine there as well. People like to be scared. If they only knew the truth."

I peeked out the window where she looked. I only noticed houses and us getting close to the hills. "Let me guess: this is the spot the Dark use for challenges like this, and they scare the people off."

Juliet adjusted her grip on the steering wheel as she peeked back at me. "As well as other things. I wouldn't be surprised if Victor lets them use the area to torment people. Or test one another's gifts. The locations is still a good place to not be found."

I motioned my understanding as I leaned a bit more in my seat. I did have to wonder how many urban legends, like this one, were caused by vampires or witches who wanted to keep areas secret or to keep out of the eyes of humans when the Immortals were up to no good. I assumed even the Light did things like this.

"Crafting these stories was a lot easier when the quicksilver mine was so far away from civilization and out in Old Almaden." Amanda picked at her fingernails and continued. "Now it's all a park."

"Yes, well, there are still rumors, and some people even believe there is a gateway to another dimension out there," Juliet added.

My ears perked up. "Is there?"

"Well, there have been some incidents with true magic out here, so I guess anything is possible." Juliet gestured with a quick glance to me.

"Even among Immortals there were still urban legends." I half chuckled at the idea.

We made our way down Almaden Expressway to where the road narrowed. Out the right window, I saw up toward Mt. Umunhum and a big cement building. "What's that?"

Juliet promptly glanced up. "Old early warning radar site. Now the radar is part of a hiking trail. The trail's a nice hike, and on a clear day the view is impressive."

"When people aren't being chased out with bat-yielding Immortals pretending to be cultists," Amanda teased.

I pursed my lips. These Immortal activities did not make me a happy camper, and challenges like this would be something I would like to see come to an end in the future. My stomach dropped with a shiver down my spine. Assuming we had a future.

I chose not to think anymore and focused on the ride. We continued on the winding road. How odd to think five minutes down the road a major metropolitan area existed. Perhaps this was why the urban legend continued. There were no lights on this part of the road anymore, and we only had the light of the car's headlights to guide us. I wasn't great with directions, and as the road continued to twist and turn, I found I no longer knew where we were.

A buzz blared out and my heart dropped as I nearly yelped.

"Message from William." Amanda stared at her phone from the back seat. "He asked a few of the Mohawks he's acquainted with in the area to help patrol tonight..." She paused and faced Juliet. "They are keeping far enough away..."

Amanda tapped out a response.

"The extra eyes will be good." Juliet slowed the car and we turned. "We're here." We continued on a dusty road for a bit before she pulled the car to a stop.

My heart thumped faster, and I took a deep breath to calm my nerves. I wasn't looking forward to any of this. No matter the outcome, or what I thought of Sahin, I didn't want this to happen. Images of how hard he had fought during the battle with my father and my father's coven flooded my memories. We all worked so well together, and now here we were. I sighed and unlatched my seat belt. I should have used the bathroom before we left. Too late now. I elected not to think about it.

There were a few other vehicles around, but not as many as I had assumed, considering the nature of tonight's event. The location had been chosen intentional to not arise any suspicion from the locals. Victor and Sahin couldn't have this type of challenge happen at the mall or in downtown Los Altos. That would be bad for everyone, and break about a dozen Immortal rules. I peeked around again, maybe there would be more Immortals coming, but honestly who knew. Counting our car, there were four and none of them were ones I recognized.

"We'll have to walk the rest of the way." Juliet opened the car door.

Once I stepped out of the car into the darkness, I zipped up my jacket against the chill in the air. I took in the scents of pine and grass and even the dampness floating around me. Out in the woods the chill burrowed deeper into my flesh. "We won't have to worry about an...incident..." I wasn't sure what else to call it.

"No." Juliet pulled her jacket tighter. "Victor understands I will have our people in the area, and Sahin should realize this as well. Neither is that foolhardy... I hope."

A click of what I assumed to be a gun echoed around us. "Doesn't mean we won't be ready." Amanda fussed with her jacket and a snap of the belt she wore with her jeans. "Never underestimate the power of greedy stupid people." Her voice had lost all its normal charm.

Out of the corner of my eye, I caught her adjusting her jacket. She put something away. "What about the others?" I thought of Deb and Patty and even William and his group. What would they do if they spotted magic or vampires or who knows what else? How would William explain the paranormal to his people?

"They'll stay out of the way as long as nothing suspicious happens. Watching from a distance. None of them would be dumb enough to interfere at this point...not even the other Dark who will be here. The fight is between Victor and Sahin, and the battle should stay that way," Juliet reminded us.

I hoped she was right.

We walked in a close group, silent as Juliet led the way. For once in my life I wanted her to use her ability on me to help keep me calm, but no warmth found its way into my being and I wasn't going to ask. My hands were sweating and my heart danced in my chest like it was at a rave. I did a partial shift to see and hear better. I didn't want to fully vamp out and get in trouble, so I figured half vamp would be enough.

Juliet didn't say anything, and I caught a glint of her fangs in the moonlight. We were both on the same page.

With the additional sight, I instantly calmed down as my senses were amped, my vision as clear as if I wore night goggles. And I had the added benefit of my increased hearing. I sniffed the air and coughed. I smelled animals including the funky wet dog smell. I wanted to gag. These aromas were not a pleasant mixture, but nature didn't always have the best scents. On occasions, like now, even the smell of death hung in the air. A wild animal, I assumed. I pushed the images of the animals to the rear of my brain, and I focused on the Immortal scents. I also took the moment to check my mental wall. No way did I want to have a vision while we were in this much uncertainty.

As we continued on I caught a whiff of sandalwood, almonds, and some other familiar aromas. But no salty ocean smell, Sahin's smell. I took another exploratory breath. We were getting close. My senses hadn't done me wrong yet. We passed a small cluster of trees and strolled into a clearing.

"At least we aren't first." Amanda glanced around, her voice intentionally soft to keep our arrival as quiet as possible.

Not much captured my gaze. We were in an open field with a smattering of trees here and there. On the ground I stepped through a mix of grass and dirt, most of it damp from the cool night air. The area was nicely lit by the full moon, so I opted to shift to my human form. No point in wasting the effort.

"Good evening." Juliet's voice sang out to the group.

"Juliet." Victor greeted us with a slight frown. "I had hoped it would be Sahin."

"He's being his dramatic self," Kirtus mentioned, and I absolutely heard his beautiful eyes roll even without witnessing them firsthand. "The patrols haven't seen him yet either."

"He wants to ensure he has the upper hand by showing up last." Victor picked at a piece of lint on his shirt. He dusted his sleeve as the lint dropped to the ground. "It's a sound strategy."

"I'm disappointed to see you all again under these circumstances." Masko offered us a slight bow. He turned and his expression brightened. "Is that the enchanting Amanda Sutherland I've heard so much about?" He stepped forward.

Amanda perked up and even stood taller, which enhanced her chest. "That is kind of you."

"Keep your dick in your pants," Joaquín grumbled. "We need to stay focused." He sniffed the area. "Do you smell anything?"

"There is always time to appreciate a beautiful woman." Masko's eyes didn't leave Amanda, but he tilted up his nose and sniffed around. "Plus, it would seem Sahin and Betty have arrived." He pointed to one of the tree lines, and as if on cue, Sahin and Betty emerged from the darkness.

"About time." Victor tapped his watch.

"In a hurry to die, old man?" Sahin snarled. He appeared already mostly shifted.

Victor remained quiet and in his human form, which I found interesting, especially given what was going to happen.

"I would like to ask"—Juliet's voice raised—"on behalf of the Council of Light and as the Light's leader in this territory, whomever is the loser, no one is killed. There—"

"Be quiet, you Light bitch," Betty sneered as her face transformed and she growled at Juliet.

"What the hell!" I shouted.

Betty made a fast movement in the direction of Juliet and the rest of us.

A growl crossed my lips as my blood burned through my veins. Already transformed into my full vampire self, I was itching to attack. The surroundings were alive. There were birds nesting in the trees. An owl took to flight, the crunch of leaves as a deer ran through the brush. Wolves or coyotes patrolled off in the distance. I was ready to lunge at Betty when a firm hand held me in place.

"Keep your boy under control," Sahin commanded. "Things are going to be different once I take out the trash. The Dark in this area aren't going to be the Light's lap dogs anymore."

I turned on Sahin, trying to pull free from the hold Juliet had on me.

"Chris." Juliet's soothing ability calmed my nerves. She caught my gaze. She, too, was partially transformed, and a wave of roses and vanilla washed over me and through my soul. "I appreciate your loyalty, but this fight isn't about us."

I unclenched my fist as all eyes were on me, including the small delegation of Dark leaders who had been at the party to celebrate Kirtus's ascension to chief lieutenant. I shook my head and transformed to myself, but I still managed to growl one more time at Betty and Sahin.

"There will be no quarter given tonight, Juliet." Victor growled. "I'm sorry." He added with force.

A tingle reached the base of my brain. Juliet wanted to protest, but she remained quiet, perhaps waiting for the fight to play out. Once Victor won, she could speak to him.

Juliet, Amanda, and I stood there in silence. I wasn't sure what to expect. I assumed there would be banter between Sahin and Victor first. A conversation. Something. When Victor rushed Sahin, I stepped back as they collided into each other. I would swear they made a clap of thunder when they struck. The battle started with no talking, only fighting, and watching.

Their movements were swift, graceful in a way, and elegant, like a choreographed dance.

Victor picked up Sahin in both hands and smashed him into the ground. This was too easy. Sahin bounced up and out of Victor's grasp in the flash of light. Sahin kicked Victor hard between the legs, and I cringed. Any normal man would have thrown up and dropped to the ground, but Victor only grunted and caught his footing. He chuckled with a pleased nod.

Sahin rushed for Victor, not taking anything for granted, wanting to attack him again while he still had his slight advantage.

Victor lifted his hand, and Sahin froze as if waiting for something to happen. When nothing did, he took a step. On the ground, several small rocks raised and shot right at him. As nimble as Sahin was, most of the rocks found their target. Sahin hit the damp grassy field with a *smoosh* and lay there a moment. Victor flew at him, and Sahin rolled out of the way enough for his arm to swing up and plunge something into Victor's side. The yowl from Victor was a scream unlike any I had ever encountered.

"Silver dagger." Victor spat blood on the earth. "So weak."

My nose was instantly assaulted with the aroma of almonds, and I became transfixed. The blood and the violence were intoxicating to me. I would feel a great deal of shame about my reaction later.

I caught a whiff of wildflowers, and the new smell acted like coffee beans when you went to smell perfumes. The fresh scent helped to clear my mind.

"You taught me to win." Sahin moved with the grace of an elk and charged Victor again.

Victor forced himself to stand tall as he held his side. He took a step and waved his free hand. Sahin froze for a split second, and as if he was connected to a bungee cord, he snapped through the air and hit a large oak tree, his left shoulder impaled in an outstretched branch.

I had issues trying to figure out whom to focus on. Victor picked up the dagger Sahin had dropped when he flew through the air. I couldn't tell if Victor's wound had healed or not, but if his cut was anything like mine, the healing would take time. And fresh blood. Still he walked stronger, and the rush of sweet almonds perfuming the area grew stronger.

I again got hit with another whiff of wildflowers.

I peeked over to Kirtus and the other Dark. None of them had pleased expressions on their faces, but they were focused on the action as well. This was the first moment I found myself able to take my eyes off the fighting. No others managed this. Even Juliet and Amanda stood transfixed, watching between Victor and Sahin.

"You need to see everything," a deep voice instructed in my mind outside my mental wall. "Do you smell them? They are here."

I scanned the area. What had happened? What was I missing?

Sahin for his part struggled against the branch, but Victor had Sahin pinned. His end was near. Sahin even bowed his head as if accepting his fate, but the glare of defiance never changed. I caught hints of the salty ocean scent of his blood as the bouquet filled my nose. There were so many scents, so much blood; so much Immortal blood. The more I focused on the blood, the more my gaze fixated on the two of them. As much as I didn't want anyone to die tonight, I was glad death would pass over Victor.

He moved closer to Sahin.

A tug in the base of my mind again accompanied by a deep voice, Marcel, I assumed, but wasn't sure. Too much was happening, and I couldn't be sure of anything. Was my wall even intact? "Betty. Watch Betty. Find their smell," the voice demanded.

"What is she doing?" I asked and pulled my attention from Victor and Sahin to her. There were three flashes of light into the trees as she stepped further from the clearing. "What is she up to?" I tapped Amanda on the shoulder.

Amanda's head snapped in the direction of Betty. "Juliet! Victor!" she shouted and pulled out her gun.

Within seconds, the trees behind Victor and Sahin rustled and burst with three wolves, but not like any wolves I had ever seen. These wolves were larger. If it weren't impossible, I would say they were the size of bears. I had to be misjudging their size.

Amanda's gun fired and the wolves scattered. Two brown wolves made their way for Victor, and the blondish one made its way for... "Kirtus!" I yelled.

He reacted faster than I shouted his name. A burst of wind and the wolf lunging for Kirtus smashed to the ground as Kirtus, Masko, and Joaquín moved closer to Victor. The four other Dark leaders formed a tight circle with one another back-to-back so they saw anything coming for them. However, they did nothing to help anyone around them. They were taking a strictly defensive posture.

I tried to move toward Kirtus and the others, but both Amanda and Juliet pulled me back. Juliet shook her head.

"I'm not going to stand here!" I shouted at Juliet. "We have to help."

Before Juliet responded, a burst of flames smashed into the spot where the wolf that was after Kirtus stood. The beast moved so abruptly the motion made it impossible to keep my eyes on the wolf.

A roar reverberated through the trees and all around. I scanned the scene to see where the sound came from. On the ground Victor had two wolves on him. Betty stood and flipped her wrist. A flash of light shot from her hand, and the branch holding Sahin snapped, allowing him to free himself. He glared at me and Juliet. Within a blink of an eye, he had his silver dagger and moved to plunge it into Victor.

"We have to—"

A clap of lighting filled the area with white light. I had to close my eyes. Less than a second later, thunder roared all around us, causing the ground to tremble, the change impossible, but the weather had gone from a clear night to a downpour. The rain and thunder caused everyone to stop what they were doing, even the wolves, and as quickly as the storm had appeared, it vanished.

Water dripped down my face and off my jacket. I had no idea what had happened.

While I glanced around at the others, roots burst from the ground, ensnaring the two wolves near Victor and Sahin.

"No!" Sahin yelled.

The blond wolf who had been after Kurtis moved to help the two that were tangled.

Kirtus raised his hand, and the ground shook and tore as it was ripped apart. The blond wolf wasn't quick enough when it tried to jump; the beast lost its footing and dropped into the pit Kirtus opened. The pit swallowed half the wolf and snapped shut in a geyser of blood. I had to look away. The smell of wet dog overpowered my senses. Every other scent in the area disappeared. A howl from the wolves, and the larger brown one snapped at the roots holding it.

More rustling from the trees as Patty and Deb appeared, both chanting.

"What are they doing here?" Sahin growled.

He fully transformed as he tried to free himself from the roots as well.

"Ensuring whatever game you were playing wouldn't work," Victor struggled to say as he snatched the dagger up, ready to strike Sahin down.

"Victor," Juliet called out, her voice hurried. "If you kill him now, we won't know the extent of his betrayal or who helped him."

Victor stood there and glanced to Patty and Deb. He peered over to the other Dark leaders who had moved closer to the action. Masko and Joaquín were holding Betty. I didn't know how I missed that, but they had her and she didn't seem to be fighting them. "Report." Victor addressed Kirtus and his other lieutenants.

Kirtus held up his phone. "I can't reach the others." His chest heaved, inhaling deeply, water dripping from his face as well.

"We've got this one." Joaquín pushed Betty's wet body more into the center of the field. "She won't use her light show anymore." He pulled her arms tighter and she winced.

"Your other men are dead, killed by the wolves." Deb's voice strained. "We can only hold this spell a short time, but..."

"With your permission?" Juliet asked with a peek at Victor.

He waved her to continue.

Juliet brushed the wet strands of hair from her face. It took only a moment, but a wave of vanilla and roses moved out from her. As the scent filled my lungs, my heart that had been pounding all the way to the tips of my toes slowed and I started to relax. The mood of the whole scene shifted. The mismatch of scents were losing out to Juliet's ability. Everyone, including the wolves, were calming down, no longer snapping at the vines. I wanted to find a nice spot to lie down and relax. Tonight had been long, and now that the event had ended, I was ready to chill out. I didn't even care about being wet. Even Victor had calmed down, his respiration normal, and he had put the dagger away and now held Sahin, who acted oddly quiet and sedate, allowing things to happen around him.

Juliet bowed her head toward Patty and Deb, and their chant changed. The two wolves no longer struggled as the roots released them. I had, as we all did, expected them to fall under Juliet's spell; however, the minute they were freed they both jumped up, growled, and ran for the woods.

"We have to..."

"Stop them..."

"They're getting away..."

"Not possible..."

We all viewed in disbelief as the wolves vanished into the forest. None of us went after them, too subdued by Juliet's calming.

"Look," someone yelled, I think Kirtus.

"Impossible," one of the Dark leaders called out and stepped forward.

The half-buried wolf had an orange glow around it. The pelt ripped from the body, and piece by piece a human form emerged.

"Werewolves?" The word fell from my mouth. The half of the wolf still visible morphed into a woman. Dead. My stomach dropped and bile moved up my throat. She had been one of the people who had gotten zapped at the nightclub. The moon, the girl, and the puppies from my vision. "Werewolves have returned."

Chapter Twenty

My head ached still in disbelief of what we had witnessed. Werewolves, and they were helping Sahin. Insanity. The worst part, the dead wolf had been one of the people from the nightclub attack. I peeked around the group. Sahin and Betty were chained up in silver similar to what I had seen when Juliet had killed Malcolm. The sickly-sweet scent of burning flesh found a path to my nose.

I took off my wet jacket and tried to shake out some of the rain as I stood there. Juliet had pulled her hair into wet ponytail.

Amanda and Masko returned from the direction where the wolves had vanished. "No trace of them." Amanda ran a hand over her hair, ensuring no strands were out of place.

"Not that we understand how to track them," Masko added, tugging at his wet shirt as the fabric clung to his well-defined chest and arms.

"Can't you follow the scent of wet dog?" I pinched my nose. "The scent is awful. I don't smell it now, but I bet if you follow the stink, you'll find them."

"Wet dog?" Masko rubbed his hair to get more of the wetness out. "I didn't notice, and I have an excellent sense of smell; that's my gift."

"Chris, was that the same odor you smelled when we went to Sahin's night club?" Juliet asked.

I pulled the memories forward. "Yes, I'm 100 percent certain."

She shook her head. "I've heard legends when Lycan roamed the earth some vampires claimed they had the scent of wet dog, but I..."

"Enough." Victor stabbed the knife into Sahin's leg. "Be lucky I'm not starting with your favorite body part, like you did to me." He dripped like the rest of us, only he hadn't taken any time to do anything about his current state.

Sahin cried out.

"We've gotten the bodies taken care of." Kirtus dusted off his hands as he and Joaquín returned to the field. "Ripped apart by the wolves, like

Deborah and Patty said." He shook his head as he rested a hand on my shoulder.

I touched his hand, giving him a squeeze.

"You have a lot to answer for, little worm." Victor twisted the silver dagger in Sahin's leg before he got up, joining the rest of us.

"Go to hell," Sahin spat.

"This woman," Deb called. "Or what's left of her." She stood. "She wasn't the alpha."

Everyone focused on Patty and Deb.

"What do you mean?" Juliet asked.

"The brown-haired female, the one who attacked Victor, that is the alpha." Patty motioned toward Victor.

More rustling in the trees as William stumbled out, holding his arm.

"William." Amanda rushed over to assist him. "What happened?"

"One of the wolves." He took the offered support from Amanda. "I followed him for as long as possible, but he was too quick. He led me off to protect his alpha. She got away."

I caught the scent of wildflowers.

"You." The word dropped from my mouth before I stopped it.

William dusted off his shirt as he got closer to the group. "I reached out to your mind to help keep you focused. I wish I did more. Once I spotted the wolf tracks, I realized something was wrong. Those weren't normal paw marks."

I rubbed my forehead. "But how did you recognize Betty? You told me to watch her."

William's eyes narrowed, and he shook his head. "I wasn't close enough to touch your mind like that; plus, your wall is getting much too strong."

I frowned.

"Once the battle ended, I radioed the others and told them to leave. That everything was fine." William gestured toward Juliet and Victor. "Figured you'd appreciate fewer eyes and I didn't feel like explaining any more than I had to."

"Thank you," Juliet agreed.

"How is any of this possible?" Kirtus pulled bandages from his backpack, giving them to Amanda.

"The note didn't go into this much detail." Victor patted his pocket.

"Note?" Juliet asked.

He dug into his pocket and pulled out a note. "This note, similar to the one I got before the party." He handed it to Juliet.

"Marcel." More of his involvement. I crossed my arms over my chest.

"Again." Amanda tightened her ponytail.

"He's manipulating things still." Juliet held the note in her hands as she read it.

"Well, I appreciate his warning." Victor cracked his neck, releasing any tension with a few pops.

"You coward," Sahin spat. He wasn't struggling, but his eyes burned with hatred and anger. "You rely on others to win your battle."

Victor walked over to his onetime friend and Called, and unzipped his own pants, glaring down at Sahin as he did. With his free hand, Victor pulled out the athletic cup he wore, dropping the protective gear to the ground next to Sahin. "We're beyond fair fights; I taught you to take all advantages, exploit all weaknesses, and you did." He sneered at Sahin. "You're angry because you lost."

"Sahin forced me," Betty whined. "He threatened me." She licked her lips. "I would never do anything against you, Victor. I had no choice. You realize that, right?" Her voice was sugary sweet, and her eyes darted to the other Dark. "You all know me. You recognize I love Victor..."

I didn't need to be a Seer to see she was lying. She was only groveling because she wasn't on the winning side like she figured she would be.

"I understand." Victor touched her cheek with the back of his free hand. His movements were faster than what my eyes could process. Within a blink Betty's head dropped to the ground, rolling away from her body, an expression of pleading still on her face as her eyes flashed two more times in disbelief. "Now for you." He walked over to Sahin.

"We still don't have information on the wolves," Juliet reminded him, her voice weak, and when I met her gaze I understood all the fight had gone. The battle had ended, and Sahin would die, if not now, before the night came to an end.

"These are the people touched by the true magic attack at Sahin's nightclub." Deborah's voice boomed but had no life in it. "I recognized the woman as did Chris."

"They struck a deal with Sahin, or he struck one with them. Protection or promises to be left alone allowing them to rebuild their numbers, help him now, and have an enemy to deal with at a later time," William added.

"And things did not go to plan." Patty shook her head, and her gaze dropped to the earth before her.

Victor glanced at Juliet. "I think we've uncovered everything we can. We will learn more once the beasts are found. Sahin can't poison my well any longer, and you and I understand his continued life would only cause more harm for all of us."

Juliet sighed and glanced at the others, appealing for any support.

"You won't kill me." Sahin laughed. "You need me. I'm your strongest lieutenant. You'll never be able to replace me, *mi amor*."

"That's where you're wrong." Victor pulled out the dagger. "I haven't needed you in a long time." He made a single motion, and Sahin's head now joined Betty's on the ground.

I didn't want to see the life drain from his eyes like I had with Betty. Sahin's death was too much. Even though Sahin had turned into a monster, he still had something there. Plus, I found the scent of blood to be overwhelming. I had drank before we came tonight, but all the blood energy got me antsy and I didn't like the effect all this blood and violence had on me.

"Such a waste." Victor bowed his head and sighed. He wiped the blood from the blade on Sahin's pant leg and stood up to his full height, the full moon behind his shoulder.

"We'll burn their bodies with the rest." Kirtus's voice filled with strength, but like everyone else no emotion accompanied his words. I figured lack of emotion was how everyone dealt with what had transpired tonight. In the coldest businesslike manner possible. A transaction. A series of motions, holding back any pain, sorrow, or anger.

"No." Victor glanced around the group. "Sahin and Betty are mine. They may have been disloyal tonight, but they are still my family. I will handle them. I owe them that at least." He glanced at the other Dark leaders. "We are done here. You have witnessed tonight's events and recognize what our world now faces, and I am still in full control of my territory. I will do what I must to protect my assets. I will answer any challenge. Do not take me for weak; it will not go well for you."

"Werewolves." One of the Dark leaders' shook his head, the words barely over a whisper.

"We will await more news from you." The female Dark leader stepped forward. "I will inform my people in Canada to keep an eye out not only for true magic but for these moon children." She bowed. "You have strong relations and even stronger allies, and I'm pleased to be one of them. Perhaps we can speak more of joining our territories."

"Thank you, Marvina." Victor had a sigh in his words. "I welcome those conversations and could use a good lieutenant especially with the vacancy I now have on our shared border."

The others remained quiet but bowed, and the four made their way down the trail to where the cars were. Perhaps, with Victor's win tonight, he would gain more territory. No one would want to mess with him, not after word got out about tonight.

A rush of wind whipped around us as the night, or maybe nature, tried to clean the air of the heavy blood scent and the stench of battle. I pulled my jacket tighter, my coat heavy but not enough to soak entirely through. Still, I wanted to get home and get into some dry clothes.

Victor turned to the rest of us. "All your assistance tonight has been appreciated. I will not forget this. Deborah and Patty, let your coven know they have a friend in the Dark." He turned to William. "William, I'm not acquainted well with you or your people; however, if there is anything I can do for you, please do not hesitate to ask. I hope we will be able to build on this night's events."

"Kind words." William's tone lifted with his words. "Thank you."

A familiar hand laced its fingers into mine. I sniffed the scent: Kirtus. "I'll come see you later." He kissed my cheek. "I'm sorry you had to be part of this."

"Don't be," I whispered to him. I met his gaze. "You're her."

"What?"

I shook my head. Now wasn't the time, but I understood Kirtus and the old queen had the same eyes, I remembered the detail from the painting on the council wall.

"Victor, when you are ready." Juliet held out her hand in the direction of the vehicles. "We have a great deal to talk about. Gregor will be waiting for word on what happened here. I had him and some of his people in the city tonight to ensure events were limited to here and didn't spill into San Jose proper." She glanced around the location. "I will have to inform the Council of this new threat as well."

"Do as you see fit." Victor brushed off the comment his voice distant as he removed the chains from Betty and Sahin. "Juliet, if I find the two wolves, they will die."

Juliet remained motionless, not responding.

"We should go." Patty walked over to William. "We'll help you to your car if you'd like."

"Thank you." William stretched for Patty's offered arm. "Juliet. Victor. Some of our folklore includes stories of the Coyote Trickster Spirit. I had hoped he was responsible for some of tonight's events, perhaps the Spirit played a part, but I'm afraid there is much more at play here, something that even predates my people's stories." He frowned. "Marcel may be such a force, but..." He rested his bandaged arm close to his chest.

The three headed off toward the trees, not to where we parked our car.

"Come on." Amanda gestured as Juliet and I made our way to our car, leaving the Dark to tend to their dead.

*

Once we got home, Gregor met us already pacing, waiting for us in the driveway of Juliet's home. He and Juliet disappeared into her office the minute the wooden doors closed behind us. Amanda squeezed my arm and went off to do who knew what. Instead of trying to think any more on tonight's events, I went upstairs for a shower. I wanted to get the wet clothes off me, and remove the stink of battle. No matter how much I tried to push the images out of my mind, they continued to race in and out, especially with all that had happened and all I had seen. The images were making it hard to keep my mental barrier up. I would really need to work on that, especially if there were going to be more situations like this.

I hope not.

The mix of the scents from the battle filled my brain. How easy succumbing to blood lust had been. So much blood ran tonight even the others had been as transfixed as me. If it weren't for William helping me to keep my focus and seeing Betty was up to no good, things may have ended up differently. Still, Marcel and William were able to reach me and I needed to fix that, but not right now. I wanted to physically, mentally, and emotionally relax.

The moment the hot water hit my skin, every pore in my body came to life. Despite tonight's event being worse than I had expected, especially finding out werewolves were now back I felt excited for what all this meant. Maybe werewolves had never been gone in the first place, and Sahin had tracked them down. I wanted to believe that, but I knew better.

No matter what, this new information and tonight's events were a game changer. I still didn't understand why they had helped Sahin. What had he offered them? If we wanted to find out, we would need to find the other two before Victor did.

The realization that Kirtus and the queen both had dual-colored eyes, one gray and one green, helped; the problem being I didn't know how to prove this to the others. It would be something more to talk about, but not right now. There had been too much, and we could deal with my thoughts and concerns once we got Gabe's report. Plus, I wanted to tell Kirtus first. Then Juliet. They both needed to know. As the water pounded onto my body and massaged my shoulders and muscles, the tightness gradually washed away. I drew in as much of the steam as my lungs allowed, and my stress vanished as a comfortable emptiness greeted me. As the steam and warm fog surrounded me, my body began to stir with excitement. Images of Kirtus and me together made their way out of the fog and filled my mind. I closed my eyes as I relaxed the muscles in my neck and face.

An aching moan escaped from my parted lips as a hand wrapped around my engorged member.

"Oh, my love," a soft female voice whispered in my ears. "I must have you inside me."

"Soon," I said, but the voice wasn't mine, the tone too deep. Marcel spoke; these words were his.

No longer me, but him, I opened my new eyes. The warm water fell from a gold spout connected to a stone wall; this wasn't my bathroom or any shower I had ever seen before. The water was warm, but not hot, and it didn't come out in a spray but more like a controlled waterfall. Where was I?

"Once we stop them, we will be together, and no one will challenge us." The body I appeared to be in control of turned and faced a woman with long black hair and beautiful, delicate features. Her breasts were firm and hips wide. Light mocha skin silky soft to the touch. Fragrant lavender filled the air, but not an oil, not blood.

The hands that were not my own moved for her face as I leaned down to kiss her full, soft lips. Our tongues met and fire burned deep inside me. We separated and she laughed as I slid my hands easily between her breasts. Stopping for a brief moment, my hands moved to each of her nipples. She exhaled in a shudder. The grin on my face grew as the edges of my lips pulled higher. My erection slid along her oiled leg. I wanted to be inside her. A passion burned between us, extinguishable only by the merging of our bodies.

Her hand wrapped around me again, gently tugging, pulling, and playing with me. The air escaped my lungs, and I leaned in to kiss once more. "I need to taste you." A remark came from my mouth in a voice that wasn't my own.

"For you, my love, anything," she whispered.

My fangs sunk into her neck, and I drank, setting all my nerves ablaze. Heaven or as close to heaven as one could imagine. The beat of our hearts were one and our souls danced. After a moment I closed my eyes, enjoying this unknown flavor. I wanted to stay like this forever, but a pull in my mind told me otherwise.

Despite the pull I needed to come, I needed to feel the release, my body too alive, and without release I would die, or at least this was what my body screamed to my brain. Climax wouldn't take much at this point, a touch all I needed. My body continued to ache.

With a pang of guilt and a large amount of protest from everything south of my chin, my eyes opened again. No longer in the shower, I appeared to be in the Council of Light chamber again, but it wasn't the one I had seen in the books. This was a throne room, with blood everywhere. The smells assaulted my nose, and instead of making me want to enjoy, my stomach flipped and I wanted to be sick. A massacre. I stood with a silver sword in my hands, my chest heaving and my muscles burning. On the floor a severed head, next to it a crown of gold and jewels. Other bodies lay about but none I recognized. All were equally decapitated and some burned. I hadn't noticed this before, but the air was heavy with smoke and the sweet stink of burnt flesh. I wanted to cover my mouth and nose and flee the sight. I blinked, hoping the vision would change, but nothing changed. My feet firmly planted, unable to move as I continued to scan the scene. What had I done? No. What had they done?

"We did it, my love." The gruff voice dripped with relief.

"None will keep us apart. We'll build a new, better way." My wife's voice sang out amongst the chaos like the song of a hundred angels.

I leaned down and kissed her forehead. My heart beat with so much love and warmth I didn't want to let the feeling go. I closed my eyes and took in the sweet oil scent of her hair.

Relaxed beyond recent memory, I opened my eyes. Something changed. Something wasn't right. My heart raced, and with each beat pain pumped through me. I knelt down and turned my wife over. Blood. The beat of her heat slowing. I found the wound and went to bite into my wrist to allow her to drink. I had to heal her. She couldn't go, not now, not with so much to be done.

"Let me save you." My voice trembled.

"You can't." Her voice weak as the life drained from her body. "But soon you will save us all." Her gaze met mine, however impossible it may be her gaze met mine, and not her lovers. I understood this. She wasn't talking to Marcel but directly to me. "Stop what is to come and fix what we have broken. The proof you need will come from the one in the strange desert city by the lake of salt. That is the only way."

"No!" A weak shout burst from behind.

I was me again. I had returned to my body, not the body of Marcel. I glanced over my shoulder.

"How did I not see?" Marcel's voice cried out as he rushed to her.

Marcel held her body. Standing a few paces away from them, I watched the same scene I had a vision of before. Before Marcel had kept me from seeing everything. But this time I understood who had killed the queen and her council. Marcel and this woman, his wife. How could they have done this? Why?

Warm fog engulfed the room, and I couldn't hear them as they spoke. Marcel tore into his wrist and held it to her lips. He leaned into her and her mouth moved, but she wasn't drinking his offered blood. How had she not been saved by him? I wasn't sure. I stepped forward and waved my hands in front of me to clear the haze. I closed my eyes and rubbed them to try to clear my vision. I took another step.

"Fuck." My head banged into the wall, and the shower controls hit my gut. I opened my eyes back in my shower. "Oh, shit." I turned off the shower. This wasn't good.

I got out of the shower and pulled on my clothes. I made my way down the stairs and found myself knocking harder on Juliet's door than anyone had any business doing.

"Chris, what's wrong?" Gregor opened the door.

"I had a vision about Marcel and his wife. And the queen and I think Gabe." I rushed through the door.

"What's all the banging?" Amanda asked from the hall.

"Chris had a vision," Gregor responded as she walked in.

Juliet stood at her conference table by the windows. Tonight, the drapes were closed and the room illuminated by harsh lamp light. I missed the warmth of the fire her office typically had.

I made for the table and pulled out a seat before I relayed my vision, without the graphic sex scene. Once I finished, Juliet, Gregor, and Amanda all sat in complete silence, studying me.

"Did Marcel ever speak of a wife?" Amanda's question broke the much too long silence.

"No. Not to me, not to anyone." Juliet shook her head. "And the queen's court... The two of them killed the queen and her court. Why?" Her nails clicked.

"This means everything we assumed about the end of the queen is wrong." Gregor scratched his goatee. "And her heir, could they have killed them all?"

"I don't know." I rested my hands on my lap, unsure what to do with them. "I only saw the two of them, but it's possible there were more Immortals involved." I massaged my temples. "I only noticed the queen, well, who I think to be the queen, . A crown lay next to her...ah...her head. I didn't see the rest of her body." My stomach sank. I really didn't want to have that vision again.

"Clearly, the comparison with the events of tonight triggered your vision," Juliet said. "The betrayal and the beheading."

"The events do seem to match up," Amanda agreed.

"There's something more." I hesitated. I wanted to wait to speak to Kirtus about this, but with this new vision... "I wanted to tell Kirtus first, but this can't wait. The queen, her eyes were exactly like Kirtus's. She had a green and a gray eye."

"Heterochromia iridium." Amanda glanced from me to Juliet and over to Gregor.

"It might be an inherited trait." Gregor pulled out his phone and began to type away. "According to this, it's possibly genetically inherited."

"How do we prove heterochromia iridium isn't super rare?" Tonight's events pushed my shoulders and the rest of me deeper into the seat.

"Hopefully Gabe will have information on this." Juliet leaned in. "Did you have a vision about him as well?"

"No, not really, but when Marcel's wife spoke to me, she mentioned the one from the strange city in the desert by the lake of salt would have the proof. That has to be Gabe. Right?"

"I can't think of any other city that would fit the description and be the least bit relevant." Juliet tapped her fingers. "If this woman wants you, or us, to fix what happened, she would speak of places you are familiar with."

"I suppose. Maybe." I adjusted in my chair to sit taller. "But Marcel and his wife—"

"We don't know who she is." Juliet frowned.

"Juliet, I'm sorry, but that lady, she's his wife. The feelings they had for each other were more intense than anything I'd ever experienced. You don't want to believe what is true, I get it, but what I saw and what I know is still the truth. They were joined together."

She clicked her nails.

"Regardless. This puts into question everything Marcel has shown you." Gregor massaged his goatee, his words soft but still holding their edge.

I sighed and leaned in my chair.

"At the very least what you witnessed throws into question his motives," Amanda proclaimed.

"Great." I frowned.

"I'm going to have to explain all this to the council." Juliet pinched the bridge of her nose. "They are not going to be happy."

Chapter Twenty-One

"A meeting of the board of directors?" I buttoned up my suit jacket as I stood from my office desk. "I assumed the call would be tonight." My voice softened. "At home."

"You thought wrong." Amanda flattened the creases of her knit skirt. She glided to the door, stopping and waiting. "Have you had a chance to talk to Kirtus?"

I shook my head. When did I have time? Kirtus had to learn his new position and deal with the aftermath of Sahin's betrayal, and I had been caught up in all the vision madness and my own training. Speaking of which, I checked my mental wall, ensuring the barrier still stood. The more I practiced, the easier getting my wall up in the background became. I equated the process to playing music in your office. You didn't always notice the songs, until the melody ended, or a favorite song popped on. And realistically the laps in time didn't feel like only two days since the challenge, but that was all it had been.

"Everything is all set up in the conference room," Amanda said.

I put on what I hoped to be one of my least exasperated expressions. "Well, this promises to be loads of fun." I pulled open my office door for Amanda, and we walked out to the main hall and headed to the lobby. The space seemed empty to me—nice, but empty, a complete contrast to Christmas, with the two-story tree that filled all the open space.

"Rachel." Amanda faced the receptionist. "Chris and I will be joining Juliet for her board call this morning."

"Okay. I'll transfer your calls to voice mail." Rachel beamed from her receptionist station as we made our way to the stairs. "Did you want me to get anything?"

"No, thank you." I tried out my work expression, going for charming but not overly creepy...at least I hoped. "We'll be fine."

We—well, maybe only me—trudged up the stairs and made our way down the hall to the conference room. I wasn't looking forward to having to explain myself to the council again. I understood their apprehension about trusting my visions. I was new, but Juliet, they had known her for years. So why were they not trusting her? The few times we had talked about the council, things appeared to getting worse between them. *Why?* I understood the idea of an Immortal monarch might not be something they all want, but if a royal court brought everyone together and got them all working together again, how was that so bad? Assuming it worked and didn't tear the Immortal community apart and by extension the human world.

Maybe keeping things the way they were would work. But the idea made me shiver. Something more was at play and I didn't recognize what. Perhaps these events weren't so much about one ruler but exposing something bigger.

My heart began to race, and beads of sweat were forming on my forehead. Images from my vision of the attack and battle in San Jose filled my mind's eye. I needed air if I was going to force myself to calm down.

This time Amanda opened the door for me, and I walked in. The conference room wasn't a bad setup. The space had the usual, a large oak conference table, cushioned chairs, a ceiling-mounted projector, conference phones, a dedicated laptop, and all the other periphery items. Overall, the meeting room met our needs well, and I loved using the space when I had both internal and external meetings. The vase with roses and orchids had been moved from the center of the table to a side table. The scents of roses and vanilla were lighter today, and part of me ached missing it.

Juliet had the automatic window tinting on full, so hardly any light peeked from the outside. She typed away as various images pulled up on the screen as it descended from the ceiling. I found her behavior somewhat funny as you wouldn't expect the executive director of the foundation but also the leader of the Council of Light to set up her own AV. I bit back my amusement, which had the added benefit of helping me to relax. The prior ED I had worked for had no clue when it came to technology and relied on everyone else to do the simplest of tasks. Seeing how independent Juliet was reminded me how lucky I was to not be at St. Elizabeth's Family Service anymore.

Literally a lifetime ago, I mused.

As the door gently closed, I spoke up. "Weren't Gregor and Victor going to join us?"

Juliet glanced up from the computer and pulled off her glasses.

Since when did she have or even need glasses? I shook the thought from my mind.

"No. I considered today's meeting best kept to us." She raised a hand. "For now."

I took my seat next to her and focused up at the wall-mounted camera for a moment. I moved my gaze to the screen, seeing the three of us in the bottom right image. Within seconds, the council members appeared on the conference call.

Garrett appeared first, and as always, he had a good-natured presence that greeted us. He always came across so cool, and I enjoyed listening to him talk with his Australian accent, which I had a feeling he turned on and off when it suited him.

Fernando appeared next. He tapped at his computer, made a few adjustments, and mumbled in Spanish. The image went in and out but shortly cleared up.

Taqi and Rahim were already speaking, in Arabic, or what I assumed to be Arabic. Given the region of the world they were from.

An appeared on screen in her corresponding box, her long black hair done up, and she sported a white top and a dark blue blazer. Very traditional, it went along with her more classic Chinese style.

Yoi was the complete opposite of An, her style something straight out of Tokyo, and I had no doubt that if I ever made it to Japan, I would see that same look on every street. It was fun, and I guess I would say anime styled, but in an intelligent sort of way. Regardless, she looked nice, and I especially dug the pink streaks of color in her hair, which were new since the last time we were together.

"Thank you all for joining us today." Juliet greeted everyone.

"Isn't Sybil joining?" Taqi asked in perfect British-style English.

"I'm sure—"

A flicker on the screen announced Sybil's arrival. "I apologize for being late. I was tied up on a personal matter."

I bit down my frown. I had a feeling she showed up late on purpose, so she could make a point or a statement or whatever. Maybe what Victor said about showing up last exhibiting your dominance would work for someone else, but not Sahin. He had ended up dead. The idea made me both want to throw up and laugh. I sighed instead.

"Completely understandable." Juliet beamed and began her update, informing the council on everything that had transpired since the last time she spoke with them.

I found the reporting interesting. No one stopped her or asked questions. I also found it odd she wanted both Amanda and me in the meeting since so far it seemed standard and surprisingly civil.

"The main question is"—Juliet concluding her update—"why did Marcel warn Victor about Sahin and who else might be involved? This set-up is difficult to believe Sahin managed alone."

My leg trembled as I scanned the screen and all the faces. None of them appeared moved or even interested.

Butterflies battling in my gut didn't help my nerves, so I did a quick check of my mental wall, feeling mortar, blocks, and steel. I took a breath.

"Juliet," Taqi began, "you're assuming this person to be Marcel. There's no physical proof to back this claim. Sahin and Betty are capable of doing such things. And my friends in the Dark have said Pedro nearly brought Victor to his knees in the encounter that ended Pedro's life." He paused and glanced off screen. "Why are we looking for some grand conspiracy when the facts point to a Dark power play and act of revenge?"

Juliet opened up a folder on the conference table, pulled out the note that had been given to Victor, and held the paper up. "This document has been scanned and sent to each of you. A note written by Marcel and I can assure you this is no fraud. Sahin may have been acting on his own, but someone in the shadows assisted him. How do you explain the werewolves?"

My head gently bobbed up and down in agreement. I stopped myself and hoped my actions remained unnoticed. From what I witnessed she laid out a strong case. They were being too stubborn.

"Maybe they were there for a hunt?" Yoi flipped a strand of hair behind her shoulder. "You know how they used to be."

"Forgive me." Fernando stared. "But, Juliet, none of us have seen these wolves but you and a few allies of yours. Not to mention none of us would recognize Marcel's hand, other than you. Even with the excerpts from his books you sent, for all the evidence provided, these may have been written by Chris or Amanda."

"Which is why I sent along writing samples from both Chris and Amanda," Juliet countered.

The burn in my neck move up to my cheeks. I peeked over to Amanda, and she sat with a collected expression on her face, quietly writing notes on a pad she had in front of her. I should have brought one as well. Padfolio would have made me look like I paid attention.

"We can have Gabe validate the age and that the book, proving that no one other—"

"Another Immortal whom you are close to and lives in Utah, which is under your control," Sybil pointed out. "Juliet, you have to understand how this all looks. Everything is happening in your area of control. Some have questioned if this is all being caused by someone close to you to help you gain more control."

Juliet laughed. "You can't be serious." She stopped laughing. "Why would anyone do such a thing?"

"Power is a huge motivator," Garrett said, "for some." He continued staring at the camera, and I wasn't sure who he might be trying to imply, but I caught Sybil frown.

"You've all used Gabe, and you appreciate his character is above approach," Juliet professed. "And as you're all aware, he's lived in all other territories of the world for his research. Yes, currently he makes his home here now. He is a neutral party and you all know that."

"Gabe is adequate." Anashe's voice came over as soft, but with firm edges. "However, I've had my people review the digital copies, and they are not convinced."

"What about Chris's vision? What about the fact Marcel distinguished the scent of the Lycan?" Juliet countered as she gestured toward me. "Are you going to discount that?"

My whole head blazed. I had no doubt that I came across like a bright red flashing beacon. I was relieved my mental barriers were in place so no one would be able to read my emotions, or at least I hoped.

"Chris has proven himself to be accurate in the past." Garrett spoke up.

Thank goodness someone agreed with and supported Juliet's position. Why was he the only one?

"And I have no reason to not trust Juliet or Gabe for that matter," Garrett added. "If you recall, we all owe a great deal to Chris and his visions."

"You would side with her." Sybil's voice held a level of venom I had grown used to by now. "We all know you and Juliet have a special relationship."

"And we all realize you haven't been happy about not being the head of the Council of Light since Juliet took over five hundred years ago," Garrett said. "What is your point, Sybil?"

"My point, Garrett, is everything happening feels overly convenient, and I for one want to remain skeptical. Everything coincided with Juliet brining on her Called."

Every part of me wanted to scream out. The tips of my extending canines were stabbing at my lips.

Juliet patted my hand, keeping me from blowing a head gasket with these people. What the hell was their problem? None of these events were my fault. I didn't want any part of all this craziness, but I wasn't given a choice.

"Now hold on. Mate!" Garrett's hands hit the table before him, and the echo bombarded the conference room as the noise thundered out of the speakers. "That is out of line."

Juliet sighed. "Please. Everyone." She raised her hand. "You are all welcome to come out here and examine the documents firsthand. Bring whomever you'd like to inspect them. We can even show you the remains of the Lycan woman." Her shoulders raised as she sat taller. "In fact, I welcome it."

"That might be a valid compromise." Rahim gestured in the affirmative. "I wouldn't mind inspecting the document firsthand, and not to be morbid but seeing a Lycan firsthand is a big opportunity."

"Oh joy," Sybil moaned. "Another glorious trip to San Jose. Why don't we move the council chamber there and convert the space to a throne room for you?"

"What?" I couldn't keep my mouth shut. "What the hell is wrong with you people?" My voice shook. "There are werewolves running around the world now, who knows how far they've spread, and you've questioned my visions. What are you waiting for? The apocalypse? Or are you afraid having a single ruler again will cause you to lose all your power and influence?" My heart banged against my chest.

"Ah, right." Sybil leaned in. "That is what this is all about. Power. According to you." She sneered. "Isn't it convenient your boyfriend is the one who is the supposed to be the heir to the throne? And how shocking, you've seen the queen and Kirtus both have heterochromia."

"That—"

"Chris." Juliet squeezed my hand. "Enough." Her voice calmed me. No anger reached my ears, which honestly surprised me. Her calm washed over me and my wall.

I bit back my response. But what did it matter? If Kirtus was the heir to the throne, he had the right to lead the vampires, but that didn't mean his leadership would have to be like the past. Everything changed, so why not this? And really I didn't think he wanted to be a ruler, so maybe he would leave things the way they are, and be more of a figurehead, kind of like the queen of England. But now they, we, had options, and with everything else happening options were a good thing.

"Chris isn't wrong," Juliet said. "Since I told you about this development, and since we've been trying to prove Kirtus is in fact the queen's heir, you've all been angry. So scared. Why? Why do you fear this change? Order and balance will return. Finally a united front where we can address these new challenges. The witches, the werewolves, and true magic."

"You are—" Taqi's voice raised.

"I'm not finished," Juliet boomed. Even the windows in the conference room rattled.

Amanda glanced up from her pad and pen, and we shared a quick, surprised look. We both continued to watch the screen and Juliet.

"As long as I'm the council leader," Juliet continued, "you will respect me, respect my judgment, and you will respect my Called. I've invited you to San Jose, to inspect the documents in question. I will ask Victor, Kirtus, and all other parties concerned to join us and you will be allowed to conduct a reasonable investigation, but I will not stand for this any longer. Have I made myself and my position clear?"

No one spoke, but there were a few nods.

"Excellent," Juliet finished. "We are adjourned."

"Juliet." Sybil's voice grew cold and warning.

I couldn't believe the balls on this woman, but there they were on full display.

"Yes?"

"For now, you are in fact council leader, but as you're aware there is a pending vote on your position. I feel this detail is important to remind you of, and another reminder—the respect you demand of his council should be shown in return." Sybil's eyes bore through the screen and into all of us. "See you soon." She tapped something in front of her and her image vanished.

I glanced at Juliet as she sat there, her head tall and her shoulders straight.

Several of the council images flickered out until only Garrett remained.

"Juliet." He lowered his eyes, and his voice grew soft. "Don't worry about the vote, and don't worry about Sybil; they'll come around. They always do." He met her gaze and offered a reassuring smile. "I'll fly out in a few days, and we can talk more."

Juliet allowed her shoulders to slip as fatigue took hold around her eyes. "Thank you, Garrett."

He waved as his image faded.

Everyone else gone, I cleared my throat. "I'm sorry. I shouldn't have spoken, but they…"

Juliet took my hand. "They were being stubborn assholes." She gave my hand another squeeze. "Chris. Amanda. I'm sorry you had to see that, and I had hoped things would have gone differently, but I needed you both here…" She kneaded the back of her neck.

"In case the meeting went wrong," Amanda finished. "That's why you wanted me to scribe the meeting for you. In case someone calls for a vote of no confidence."

"Wait." Confusion swept over me. "Can they do that?"

Juliet nodded in the affirmative. "But a no confidence vote hasn't happened in a long time. Even when I took over for Sybil, the vote had been nearly unanimous and there were other circumstances in play." She rested her arms in front of her chest.

I kept my mouth shut, but I wouldn't lie; I needed to know. "I had no idea things were so difficult with the council," I said. "And my outburst didn't help."

"Since the incident with your father's coven, the Council of Light has been holding me accountable for us nearly being exposed and, of course, true magic getting into our world."

"But that wasn't you. We stopped the coven. And no one could have stopped the magic seepage."

"We know. As does Garrett and the others. But Sybil and Fernando…" She sighed. "Now with the prospect of an heir to the royal throne. Especially being found here in my backyard."

"They think you are behind all this," Amanda scolded. "Think you are fabricating this so you can gain even more power. They are worried the changes would be like when you became leader before."

"Sadly. Or, at the very least rule by proxy." Juliet clicked her fingernails. "They see my relations with the Dark, the witches, and even William as a consolidation of power." She leaned in her chair, appearing so small and fragile. "Even though most of them hold similar relationships in their territories."

"But it's not you," I said.

"But they are worried history will repeat itself, and I can't blame them." Juliet's shoulders sank.

"Well, I can." I sat taller in my chair, annoyed as all hell at this recent series of events.

Chapter Twenty-Two

"Everything is a complete mess." I moaned and put my skewer down. I leaned deeper into the booth seat, allowing the softness to surround me. This should have been a relaxing dinner in Saratoga. We sat in the same restaurant Amanda had set us up in all those months ago. I really enjoyed the blood cheese fondue, but with everything happening I found myself unable to unwind. Still, dinner tonight continued to be a nice break from only drinking blood.

Despite what had happened with the Council of Light, I needed to spend some time with Kirtus. Plus, Juliet had asked me to update Kirtus on what had happened with the council and tell him the council would possibly want to meet him and see Victor if available and convenient. The melted cheese and blood released a small bubble, and I took in the aroma.

"Jesus," Kirtus whispered as he stirred the mixture prior to dipping a small boiled potato into the red cheese.

"It's been a complete joy." Another bubble popped in the cheesy mixture. "They were awful." I shook my head as I peeked around our section. No one else was around, a nice benefit of being an Immortal guest, but I still needed to be careful with what we talked about. "There's something else." I leaned in and stretched for Kirtus's hand.

"Okay." Kirtus extended the word longer than needed as his eyes narrowed and rose.

"When I had my vision, I scrutinized the queen's face..." I lowered my voice to barely a whisper.

"And..." Kirtus said.

Kirtus's hand had a slight tremble to it, and there were hints of dampness. I took a deep breath. "The two of you have the same type of eyes, one green and one gray."

"Fuck." Kirtus pulled his hand away before running it through his hair. "There is no way to prove that."

"Gabe is working on the information we provided him and seeing what can be confirmed," I added.

"I'm not... This...this can't be happening. I'm not a king. I'm barely a lieutenant for Victor." He shook his head in the negative. "No one will accept me."

"It's looking that way."

"The Dark are a mess right now. Some of the leaders in Mexico, Central America, and South America are furious with Victor." Kirtus leaned forward. "They expected Pedro's death because many of them were at the meeting, but now with Sahin and Betty..." Kirtus reached out with both his hands, taking mine, his pulse rushing. "They're calling for Victor's removal."

"You can't be serious."

"Pedro had clearly been poisoning the well for years. I think he would have challenged Victor at some point. At least according to the rumors."

"So now what?" I shook my head in disbelief. "The council isn't going to love any of this."

"Victor has been shoring up his allies and either physically or financially threatening those that might challenge him. He's even reached out to a couple of folks in Europe. I've been working to liquefy some of his assets and buying more of his holdings and investing in stocks in Russia and throughout the EU and Asia."

"This is a freaking mess."

"Is everything okay?" the female server asked as if from nowhere. "Would you like more of the dippers? Potatoes? Bread?"

Kirtus beamed up at her. "No. I think we're good. This is amazing."

"I'm glad you're enjoying your meal." She offered a slight bow of her head.

"Yes, indeed. Can we get another bottle of this?" I pointed to our empty bottle of red. This one had almond undertones and went really well with the blood cheese.

"Sure thing." She picked up the bottle, filled both our glasses, and took the empty with her as she left the table.

"Think she heard?" I watched her walk off.

"Even if she did, it wouldn't matter. Jack has a good talent for picking staff who are both efficient and discreet. People come here all the time and talk business." Kirtus tapped his glass. "That is why this is a popular place."

"Makes sense, I guess. I still remember our first date here. Things were a mess then too."

Kirtus laughed. "That wasn't that long ago. God, I was so angry at Amanda for setting us up..." He raised his gaze to meet mine. "But I'm happy she did."

"Me too." I speared a chunk of bread and dunked it into the cheese. I took a bite and savored the nutty flavor of the cheese, not minding the texture of the bread. The red in the bottle had been a nice complement, and I looked forward to having another bottle. "What do you think will happen? I mean this sort of thing must happen all the time, right? They work it all out."

Kirtus's expression dropped, replaced with concern and worry. "No, nothing like this has happened. Canada, the US, and Mexico are never like this." He rubbed his chin. "Everyone is worried. If we're not careful, events will start to affect the humans, which would be bad for everyone, especially with how interwoven global economics are. How can anyone manage this...especially me?" He snorted and shook his head.

"Everything will be fine. I have no doubt all this crazy will pass and things are going to be fine. Look, you can do it. You, my dear man, can do anything. I have complete and total faith in you."

"You have to say that."

"I don't have to say anything." I laughed.

"Keep laughing. We may need it if everything falls to shit."

"You don't think..." I glanced around again. "My vision will come to pass. The fighting and...well...basically war?"

"I hope not." Kirtus rubbed his chin as he closed his eyes. "If something happens here, fighting will spill out everywhere. People are blaming Victor and Juliet for a lot right now, but they forget these two have the most stable areas in the world; even the other Dark leaders who happen to be in Juliet's region enjoy stability thanks to her. They would never admit it, but if something happens here..."

"We'd all be screwed."

"Which is why I can't do this...King thing. I'm not Juliet and I'm sure not Victor. I don't have the political capital they have and not to mention I'm only a child—"

"What?"

Kirtus raised a hand. "In a manner of speaking. Juliet is, what? Fifteen hundred years old."

I didn't interrupt or correct him.

"Victor's 1400 years." Again, his hand ran through his hair. "They have all that experience, and here I sit. There is no way. If they can't even keep their own people from butting heads, how will I be able to do it with both groups?"

"You're forgetting they aren't alone. Juliet has...what? Nineteen governors, plus me, plus Amanda. She has a huge team of people supporting her." I grasped for his hand. "And Victor had four, plus you, plus Daniel when he... Not to mention whoever else he has sway over."

"Still, they both have the influence and experience." Kirtus huffed.

"Well, you'll have a group of people around you. The queen had a council. Why not you as well? You can even have the Council of Light as it stands...well, maybe not Sybil. To keep the balance you invite an equal number of Dark leaders. That way everyone has a voice." I tried to bring forward my most sincere expression.

"Maybe." He sighed. "I mean, like we were talking about before, perhaps a change needs to happen, pull from the old and...gah."

"Hey." I took his hand. "It'll work out; you can sort all this drama out. I'll be here to help too."

"Let's focus on getting through all this current crap before—"

A buzzing from my pocket caught my attention, and I pulled from Kirtus to retrieve my phone. Before I answered, his phone buzzed.

"This can't be good." He pulled out his phone as well.

I tapped Accept on my phone, seeing Amanda's picture. "Hey. What's up?"

"Chris. Thank Christ." Amanda's voice was hurried. "There's been a werewolf attack."

"What?" My voice shook, it was louder and sharper than I wanted. But I couldn't help it. Another attack on the house, or where? Perhaps my vision decided to come to pass? "What?" I repeated softer.

"They attached a group of Darks. We don't have all the details, but the attack was bad. They killed one. Juliet wants to meet—"

"We're on our way." I hung up the phone.

Kirtus was already standing, holding his coat and digging into his wallet.

"No, dinner is supposed to be my treat."

"Does it matter?"

I pulled out my wallet and dropped two hundred dollars in twenties. I grabbed my coat and stuffed my phone and wallet back into my pockets. "So much for our quiet evening."

"Once you drop me off, I have to go meet Victor," Kirtus said as we made our way toward the exit. "I can't believe this."

"I can. They were pissed, and we killed one of their own. Are you familiar with who?"

"Alan. He went out with Jen and Jon."

"Have I met them?"

"Nah, they're young and part of the group Victor told to get out of town when we were dealing with..." He glanced at me.

"My dad."

He frowned as his gaze dropped from mine.

We passed through the heavy drapes and opened the main door as the cold bit at my face. I pulled on my jacket and we headed to my car. "If everyone was on edge before, this isn't going to help."

"I'll inform Victor about the Council of Light coming to town. I'll be available, but I can't speak for him."

I understood, and if I had to guess, Juliet gave him a heads-up already. Things were escalating, and all I thought of was my vision and all the death and destruction. I only hoped we got everything under control and stopped what I witnessed from happening—because, if not, tonight was only the beginning of the slaughter.

Chapter Twenty-Three

Meetings and lonely nights greeted me for the days since we got the call about the werewolf attack. Juliet and Victor met to talk about the attack and how it might not be wise trying to kill the wolves involved. That there might be another way. Amanda, Kirtus, and Gregor met with them from time to time. Some of the meetings happened at the house, some happened at Victor's penthouse, and others at locations I wasn't told about. For them, these events were all about damage control and dealing with the Council of Light members who had come in early to evaluate all our claims and the follow-up with the nightmarish conference call at the end of February.

While Juliet and the others were dealing with that, she asked me to take care of the office, keep up appearances, and ensure if I heard anything strange to let Juliet know. Working in the office wasn't too bad, but since the attack, a tickle grew in my head, unease nested in my thoughts. I mentioned my restlessness to Juliet, so she was aware, but with nothing to act on, there wasn't much to do. I talked to William, and he suggested I lower my mental walls and try to use my ability and focus on a past vision, or Juliet, or one of the others, but nothing appeared when I tried. This uneasy tickle was more about the feeling that something wasn't right and we were moving closer to danger. I couldn't put my finger on when or where yet.

Sybil, Garrett, Fernando, and Taqi brought their own staff and people they trusted to conduct their own investigations of the Lycan attacks, of the documents showing Kirtus as the heir, and even into the events caused by my father. I didn't like constantly being asked the same questions, but I played nice. I didn't want to piss off Sybil any more, and I certainly didn't want to give her any more reason to question Juliet's motives. Also, I hoped by being as accommodating as possible my worries would lessen.

They didn't.

With everyone and everything happening around the estate and as annoying as being kept in the dark about much of the investigation was, I understood. I, along with my gifts were being investigated. I had visions and my visions were part of the investigation. Sybil and Fernando doubted them, and sadly even Taqi questioned their truthfulness. So, Juliet and I didn't want contamination. If the council wanted to test me again, we wanted to ensure no one could doubt the information I had. The idea made sense, but it still bothered me, especially since I didn't get to spend any more time with Kirtus.

My whole body missed his touch and our alone time together.

I checked the budget report on my computer, making sure everything at the foundation had been wrapped up for the day. There always seemed to be some report that needed to be written or some budget that had to be approved. Busy work, but not my favorite part of the job. Plus, tonight, we had the premeeting where everyone was going to be at the house, and I needed to be there, in case, I suppose, they needed to probe me more. I frowned, moved my chair from the desk, and stood. I pulled on my suit jacket and made my way out of my office. The front desk sat empty. "Good." I nodded, pleased. Rachel had left for the day; I hated when staff worked late.

Short of a fire, we never had any reason for the staff to work long hours, especially when they received no additional compensation. I had hated doing that when I worked in Reno, and I wouldn't allow that kind of work environment here. I'd had this conversation several times with Juliet, who agreed, as did our leadership group and the board. If they didn't like the change or agree, they were invited to step down...well, not Juliet, but the board members and members of leadership.

In my car, my mind focused on Kirtus and how lonely I was. My body stirred at the idea of his touch, but I pushed the thought away. There was no point in getting myself worked up for something that wasn't going to happen, at least not any time soon.

Grr.

Honestly, I couldn't remember the drive home. My mind focused on everything else, and despite my best efforts the nit in the back of my brain worked overtime. Not making matters any easier, my worry for Juliet landed front and center. What if the council tried to remove her? What if they didn't believe us? What if all this led to the war from my visions? Nothing I did helped. Not even singing along with the radio.

I parked the car and checked my mental wall. I hoped keeping my mental barriers up would help me tonight, so I focused on the wall and ensured I pulled up every detail, even concentrating on the scents around it. Once it was fully embedded in my mind, I made my way into the house. Our guests would be here soon. If they weren't already here.

I made my way from the garage through the kitchen, hanging my car keys on the board so they were easy to find by the staff. I didn't want to risk the wrath of Lecomas again. I massaged my temples as another tug at my brain ached; now this pain seemed like something knocking on the wall. I pushed the pain away. I left the kitchen and headed down the hall to the front of the house. I stopped as Patty and Deb took off their coats, giving them to Amanda. I love seeing the confidence and power in these women. Where some people would think they would be meek and reserved, they weren't and they wore their self-assurance well. "Hiya." I waved.

"Chris." Deb greeted me and took my offered hand.

"Any new visions?" Patty asked, not entirely returning my welcome but not pushing past me either. I counted her ambivalent expression as a win.

"Nothing new." I kept my answer brief. I didn't know how to bring up the whole bad feeling I had.

"It's awful what happened." Deb grimaced.

The new scent of cucumber and watermelon tickled my nose and of all things helped me relax the most. I peeked over at her.

"At least there haven't been any fresh attacks." Amanda hung up their coats. "I wish we were able to track the Lycan down. We know who we are looking for, but somehow they have become masters at making themselves vanish."

"Clearly they are being helped." Patty frowned. "The question is, by who?"

Our group made our way into the living room. "Would you like something to drink? Water? Wine?" I offered. "Juliet and the others should be along shortly." I glanced over at Amanda for confirmation.

"She, Sybil, Garrett, Fernando, and Taqi have been meeting all afternoon," Amanda said, her tone neutral, which filled me in enough to understand things were not going well. The five of them meeting also explained why I had sat alone at the foundation.

"Are we going to meet with the full council? What about Victor?" Deb waved off my offered glass of water or wine.

"Water please." Patty grabbed a pillow from where she sat and moved the cushion to the side.

I filled up a glass and handed it to her.

"Friday. That's when the council meets in full, with everyone, including you and William. This has all been about them doing their own investigations." Amanda crossed over to one of the occasional chairs, sitting. "Victor won't be here tonight. As you can imagine, he's busy dealing..." She faded off.

He needed to dig out of his own pile of shit. The recent attack on three of his Dark didn't look good for him or anyone really, I supposed.

"Is William joining us?" Deb asked.

"Yes." Amanda checked her watch. "I'm surprised he's not already here."

The back of my mind tingled. Was he okay? My stomach dropped. I'm sure he was fine, but I couldn't be 100 percent sure.

A knock at the front door called out, and I moved to go answer as the staff were gone for the day and we had no need for them to stick around for tonight's meeting. As with Deb and Patty, I sensed William before I opened the door. That helped me relax. I wondered if their powers and abilities comforted me. Kind of like Juliet. Also, it might have to do with all the training and the fact the Patty, Deb, and William had all worked with me at one point or another. Regardless, I enjoyed his scent of wildflowers.

I pulled open the door and greeted him. He studied the markings on the doorframe. "Seems like my wards are still in place."

"I think so."

He extended his hand and we shook. "It's good to see you." He held my hand longer than needed and peered into my eyes. "Is something wrong?"

My lips pinched together. "This is all like before. Something hasn't been right since the night of the attack, and now with the investigation, I feel like we're marching closer to everything falling apart."

"And trying to focus on what is happening or your other visions hasn't helped."

I shook my head.

"Have you talked to Juliet?"

I nodded.

"Good."

"But with nothing to act on—"

He waved off my concern. "She knows and that is something."

I couldn't disagree. Something had to be better than nothing, I supposed. "We are gathering in the living room." I pointed to his coat. "Can I take that for you?"

He pulled off his jacket. I hung his coat up, and we made our way to the living room.

"We have to try and convince them Chris's visions—"

"Can't be questioned," William said as we walked in. "And we are not making any of this up."

"William." Deb and Patty both stood.

"As always a pleasure." Amanda welcomed him.

"I wish it were under better circumstances." William greeted her in return.

"I see all our guests have arrived." Juliet entered from the dining room, Sybil, and her air of superiority, next to her. Stationed by her side, Fernando didn't look pleased. None of them did. Garrett and Taqi came in last; the only one mildly smiling was Garrett.

"Mate." Garrett took my hand, giving it a hearty pump. "Good to see ya. Sorry about all that fuss the other day."

"It's good to see you." I hoped my palms weren't as sweaty as I supposed they were.

Everyone made their introduction, and before long we went right into the outcomes from their various investigations. I expected the tension to be thick enough you would need a knife to cut it, especially considering how the conversation had ended on the conference call, but tonight everyone acted well-behaved. Including me.

"I have to concede my people believe the documents you provided are legitimate"—vindication at last—"but, with no way to verify Chris's visions, I'm unclear how we should proceed, what you propose especially with what is happening with the Dark." Taqi sighed.

"I believe the path is perfectly clear," William said. "You must accept Kirtus as heir to the throne, deal with the change as you see fit. From there we move on, united, to deal with the werewolves and true magic. These things will not go away simply because we ignore them or choose to not believe in them."

Taqi crossed his arms in front of his chest.

"Burying our heads in the sand and pretending none of this is happening won't help, especially since these events will not only affect us here in North America, or even the West Coast," Deb said. "Even with our networks all paying attention and knowing what to look for, this recent attack isn't helping any of us."

"And how are you covering these events up?" Fernando asked through his rich accent.

"Gang violence." Amanda fussed with her hair. "It doesn't look good, in general, but gang-related shootings is better than the truth."

"You make it all sound like this will bring about the end of the world." Sybil's tone underplayed the importance of what we were discussing.

The heat in my neck and cheeks grew; clearly Sybil didn't believe my vision or she downplayed the second sight for whatever reason. I winced at another tight pain in the back of my head.

Juliet peeked over at me.

I offered a slight shake of my head to tell her I was okay, or would be; either way I wasn't going to make a scene...again.

"I can't believe these attacks are so troublesome for you," Sybil judged. "They can't be hard to find. Just follow your nose." She tapped the end of her nose.

"I agree." Taqi nodding as he glanced around at the others.

"That's the problem; every time we follow them or track them, the scent literally vanishes and the trail goes dead," Juliet said.

"Clearly they are getting assistance," William pointed out.

"By whom?" Sybil asked.

"One of you, perhaps," Patty suggested. "Because you don't like the idea of a single leader."

"Hardly." Sybil waved off the comment, but the bug in my brain kept my attention on this point. There may be something to it, that I didn't want to forget, or let be forgotten or missed.

I had a feeling she played this cool, but something bothered her about this. She played at something, but what?

"Regardless—" Sybil waved her hand, brushing off the comment. "—there hasn't been a royal leader in any of our lifetimes. We wouldn't even know what to do."

"Create something new," I chimed in, unable to keep my mouth shut, but keeping my tone and voice level and calm. "No one says a new court has to be anything like the former royal court. Kirtus might not even want to be a vampire king."

"Oh, are we to get another lecture from your Called, Juliet?"

I inhaled deeply and bit down hard on the inside of my cheek. No point in getting upset—that was what she wanted, and I wasn't going to play her game. Not tonight.

Amanda offered me a quick smile and slight tilt of her head.

That made me feel a bit better.

"We don't need a Vampire king or queen any longer," Fernando said. "We've moved beyond that. Our world works fine. Yes, there are issues with some of the Dark, but this is nothing like it used to be. The world is a much safer and well-connected place. Plus, what assurances do we have that this isn't some elaborate trick of the Dark? Or Victor?"

"Seriously, mate?" Garrett asked. "A trick. To what end?"

"Power. What else?" Fernando raised his brows and leaned back.

"The idea is worth exploring," Taqi added, leaning in and focusing on Juliet.

"You all heard Chris's newest vision." Juliet visually connected with each person present. "You've seen my books, you've seen the note left for Kirtus and Chris, you've listened to firsthand accounts from Patricia and Deborah Carson"—she gestured to the both of them sitting here—"as well as William Marshal"—she nodded at him—"and you studied the remains of the Lycan woman." She relaxed her shoulders. "You've talked to Victor and Kirtus. You've seen the report from Gabe confirming his findings. You've seen the material with your own eyes. And yet..." She trailed off.

"All true, but the rest of the council won't be here until Friday, so I don't see any point in rushing to action tonight," Sybil said. "Matters would be different if you, or Chris, brought forward actionable theories or events. But you have none."

"What about my vision on the attack at the SAP Center in a few weeks?"

Sybil chuckled. Fernando huffed and raised his eyebrows, holding back what I thought to be a much wanted roll of his eyes.

Their reaction pissed me off, and I felt my fangs extend. I drew in as much air as my lungs allowed. A tightness poked at my forehead. The scents of roses, vanilla, wildflowers, cucumber, and watermelon all pushed against my wall, forcing my anger and me to relax slightly.

"That is nothing to laugh off," Garrett condemned.

"I would agree," Deb added.

"These difficulties are something for us to discuss more when the others arrive and we can address all theories and the pending issues." Sybil focused on Juliet for that last bit.

"However, Sybil, perhaps presenting a united front is a good idea," Taqi said. "The potential attack, the information we've studied, and after talking to everyone, we need to address this as both William and Patricia have stated."

"Sybil. Fernando. I understood the purpose of the meetings of the last few days was to come together and present a united front to the rest of the council," Garrett questioned. "So we can plan for what to do next."

"No." Sybil pointed to the members of the council. "The purpose had been to meet with Victor, William, Deb, and Patty and to ensure we have all the information before we make any decisions. We needed to validate what we've been presented with, and now we can discuss it in greater details with the others. But I'm in no rush to make any decisions at the moment, and I'm afraid I have to agree with Fernando; it's possible this is a trick of the Dark. As for this attack, as we observed with Chris's visions over the holiday, they are easily manipulated."

"Not since his training," William said.

"His mental defenses are impressive," Deb added, and Patty nodded her agreement.

"And none of us have a way of verifying this," Sybil remarked.

"Test him." Garrett pointed at me.

"The only ones who can test him are the people we are also questioning," Fernando reminded the room.

I massaged my temples again. Everything tonight had been pointless, and the nit in the back of my brain hammered now.

"We're finished for the night; we will talk more once the others arrive and we can all meet. The meeting will also include Victor and a delegation of Dark leaders as well and our friends here tonight." Juliet stood and motioned to Deb and Patty. "Chris. William. May I speak with you both?"

I stood, made my goodbyes with the others, and walked with Juliet and William. We moved into the dining room, not even going to Juliet's office. She closed the double doors as the others lingered in the living room.

"Chris, what's wrong? You're not upset at them not believing in your visions of the coming attacks." Juliet touched my arm. "I've sensed a shift in you. Are you feeling all right?"

"Something's been off tonight, and my unease has gotten worse the more we've talked."

She glanced at William.

"I noticed a darkness, or something like a darkness as well. Chris said he spoke to you about it earlier."

She nodded.

"I haven't seen anything, but this feeling of dread like we are marching closer to my vision. Tonight didn't help, but everything got worse when Sybil brushed off the idea someone might be helping the werewolves. Perhaps the Dark? Part of my vision showed betrayal; maybe that has something to do with this apprehensive feeling." I rubbed my forehead.

"No. Not any of the Dark. Not after the attack. The idea any of this is them. No." Juliet rubbed my arm. "Can I get you something?"

I shook my head.

"One of the Light?" William suggested.

"No one in the room tonight would do such a thing," Juliet said. "None of my people in the area would either."

"Are you so certain?" William asked.

I glanced over at Juliet. No response.

That said more than any words. Who did we trust if not the members of the Council of Light? I pinched the bridge of my nose, hoping the pressure would stop the pounding in my head.

Chapter Twenty-Four

Returning to the Night Stalker, realizing all that had happened, was sad. Sahin might not have been my best friend, but knowing he had died and would never be seen or heard from again, I wouldn't have wished that on anyone. And now his club had closed, transitioning over to Victor to be rebranded, with all trace of the former owner gone, a gloomy prospect for sure. As I glanced around the club, the idea of erasing a man amazed me. Soon no one would ever realize Sahin had existed. The more I pondered these events, the more I personally believed Sahin had been manipulated—the question was by whom. Who had the most to gain? It wasn't us, but maybe my visions were being manipulated again, however unlikely. The meeting earlier in the week didn't help my confidence.

I had no one to talk to either. Alone to face this...again.

I sat on a bar stool behind the delegation from the Light, basically every member of the Council of Light, plus Gregor and Gabe, in his wheelchair. Amanda sat next to me as we listened in to what got reported. Juliet wasn't kidding when she had said she opened up this meeting. If you wanted to take out the Immortal power structure, now would be the time. The best part, for me, was seeing how annoyed Sybil had been when she arrived.

From what I had gathered from Kirtus, tonight was the first time since the end of World War II when members of the Light and Dark met, in any great number, to discuss the future of the Immortal community and the potential of some impending attack or conspiracy. And, to my surprise, the first time, ever, that any outsiders—William, Patty, and Deb—were invited.

I tried not to squirm in my seat, but I still had the pull at the back of my mind that made me worry and kept my palms damp. No matter what, I ensured my mental defenses were in place. I had no idea who had what ability, and I didn't want anyone to take advantage of the situation tonight. Plus, I worried Marcel, who had been quiet for too long, may decide tonight would be a good night to take advantage of me. I fumbled with my shirtsleeves and tried to concentrate on the room.

Instead of one table, a grouping of tables created a triangle. I supposed this arrangement had to do with showing no group held more importance than any other. Still, to my eye the display came across as strange since the setup sat in the middle of what should have been the main dance floor. Juliet had told me everyone considered this club to be a neutral enough space no one would feel like they had the home advantage.

I didn't see why everyone cared so much about who had what and if one group supposedly mattered more, but this made them comfortable, so whatever.

I peeked over to Kirtus; he sat at the table with Victor, Masko, Joaquin, and other leaders of the Dark who were new to me. Some I recognized from the challenge between Victor and Sahin and a few others from when Kirtus got promoted to his current position of chief lieutenant. But there were a couple more I had no idea who they were, and no one bothered to introduce me. I hoped to have seen some of the folks I had already met, but Kirtus mentioned many of the Dark leaders here had been escalating their consolidation of power. From the extreme glaring going on, not only from the Dark but also from the Light, I had a feeling these were the main leaders everyone dealt with on a regular basis.

"To answer your question…"

Gabe's speaking pulled me from my thoughts.

Gabe swiped the blond bangs from his eyes, continuing. "In my opinion—" Gabe rolled closer to the table. "—everything—the letter, the books, the note, all of it—is legitimate. I've found nothing to contradict them."

Right now, in this moment, Gabe was the most powerful person in the room, wheelchair or not, and I found myself impressed by how only his mind and what he knew mattered. So many could learn from this moment; a shame most would never know what happened here today. If anyone noted his chair when he arrived, they didn't show it, because the wheelchair didn't define him, just like being gay didn't define me. I would be lying if I wasn't curious as to how an Immortal lost the use of his legs and needed a mobility device, but that information wasn't needed for our conversation and it didn't affect the work he did, so really why should I care?

"And why should you?" An's voice was polite as she offered a nod of support.

"And what about the claim Kirtus is the heir to the last queen?" Sybil asked as she tapped her fingers on the table.

"I checked every source I have," Gabe announced. "The queen had heterochromia iridium as does Kirtus, and based on the book provided from whom I believe to be Marcel, the line is unbroken leading to her human sister." He maneuvered the chair, so he faced Kirtus. "Kirtus is her heir and our rightful king, should he choose to take on the responsibility."

The room broke out into whispers and mumbles.

"I, for one, welcome the news," Victor affirmed. "For too long have we been bickering and fighting amongst ourselves; a single voice, perhaps with a wise council, is exactly what we need.

"I have to agree with Victor," Yoi said, flicking her now fully pink hair over her shoulder.

"Thank you, Yoi." Victor dusted off an invisible piece of lint from his shirt. "The matter of a king or queen has been debated for centuries; now we have the answer, and it's what we choose to do next that dictates our future."

"I would also agree," a slim Asian man said. He was also one of the new-to-me Dark.

"Why am I not surprised?" Sybil grumbled through a frown. "Kirtus is Victor's second-in-command. This only goes to strengthen your position."

"Does it?" a woman with brown eyes and brunette hair questioned. Another member of the Dark delegation. "Kirtus is no friend to many of us."

"Be that as it may, he is still of the Dark," Masko reminded the group. "And he has many qualities that should be admired."

"Oh really?" Sybil shook her head.

Victor leaned forward. "Jealous, because no one can say the same of you?"

Sybil stiffened.

"I'm not suggesting any of this would be easy," Masko continued as if he hadn't finished. "But there are wise people here on both sides of the table. Why not come together and speak with a single, united voice?"

"Should we all join hands and sing 'It's a Small World' as well?" Fernando quipped.

There were laughs from both members of the Light and the Dark.

"Enough," Juliet said. "Thank you, Gabe, for all your work."

"My pleasure." Gabe rolled over to the rest of us.

As the others made their comments, which I chose to ignore, I offered Gabe my appreciation in the form of a quiet bow. He had made the best case possible, and given all the data he had provided, I wasn't sure how any of them would be able to deny the truth.

Juliet raised her hand. "Please. We are here to—"

"This is ridiculous." Fernando banged his hand on the table. "I've said it before, and I'll repeat it here. This is a trick. A scheme from the Dark, to get one of their own into a position of power. We've seen what happens when they disagree. Do we want to live like that? Duels for power? No!"

"How dare you!" The same brown-haired female Dark leader from earlier growled, standing.

"Are you saying a new council with the Dark would be anything different?" Sybil barked.

"Taya, please sit. Your grandstanding will do no good." Yoi stood as well, which honestly surprised me.

"Yoi, do not test—"

"Everyone sit," Juliet insisted from her seat. "I suggest we hear from the one this affects the most. Kirtus, what do you have to say?" She pointed to Kirtus, and the others returned to their seats. "This affects you more than anyone."

As he moved, I caught brief hints of his sandalwood scent, causing a stir in my heart.

Kirtus cleared his throat and scanned the group. The suit jacket he wore made his shoulders straighter, and he managed to make eye contact with everyone. "I'm no king. I may be the queen's long-lost heir, but I'm no ruler."

My heart beat faster seeing him talk to everyone. He might not be a leader yet, but seeing him like this, he had the makings of one.

"You won't be alone." Masko crossed his large arms over his barrel chest.

"You would have help," Gregor added.

"I appreciate that," Kirtus acknowledged. "However, several of you don't even know me, so why would you trust me?" He walked away from the table. "All I can say is for those of you who are familiar with my story, you understand I'm not fully of the Dark, nor am I fully of the Light, but I do believe we can all work together. I've seen cooperation in all of you. You wouldn't be here tonight otherwise." He motioned around him. "If we can pull everyone together and work together, there is nothing we can't do, and there is a lot we have to deal with."

"And you think you can help us do that?" a blonde-haired, blue-eyed woman asked; she sat next to Taya and had been quiet through most of the meeting.

"I think I'm in a position to see both sides," Kirtus said. "I've always been an outsider, and that gives me a unique perspective."

"I suppose we'll find a way to make it work, but there would need to be a lot of negotiations; I refuse to be brushed aside and ignored," Taya, from her spot on the Dark's side, stated. "My territory and my people are mine. They trust me."

The others from the Dark's table nodded.

"Leadership can be learned." Rahim's gaze met the others, still his voice was barely a whisper, which caused the others to lean in to hear him speak. "I had a lot of help when I first took over my territory."

"And you have such a peaceful area of control," Sybil rebuffed.

"We would all be of assistance." Taqi's tone fell flat, like he said the words but didn't believe them. "Should a royal council be agreed upon, perhaps we return to some of our more forgotten traditions—" He glanced around the table. "—and locations."

"Now is the time to pull together," Deb spoke up. "All of us, putting aside our past. We would be happy to work with a united Immortal community as would many of the covens."

"I believe all the support and assistance would be welcomed," Juliet said.

"And it would all be controlled from here. Right?" Sybil stood and pointed to Juliet. "Fernando is right; this is a power grab like before. But not from the Dark, although I do not doubt Victor and his band of minions had their hands in this too—the vision, the witches, the attack, everything planned by you." She glared at Juliet. "How long have you been plotting this? How long have you been planting the seeds in your Called? You are getting what you want. But we won't stand for it. We can't. Do you all want to be ruled by Juliet and, by proxy, Victor?" She glanced at the others around the table. "Are you going to allow this? Am I the only one who can—"

I didn't see Juliet move, but when Sybil hit the floor with her chair toppled over and feet in the air, I figured out what had happened. Juliet had transformed into her vampire form with angry brow, ridges, and fangs, glowering at Sybil. Juliet must have either used her power on Sybil or punched her, both of which I approved of but now thought better of.

"Juliet!" Fernando yelled. "You are no better than the Dark. What's wrong with you?" He met Sybil and offered his hand as she dusted off her dress and picked up her chair.

"Now hold on!" Victor stood. "We've done nothing. If you have problems amongst yourselves, I suggest you deal with your issues and leave us out of it."

"We expect better from the head of the Council of Light," Anashe warned, watching the events unfold. "Victor, perhaps some of your Dark influence has rubbed off on Juliet. Perhaps that has caused this outburst."

"I beg your pardon!" Victor snapped.

"Beg all you want, but I have a feeling you're behind some of this." Sybil's thin finger pointed at him.

"Enough!" Juliet shouted, and the room buzzed with energy; even the lights glowed brighter. "I've done nothing to warrant such disdain from you or anyone on this council. Yet you continue to be angry with me for something I had no control over and never wanted. You, not me, thrust this responsibility on me."

"Juliet, please." Kirtus stood, but his voice faltered.

He needed to be strong here. They needed him to be strong.

"With the understanding you would abdicate once situations improved in Europe, but you didn't." Sybil ignored Kirtus as she spoke.

Sybil hovered off the ground. This might be so that if Juliet did something again she'd be able react faster.

"You held on to power." Sybil pointed. "And now you are trying to get even more, consolidate everything under you."

"Sybil, please," Kirtus tried again.

"They voted to keep me in and have done so continually. You *chienne!*" Juliet barked.

"How dare you." Sybil transformed, her fangs appeared, and hard, angry ridges appeared on her forehead.

Amanda stood next to Juliet, as did Gregor. French was not a language I understood, but there are some words that didn't need translation. They weren't the only ones standing; most of the table was now on their feet. The situation had deteriorated.

Kirtus needed to speak up, take control, but he was shocked into silence like some of the others. I tried to make eye contact with him, but why? Everyone watched the Light. I pinched the bridge of my nose as the building pain in my head got harder to ignore.

Most of the Light were now snapping at one another, and sadly many of the Dark were chuckling and egging them on as they observed. This was a sight I had never expected I would see, and as events continued, the pain in my brain had tears dripping from my eyes. I swiped my hand at my eyes, then pinched the bridge of my nose trying to keep the pain at bay.

"Ladies. Please." Victor's voice boomed as he held up his hands, ready to act to stop them, his narrow gaze more worried than amused.

That should have been Kirtus, but he stood next to Victor frowning.

Juliet took a partial step forward and returned to her human face.

The Light all quieted, and even Sybil relaxed as she, too, returned to her human from. To my surprise the only one who didn't seem affected was Gabe. I wasn't sure why this would be the case; maybe his response had to do with his neutral stance in the Immortal community. He sat in his chair, moved away from the commotion, watching, like me.

"I believe now is the time for everyone to calm down," William said. "You don't want to say or do anything that might not be able to be undone later." He pointed to the chairs. "Please."

"William and Victor are right," Sybil agreed. "Thank you for your level heads."

Another sharp pain hit like a hammer, and I squeeze my eyes shut, raising my hands to my ears and pushing to make the pain stop. When I opened my eyes, I stood in the club, but there were no tables. Standing at the bar, Sahin spoke into his cell phone, and I got whiffs of the ocean.

"What the hell?" I glanced around; the pain and everyone assembled had gone. Sahin stood in a gray suit alive and well again.

A vision.

"You want to help me?" He laughed, and the sound echoed though the space.

I rushed over to get a better listen of the conversation, but only heard his end.

"Why should I believe you?"

I scanned around to see if anything would give me a day or time, but nothing appeared, so I focused on him. "Please say something I can use."

"Everyone knows Sybil and Juliet don't get along; that's nothing new." He shook his head. "You think you can do that?" A pause. "Many have tried, but despite their disdain they always pull together in the end. Take what happened with Chris and his father the witch." He adjusted his stance and pulled over a bar stool to sit. "I still don't understand how that will help me."

A sudden rush of energy ran through my body; this was important. With luck I would get a name or something that would prove Juliet wasn't playing games or doing anything Sybil and Fernando were accusing her of.

"So, if I get rid of Victor, with the help of the new werewolves, you can get rid of Sybil and Juliet and take over the Council of Light. And how do I know you can deliver the wolves?" A scowl crossed his lips. "Ha, what about Kirtus? That *lund k laddu* won't be an issue once Victor's gone." He fell quiet again. "Okay, I can see how that benefit me as long as you don't screw me over; it would be unfortunate if something happened to you as you ascended to your new position."

The doors to the club opened and Sahin stood.

"Send me the details. No, not here at the club. I'll text you." He glanced to the front of the club as a couple of his staff walked in.

"I gotta go. We'll chat more soon." He ended the call and slipped his cell into his pocket with a chuckle. "Who'd have imagined someone like that would be sitting on the Council of Light?" He adjusted his tie and walked over to his staff. "Tonight's going to be a great night, folks."

I blinked and my vision shifted. I stood in the middle of a freeway. To my right as the cars zipped past me, a sign: Redding, Truckee, and Bakersfield. There were no mile markers; the sign only had the names, but that didn't make sense. Redding was north of the Bay Area, Truckee was on the way to Lake Tahoe heading east, and Bakersfield was southern California. I scanned the area some more. In the sky a large full moon hung like a beacon. In the distance, the sound of howling reached my ears. "Wolves." I tried to see if I spotted anything else, but there wasn't anything more.

Another car zipped right through me, and I shuddered. "Wolves. No. Werewolves, there are werewolves now in those places. New packs."

I shook my head and blinked again. My eyes opened. This time everyone scrutinized me. My stomach dropped as my neck and cheeks warmed. At least the pounding in my head had vanished. I mentally reached out for my wall—still there, nothing had broken in, so this must have been a true vision, one that wasn't compromised by any outside influence. I wanted to close my eyes to rest, but I doubted that would be allowed now.

"Who helped Sahin?" Taqi asked, his tone demanding, and his scowl deepened. "Who is betraying the Council of Light?"

"I don't know."

"What about these new werewolves?" Joaquín asked.

"I'm not sure."

"Back up," Juliet instructed. "Please." She, Amanda, and Kirtus circled in around me, so I could breathe. "Chris, what else did you see?" Her tone soft, she pushed her calming on me. I allowed it.

I shook my head.

"Oh, how convenient," Sybil quipped. "And of all nights."

"You can't doubt his vision," William said. "You just witnessed his power firsthand."

"We witnessed an excellent performance." Anashe adjusted her blouse. "And it all falls in line with what we already are aware of. William, you were a litigator. How would you view the evidence before you? How would you proceed as a man of law?"

William fell silent.

"Unbelievable." The blond member of the Dark's tone sounded impressed or amazed.

"So, we find out the Council of Light worked with Sahin and now they try and hide the news." Ponleak shook his head. "Victor, you work with them, and this is how they repay you."

"Juliet?" Victor said. "You speak for the Council."

"No!" Sybil countered, clapping her hands together. "Enough. I'm calling on a vote of no confidence. We've had enough of this manipulation. We vote now."

"Sybil. You can't be serious? Now is not the time," Juliet said.

"Now is the perfect time," Fernando agreed. "For all we know, you helped Sahin. Perhaps even the wolves, costing the lives of those three Dark."

"Didn't you hear what Chris said?" Deb spoke up. She handed me a glass of something red; I assumed, by the orangey smell, blood. I wondered for a second where it had come from but was grateful and didn't want to think too much about the new drink.

"I did not sense any trickery." Patty closed her eyes and scanned the room as if confirming what she already stated.

"And we are supposed to trust two witches?" Taqi asked. "Your kind was responsible for the events in December."

Both Deb and Patty glared at him but didn't speak.

My hands trembled; those were different witches. Not all witches were the same. Why not trust them? This wasn't happening!

"Please everyone." Juliet lowered her tone. "I suggest we adjourn the meeting and—"

"I'm sorry, Juliet," Garrett said. "But a vote of no confidence has been called; we need to vote."

My heart sank, and I had to hold the glass of red with both hands. Even Garrett supported this.

"Can't we wait for a private session?" An asked as she glanced at the nine council members. "That would be my suggestion. I would like to discuss this more."

"What? So you can plot and plan behind closed doors." Taya leaned in. "No, vote here, unless you have something to be afraid of."

"Victor, perhaps we should give them privacy." Masko glanced to his superior.

"As a neutral party, I'm happy to offer an arbitration," Gabe suggested.

Sybil's eyes narrowed on him.

Gabe held up his hands. "Fine, no arbitration or mediation. I shall witness as an impartial party."

"Fine, you want to vote, we vote," Juliet conceded. "A call of no confidence has been enacted. If you want me to step down, raise your hand."

The room grew quiet as all eyes were on the members of the Council of Light. I finished the last of my drink, unsure what else to do. I would be lying if I said I wasn't worried at how this would affect me and Kirtus. I shook the idea from my mind only to be filled with worry about what would happen to Juliet, to all of us. This wasn't really happening. How could it? The immortals were pulling themselves apart. Just like my vision. Sybil's hand raised first, followed by Fernando's. I wanted to be sick. I glanced over to Kirtus, hoping he would offer me some kind a physical reassurance, but he, like the other leaders of the Dark, were all transfixed. I peeked at William, Patty, and Deb and they stood in silence.

When I peeked at the Council of Light, two more hands raised: Taqi and Anashe. I couldn't believe the vote.

Juliet scanned the council members. "It would seem—"

"I'm sorry, Juliet." Rahim raised his hand.

Juliet's whole body slumped.

"Mate, come on, you can't be serious." Garrett gawked at Rahim.

He didn't react and kept his hand up.

"This should have never happened," An said. "I still want to pass a motion. We postpone this vote."

"Five to four." Sybil leaned back and tilted her head in an overconfident and overdramatic nature. "Unless, Yoi, you wish to increase the vote to six to three?"

"No," Yoi said. "You have gotten what you want; you've removed Juliet. I will support this vote, but I do so under protest."

"Noted." Sybil glanced around at the tables. "As I have called for the vote, I will assume control of the council for the time being, until we can have a proper vote on a new head."

Gabe and Kirtus both shook their heads.

We were done.

"Don't you see this is falling right in line with Chris's vision?" Juliet struggled to keep her tone level.

"Or we are stopping a well-orchestrated plan," Fernando said. "Juliet, I'm sorry this happened this way, but what choice do we have? There is too much unknown and what is known may easily have been put into play by you, or—" He studied me. "—someone close to you." He faced Sybil. "You have my full support."

"Thank you, Fernando." Sybil beamed. "Juliet, until we fully understand you and potentially your Called's involvement with the Dark, Gregor will speak for your territory. This matter is settled." Sybil's gaze narrowed on Victor and the other Dark. "Watch your step. Things are going to be different. The days of the Light pussyfooting around the Dark are over. We will not tolerate your meddling. If we find out you played a greater part in any of this *king* business, it will be war."

"Who do you think you're speaking to?" Victor shifted and growled at Sybil. "We've had nothing to do with any of this, and if it's war you are looking for..."

"Sybil. Enough," Yoi warned. "You will not overstep your authority. Not at this moment, not when so much is uncertain."

"None in my territory will support a war with the Dark," Garrett said. "You want a war, you fight on your own."

"None in my territory will either." Gregor stepped forward and rested a hand on Juliet's shoulder. "I will continue to work with the Dark of this territory as my newly appointed senior governor has done in the past when she led this territory and the Council of Light."

Sybil's eyes narrowed on Gregor, but if I understood the Light's rules of governance, she had no authority on how Gregor ran his territory, so he easily appointed Juliet as his senior governor, unless they banished Juliet or did something more permanent.

I exhaled, a small bit a tension escaping my shoulders as Gregor offered me a slight wink.

"My territory is in no position to support such a pointless endeavor," An added.

"Seems like the Light are not as unified as they have been in the recent past." Joaquín focused his comment directly at Sybil. An amused mocking tone bit around his comment.

Tonight had been an awful chess game, and I didn't understand the rules. I wanted to yell at them. This was madness, but given the pained look on Juliet's face, I said nothing. Plus, not speaking seemed the best option as I suspected once I opened my mouth the glass of red I had just drank would be up and out.

"Clearly the Immortals here have much to work through." William scooted his chair back. "Until such time as you can present a unified front, I'm sorry; I cannot be involved."

Deb gestured to Patty.

"Our coven will, unfortunately, need to pull our offer of assistance at this time," Patty said. "I'm sorry, Juliet." Both she and Deb made their way to the club's exit. Patty turned and faced Sybil. "I will be notifying the other covens as to what has transpired tonight. I doubt they will be willing to help either."

"Chris. Juliet." William bowed his head. "I'm sorry." He caught up with Deb and Patty, and the three walked toward the doors.

"I will adjust the territory records accordingly to reflect the changes tonight," Gabe submitted. "I have nothing more to offer at this time. I will take my leave as well." He wheeled to the doors with the others. As the doors closed, the echoing of steel blared throughout the club, like the doors of a crypt when the dead were being sealed in their vault.

"We're screwed," I whispered as Juliet took my hand.

Chapter Twenty-Five

I want to say life had changed dramatically since the blow-up at the Night Stalker, but if I'm honest, it hadn't. In the two weeks since, everything grew calm. I still worked at the foundation, as did Juliet. In fact, she came to the office daily, so did Amanda. Kirtus and I had been spending more time together, which I think we both appreciated. Having him to lean on and providing whatever support I offered to him, we had a nice break from this new reality. Everyone appeared on the outside to be doing fine, but the quiet moments were when darkness creeped in.

But, overall, we were fine.

Well, mostly fine.

Okay, not fine.

Our smiles and moments of calm were an illusion we created to make each other feel better.

Everything had been screwed up, and I hated it.

Anger radiated off of Kirtus because of his lack of leadership and coming off weak as things fell to shit. He kept swearing he would never act weak again. He would never lose control of his council the way he had that night. If anything, the events of the council vote made Kirtus more determined to get everyone working together. His new attitude was an amazing shift to see for someone so reluctant to lead, but I couldn't be more proud of him, and more importantly, I believed he now had the pride in himself he needed.

Gregor had been meeting with Juliet after work. He would arrive at the house around six o'clock and leave well past midnight most nights. One night, about a week after the breakdown at the nightclub, Rei and Maria, Juliet's (now Gregor's) senior governors from Canada and Mexico respectively, arrived for an in-person meeting, and my only interaction with them was a brief hello. Despite not getting to spend a lot of time with them again, like I had several months ago, seeing them had been a nice treat, feeling how supportive they appeared to be. Despite seeing him arrive at the house, Gregor never spoke to me, and Juliet didn't share what their meetings were about.

One good thing about all of this. I managed to continue my training with William. The training was always held at his house, which helped, but I didn't have any new visions. I had heard through William that the werewolf packs in my vision had been confirmed by members of the witch community, but not found. Like the pack located here in San Jose, they were impossible to track, and without everyone working together, finding them didn't seem likely.

My time with William turned into some of my greatest learning. We spoke of both the Mohawk Nation and his nation, the Muwekma Ohlone. By no means did I become any kind of expert, but I tried to learn. I wanted to respect him and his culture. My neck and cheeks warmed because I was so ignorant at times, hearing him tell me the stories of his family. There were some aspects I wasn't totally clear on; he mentioned witchcraft was a big no-no for his people. The ban on witchcraft had something to do with their Great Law of Peace, but when I asked how he helped us and Patty and Deb, he got an odd expression on his face and told me that wasn't for me to worry about. When I asked him about his magic, his abilities, he asked me never to refer to his gifts like that. So, after that I made sure to only refer to him as a Healer, and I didn't mention his gifts again.

When it came to Deb's and Patty's silence, sadly, no one had any contact with them or anyone in their coven. The witches had dropped off our and William's radar. And I wasn't sure how worried that should make me. I tried to push the worries from my mind, but all my concerns seeped into my thoughts, even at the office.

I persisted in staring at the computer screen not seeing the grant proposal in front of me. How long had I been working on this? I closed my eyes and focused on my mental wall to help focus my mind, but that didn't help. A rap at my office door forced me to glance to the door.

"May I?" Juliet asked. Her cream-colored blazer draped over her arm, revealing her sapphire silk blouse. As always, her appearance was impeccable. I even got a hint of a gold necklace through the open collar of her shirt.

"You don't need to ask." I stood. "Is there something I can help you with?"

She closed the office door and glided over to one of the chairs in front of my desk. "I wanted to see how you were doing. Especially since I haven't been able to spend much time with you."

I returned to my seat as she took the one across from me. "I'm fine." I leaned forward. "I'm more worried about you, especially with how things ended."

She offered a grim expression and a slight chuckle. "The changes have been a challenge, but Gregor, Rei, Maria, and I were prepared for something like this. Sybil..." She sighed. "Sybil's been trying for years to reclaim the head position. Now the seat is hers."

"Won't they need to vote?"

"Oh, they will. Immortal politics are strange. The council hasn't changed in hundreds of years; there's never been a need. Even though they've voted me into this position every time there has been a call for a vote, the election has always been more of a formality." She sank into the chair. "But since—"

"Since I became your Called, things are different."

She frowned as the click of her nails echoed around the space.

"So, if I hadn't become your Called..."

She reached across the table and took my hand. "Nothing would have changed. In fact, things would be worse. The witches would have attacked us, we would have been ill-prepared, and the world we live in now would be much worse. You saved us."

"Did I? Or did I cause all this?"

"Chris, don't think like that. No one can say what Marcel would have done, but I doubt his plans rested solely on you being my Called. Marcel's plans have plans, and those plans typically have plans."

"Just like yours."

She chuckled, removing her hand from mine and adjusting her blouse.

"With Gregor on the council, do you think he will get them to come around?"

Juliet sat quiet, which gave me my answer.

"So, Sybil will be head of the Council of Light for however much longer that will last, and she'll push for war with the Dark, or whatever, because they are going to push for Kirtus to be the one rightful leader. Meanwhile, the werewolves will grow in number and remain unchecked." I massaged my temples. "Oh, and everyone will be ignoring true magic."

"I don't think events will come to war. Sybil, despite her many flaws, should know better. The change in the council sadly had more to do with me than anything else."

"You think she'll come around to Kirtus being the heir?" I frowned over at her.

"Perhaps."

"No one can deny these facts for long." I peeked at the papers on my desk. "They all have the information from Gabe. They can't ignore that...can they?"

"No."

"But they are worried about what will happen to the council?"

"According to Gregor, when he updated me and the other governors, the council has been split. Several members don't want Sybil as the leader, but they don't want me or him either." She rotated her neck until a pop escaped. "So, the council's fractured."

"You don't seem worried."

"No, typically a motion, or vote, means someone wants something... It's politics."

"But what do they have to fight over?"

Juliet's eyes perked up, and the edges of her lips rose at my question. "Other than power and prestige? There are financial gains to be had, contracts to be negotiated, engagements with humans to be addressed; supporting another member of the council is always a big one."

"I never thought about it."

"Unfortunately, Immortal politics is like everything." She leaned forward. "An example is I didn't allow—and I suppose Gregor will keep this law on the books—open hunting in my territory. Meaning feeding is either done in private between two consenting adults, Immortal-owned and operated dining establishments, like what you've been to, or in private clubs, all typically owned by a member of the Dark. That's an agreement I made with the Dark Leaders. Most follow this agreement, others pretend to, so they don't get in trouble."

"Okay."

"The 'no hunting' law keeps things from getting out of hand. Imagine the potential for bodies to be found from accidental killings; it would be a nightmare for everyone. Especially here in North America. But this isn't the case in other territories. Now, say, Gregor tried to get Taqi to vote for him to become head of the council. Taqi may request his Immortals be exempt from this law allowing them to feed however they want."

"Wait, seriously?"

"The hunting law is an example of a point of negotiations, but still he might ask for such a concession. He's not a fan of civility and tends to be much more traditional in those manners. I'm pleased he never pushed."

"I would have assumed there would be no actual hunting in the sense of open feeding."

"You'd be surprised what some members of the Light allow in their territories."

"Who do you think will win?" I closed the files on my computer since I wasn't working on them anymore, and I doubted I would get to them.

"Unless there is some unknown factor, Sybil."

"What about the traitor among the Light?"

"I've been thinking that over since your vision of Sahin. I wish you heard or discovered who he spoke with. That would have been helpful."

"You don't believe me?" I tried to keep the hurt from my words.

"Of course, I believe you. I have no idea who the traitor might be. Ruling out both Sybil and I, since we were the focus of the conversation, it may be anyone."

"Really? Even Garrett or Fernando or Yoi?"

"Chris, we all have our deals we cut. Victor and I have a special relationship, and every member on the Council has called our working bond into question. Getting rid of him, and putting in someone, like Sahin, who now owed you a favor, that is a big motivation, especially if Sybil and I were out of the way. Victor's area of control is huge, and his influence has only grown since Christmas. He's a brilliant man who doesn't bind himself in rules that don't benefit him. With Sahin gone, Victor will benefit greatly from his death. Especially among some of the Dark leaders in Europe."

"I can't see Garett screwing you over."

"Honestly, neither do I, but over the years, I've learned to never take anything for granted."

"And what about the vision of the attack?"

"Have you had anymore visions about what may come?"

"No, not even when I've been with William. It's like everything is in a big cloud. Some of the vision has come to pass; the council fractured, the deception, the wolves, so I don't know."

She nodded.

"But whatever is going to happen will be this month, and we only have a few more days." I ran a hand through my hair. "When I asked William about when and how everything falls apart, he said it's possible the timetable had shifted."

"The butterfly effect." She clicked her nails. "We are in flux, things are changing, and your foresight hasn't caught up."

I rubbed my head. "I wish I did."

A slight tap on the door pulled my attention.

"Come in," I called out.

Amanda opened the door, and we were greeted by her sea-foam-green business suit and her signature perfect hair and nails. "I'm heading out, and figured I would peek in and see if either of you needed anything."

"Thank you, Amanda." Juliet stood and slipped on her blazer. "Why don't you both head out? I can finish up here."

My eyes narrowed as I focused on Juliet. "You sure?"

Juliet waved us off. "Yes, I'm sure." She met my gaze. "I'm sorry we haven't trained since that one night at the house. If you want, talk to Kirtus and see if the offer still stands to use his barn. If so, I'll pull something together."

"Thanks." I closed out my system as both Amanda and Juliet chatted. Even though I worried about what lay ahead of us, I looked forward to being done with the day. I shrugged on my jacket and met Juliet and Amanda at the door.

"See you at home." Juliet's weak gesture of her hand greeted both Amanda and me.

Juliet made her way up to her office.

"How is she, really?" I asked as Amanda and I made our way to the parking lot and our cars.

"She's not happy about any of what has transpired, and she been working her channels to find out who screwed over the council." She glanced over at my car. "I left the keys with Juliet. Do you mind taking me home?"

"Not at all."

We piled into the Fusion and headed for home.

"When are you going to get your new car?"

"When all this craziness is over."

"You sure you want to wait that long? It may never be over."

I sighed and flicked the blinker, waiting for the light to change to make my turn. "I know." I banged my hands on the steering wheel. "God, I can't believe all this."

"Everything will work out. You have to have faith."

"I hope so." My stomach worked its way into a giant knot.

".Juliet will be fine. Who knows? Maybe the change will do her some good. She has been through worse."

"Has she? Marcel, werewolves, the council, true magic, all that seems like a lot to me."

"You don't get to be as old as Juliet if you let situations like this get to you. Yes, it's a lot, but she knows what she's doing." Amanda patted my leg. "Have faith."

I chewed on the inside of my cheek. I hadn't even been an Immortal for a year, so really what did I know? For the first time in months, I wished I would have a vision, to see how this all played out.

Chapter Twenty-Six

I had a bad feeling all day that put me on edge. Today was destined to be the day of the attack at the SAP Center. The San Jose Sharks were playing the Anaheim Ducks, and there were going to be thousands of people present. As a precaution Gregor issued a statement to all Light Immortals to stay away, and to my surprise, Victor had done the same for the Dark. Still, I didn't feel any better, and no amount of mental concentration or relaxation techniques made the difference. As agitated as I had been, I forced myself to relax, but I was still unable to shake the feelings of dread and darkness all around me.

"Hey." A gentle pat on my leg warmed my cheeks and my heart. I glanced over to Kirtus. "Try and relax; you're growling," he said.

"I am?" I shook my head and gulped at the air around me. My jaw ached from how hard my teeth were clenched.

"I thought that was your stomach," Amanda quipped, but only a hint of glee reached her lips. She put her glass of wine down. "Today is stressful, I get it, but there is nothing we can do at the moment."

"Isn't there?" I huffed. "Maybe we should be there. Perhaps, by us not being there we are..." I shook my head. The exhale of breath I had been holding escaped my lungs.

"Everyone has been told to stay away," Amanda mentioned, sipping her cocktail. "There won't be any Immortals at the game tonight, which is too bad. I hear it's supposed to be a great game." She tried to grin, but no amusement touched her expression.

"I'm sorry." I focused on the restaurant and my surroundings. We were having dinner at the Capital Club in downtown San Jose. Kirtus had a membership, and the spot had the most impressive views of the city. I glanced out the window and caught sight of Victor's building, the old one with the cupola, and the SAP Center beyond. "How is Victor doing?" I asked.

Kirtus tilted his head and sighed. "With the way things are going, he's planning for a confrontation with the Council of Light. I've hardly seen him, which isn't good—"

"You were supposed to be smoothing those waters." Amanda's finger tapped the bottom of her glass.

"Sure," Kirtus said. "The council won't talk to me or see me, and Victor has entrusted me with things here while he's been dealing with..."

The server came by and dropped off all our salads and refilled our glasses. This restaurant, sadly, was a strictly human location, but they allowed you to bring in your own wine; however, they charged a corkage fee. Still, we had our red, but we had to eat too, so dinner would be a mixed bag for Kirtus and me. Amanda, however, loved the food here, so at least one of us came out ahead in the dinning arena.

A roar of cheers came from the bar area, and we all faced the booming crowd.

"I guess the Sharks scored." Amanda frowned. "What a shame the box isn't being used tonight." She shook her head.

Kirtus nodded.

My vision played in my head. The overwhelming fragrances of blood both excited me and made my stomach sink. The attack at the SAP Center tickled at the back of my mind. Something hovered in the darkness waiting to strike. A quiver ran from my toes to my ears. I might not know for sure, but I had to trust my gut. Immortals present at the hockey game or not made no difference; something evil waited there, and people would get hurt.

I had to be there.

Now.

The roar of cheers lifted me from my chair for the last time.

"We need to go." I glared at Amanda and Kirtus. "I don't care what the others have done or are going to do. There is a darkness, and we have to stop it."

"If you're sure, that is all I needed to hear," Kirtus said.

"Is that why you picked the Capital Club for dinner?" I shrugged on my coat.

Kirtus winked at me.

"So much for dinner." Amanda stood and pulled on her jacket.

We left everything at the table and made our way to the elevators. Kirtus chatted with the hostess as we kept walking, and another round of applause from the bar erupted. I hit the down button on the elevator. By the time the elevator opened, Kirtus stood next to me and we walked in.

Amanda pulled out her phone and made a call.

Another pull at the back of my brain caused me to stumble and I was forced to use the elevator wall to steady myself. Either my worry or something more hovered near me, like a pin in the spine of my neck. Either way I needed a moment. I focused on my mental wall. I walked along the edges, holding my hand out, the hardness of the steel and stone ridged under my touch. I sniffed the air and took in the smells of mortar, brick, and steel.

There were still hints of blood from the arena, but they were fading. *Finally.*

"You okay?" Kirtus rested a hand on my arm.

I moved my head in the affirmative while allowing my lungs to refill with much-needed oxygen.

Amanda hung up the phone. "You owe me for this."

Kirtus peeked over his shoulder at her. "We'll come back."

"Oh no. I'm thinking something nicer, more prestigious. Something south of here."

I scowled at the two of them; how they were so flippant right now? I wanted to bark at the both of them. I clenched my fist, my nails digging into my palms. Nothing happening was their fault; they weren't feeling what stalked me, and they were trying to keep me calm and my mind distracted. With each tick of the clock, the world got darker and emboldened a mental push on my mind's walls. The attack wasn't like before; this energy came from all sides.

Kirtus shook his head. "The Club?"

"Definitely, and I want an extended weekend at the Grand Californian with a private dinner at 21 Royal."

"Ouch. You know what that'll cost?"

"Absolutely, and I'm worth it." She winked.

"Yes, yes, you are. I'll give Danny a call and see what he can work out."

"What are you two jabbering about?" I snapped. "The Club? The Grand Californian? 21 Royal? We have more important things to worry about right now." My fangs were extended and biting into my lips.

Kirtus forced a pleasant appearance, but the strain shown around his eyes. "Hey. It's okay. We're going to get there." He rubbed my arm.

I huffed and shook my shoulders, and my canines retracted as I forced what I hoped would be viewed as reassurance on my face.

"Club 33 at Disneyland." Amanda continued the conversation as if nothing happened.

I appreciated the banter. She was really trying to help me relax; they both were.

"He's a member. If everything works out, we'll go." She winked. "It's fun. They have an amazing selection of reds, or so he and Juliet say."

"Not to mention, the service. David, June, and Glynndonna are amazing." Kirtus beamed if only ever so slightly.

"Wait." Even though the heat of anger rose from the pit of my stomach to the top of my head, especially given what lay ahead of us, my curious nature got the better of me. "You mean Disneyland caters to us?" I pointed between Kirtus and myself. I tried to wrap my head around multiple things, and the elevator ride down wasn't helping.

"Disneyland is the happiest place on Earth. For everyone, not just humans," Kirtus said as the doors opened.

"Yep." Amanda's posture changed to all business. "I got us access to the box seat at the SAP Center. If something is going to happen we'll be right in the middle of...whatever."

Getting to the SAP Center played out as an easier journey than I figured. Given the game had already started, traffic wasn't a problem, and neither was parking. Kirtus knew right where to go and how to get us there. Amanda spoke with Juliet, or maybe Gregor, or both.

I tried to breathe. I closed my eyes and focused on the hockey game and the SAP Center. I wanted to recall the images of the attack, but only a cloud met my efforts. Not even the sickening sweet smells of all that blood came to mind.

"Chris." A female voice soothed my nerves. "We're here."

"Patty?" I asked.

"William, Deb, and I are here."

"Where?" I opened my eyes. "Patty, Deb, and William are here," I conveyed to Kirtus and Amanda, whose confused expressions met what I deemed to be a pinched expression on my face, if my clenched jaw and aching temples were any indication. I should have been surprised by this, but I wasn't. They weren't Immortals and weren't bound by the rules or the mandates of Gregor or Victor, so why wouldn't they be here?

Just in case.

"Have them meet us at the VIP entrance," Kirtus instructed.

I tugged at my coat before I sent the mental message out. "Meet us at the VIP entrance."

"See you there."

"How are they here?" Amanda asked.

"We can ask them when we get there," Kirtus said as the car came to a halt. "We'll have to walk from here."

We moved down the street and passed the park with the carousel, making our way to the building. The SAP Center stood as a big silver tank near the San Jose main train station and across from a big part of the river walk park. The set-up was nice, and the building, despite being older, still looked cool. We made our way to the VIP entrance. Waiting for us were the witches and William. I sniffed the air and didn't pick up anything strange.

"What are you doing here?" Amanda asked.

She gestured at us. "Same as you," Deb said.

"Chris's vision." William adjusted his coat.

"Where have you been?" I asked Patty and Deb.

"We've been busy." Patty directed us to the entrance. "Are we going to keep talking or are we going to stop this?"

"We're not even sure what this is," Amanda mentioned as she ushered our group to the entrance. "For all we know, we're going to watch the game."

"Doubtful." William frowned. "Or we wouldn't all be here."

A chorus of nods was the only response as we made our way through security and into the building and headed to the private box. How we got in and through all that was a miracle of Amanda's doing. There was nothing she couldn't do after all. As I found out later, both Victor and Juliet had VIP boxes here. I mean, sure, why not, right? Still the private box got us in and that was all that mattered. But the deeper into the building we marched, the more the tether of my mind reeled me in. Something would happen here, Immortal or not, but this knowing wasn't part of my vision. This feeling meant something else. I wanted to lower my mental wall, but I worried whatever stalked us out there might use that opening as an opportunity to attack me or the group and I didn't want that to happen. So, I kept the wall up.

William nodded at me, and I took that as his approval for my current course of action.

My mental barriers stayed in place.

Once at the box, nothing special caught our attention. We all moved to the windows and watched the game. There were fans shouting and having a great time. The players on the ice were fine. For all intents and purposes, everything appeared ordinary. The hockey teams came across as giving the game their all, but I wasn't here to enjoy.

"Normal?" Amanda said. "I don't see anything."

"Neither do I." Kirtus continued to scan the area.

"Something's not right," Patty said. "Do you feel the darkness?"

Deb gave her sister a quick bow.

William and I both shared a look, signaling me he sensed it as well.

I scanned the arena and opened my mind ever so slightly to see who wanted to talk. A risk, but one I needed to take. I focused on my mental wall, all the details and the scents that went with it. I stood at the wall feeling the hardness and moved to a section of the barrier and pushed. I allowed this small section to loosen, not to fall, but drop enough to allow contact. Pulling up my wall and making the change only took a moment. His earthy scent filled my nostrils; he was here. He wasn't going to use anyone else; he had to do this himself, and that scared me more than anything. I moved my head to follow his scent. Confident of the location, I opened my eyes and squinted, trying to focus on the area of the arena he should be.

Three blinks of my eyes and I found him.

"There," I whispered and pointed. "Marcel."

Everyone stopped and glanced where I pointed. A man with salt-and-pepper hair and crystal-blue eyes. His jeans and polo showed off the softness around the middle; still, his strength came not from his body, but from his mind. The people around Marcel were quiet, none of them cheering or reacting to the game. They were all blank. He had them well under his control.

Why is he doing this?

I wished a big battle like what we had with the witches at Christmas occurred, something everyone had experienced with me, but the moment I pointed out Marcel and the humans around him the world melted away and he and I stood at center ice. Everyone else vanished.

"I knew you would come, little one," Marcel said.

"What are you planning? Why are you doing this?"

"The Dark and the Light need to understand. They need to see, and until they do, I can't rest."

"Why not come out? Why not work with them? Meet with Juliet and Victor. Meet with the Council of Light—"

"They've corrupted the council. Filled it with infighting and power struggles. In your short time, you've seen how they work. They will be the end to us. To you. You understand as well I as do."

I wanted to tell him he was wrong, but I couldn't. He was right; I sensed the shift, the pending doom, the same way I felt my toes and fingers. I shook my head. "What do you want us to do?"

"Restore the royal council. Kirtus is the true ruler, and they know it. Bring the witches back; return their seat at the table; offer a seat to the Lycan."

"You want us to tackle world peace as well?" What he wanted, what he asked was impossible. How was any of this going to work?

"Do not make light of these changes. Now is the time to restore the balance for everyone." Marcel stepped forward. "You were brought to my daughter for a reason, and you will fulfill this task set before you."

"Chris. Step back."

The command came from William.

I did as instructed.

"William Armija." Marcel faced him. "The Muwekma Ohlone Healer. You have trained my grandson well in such a short amount of time." He pointed. "Your part in this is more critical then you or your ancestors had imagined. As are the roles of Patricia and Deborah Carson." He snapped, and both Patty and Deb appeared.

"What do you want?" Deb asked.

"How are we here?" Patty glanced around the rink.

"You are here because I wish it," Marcel answered. "All of you are here for one purpose, and that is to restore what was destroyed long ago."

"We appreciate what you want, but you are asking the impossible," William said.

"Let us expand to those that are needed." Marcel closed his eyes, and within a moment Juliet, Victor, Kirtus, Gregor, and Sybil were all present.

"Marcel!" Juliet exclaimed.

"Impossible." Sybil peeked around the empty arena. She rubbed her legs and her arms.

"Chris," Kirtus said.

"Mind games?" Victor scowled and tried to transform, but every time his transformation began he returned to his human state. "Not possible."

"Juliet." Gregor stepped forward and rubbed his head.

Everyone had confusion plastered on their faces, and I couldn't blame them. How was any of this possible? And why hadn't he done this before? If a mental virtual meeting was so easy, he should have saved us a lot of time by doing this before.

"I needed your strength and theirs." Marcel turned towards the witches and William.

"Batteries?" Kirtus said.

"As well as all the minds here tonight." Marcel glanced around the arena. All the shadows of the people present were visible, strands of green smoke coming off each of them and swirling around us on the rink.

"You're using these people." Juliet waved her hand. "How? You'll kill them." She growled; she wasn't able to transform either.

"They will be unharmed and unaware." He glared at her and she backed down. "You have all been so foolish, so childish. She has given you a child with her sight, and you question him. He has shown you the way forward, and you fight him. You fight each other. He has a gift not seen since my time, and yet you treat him like a school boy who doesn't comprehend what he doesn't know yet. The royal court must come to pass. Kirtus is the king, the heir of the queen; your own people have proven this and yet you still fight and bicker. Enough. You will not keep me from rejoining my love and my rest."

"So that's what this is about," William said. "She cursed you."

"No, not cursed, never cursed. Enchanted. I have to fix what we destroyed so long ago. We were wrong and now, finally, I can right the wrong and rejoin her."

"The queen," I said.

Marcel laughed. "No, little one, but you understand who I speak of. You've seen her and have witnessed her love for me."

My cheeks warmed at the memory.

"What about us, the Council of Light?" Sybil asked, taking a step forward, a sneer still encrusted on her face. "The traitor?"

"You petty woman. Always looking to blame others for your shortcomings. You wanted all the power and yet you removed your strongest ally." He glanced at the ceiling and shook his head. "The two of you work so well together, and yet, you fight like..." He laughed. "I suppose some would call you sisters, and I believe that fits."

"Who is the traitor?" Gregor asked.

"I cannot say."

"But you know," William said. "How can you claim to be neutral when you still allow this strife to continue?"

"As you are aware, Healer, some truths must be learned on your own. You understand this better than most, and for that I'm sorry."

"He's right." Patty met the gaze of the others. "If he told us, would any of you believe him?"

"Why wouldn't they?" I said, but mine was the only voice speaking.

Victor chuckled. "So innocent and honest." He rested a hand on my shoulder. "Marcel is correct about one thing; we have misjudged you more than we should." He glanced to the others. "We would need the proof; these aren't like the old days."

Juliet, Gregor, Kirtus, and Sybil all agreed.

"Which is why nothing more can be learned of that matter now." Marcel raised his hands to the ceiling. "You nine are aware of what you must do. You now realize who your leader is. If you do not restore what has been so long missing..." Whiffs of black and red smoke filled the space around us. "This is your future."

The arena melted away, and in its place stood a burned-out shell of a building. Skeletons and bodies littered our surroundings. We all rose from the rubble. The higher we floated, the more of the location came into view. The sickly sweet scent of decay tickled my nose. Outside the hockey arena more death and destruction. Buildings on fire, cars tossed like toys, no one alive, only bodies of the dead. Bodies of humans, witches, and Immortals. All part of the future.

"Chris, is this what you saw?" Juliet's voice trembled.

I nodded.

"How far?" Sybil asked.

"Does distance matter?" Victor asked.

"All this death," Deb gasped.

"God in heaven." Kirtus had tears in his eyes.

We all turned toward the north in the direction of San Francisco. A bright flash blinded everything around us. There should have been pain when I stared at the blast, but nothing, the shape that of nightmares. No movie or even historical images showed the horror I witnessed justice. A mushroom, they say; a blast of heat and nothing, they claim; but the explosion was so much more—fear, terror, death, silence, all wrapped in a bright light.

"We caused this," someone said.

The flash of light grew brighter, blocking out more of the destruction around us. The air grew hot and silent. The luminosity filled more of my vision. I closed my eyes. I had no choice; the light blinded me. When my eyes opened, I materialized in the arena. We were all back. Cheers forced me off my feet.

"Where'd he go?" Amanda questioned.

A buzzer echoed and the announcer called the end of the first period.

"What the hell?" Kirtus grasped for the rail in front of him. His free hand made his way to the bridge of his nose. "Oh, my head."

"What?" Amanda's gaze bounced from each of us.

"A group vision." William shook his head gently. "I think we need to go and talk to the others."

"Who?" Amanda's voice grew louder. "Can someone please tell me what the hell is going on?"

"In the car." I took her arm. The others were massaging their temples, not that I had gotten used to the pain, but the vision was new for all of them, especially Kirtus, who Patty helped walk straight. The prophecy might not have been a battle, but this shared vision acted as something none of them would forget. At least that was my hope.

Chapter Twenty-Seven

The drive to Juliet's was a mass of phone calls and no conversation. Everyone had their cell phones out, and I played the driver, since no one called me, and I had no one to call. Within moments of the vision, everyone's phones blew up with calls. They had all been there, and now events were all laid out in front of them. If they were going to deny the vision or fight for a lost cause, it would be all our deaths and I doubted anyone wanted that. None of their egos were that large, or so I prayed.

We were sitting in the living room of Juliet's home like so many other times before except this time I wasn't the prop as usual. Everyone questioned me and rubbed their heads to massage away the pain of the shared vision. A bottle of red sat next to me with a crystal glass. Bottles of red were on hand for each of the Immortals present should they need it, and wine and soda bottles were present for the humans. It had been about an hour since the mass vision, once Gregor arrived the last person to pull in was Sybil. Amanda wheeled in a monitor with speakers, the monitor filled with Sybil's whiter than normal face. The dark circles under her eyes were something I hadn't ever seen before. Everyone but her was a local, so this the only way to pull her in to the conversation.

"I had no idea." Sybil played with her monitor as the audio clicked on. "I'm sorry." She focused on me. "I was asleep and yet... How do you deal with the pain?"

"You get used to the pain and headaches," I said.

"Can you ever forgive my arrogance?"

"There is nothing to forgive."

"Thank you." Sybil glanced at the others. "I'm sorry for all of this." She rubbed the side of her head.

"Marcel is always about the drama, but he wasn't a Seer or a Psychic. So how?" Juliet glanced my way. With a shaky hand she sipped her glass of red.

"His power has to be an enchantment from his wife," I said. "I don't fully understand how her power works, but she's strong, like he mentioned, and given how long she had lived and all her knowledge, it's possible she passed on some of her abilities to him."

"I'm not questioning given what we witnessed, but can you do that? Is what happened possible?" Gregor asked as he nursed his drink like a man suffering from a hangover.

"With training." Patty massaged the bridge of her nose. "That ability would be similar to how Deb can enhance my powers, but the bond would have to be strong."

"Like that of a family member or a spouse." Victor squeezed his eyes shut for a moment before opening them. "So, she was the witch from the royal council and Marcel's wife."

I agreed.

"All their power to bring back the royal court. And this will stop what is to come. I can't believe not having a royal court would lead to a nuclear exchange," Kirtus said. "From the direction of the blast, the hit had to be San Francisco."

"And we still have no idea if the attack only affected San Jose and the Bay Area," Gregor massaged his temples. "But an attack on a major US city, we can be assured something like that won't lead anywhere good."

"What we witnessed happened all over," Patty confirmed. "I had the feeling in my gut this moment one of the last..." She glanced around the room the glass of water in her hands quivering. "For us all." She sipped the water.

"Which is what Chris has been saying all along," Amanda huffed.

"But now we can stop the attack," I said. "We all have to work together."

"I would have to agree." Juliet massaged the bridge of her nose.

"I shouldn't be curious, but we never did get to see a time frame," Victor added. "Is the nuclear attack a day from now, a week, a year, ten years? How will we know our changes worked?"

"Does it really matter?" I faced Victor. "The vision is more about us working together and stopping all the pettiness. If we don't, we're all dead regardless unless Immortals are immune to nuclear blasts, fallout, and radiation."

The room hung in a dreary quiet reflective of my mood, if not the others.

After several eyes meeting one another, William spoke. "Who has the information on the prior royal court? Marcel's suggestion to reinstate the council is what we are going to do. There can't be any question now."

"Yes," Kirtus said. "That is what I would like... We need to come together, and I can't do it without you. All of you."

"Clearly, we have to put aside all our personal feelings." Sybil's voice sounded more tired than anything, but I'm sure a hint of snark reared its ugly head...still.

"So, you are now supporting the plan?" Juliet asked, a small level of venom in her tone.

"I don't think there is much choice or doubt as to what needs to happen." Gregor rolled his head around his neck, releasing several pops. "Addressing this event will be the first point of order after a new head of the Council of Light is elected."

"And given both our support, the change will pass," Sybil added.

"What about the traitor?" Deb asked.

"I've contacted Gabe." Amanda fussed with her hair. "He's going to do some research for us, especially now since we're all playing nice."

"Good." Kirtus stood up. "Look, here's the thing. What we all saw is beyond terrifying, and I realize what is being asked of me, but I can't do this alone, and Marcel confirmed as much." He cleared his throat. "This is what I would like to propose. The Light already has their council of nine. I would like to have the Dark do the same, nine members. A total of eighteen members on the council. I suggest an advisor position from the witches, elected however they see fit, and an advisor position for the Seer. Also, I want to bring in the Lycan as suggested by Marcel."

"Offer them an advisory position as well?" Juliet asked.

"You can't be serious." Victor's voice raised louder than it had been all night.

"Do we have a choice?" Gregor asked. "I'm not thrilled with the idea either, but..."

"Kirtus, what you ask..." Victor sighed.

"Is a lot." Kirtus nodded his head in understanding, keeping his tone solid and resolved. "I get it. I was there, but I think part of what we witnessed tonight might be a warning. If humans find out about us and about the Lycan, how long do you think before fear and panic causes someone to push a button? We've all been apart or witness to some of the mad men and women in power."

Silence from everyone.

"Yes," Kirtus continued. "If we do not interfere with the Lycan and if they agree to our legacy of secrecy, the vision won't come to pass." He glanced at me.

I nodded. I couldn't be 100 percent certain, but everything in me told me his assessment was correct.

"That is a lot of 'buts.' And you are assuming we can find the moon children, Lycan, whatever." Gregor shook his head.

"I think I can help," Victor said. "I've been working on tracking them down. My intentions are not as altruistic, but if finding them will keep the peace..."

"Good," Kirtus said. "And thank you."

He bowed.

"Listen, this is all new territory for all of us," I reminded everyone, "but if we are to bring the Lycan into our fray, we can't hunt them down; same with the witches. We are all going to need each other."

"At least for now." Sybil's expression dropped and her mood was dour.

Everyone focused on the monitor.

"This isn't going to be easy, and you are asking for a lot to be buried in the past." Sybil motioned off screen. "We still have no clue who betrayed us, and I can't promise I won't want them dead. And as much as I want to take Victor on his word, they cost him a great deal."

"Sybil's right," Juliet agreed. "There is a lot of hurt right now, even in this room. We all have a goal, and we are all scared. Working in a state a fear for the greater good never works out. The plan for a returned council with the advisory seat is a first step in the right direction, but the change is just that. A first step."

"So, we are doomed to fail." I crossed my arms.

"No, but we have to understand what we are up against," Victor said. "It is true I don't enjoy the idea of playing nice with the Lycan, but..." He sighed. "If I'm honest, they did me a favor, Betty, Sahin, and Pedro have been a problem for at least a hundred years now, and having them gone, as difficult as their deaths are, will be for the best." He nodded. "That said, I believe we can agree to a council of eighteen, with equal Light and Dark, as long as the rulers of those regions can continue business as usual."

"I don't want to micromanage, so we won't change what is already working." Kirtus faced the others.

"Good." Victor gestured his approval. "A less bitter pill is easier to swallow."

"I believe the covens would agree as well." Deb glanced over the Patty.

"As long as we are left alone," Patty added. "And working with each other would be a good change, giving us all a more united front in dealing with more dangerous matters."

Deb leaned back. A sigh of agreement offered her approval.

"Perhaps creating a Law of Peace that would oversee all groups, but allow each group their own sovereignty," William suggested.

"Like your people have?" Juliet tapped her chin.

He nodded.

"That is something to consider." Kirtus pulled out his phone and tapped away. "I don't want to be balls-deep in paperwork and telling people what to do; plus, I don't want people to have to ask my permission for every little thing."

"We are taking the best of what works and revamping what once was," I said. "Is this plan going to be something all groups can live with?" I ensured not to say 'like,' as I figured no one was going to 100 percent like this plan.

"Once you have the outline drafted, I will take the proposal to the other Dark leaders," Victor offered. "There will need to be negotiations and perhaps a few duels to get the playing field down to nine people that will work together, but despite what the Light think, we are reasonable."

"Sybil? Gregor?" Juliet asked.

Gregor rested a hand on his forehead after waving his agreement.

"I think once we clean our house, this is doable." The clicking of a keyboard came through as Sibyl spoke.

"And what about Chris?" Kirtus asked.

I glanced at him, my lips tight and my brow lowered. "What do you mean?" I asked.

"Given his visions in the past and what we've all experienced tonight, the Dark will fall in line; plus, I trust him," Victor said.

"As do I," Sybil said, surprising me.

"As an advisor, he will have great power, but that influence can't go unchecked," Juliet warned. "We will need to see to that."

"Agreed," Gregor said. "Chris, we have to make sure you don't *see* things that may only be advantageous to one group. If there is any question of impropriety..."

"How can I ensure that?" I glanced around the room, meeting as many eyes as possible. "I don't have control over what I see."

"Training." William touched the side of his face. "And the witches will have a seat on the council, so they can provide verification or to do as I've done and have Patty and Deb join you in your vision and see for themselves."

"We will try and find other Seers," Juliet offered.

"Chris is the only Immortal Seer in how long?" Amanda asked.

"True, but that doesn't mean there aren't others out there. We need to find them," Gregor said. "In the meantime, we do what we do now: check and verify every one of his visions. We don't act without doing the best vetting as possible, and we will need to figure out how to vote on actions."

"We are not going to hammer out all these questions tonight." Juliet sat forward. "Might I suggest you work with your groups and meet again in a week?"

"Reasonable," Sybil said.

"Okay." Kirtus placed his smartphone on his leg. "I guess we are adjourned for the week."

Once Sybil left the screen, everyone made their excuses and made for the door. Exhausted didn't describe my current state, and I had no idea the current time until I pulled out my phone. I display showed we were well after two in the morning. I invited Kirtus to spend the night not only so he wouldn't be alone, but because he looked spent. Everyone seemed drawn and tired. The vision had taken a lot out of the group, so sleep would do us all some good.

*

Over the next couple of days Gregor, Juliet, and Sybil had been working with Victor and Kirtus on what this new Immortal royal court would look like. Which left me to my own devices, not that I minded. After the initial conversation with everyone, the thing I discovered about vampire government was our politics were more complicated and had a longer history than my new mind comprehended. This gave me time at the foundation and time training with William, which I enjoyed more and more these days. It's silly to say this, but my time with him was nice, especially getting his guiding hand and his wisdom. Maybe someday I would be that wise.

"Tell me what you see." William's voice came through a speaker in my mental wall. Instead of pulling apart my internal barrier, William suggested I create a way for others to communicate with me that I controlled. At first, I figured a phone would be a good idea, but once it rang a couple of times I chose against it, so I changed to a speaker system that I could turn on when I wanted to communicate, or allow communication, and off when I didn't want to be bothered. For tonight's training I had the speaker on to talk with William.

"A moon, fields, and trees." I glanced around my surroundings— nothing I hadn't seen hundreds of times already.

"Focus on their scent."

I inhaled, pulling up the image of a wet dog, the musty, funky smell of water and fur. The aroma wasn't pleasant, but one I easily brought from memory. I rubbed my nose out of habit to try to nix the scent from my brain, but I kept focusing on the funk despite myself. I walked forward, the grass crushing under my feet, the moon's rays tenderly caressing my face. "Nothing."

Greeted by silence, I waved my hand in front of my face and kept walking and searching. I hoped to see if I was able to track down the Lycan. Victor mentioned he might have a way of finding them, but I didn't want to leave the Lycan's location up to him, especially since he wasn't fond of the idea of keeping them alive. Honestly, they should be punished for what they had done and what they had caused, but understanding they had been manipulated and created out of no fault of their own, it wasn't black and white anymore. "I'm still not sensing anything."

"We need to find them."

"I'm aware of that, but I'm not having any luck tracking them like this. I've barely seen them, and I only have a scent to work off. Plus, they may be out of the area."

"Fine. We'll try again later. You could use a break."

I shook my head, clearing my field of vision and pulling up my wall. I ran a hand over the familiar solid texture, noting my built-in speaker system. I walked over and toggled the switch to off. Happy with the wall and my surroundings, I opened my eyes.

The soft couch under my butt and supporting my back felt incredibly wonderful and familiar to me, a warmth and comfort like home to me now. Across from me William sat in his recliner.

"I'm sorry I can't find them."

He waved off my apology. "It's fine. We'll have to try again. Have you heard any more from Victor?"

I shook my head.

"They are busy, I'm sure."

I shifted on the cushions, allowing the softness of the couch to take all my weight. "I don't understand how Marcel was able to get everyone like that. I didn't even think a mass vision was possible. Especially over the distances."

"Given what we understand about your abilities, with training and time, you may be able to do something similar."

"But what he did..." I sighed.

"He had a lot of life energy to pull from. There are close to 20,000 people in a concentrated area, plus you, me, Patty, and Deb. We all acted like batteries."

"I'm glad everyone believed him."

William chuckled. "There are many things we can choose to ignore, especially when we don't want to look with our own eyes, but confronted as we all were in the moment, there was no choice..."

"But he could have pulled us all in at any time. Why did he wait?"

"I don't believe he could have done it any earlier. Everyone either already believed him or had doubts in what they believed. With the information Gabe presented at the council meeting. With your additional vision of a traitor in the Light working with Sahin. With what had happened with the Lycan. The only barrier he had to overcome was ego." He grinned. "And ego is the first thing to go when people are confronted with complete and total annihilation."

A shudder ran down my spine at the images he had showed us.

"What do you think will happen to him, now that everyone is working together to reunite the Immortals?"

"I would like to rest." Marcel moved from the hall that led to William's kitchen.

William and I jumped to our feet.

"How did you get into my home?" William shouted.

"Your back door was unlocked."

"And how did you get past my wards?"

"I'm not here to cause harm or hurt anyone. I need your help, and I didn't think you would agree if I asked." Marcel watched William, then turned in the direction of the front door.

A knock at the front door called out.

"Good, she's here," Marcel said with a peek to the front door.

"Who's here?" William demanded.

"My daughter." Marcel pointed. "Chris, do you mind letting her in? She's agitated at the moment, and we don't want anything to happen to William's door, or worse, his home."

I glanced over at William who nodded, and I rushed to the door to let Juliet in.

"Are you okay?" She hugged me.

"I'm fine, but..."

"I got a message you were in danger, and I realized you were here with William." Her head shifted and her body went ridged in my arms. "Marcel."

I stepped aside and closed the door as we moved to the living room where Marcel sat. He projected a sea of calm amongst all our anger and confusion.

"Marcel, what is this about?" Juliet demanded.

"My daughter, please sit." Marcel gestured to the chairs and sofa. "Everyone please sit and I'll explain."

William frowned but returned to his seat. Juliet and I sat next to each other as all eyes were on Marcel.

"It's been too long." Marcel leaned forward, focusing on Juliet. He dressed similarly to what he had worn at the arena—jeans, a simple purple polo shirt, and a tan jacket. "You are so amazing. Everything I wanted you to be. I couldn't be more pleased."

"Marcel." Juliet's voice cracked but there was still a warning in the use of his name.

He raised a hand. "Very well." He sighed. "I was created in 797 BCE. Which makes me the oldest living creature on this world, but long life is a mistake. I shouldn't be here." He frowned. "But I, but we, oh, Tina and I, we were so wrong, so stubborn. We thought we knew what was best. Sadly we didn't." He glanced at Juliet, then to me. "Phontina would have loved you both so much: you, Juliet, have her heart and her strength, and Chris, oh little one, you have her gifts and the ability to not let them rule you."

His expression shifted to that of an old man walking through memories that pulled at his heart, and for the moment I took joy in sharing this with him. When I glanced at William and Juliet, they both seemed to be willing to indulge Marcel.

"Tina, well, Phontina, had been a powerful witch like Deborah and Patricia. She was the liaison to the court. She held a position of power and influence. So naturally, neither the royal Immortal court or the witch council would allow us to be together. In their vast wisdom they believed we needed to stay apart. They were afraid of what might happen."

"But keeping you apart caused what they feared," I said. "The two of you..."

Marcel held up a hand to stop me. "We were so in love and so stupid. We plotted and planned against both the court and the witches. When we were finished the queen and her heir were dead and the court fractured between the Light and the Dark. The witches were equally as angry. Cities burned, so many people lost and lives destroyed, for what? So Tina and I might be together. A mistake, one the world did not recover from for hundreds of years. When the remaining members of the court found us, we fought in the council chamber. Tina...mortal, powerful, yes, but still mortal..." He took a deep breath. "When she wilted in my arms, I pledged to her I would avenge her. But she made me promise to fix this. She had a vision of you. Somehow, I still don't know how—"

"But...but what I saw...it's only a vision." I shook my head. "She spoke to me when you held her, but not really...right...that...I don't know, whatever...only had been my vision. Wasn't it?"

William rubbed his forehead. "She was able to reach out, pull Chris's consciousness through time and space. Amazing."

"I can't be sure, little one, but there is something. Someone had been there with us. Maybe you traveled to that point in time; maybe she pulled you there. But I promised her I wouldn't rest until I repaired what damage we had caused."

"She enchanted you with long life." William surveyed the ancient Immortal.

Marcel nodded.

"That's why you want to return the court." Juliet clicked her nails.

"I studied humans, witches, and vampires for years. I vanished from the world to wait. I kept track of the queen's sister and followed her heirs. I had to ensure there would be an Immortal heir someday."

"Kirtus," Juliet said.

He shook his head again. "Once in a position to ensure the royal line, I waited. Finally, she sent me a sign and I found you." He glanced at Juliet. "You were of my blood, so I called and you answered. I embraced you making you of my blood. You were my only Called. Once I had trained you and before I destroyed your beautiful heart, I left." He licked his lips. "But I had never gone far. I always watched. I realize I wasn't an easy father for you. And you blame me for Gius; I couldn't deny you that kind of love as much as his aging and death hurt you." He leaned closer to Juliet. "Please understand I did and still do love you."

Juliet took a shaky breath. "Yes, well, you are getting what you want. The council is to be reinstated. What more do you want from us? You've gotten all you want."

"No. That's why I'm here." His voice calm and level, Marcel glanced over at William. "Healer, you are the only one who can break the enchantment. You and your people have a connection to the earth that I nor the witches understand. But more than that I recognize the pain we share. Our shared pain gives you the ability to undo what Photina did so long ago." He got up from his chair, crossing over to William. "Will you free me?"

"No." I stood. This was unacceptable.

The weight of everyone's gaze made my heart sink.

"We need you." I glanced around, meeting their eyes as I spoke. "You don't get to come and drop this on us and leave. We need you. Kirtus needs you. Think of how much help you can provide the new royal court." I ran a hand over my face. "Look, you have an understanding of the court and all the history. Plus, you knew the queen. That would be helpful for Kirtus now. How are you even sure this will work? People and attitudes change."

"Because I have faith in you, Juliet, Kirtus, and all the others," Marcel responded. "You are all modern with modern ways of thinking and living. I would only cloud your future with my past."

"Juliet, you can't agree with this." My whole body trembled.

"Chris..." She shook her head. "If this is what Marcel believes would be in all our best interests, I have to honor his wishes. It's his life."

"No. His death isn't only about him. It's about all of us. He doesn't get to choose for everyone," I countered.

"Chris." William's voice drifted to my ears, comfortable and warm as the sofa I so enjoyed. "Remember what I said about ego?"

"What?"

"Emotion and our feelings are equally as bad. Are you thinking about what is best for everyone or for you? If this is Marcel's desire to be reunited with those from his past, why shouldn't we help him?"

"So, you'll help me, Healer?"

A long pause as William sat there, glancing over to a wall of photos. They were of him and his family. "What you ask and what I think I understand about our shared pain..." He sighed. "How are you so sure?"

"The past," Marcel said. "Tina drew from the power of the earth and from the council itself. I will need you to break the connection and use this." He pulled from his jacket a silver dagger.

All three of us moved closer to view the dagger as it glittered in the light of the room.

The hilt flashed, made of chrysocolla, sodalite, and amethyst gemstone in a repeated horizontal pattern with copper bands going around the stones. The blade had to be solid silver, from what I could see, with edges that appeared to be able to cut paper or flesh with ease. On the blade itself there were engraved images and patterns. They appeared Egyptian, if I had to guess.

"The blade of Ma'at." Juliet stepped back, her voice barely audible. "But the blade is a rumor, nothing more. An all-powerful dagger that can kill any Immortal." A visible shudder broke her typically solid stance.

"Wait. What?" Juliet's reaction sent wisps of fear into me. "You never told me about some badass dagger."

"The dagger is a legend from ancient Egypt, and you hardly take what the ancient Egyptians believed as truth. They worshiped cats after all."

Marcel shook his head. "My daughter, so judgey, you disappoint me." A slight frown pulled at his lips. "Regardless, the dagger can't kill you as the legends said. There is more to the knife's power. It's like the fine print of a contract."

"And I'm the fine print." William pursed his lips.

Marcel's gaze lowered.

"As I told you, you have a connection to the earth and to Ma'at. We share the pain of watching the love of our lives fall to death by our hand."

Marcel's comment caught my attention, and I glanced over at Marcel, but said nothing. Now was not the time for more questions.

"Your gifts or talents, whichever you prefer to call them, embody harmony of the universe, truth, and justice, everything Ma'at represents. You will be able to use this dagger on me, sever my connections to this world, and allow me to rest."

"What happens to the dagger?" William asked.

"Something for you and Juliet to decide. As I mentioned, you, as far as I'm aware, are the only one who can wield the dagger's power. When Photina died, I didn't want to live. I searched for the dagger, and once I found it, over the next hundred years I had thousands of humans, Immortals, and witches try this dagger on me to no effect. Once I understood I couldn't escape my task, I studied the dagger and the legends, all of it. I admit I experimented on Immortals as well. Some died, but the majority lived."

"So, what I'm hearing is this might not work," I said with a hint of relief.

"No, the dagger will work. The time has come for me to rest."

"And you're sure of this how?" Juliet asked.

"The hieroglyphics have appeared on the blade; they were not there two weeks ago." Marcel outstretched his hands, offering the blade. "Take the blade, Healer." Marcel encouraged the William.

William picked up the blade, and a bluish-purple glow emitted from the hieroglyphics. "Impossible."

"The blade recognizes the hand it belongs in." Marcel pointed to Juliet. "Please give her the blade."

William stood, then crossed over and handed the blade to a reluctant Juliet. Once the blade left William's hand, not only did the hieroglyphics stop glowing, but they faded.

"Amazing." Juliet turned the dagger over in her hands as the inscription continued to vanish.

"Juliet, now please hand the dagger to Chris."

I extended my hand, and she gently placed the knife in my hands. Once in my grip, the dagger had nothing etched into it any longer. "I don't feel anything."

"Nor should you." Marcel crossed over to me and took the dagger. The moment it left my hands, the wording returned. "This is the dagger of Ma'at, used to judge those who are bound for the afterlife. Neither of you are meant to die for a long time."

"But Ma'at used a feather to weigh the souls," Juliet said.

"Correct." Marcel handed the dagger to William. "Perhaps the dagger was for her protection, or ornamentation, or for any other number of reasons, none of which matter to me at the moment. All that matters now is my family is here, the means of my release is here, and shortly I'll be united with Tina."

"You want to do this here?" William asked.

"You want to do this now?" Juliet questioned.

"You've got to be kidding." I ran a hand through my hair.

"I assure you I'm not rushing into this. Please, I have done all I can. I've told you all you need, so now I can say goodbye properly," Marcel said.

I couldn't believe all that happened around me. Everything had been explained and handed down in such a short amount of time. Honestly, I don't think the others believed this. Still, here I stood in William's backyard, unsure what would happen when he stabbed Marcel in the heart with the dagger. Would his death be some nightmare image I would never be able to unsee, or would Marcel's demise be something different, something more peaceful?

Marcel stood with Juliet as they spoke in hushed voices. I couldn't imagine what he had to say to her. What does a father tell his daughter on his deathbed? I glanced out over the valley as the lights twinkled, reminding me even more of a jewelry box glittering open for all to see. I peeked over at William; he mumbled something, maybe chanted in his native language. He sought some kind of guidance or peace I wasn't sure would be found tonight for any of us.

I continued to watch. I caught the scent of wildflowers as a hand pressed down on my shoulder. "Why are you agreeing to this?"

"Because I had to do the same thing for my wife." William spoke barely over a whisper. "The brain cancer ate her alive. She begged me for weeks to help her end the suffering. I had to ask myself if letting her live was best for her or best for our children and me. The choice had not been easy... I loved her." William's voice weakened. "In the end I did what she asked."

"And your son and daughter?"

"They were angry and hurt, but they came around." William sighed. "They viewed all the pain and what that beast of a disease did to her. With the doctor's help, we released her, and I witnessed something that night I never imagined I would see again—well, not in this life: the woman I loved smiled one last time."

"So...it worked out?" I asked.

"No, but allowing her peace had been the right thing to do."

There were tears on my cheeks, as I remembered my mother and how sick she had been, both times. Seeing her that final time happy, young, and beautiful again, how could I disagree with him? I wiped my tears from my cheeks.

Marcel and Juliet crossed to us, each movement not lost on me. I noted the sway of Juliet's steps, how Marcel walked chest first, his arms slightly bent, a walk of determination. Juliet's hair shifted ever so slightly, sadness hovering all over her face.

"I don't suppose we can talk you out of this?" I wanted to give it one more shot, even though the answer wouldn't change and I understood I was being selfish.

Marcel shook his head. "I'm sorry for everything I put you through. If I had another way..."

"You would have done it. I understand." I didn't like all that had happened, but at this point, given all that occurred, there weren't other options. Sometimes this is how life worked out. Life isn't fair and no one is owed anything; you make your own life and do with that gift as you see fit, with only yourself to blame for the choices you make. Still, things happened for a reason. I worked my expression into as close to reassurance as possible; at least that was my hope.

"I'm not one for lengthy goodbyes." Marcel took my hand. "Be well and live a good life. There is nothing wrong with making mistakes so long as you learn from them."

Advice from an ancient Immortal, nice, but I had hoped for something more profound. "I wish we got to know each other better."

Marcel laughed and turned to William. "Well, Healer, are you ready?"

William turned to the patio table and picked up the dagger of Ma'at. The dagger appeared so small sheathed and only took a second or two until it was freed. As the dagger began to glow again, he licked his lips. "Given all I've seen this night, I suppose I'm as ready as I can be."

I wasn't sure what to except. I understood what needed to happen, but I wanted there to be some kind of ritual, some final words, something to bring this chapter to a close, but nothing. William walked over to Marcel. Marcel opened his shirt to reveal a hairy chest, an area where his heart beat, so William could pierce him.

"I release you." William spoke as if he were a young man again, but his facial expression a mix of different emotions, not all of them readable.

"Thank you," Marcel said as the dagger made its way into his chest.

William took a step back as we were all transfixed on what came next.

A gasp of air escaped from Marcel's mouth as his lips worked into a satisfied expression. Tendrils of blue and purples leisurely made their way out of the dagger and lazily moved over Marcel's body as if wrapping him up in a cocoon. All sound vanished and even the air around us grew still, as if time stopped, but the process took no more than a couple of seconds. Marcel was now a glow of purple and blue, and within a shimmer he burst into a million points of light and gradually faded away, the blast of color a beautiful peaceful moment only broken by the dagger as it hit the patio floor.

William kneeled and picked up the dagger. The weapon no longer glowed, and the markings had again vanished. He turned the dagger over in his hands a few times before resheathing it, offering it to Juliet. "You should keep this. I'm sure you have a safer spot for this weapon than anything I can come up with."

Juliet's hand shook as she wrapped her fingers around the dagger.

I wasn't sure what to say, so I put my arm around her shoulder and squeezed. When my father and mother had died, a pain ran out from my heart as if I had died with them. I empathized with the pain she must be feeling now. "I'm sorry."

She leaned into me more. "He's gone." Her body and her words shook. "Marcel returned to my life, and now he's gone again. There is never enough time to say all you want to say. I could have spent another five hundred years with him, and I doubt the pain would be any less. He had been my father and my family." Tears ran down her cheeks.

I took her into my arms and hugged her. We stood on William's patio hugging as all the lights below twinkled at us, and I wondered if some of those lights were Marcel.

Chapter Twenty-Eight

Lying in bed, I examined the ceiling, the sun's light barely creeping into the room. Kirtus's arm rested under my pillow and his free hand rested on my chest. Soft wheezes escaped from his mouth, and if I listened long enough, the rhythm of his heartbeat would lull me to sleep. The warmth of his body was a pleasant reminder of life and living. After Marcel's death, hollow emptiness surrounded me, and it wasn't only me. Juliet wasn't herself, but she hid her emotions better. Work still had to be done, and from the small conversation we had when I returned home, Marcel had told her where to find the pack of Lycan. He also informed her he had sent Gabe some additional information on who the traitors were, but she wouldn't say anything more. Honestly, I didn't want to press for details. Something in my gut bothered me about this traitor business, but I couldn't put my finger on just what.

I closed my eyes and sniffed at the aromas around me, breathing in the familiar sandalwood scent of Kirtus, noting nothing would have made me happier than to fall asleep.

Kirtus stirred and adjusted his hand on my chest, slowly sliding it down past my stomach, finding the waistband of my briefs and making his way to my dormant organ. The feel of his touch as he massaged me made my heart skip a beat. On my side his excitement stretched out poking me. His touch was electric, and a small gasp from his lips reminded me how much I wanted him and how long it had been. I needed to feel him. I wanted him to be inside me.

It only took moments for my body to respond, indicating my desire. He kissed my neck and moved to my mouth. Our tongues danced until he broke off the kiss.

He nibbled my ear, then whispered, "Are you sure?"

"Yes, please," I whispered.

Kirtus continued to kiss my ear and neck, making his way to my chest and down, pulling off my briefs with his teeth and some help from me. I gasped for air as he took me into the warmth of his mouth. Staying like this forever, this moment, alone with him, enjoying our bodies together, was all needed. There were times when we were frantic, aching for each other, needing haste, but times like this where we didn't need to rush, only enjoyment and sensuality required, made these moments together all the sweeter. These times tended to be my favorite.

He shifted his body, and I found my own prize waiting for me. I eagerly accepted his member and enjoyed every whiff of his sandalwood scent. We stayed like this for hours or maybe only a moment, but when we were together, I lost all sense of time. Once he removed me from his mouth and shifted a bit, indicating he would like to change what we were doing, I released him as his chuckle sent tingles through every part of my body.

As our bodies moved, the drawer next to the bed opened. A rustling sound bounced around the room making its way to my ears. The noise ended as quickly as it begun. With talented hands, Kirtus sheathed himself. Finished, his fingers massaged me as he applied a warming lubricant. Once prepared, he lovingly pressed himself against my opening. I relaxed and welcomed him into me.

Kirtus played my body like a well-tuned piano. I loved every motion and every shared breath. Being connected to him like this was as close as any two people could be. Again, I became lost in the moment. How long were we like this I didn't know, but our shared climax came with a thunder, and by the time we were wrapped up into each other's arms, the room was now entirely washed in morning light, even with the shades drawn. We had both fallen asleep, so when I stirred again, he startled.

"I didn't mean to wake you," I said.

"No. It's fine." He faced me, kissing my lips. "I need to get up and take a shower." His bottom lip folded down into a small pout. "There is a lot to do before the meeting tonight."

"Ugh." I scrunched my nose. "Don't remind me."

He rolled over, revealing his naked body, his chest covered in a light dusting of red hair with a trail leading to his now satiated penis. I loved seeing his body like this, seeing him in this state, recognizing we had shared with each other something special and for the moment we were both satisfied.

"What?" He checked his body.

"Nothing. I'm basking in the glow that is you."

"Right." He got out of bed and made his way to the bathroom.

I exhaled, watching him leave the bed, his perfect butt teasing me as he walked off. My body stirred and I wondered if I should go and join him in the shower.

*

"Did you see the text from Amanda?" I asked, finishing off my bowl of fruit and second glass of red.

"What?" Kirtus called from the kitchen.

"I guess something happened in Egypt." I swiped over to the news on my phone, but I didn't see anything, or nothing came up in my feed. "I'm not finding anything about it. Maybe I should call her."

"Leave that poor woman alone. We're going to see her soon enough, so you can ask her later."

Part of me wondered if the news had something to do with Marcel's passing. After Marcel's death, I found myself anxious to see Juliet again and find out if the two were related. Luckily, traffic on the weekend was nothing like during the week, so the drive to the foundation was easy. As I parked my car, I noted all the other vehicles present. I forced air into my lungs, trying to calm my nerves. I wasn't so much nervous for me, but for Kirtus. He had been working hard on his new vision for the Immortals. I hoped the meeting went as well as the initial meeting had.

Kirtus pulled on his suit jacket and fixed his solid purple tie. He closed the passenger car door and opened the back door, pulling out his laptop and everything he would need for the conference call. Thrilled nothing required my attention, I wasn't on the council, nor would I be. I served strictly as an advisor, and that position suited me just fine, especially since my services would only be needed when called upon or when I had a vision about some form of death or destruction.

"There're, my two favorite boys," Amanda greeted us as we entered the lobby. She gave each of us a hug.

"How's Juliet?" I asked as I returned the hug.

"She's putting up a good show, but this pain is going to take time," Amanda said. "But also, I think she's relieved."

I looked forward to spending some time with her once things settled down a bit, assuming that would ever be the case. "Why the text about Egypt?" I decided now was a good time to ask.

"Oh right." Amanda stopped at the stairs before heading up to the conference room. "The old council chamber is gone, destroyed in some kind of sink hole, the same day Marcel died."

"What?" Kirtus whistled.

Amanda rested her hands at her side. "And Taqi and Anashe are missing. It's a mess."

"Why wasn't I informed?" Kirtus huffed.

"Gregor didn't say." Amanda frowned. "I suppose they were waiting for news, or tonight to tell everyone." Amanda pulled up her phone. "I did text you earlier, but you didn't respond."

"I didn't think…" Kirtus shook his head, his lips pinching together. "Fuck." He sighed. "Look, in the future, if anything major happens, I need to be informed right away. I'll tell the others as well. We have to start working as one cohesive group." He massaged his temples. "I'm going to need a Keeper at some point to help me with all this. I can't rely on Amanda."

"I have a person in mind," I said.

"Who?" Amanda asked.

"My friend Cindy," I suggested. "She's amazing and I think she would be a great help."

"I liked her." Amanda grinned. "She's feisty."

A swell of pride rose from my toes all the way up to my mouth where I hoped my delight showed.

"But she's your friend. What about you?" Kirtus asked.

"Well, the way I understand it, technically I'm going to be under Juliet's charge for some time, and by the time I need a Keeper, Cindy might not be…um…available anymore." I didn't like the idea of outliving Cindy. I wasn't stupid, I understood that would be the case regardless, but seeing her and having her around in my life for a long time would be great. Plus I didn't really want to have her work for me like that. I would feel guilty, but working for Kirtus in Keeper capacity might work. Plus, he would be the king, so the job a big step up from working in a Reno nonprofit. "You don't have to decide now. It's an idea."

Kirtus took my hand.

"Shall we get going, so we can get you set up?" Amanda pointed up the stairs.

*

Like the foundation board meetings, this one started off no different, a lot of talking and complaining with a fair amount of grandstanding on all sides. Much of what they presented was information familiar to me and items we had talked about after our shared vision. For as many complaints as the group had, everyone managed to be receptive to the changes and pleased to learn their lives, territories, and business would be unchanged. What made this so painless, I believe, was all the infighting had occurred with the Light and all the killing had transpired between the Dark. The members of the former Council of Light regarded these changes as a way to minimize the influence and power the Dark would gain, and the Dark considered these changes as a way to have more control and influence in global matters. Plus, with the worry over true magic and the werewolves, which no one fully understood how best to proceed, gave the gathered a reason to work together, pushing less important matters aside.

This new united front made the most sense to everyone.

The questions I had running around my mind: How long would the united front last? If something went wrong, really wrong, would they blame Kirtus and break this new court? If either the dealings with the werewolves or the handling of true magic backfired, they might all blame him and accept none of the responsibility.

Heavy is the head that wears the crown.

"Now that is all the old business." Kirtus motioned. As the king, he ran the meeting and I was glad to see him at the front of the table. Being flanked by Victor, Masko, and Joaquín on one side while Gregor, Garrett, and Sybil were on the other only strengthened his position. He was surrounded by strong allies, which only fortified his standing. Others were here as well. An, Yoi, and Juliet (as a former council member and observer; plus since she had the most experience with the council and setting up this new system, Kirtus had requested her presence). Fernando and Rahim were on the video call, as were Taya and a few other members of the Dark.

Also missing were Taqi and Anashe, but they were represented by their senior lieutenants. I couldn't remember their names as there were so many names being tossed around I needed a score card to keep track of them.

"There are a couple of issues I want to bring to the full council." Kirtus cleared his throat, then tugged at the cuffs of his shirt, his fidgeting minimal, but I had no doubt the others noticed. "First, from this point forward I want to be kept apprised of all large situations affecting your territories or your groups. I appreciate there is a tendency to insulate yourselves or try and handle incidents on your own, but I'm here for you, and I want to help. In that vein, I understand Taqi and Anashe are missing and have been since Marcel's death."

Garrett frowned, Gregor's ears started to turn red, and Sybil lowered her head.

"In the future, I would expect my council to do more than text me this information." Kirtus's shoulders were ramrod straight, and he made eye contact with each member of his council.

"Apologies." Sybil bowed her acknowledgment.

"We should have—" Gregor's tone strained as a frown crossed his lips

"It's fine," Kirtus relaxed his shoulders. "We're all learning, and things like this are bound to happen from time to time." He waved off their apologies. "Let's try and have less of these things happen in the future."

"Well, you can count on all our support." Victor sat tall. "We won't make a silly mistake like that." The prideful expression on his face showed he enjoyed this more than he should.

"I'm glad you feel that way, Victor." Kirtus faced his former leader.

Victor shoulders were firm as he met Kirtus' gaze. "Anything for our...king."

"Excellent. I understand you have been in the process of taking ownership and remodeling Sahin's former club, the Night Stalker?"

"I have." Victor eyed him.

"I am requesting you sell me the building for $1000 so we can use the space for our new council chamber."

"What?" Victor's voice raised.

I had to bite the laugh that was going to break out of my mouth.

"As much as I appreciate Juliet allowing us to use her foundation, I think it's important for the council to have a neutral location, one built and designed for the running of our community, and considering the trouble caused under your watch, that location only seems reasonable." Kirtus examined him a moment. "Don't you agree?"

"I...well, of course...but $1000, the land is worth...well, much more."

"Consider the sale as part of the reparations you make to the crown and our community. This donation will also go to your annual dues you all will be paying the crown." Kirtus glanced over to Amanda and bowed his head slightly.

Amanda stood and effortlessly passed out a folder for each of the members to review. When she finished, she returned and typed on the laptop. "Everyone should have the documents."

"Thank you." Kirtus pointed to the papers. "Not to take up too much time on the matter, but instead of each of the council members being taxed, you will all pay annual dues to the crown. The amount will be the same across the board, and every two years we will vote on an increase. The funds will not line my pockets but go to running the council and providing funds for our community. The financials will be audited by an outside audit firm to be selected at a later date, and by the full council." Strong and sure, this must be how Kirtus spoke to his clients. "Also, for many of you these dues will provide you with tax shelters you desperately need."

No one commented as they studied the documents.

Kirtus glanced at Victor. "With your generous contribution to the council, I will have your construction company awarded with the contract for the remodel and improvements so you'll still make a profit, smaller, but still a profit."

Victor's lips were pinched together, but when he managed to speak a polished tone exited his mouth. "Thank you, Kirtus."

"Excellent. Now, Taqi and Anashe are missing, believed to be in the former chamber. Is that correct, Rahim?"

"Yes, that is what I understand, but..." His serious expression hadn't changed the entire time, and despite what had been happening during the meeting he continued to glance off screen.

"I would like to ask our Seer to search for them or find any trace of them." Kirtus gestured toward me. "Assuming you are willing to assist us?"

"Anything I can do to help," I said. "Do you want me to try now?"

"Are you able to have a vision on such short notice?" Juliet asked.

"Well, I can give it a shot." I wasn't 100 percent sure I would be able to contact them, but the king asked, and I couldn't refuse. "Please turn down the lights and I'll need complete quiet." There were a few mumbles as Amanda got up, closed the blinds, and clicked off the light.

I closed my eyes and focused on Taqi, trying to pull up everything I remembered about him, how he spoke with a perfect British accent, his less-than-friendly demeanor most of the time, but I tried to focus also on his strong beliefs and appreciation of tradition. For Anashe I focused on her beautiful rich dark-colored skin and the vibrant colors she would always wear. The one thing Taqi and Anashe both shared was their strong faith and firmly held beliefs in tradition. The last piece of information I concentrated on was the Council of Light chamber. The information was a lot to pull into my mind, but the images sluggishly fell together.

I continued to direct my thoughts to the picture I created, pulling in all the details I remembered. The more I concentrated, the clearer the representation became. Gradually blue and purple points of light joined the image, and as more of the points of light came into my vision, the less of a picture and more real the room became. Taqi and Anashe spoke. Taqi was animated, his hands gesturing left and right. Anashe nodded, a frown planted on her lips. I couldn't make out their conversation, but Taqi wasn't happy.

The longer they spoke, the more the blue and purple points of light turned into tendrils that poked into the cracks in walls, ceiling, and floor. They grew in strength and brightness. In a flash of color, the walls and ceiling crumbled. Taqi and Anashe tried to move or run, but with the flash of blue and purple the room collapsed around them not giving them time to escape. A thrust of bodies hurried to get under the table, to use it as a brace, but smoke blurred and covered my vision. Within a few seconds, the images were gone.

"They're trapped." I moved my head, trying to find them. "Alive, I think, but trapped. Still in the council chamber."

"What do you mean?" Kirtus asked.

"They found a space between the table and the wall. You'll find them there."

"How long ago?"

"Days. Hours. I can't be sure." I waved my hands in front of me to clear the smoke. A dark figure lay under the remains of the table. I believed the person to be Taqi. "I don't see Anashe, so maybe only Taqi, but they are there." I opened my eyes, and the room came into focus. "When Marcel died, his link with the council chamber broke and the building couldn't take the stress, or his energy destroyed the space. I'm not sure which, but the power held him here. The energy the same blue and purples we observed when he...when he died." I took a deep breath through my nose and exhaled it from my mouth.

"You searched the area?" Garrett asked, Taqi's stand-in, his Australian accent not as fun or as friendly as usual.

"We have been trying," Taqi's proxy said. "But the area is old and hard to get to."

Kirtus faced the monitor. "Rahim, contact Gypsy, and ask for assistance. I can contact him as well and make the request if needed. Costs can be addressed through the council emergency fund..." He peered around the room. "Part of your new dues in action."

"Thank you. We'll have our people find them and coordinate with Gypsy," Taqi's female stand-in responded. "Thank you, Seer." She offered a stiff bow of her head.

"Don't thank me yet," I replied. "I hope they are both alive, but honestly I can't be sure."

"Understood." Kirtus rested his clasped hands on the table. "Thank you, Chris."

I massaged my temples and ensured my mental wall remained up. Holding these defenses got so much easier to keep in place, especially when I used my seeing ability.

Chapter Twenty-Nine

The water danced around the edges of the pool as I sat on the patio enjoying the morning light. I glanced at my phone, sitting beside me as lifeless as the empty seat next to me.

Four weeks had passed since the council meeting, and I hardly spent any time with Kirtus. The few times when we did manage to meet up, he was distant and distracted, which had me worried. He said he was fine, but I had that tickle in my mind telling me otherwise.

I peeked at the phone, hoping maybe thinking about him would cause him to text me.

Nothing.

The last time we talked he explained he was busy with the council members and getting the court working. I had hoped building a new court would be something we might work on together, but my offers of help were brushed off. I will admit I wanted to use my gifts to see if I might spy anything, but doing that was a slippery slope that would be wrong and I didn't want to spy on him. I cared for him and I didn't want to mess things up. Even though he was being a jerk right now.

Ugh.

"Decided to enjoy the patio." Juliet's voice rang out from behind me. I hadn't smelled or sensed her arrival first. I must have been too focused on the pool or my thoughts. Or the blank screen of the phone.

I glanced over my shoulder, catching a whiff of her vanilla and roses. "Good morning." I forced the worry from my shoulders and neck, trying to show a posture or relaxed calm. "It had been too long since I'd enjoyed the view, so I figured why not."

"Why not indeed?" She strolled over. Her cream-colored slacks made her ruby top that much brighter in the morning light. "Mind if I join you?" She put down a freshly opened bottle of red and two glasses.

I stood and pointed to a chair. "You don't need to ask; this is your home, after all."

"Still, it's the polite thing to do." She sat.

I returned to my seat. "How are you?"

She poured us both a glass, putting the bottle on the table. She picked up her glass, took a sip, before placing it on the table. "It's been a month since Marcel's true death, and before that he had been dead to me for 850 years." A soft sigh escaped her mouth. "You would think I wouldn't be bothered, but..."

A hint of sadness and sorrow floated over me, belonging to Juliet. Realizing she wasn't denying her emotions helped me relax, as odd as that may be. "I doubt time matters. With both my father and mother, I assumed I had long gotten over them, but with what happened at New Year's, all those feelings were right back, knocking on the door." I tapped my temple. "My parents' death is still hard for me to work my way through. The loss is...painful."

"At least this time, I got to say goodbye and be there for him at the end." She glanced up at the sky. "I couldn't have really asked for more."

I peered out over the pool deeper into the backyard. "I'm not sure what you believe, but I don't think they leave us. I think they are there, right at the tree line watching over us. Out of our sight, but still there."

Juliet nodded, following my gaze.

"Their presence still there, right out of sight, wouldn't surprise me." She brushed invisible lint from her blouse. "As I mentioned when we first met, this is a big world and there is a lot we don't understand." She sipped her drink again. "And it's nice to be surprised especially at my age."

I chuckled. "I'm glad I'm not the only one who's astonished by our world." I sighed again. "Like with that dagger. I mean holy cow. That's crazy."

Juliet flicked her dark blonde hair over her shoulder. "I've spoken with Kirtus, none of the others of course, but it's important and he should be informed. The dagger will be stored in a secure vault at the new council chamber. He is going to work with Gabe to also have a subbasement for archives and research. I will donate many of my tomes, as well as Marcel's."

"Really?"

"Well, not everything, and I'm going to have what I donate digitized so I have my records." She flattened the creases of her ruby blouse. "Victor, Sybil, Garret, and all the council members are doing the same. Even Luka and Elena."

"Who?"

"Two of the Dark who will be on the royal council. I suppose." She tapped her chin. "I've had dealings with them in the past. They are reasonable, kind of like Victor, but Luka and Victor don't get along, so that will be interesting to witness." She chuckled.

"A lot is changing."

"Indeed. Anyway, we've asked several older covens to consider donating their records as well. The facility will be open to all for study. A historical library is part of what Kirtus's dues will pay for." She laughed. "Another brilliant idea of his. Leave it to a financial consultant to figure out a way to get Immortal council members to part with money."

"I'm glad everything worked out." I picked up my glass of red, took a sip, and placed it on the table, doubtlessly harder than needed but with a quick glance at my phone. I was still perturbed by him.

"Oh, he's brilliant and everyone likes him. Showing his dominance at the meeting had been a smart move on his part." She sipped her drink. "He'll need to do more of that at the start, so he's not taken advantage of. I worried he might get walked all over, but I don't see that happening."

"Speaking of being walked over." I followed her sip of red with my own, picking up the hints of something tart and tangy. "What about your spot on the council? Are you getting your rightful seat returned?"

"Perhaps," she answered with surprising honesty. "I gave Kirtus the information Marcel gave me, about the wolves and what he found out about Sahin. They were going to investigate and let me know at the council meeting next week, but I haven't heard anything yet." She shifted in her chair. "Honestly, I'm enjoying only having to deal with the foundation and, of course, the West Coast territory; the change is a nice break. Maybe I'll pen a novel."

"You're not worried?"

She rested her hands on the table. "Like I said, I'm enjoying my break."

I didn't want to believe what she said, but from everything I sensed off her she wasn't covering anything up or trying to protect me from some awful truth. "You don't strike me as the type of woman who enjoys too much free time." I eyed her.

Juliet laughed and patted my hand. "I never said I wasn't busy. After all, I have a son to watch out for."

*

I loved when Juliet drove the Mustang. It was so much fun, especially with the top down, the weather perfect under a bright starry night. I had on a light jacket to protect me from the rushing wind as we drove. A shame the drive to downtown Los Altos wasn't longer, but the foundation wasn't far from the house and with the Night Stalker/royal council chamber well under construction a trip there would have been pointless. Considering all the work going on at the construction site, I wasn't sure how long it would take for the building to be renovated and reopened.

From the approved plans the building would be impressive, underground parking and two levels of sub basements both for research and archives. On the main two levels would be the club, with a private VIP section for Immortals on the third floor. There would be an outdoor patio accessible from both the second and third floor as well. The top three floors above the club would be for the royal council and offices for Kirtus and his advisors. I couldn't wait to see the space when complete, and, I'll admit, I was curious to see if I got an office since technically, I counted as an advisor to the crown.

We found parking easily enough; however, all the other vehicles here surprised me.

"Are we late?" I zipped up my jacket.

Amanda checked her phone.

"No, Kirtus asked the others to arrive early, along with the council. They had business to take care of, and since today is a Saturday, I didn't see the harm." Juliet pulled off the scarf from a top her head, fussing with her hair. Even in jeans, boots, and a deep royal-blue blouse, she radiated beauty.

I checked my reflection in the car window. Instead of my typical business attire, I wore dark jeans and a lavender striped dress shirt with my tan jacket. Our casual wear was kind of odd, seeing as this would be the first full court meeting and we weren't dressed up.

"You look like you miss your suit," Amanda teased.

"Hardly...well, maybe... You know how you get used to things." I adjusted my jacket sleeve. "I'm surprised we're all dressed so casually."

"I don't mind; it's nice to be out of my skirt and in jeans and sweater." Amanda dusted off her dark blue jeans and tugged at the base of her lilac sweater.

"Shall we head in?" Juliet pointed to the office.

"It's so strange you weren't informed to what's happening and you aren't in charge." I glanced to Juliet.

"Part of not being on the council—"

"For now," Amanda said with a firm nod of her head.

I wondered if she knew something I didn't.

We made our way into the office and were greeted by Terrie, Ben, and Max. I was only surprised to see Ben present, as he was human, but Amanda accompanied us, so I guess I shouldn't have been surprised.

"They have you on guard duty, I see." Juliet greeted each of them.

"First meeting and all." Terrie focused straight ahead. She didn't seem like her normal self. She wasn't always the chattiest, but tonight with her stiff shoulders and neutral expression, she appeared cautious.

"Nice to see you." Max's shoulders were stiff and each word he uttered harsher than what I expected from him. "I'm sorry about all that..."

"Don't even think of it." Juliet remained pleasant as always. "I'm happy I can still be of help to the crown."

Max nodded.

"Hiya, Chris. Amanda." Ben gave each of us a quick hug. He never changed. His hands found my rump pretty fast. "I think they are waiting." He pointed. "I doubt I need to show you the way."

"We can manage." Amanda beamed good-naturedly. Ben had found her bottom as well.

"See you all later." I waved. Instead of climbing the stairs to the second floor and the board room, we made our way to the rear of the office, past the cubicles and the staff offices to the large meeting room where we held staff meetings and other large gatherings. I appreciated the open space because it didn't make the office feel so claustrophobic.

Standing at the double doors were Masko, dressed in form-fitting jeans and a duster jacket, and Joaquín, in loose-fit jeans and a plain black T-shirt. Neither were smiling.

"Wow!" Amanda said. "The big guns tonight."

"You can never be too careful." Joaquín greeted us, and I would have sworn he flexed his muscles to emphasize his point.

A tight pull on my neck called my attention, to what I wasn't sure, I glanced around the space but nothing appeared out of the ordinary. Still a cold shudder ran down my spine.

Masko knocked on the door and slipped into the room.

So odd not being granted access to spaces, on any other day, I would be able to walk into without a second thought, and I didn't enjoy this intrusion. Even though Juliet had a polite appearance, the slight clicking of her nails signaled she wasn't as pleased as she made out to be. And I frowned a bit at the slight mix of scents from the conference room. Usually, the house and foundation were awash in Juliet's scent of vanilla and roses, but not tonight.

Masko opened the door. "Sorry, I had to make sure they were ready for you." The frown on his lips was echoed in his eyes, and his tone held as flat as his expression. Not so much as a grin from him and he was the one I considered the most friendly.

"Of course." Juliet beamed brightly.

Masko held the door open, and we walked in without another word.

I always had unreasonable expectations when it came to events like this. In my mind the room appeared decorated in tapestries and shields with torches surrounding the perimeter. A makeshift throne, something theatrical with a high back on a stage, kind of like what Victor had had at his party at the Fairmont. Disappointedly, the space reflected our large conference room with all the tables placed in such a way to create a U-shape with the open end facing the wall and the projection screen lowered for a presentation. I also noted a laptop ready as well. The rear window had all the blinds drawn, so only the lights in the room illuminated the space.

Another shudder of discomfort scurried down my back.

There were nineteen people present, with Kirtus at the head of the table facing the projection wall. All the council members were seated around the table in no particular order, as far as I knew. Each council member had a name plaque in front of them, which helped me, and others, so we didn't have to remember names. I scanned the room for members I recognized. I found An, Yoi, Garret, Fernando, Gregor, Sybil, Rahim, Taqi, Taya, and Victor. There were a lot of new faces too. I found Luka to be huge, a bear of a man. He donned a dark suit, unlike everyone else sporting casualwear. He had attractive puffy lips, but I doubted he would appreciate the comment. I also found Elena, a small woman with blonde hair and blue eyes, pretty, and again not what I would expect to see from the Dark. Gypsy with his dark hair and dark eyes to match was present, and despite my feeling of unease, the idea of his nickname gave me a moment of levity.

"Juliet," Kirtus greeted, pulling me from my scan of the room. "Thank you for allowing us to use your meeting space again."

"You are always welcome," Juliet responded. "But I can't say I approve of the new carpet." Her eyes moved to the floor.

I glanced down; under my feet, the floor had been lined with plastic as well as the lower parts of the walls.

What the fuck!

"Yes, well..." Kirtus glanced my way.

"Chris. Amanda." He offered each of us a slight bow.

"Kirtus?" I raised an eyebrow, glancing at the floor. My head ached, and the beads of sweat on my forehead ran down my cheeks.

"Thank you for coming," Kirtus said. "This has been a trying time, with the investigation and the loss of the original council chamber in Egypt." He still hadn't offered an explanation or offered us a place to sit, which made my stomach drop and my heart start to pound harder.

I peeked around at all the council members. The only ones to meet my eyes were Garret and Sybil, and neither were pleased.

"I want to thank Chris," Kirtus continued. "If not for you, we might not have found Taqi. Sadly, Anashe wasn't as lucky."

I frowned; it would have been nice to know Taqi had survived. When I hadn't heard anything, I had assumed the rescuers were too late and, annoyingly, Kirtus refused to speak about council business. I battled against a scowl and struggled to keep my voice polite. "I'm glad to help."

Kirtus tapped the table in front of him. "Now, to the matter at hand." He pointed to the door. "Amanda, would you be so kind as to let Masko and Joaquín know we are ready for Gabe?"

Amanda offered a confused nod. Clearly she wasn't sure what was going on either. Everyone acted insane. My mind jumped to a dark place. Were they planning on killing someone? Killing us?

I struggled to keep myself under control.

"Gabe?" Juliet asked, and a push of calm floated toward me.

God, I hate that.

I calmed down some, but I still internally freaked the hell out.

"He finished his investigation," Kirtus announced.

"If I may, Your Majesty," Garret said. "I don't see the point. The Council of Light has been absorbed into your royal court. Can't we move on? What is done is done."

"I must say I agree." Taqi peeked around the room as if plotting an escape route. "Haven't we been through enough?"

"I would like to restate my protest to this entire proceeding." Gregor sat taller his words gruff and annoyed. "Juliet and Chris—"

"We've been through this in executive session," Kirtus interrupted. "I've heard your arguments...all of them." He glanced around the room, meeting some of the Light member's eyes and some of the Dark member's eyes. "Gabe has traveled here from Utah. I would like to hear his final report, and I think it's only fair all parties involved hear what, if anything new, he has to share."

Juliet shifted on her feet, and in the back of my mind something caused a tug of worry, but I wasn't sure who the pang came from. The worry may have been mine or any one of the council members. I mentally tried to focus on that worry, but there were too many minds, too much turbulence. My inability to figure out the near future annoyed me, and my desire to not be here anymore grew stronger. I peeked over at Juliet.

Nothing.

The doors opened and Gabe rolled in. He wore a pair of Dockers and button-down light blue shirt.

"Thank you, Amanda," Kirtus said. "If you don't mind, would you guard the doors and ask Masko and Joaquín to join us?" His face was polite, but darkness hid behind his green and gray eyes. "Amanda," he added. "Under no circumstances are you to open those doors again until instructed by me to do so. Am I clear?"

Amanda glanced at Juliet.

Juliet dipped her head, signaling Amanda it would be okay.

"I...Juliet..." Her lips pinched together.

"Do as the king instructs." Juliet motioned to the door.

"Yes, Kirtus, I mean Your Highness." The tone dripped with venom as daggers shot from her eyes.

What the holy hell is going on? I wanted to pull both Juliet and Kirtus to the side. Call a time out. Everything happening was complete madness, but with everyone here I doubted that would get anywhere and I wanted to trust Kirtus. I wanted to trust the people on the council, but honestly the beating of my heart and the sweat dripping down my spine told me otherwise.

Juliet spared a glance at me with a shake of her head, signaling me to not react.

I stood in place as bile rose from my stomach and burned my throat.

Amanda knocked on the door. "Do you mind?" Her tone remained polite, but strained.

Both doors opened and the two men walked in as Amanda closed the double doors behind her. She glanced both at Juliet and me one more time before the doors sealed, like she closed our tomb.

"Thank you for joining us, Gabe. I appreciate your time and your commitment." Kirtus stood and gestured Gabe to come fourth.

"It's my pleasure, even in these trying times." Gabe wheeled over to the center of the *U* and inserted a flash drive into the laptop. "It'll take a minute." He tapped away on the system.

"As you're all aware, Gabe has investigated many things for me since March," Kirtus began, his tone cold but professional.

Another tug of fear and panic pulled at my mind.

"With all that happened, I never felt right about Juliet's ousting from the Council of Light," Kirtus continued. "What happened with Sahin, the dealing with Marcel, and let's not forget the werewolves." He licked his lips. "And we still have the issue of true magic. So many events in such a short amount of time, sadly most of these occurrences have to do with Juliet and her Called, Chris."

I browsed the plastic cover over the carpeted floors. Another shudder ran down my spine. Clearly, we were in some kind of trouble. But we didn't do anything. I scanned the room, and my heart pounded more like a drum in a band than something to pump blood through my body. Hearing Kirtus's voice at all amazed me.

"I never did trust her." Taya frowned. "It wouldn't surprise me one bit that she was behind what happened to Sahin and the others and for this mess with true magic."

"Taya, please." Victor glared in her direction.

"Taya may be correct," Luka said, his Russian accent heavy. "Just because you had a special relationship with her doesn't mean we are all as fond of her."

"Luka, now is not the time," Elena chided, unfazed by his size.

"Please, can we get through this?" a darker Asian-appearing man asked. He looked so thin and small compared to Victor and Luka. He didn't look Chinese, or Japanese. Honestly, I wasn't sure about his nationality, but if we were about to die, I didn't think his race mattered.

"Yes. Please." Kirtus speared a polite grin his way. "Thank you, Ponleak."

On the screen appeared a list of files. "I'm ready," Gabe announced and pointed a device at the screen.

Kirtus bowed.

"These are the audio and video files I pulled from the security cameras at Sahin's club and his home," Gabe began. "Also, here are the phone records from Sahin's cell phone. I've also pulled phone records from all the former Council of Light members and all the Dark Leaders on the court's council."

"You did what?" Rahim pulled away from the table.

"This is a clear overstep." Yoi leaned forward and glanced over at Kirtus.

"I assume you had the king's authority?" Victor asked, his voice calm and too nonchalant for my liking.

"I had his full authorization," Gabe continued. "Now, if you all care to—"

Gabe was about to click on the first file when a chair slammed against the wall and one of the tables flipped over, hitting the floor with a thud, shaking my soul. Not to be undone, a sudden bang echoed through the space as something hit the wall. Different yelps and roars boomed through the conference room as everyone appeared taken by surprise. Even Juliet stepped closer to me, taking a more protective stance. Held against the wall by Joaquín was Taqi. Several of the other members were up on their feet watching the interaction. Elena offered a hand to Luka to help him up as he had landed on the floor next to where Taqi had been sitting. Yoi and An were assisting Gypsy and a couple of the other members who were pushed out the way, but everyone gave Joaquín and Taqi a wide berth.

My eyes and head pounded as the adrenaline coursed through my veins. Shifting from left to right foot, I found my body hard to keep still, but I wasn't going to move in case something else happened.

"Where are you going, Taqi?" Kirtus asked, his tone deathly calm. "Aren't you interested in learning who betrayed the council?" His gaze narrowed in on him. "Your former council." He stepped closer to the man who had transformed into his vampire form. "Or is that old news to you?"

"What is the meaning of all this?" Ponleak demanded.

"Highly irregular," Fernando stated, moving back so he would be able to act if need be.

"Fuck you! All of you," Taqi growled, struggling under Joaquín's hand. "You're going to be ruled by the likes of him, this Dark piece of shit. Or her." He spat in Juliet's direction. "This isn't a royal court; this is nothing. You know nothing about a royal council or how things should be run. None of you deserve the positions you're in! None of you have—"

"After reviewing—" Kirtus stared, his booming voice drowning out Taqi's blather. "—the files and seeing what you were up to... Working with the werewolves, working with Sahin to overthrow Juliet, putting yourself into power. You even planned to hunt down the Lycan and slaughter them once you were in charge and to cancel all treaties with the witches." He shook his head. "The one thing I'm surprised you weren't planning was to round up all the humans and put them into farms for their blood. But I guess you're not even that stupid." His frown deepened. "And all this for what? To bring back a world that no longer existed? A world *you* weren't even around for. A world you only understand through stories and your own rose-colored study. Why are you so afraid of change?"

Taqi tried to speak, but Joaquín's squeeze kept his words from forming.

"After tonight's meeting I will ensure the Lycan alpha and the witches are aware of what you were planning." Kirtus shook his head. "Victor, I hope this will help to satiate your lust for vengeance on the Lycan?" He peeked over to Victor, whose scowl focused on Taqi.

"Given this new information..." Victor observed Kirtus.

"As king—" Kirtus focused on Taqi. "—I find you guilty of treason to the crown and a traitor to your former leader. You are a threat to this court and to all immortals. Your planned actions against the Lycan and the witches are contemptible."

Taqi struggled more under Joaquín but got nowhere for his efforts. Joaquín clearly had amplified strength, even for an Immortal.

"I have spoken with the alpha of the Lycan and our current witch representative; they have both agreed to let me deal with you. On their behalf I damn you and those actions against them." Kirtus shifted to his vampire form; he now stood face-to-face with Taqi as Joaquín continued to hold him. "You could have been part of this, you could have stood with this court, but you decided you knew best, holding on to a past that never would return. You, Anashe, and..." He turned and pointed to Rahim. "Masko, if you please."

Rahim squealed under Masko's burning grip. "I'm sorry."

The stench of burnt flesh hit my nose, and I tried to push it out of my mind.

Rahim didn't try to fight Masko, so the fire or heated hands at least stopped.

"They threatened me." Rahim winced. "If I didn't help them, they were going to cause even more violence in my region, working through human agents. Our part of the world is turbulent enough without the two of them causing more trouble. Everything you told us is true; he and Anashe were plotting all of this since Chris had been Called. They were afraid of him and his ability. They spoke with Sahin and learned of Chris's potential. His gift terrified them. Once they saw him to be a true Seer, they were going to kill him as well, once Juliet had been ousted from the Council of Light."

I gulped. Did I have that large of a target on my back? No wonder Juliet always wanted to keep me close.

Rahim peered around the room, licking his lips. "I didn't want to oust Juliet, but I didn't have—"

"Silence!" Kirtus bellowed. My bones rattled, along with the windows of the conference room.

Rahim fell silent, tears starting to drop from his eyes. He didn't move as Masko tightened his grip.

"Your testimony is not needed nor requested," Kirtus commanded. "I'm the king. I'm the rightful heir. We are one council, one people; you are either part of this court or you are an enemy of our court." He turned to Joaquín. "Release him."

Everyone hurriedly backed away. Clearly everyone understood Kirtus had plans and didn't want to be in the way or get caught in the crossfire. I went from being scared as hell to angry enough to spit nails. What Taqi had done to all of us and now what Kirtus had planned to do when Taqi was free from Joaquín's grip filled me with a rage I didn't know I had in me. A quick burst of pain rushed through my face as I shifted and a growl rumbled out of my mouth. Juliet grabbed my arm and with a mental thrust forced calm into me. I grabbed for the chair to steady myself before I crumpled to the floor.

I really hated when she did that.

Joaquín's brows furrowed but he did as instructed. Taqi dropped to the floor and made a break for the doors, but he got at most five feet before Kirtus pounced. The attack took only a moment before Taqi's head no longer rested on his shoulders, the open wound now a fountain of blood and gore.

Kirtus growled and, as if adding insult to injury, plunged his hand into Taqi's chest and pulled out his heart.

Bile grew in my throat, and I coughed to choke it down.

I would never get used to the ripping of flesh and all the blood. I had so many images running around my head, and sadly the one that continued to stay at the front of my mind, thanks to Juliet's calming, was that we had an all-staff meeting next week and how were we going to get this all cleaned up in time.

Kirtus turned to Rahim. "You are not ready to serve on this council, but I can't take your life for wanting to help your people. Nothing I found in any of the files implicated you, yet you allowed this; you should have come to us, but you were weak and afraid. That is not leadership. But for weakness I can't take your life. You will be removed from the court, replaced by Mendi for the time being." Kirtus pointed at him. "Oh, and, Rahim, I will inform the Lycan and the witches of your part in all this as well."

"But I..." he sobbed.

"Remove him from my sight," Kirtus demanded. "And take that garbage out as well." He pointed to the remains of Taqi.

Masko bowed his head. "As you wish." He glanced over to Joaquín who pulled out a plastic bag from his pocket for what I assumed to be Taqi's head.

I shuddered at the image and turned away from the gore.

I gulped down hard at the possibility the dead might as easily have been us, if Taqi and Rahim hadn't been so foolish.

"Please ask Amanda to join us. I doubt she will argue." Kirtus's face returned to normal. His ridges smoothed down and his canines returned to their human form. He returned to where he had been sitting and pulled out a towel from what appeared to be his briefcase or satchel. "Juliet, please forgive me and this spectacle. I will ensure everything is cleaned up and returned to normal." He glared at Taqi's dead body before turning to the rest his council. "If any of you have a problem with how I plan to lead this council, now is the time to step down." He scrutinized those in attendance. Everyone stood in some kind of frozen state, but no one spoke. "Gabe, thank you again for your assistance. Please provide each member of this council with copies of your files for their review, in case any are under the impression my decision is unwarranted."

"The files and reports have already been sent to everyone via a secure server link including the Lycan alpha Ashley, William, and all the witch covens, including those in Rahim's territory." Gabe typed on the laptop, and the file on the screen vanished. "I'm sorry this had to happen." He addressed the group but focused on Juliet. "Once I followed up on the information you gave me and, with what I found on my own, I talked to Kirtus, to see how he wanted to handle this."

Juliet nodded. "I'm glad the information Marcel gave you helped."

"You didn't know?" I asked.

Juliet shook her head. "I trusted Marcel, and I trust Kirtus, so I had nothing to worry about."

Her faith was endless. Yes, I believed in Marcel and, God, I love Kirtus, but this level of trust and faith, I wasn't so sure I had. Maybe someday.

"Juliet," Sybil said from where she stood watching. "I'm sorry."

"We both are," Fernando added with a deep bow of his head. "I had no idea Taqi would do something like that. He played all of us."

"And yet our king had been the only one with no bias and acted accordingly." Ponleak rubbed his chin.

"If I had any questions or concerns about your leadership before, none remain." An bowed her head toward Kirtus.

"Unfortunately, we are not as far apart as we like to think we are." Victor faced Fernando and Sybil. "If we are being honest, I assumed you and Sybil set up Juliet."

Fernando rested his hands on the table. "I wish I could say I don't deserve that, but..."

"Taqi had one thing right." Luka called everyone's attention to him. "We don't deserve the positions we're in if we don't start to trust one another and work together. I may not agree with many things you all have done, and many of you do not care for how I lead, but I hope you appreciate I do respect you."

"Agreed." Taya motioned to the others. "Sadly, trust will come in time, and I would like to ask perhaps the king consult the full council before executing one of our members."

"That is a fair point," Kirtus conceded as he continued to wipe the blood from his hands. "Which is why over the next few weeks we will pull together a royal inquiry panel of judges who will, from this point forward, rule in such matters; they will be outside my control and report to this council. I may be the king, but I should not be judge, jury, and executioner. That is not how I want to rule." He dropped the now bloodied towel on the table in front of him.

"We will need to ensure safeguards are in place so you are protected," Victor added. "We don't want this inquiry panel of judges to have too much power. We've seen how that can be a pain in the ass."

"Agreed," Sybil said.

"I would like to assist the king in setting up this judge's panel." Gregor picked up a pen and made some notes.

"Yes, the offer is appreciated," Kirtus said. "One more thing I want to make clear to everyone here. I don't plan on making a habit out of such displays, but understand all of you, I will not walk away or cower from my responsibilities." He eyed me. "No matter what the cost."

That explained him being so distant over the last few weeks. The burden he carried was going to be a challenge for not only him but for us as a couple. I offered him as much mental assurance as my mind and body allowed, not sure what more to do at the moment. He had saved me from a death I hadn't known was coming. How do you thank someone for that?

"Now, unless there is anything more, I have cleaning to do as I have promised to return this space to its pristine condition." Kirtus sighed, with a glance to all the blood and gore.

"You don't have to—" Amanda glanced around. She had entered without my knowledge and seemed much more at ease.

"This is my mess, and I shall clean and take care of the body. I would never ask of anyone what I would be unwilling to do myself." For the first time tonight, Kirtus beamed and had a sincere expression on his face. "Now, please everyone go. Enjoy your night. And we will see you in July. This council is adjourned."

"Juliet," Gregor called out. "I'd like to speak with you, at your home, if you don't mind."

"You are always welcome. All of you are," Juliet added, peeking around the room. "My home is open to each of you. Please allow me to host you all this evening."

Despite what had happened, Juliet always managed a graciousness about her. Considering the horrid events of the evening, like the others of recent times, no merriment reached her tone, only honest hospitality.

I moved over to Kirtus who pulled off his blood-splattered jacket and tossed the garment onto the plastic-covered carpet. He rolled up his sleeves, getting ready to work. In the corner of the conference room lay a large duffel bag. The bag, I had no doubt, would be filled with everything he needed to do the job. "Do you want help?"

"That's kind of you, but no, I need to do this on my own." He took my hand. "I hated everything about tonight, about the last several weeks, and I don't want to drag you into this kind of situation again. When I found out they were going to try and kill you..." He squeezed my hand. "I wanted to tell you, to tell Juliet, but I had to deal with him, this matter now my responsibility. Sadly, I'm going to have to institute a royal guard. Matters of safety were something we spoke about tonight, but considering all this..." He glanced over at the mess on the floor. "I wanted them dead and to suffer." He pulled me close to him. "I'm sorry you had to be a part of this. I wanted to tell you."

"I wish you did..." I sighed. "But given what you had to do and the fact my life hung in the balance, I understand you having to keep quiet. All this"—I waved my hand—"will get better as you pull in more resources. Add this panel of judges and, I guess, the guards, it will become easier."

"I hope so. But tonight I couldn't risk Taqi finding out what I had planned. I had to make his meeting seem like he had gotten away with his plan. Fernando and Sybil unknowingly helped with that, as did Taya and Luka." He frowned and lowered his voice. "I hope I made my point clear to everyone tonight; I will not tolerate backstabbing."

I peeked over my shoulder as everyone exited the space, leaving the mess as instructed, but I did note the chairs and tables had been moved out of the way and the screen returned to the ceiling. "I don't see how you will be able to avoid it."

He frowned. "I hope having this royal inquiry panel of judges will help. If not, I'll have to do this again, and that is something I'm not interested in doing, but I will if I need to." He closed his eyes and shook his head.

"Well, for what my words are worth, you scared the pee out of me. So I would say mission accomplished." I was still sad and upset at what had happened, but I understood why he had done it. I didn't like it; I doubted anyone did. "You sure you don't want help?"

"No. My kingdom, my mess, my cleanup." He moved over to his duffel bag. "Hey, maybe tomorrow we can meet up. Take a break from all this." He gestured with his hands.

I walked over, leaned in, and gave him a kiss on the cheek. "I'd like that."

Chapter Thirty

The construction site continued to be a dusty mess, even after being cleaned for the night. So much work had transpired that nothing about the space appeared as it once had. At least Victor's company had made solid progress on the building, given how fast they were moving. Maybe the new club and council chamber would be ready in a year. At least when I cheated—I shouldn't have—and used my foresight, from what I figured out the space would be opened. Of course, I fully understood the one main truth about my gift; life affected these visions, so things may change.

"What do you think?" Kirtus outstretched his arms, and despite dust in the air, I made out his sandalwood aroma. The scent already permeated the building. And I would be lying if I didn't take great comfort in that smell.

"Wow, this place is a mess." I beamed in his direction.

"Well, yeah, but they're moving along, don't you think?"

I took his hand, enjoying the warmth and the contact.

We walked around the main floor. Not much to see, but I found my way over to one of the construction tables and thumbed through the blueprints.

"You can read these?"

"Blueprints, sure, why? Can't you?" I pointed to where the stage had once been. "There's going to be a private lobby back there, where the elevators are, right?"

"Yep. To the right of the new stage with its own private entrance, green rooms, and storage area." Kirtus glanced over my shoulder. His words were a soft tickle on my neck and I inhaled taking in as much of his sandalwood scent as possible. "The elevators will lead to the parking garage. You'll need a fob to access the more private places. There will be a security desk as well, with one of the new royal guards."

I tapped the blueprints. "So, we're hiding everything in plain sight?"

He laughed. "Pretty much. People who are supposed to know will. Everyone else won't care as long as the music's good and the drinks flow."

"What about the official permits?" I was genuinely curious; would the building be all one big black-ops project, or was this club and meeting space all on the up and up?

He grinned down at me. "Your good boy light is shining." He chuckled. "Everything is legit. The subbasements are shown as storage with a wine cellar and all that. There will be a few offices down there, but that can be explained away as club management space. What's above the club is office space and meeting rooms. There is nothing dodgy...well, not too much."

I closed the floor plans and browsed around the space. "Hard to believe this will be a club again."

"And a research facility, storage and archive area, Mystical Inquiry Panel of Judges Court, royal guard office, and the Immortal royal court. All right here in the heart of San Jose." He tapped his finger on the table. "I think I told you we'll have backups of all the data kept here, in Utah out with Gabe, and another location in Europe. I don't want to lose any of our history." He leaned against the table. "I wonder if this is what building the original court in Egypt had been like?" He studied me. "Do you think Marcel would have known?"

I stuffed my hands deep in my pockets. "If he did, he never said anything to me, but I don't think so. He wasn't that old."

Kirtus glanced around the open two-story tall space. "The club here is going to be impressive." He pulled me over to him and kissed me. "I have you to thank for this."

"Not just me," I reminded Kirtus.

"No, but your visions helped get us here." Our eyes met. "I don't want to fuck this up."

"You won't." I couldn't guarantee that; no one could. He would do his best, and that was all anyone can ask. Yes, he was going to have a lot of support and a lot of help. Surely some of the help would be bad, but I believed most of the help would be good. "Come on, let's get things set up for the reception."

*

Everyone walked around the big empty, as I referred to the space. A table had been laid out with bottles of wine and bottles of red. Next to those tables were one of the five food stations. On easels were artistic renditions on printed foam board, all showing what the building would look like in the future. Tonight there was nothing fancy planned, a simple reception for the council and other guests to see the space. This party was also the first event where the new royal guard would be trained for events of this nature. Several larger coven leaders had been invited as well as William. All the royal court were present with their Keepers and their Called, if they chose to bring them. I took time to meet the replacements for Taqi, Anashe, and Rahim.

Jawaria, Taqi's replacement, seemed nice enough. I liked her a lot more than I had liked Taqi, which I thought to be a good thing. We talked about my abilities, for which she sounded genuinely interested. Arno, the gentleman that took over the seat left open by Anashe, seemed quiet, trying to figure out all the players; he struck me as more of an introvert, another good thing. Mendi, Rahim's former senior lieutenant, impressed me. A no-nonsense man, which made me wonder how Rahim had ever gotten into power. He did mention Rahim, who appeared much happier now that he wasn't on the council and enjoyed life in Tel Aviv. Good for him, I guess. For me, the new members boiled down to how well they would work with the council, but from what I observed they all appeared fine, and I didn't get any negative feelings off any of them, nor did I see anything bad when I examined them for Kirtus.

"Enjoying the evening?" Juliet handed me a glass of red.

"I suppose." I took the offered glass. "It's certainly better than the last meeting."

"Cheers to that." Juliet and I clinked our glasses.

Juliet tasted her red. "I'm pleased to see the newly appointed judges panel are all here."

"I don't think they had a choice." I sipped my drink. "They might be a mix of witches and Immortals, but Kirtus impressed on them that despite them being autonomous, he ruled and expected them at all royal events."

"His plan to include three witches—genius," Juliet added and put her glass down. "Their participation will provide a bit of balance, especially with the six Immortal judges."

"True. Has anyone heard from the werewolves?" I scanned the room. "I don't see...Ashley or...um...Mark."

"Gregor and William were able to track and find them, again thanks to Marcel. They were invited, but..." She slipped her handbag from one hand to the other.

"Kirtus has met, at least twice, with Ashley privately since the last council meeting, but I don't know what about."

"Trying to keep the peace," Juliet suggested. "Especially after what Taqi, Anashe, and Rahim tried."

"And what are you two plotting?" Victor asked with the smoothness of a politician as he joined Juliet and me.

"We're talking about how Taqi tried to screw everyone over, and our missing guests Ashley and Mark." I had no desire to hide anything from him. He understood more than I did anyway.

"Ah, the moon children." He glanced around the space. "Perhaps this space isn't dirty enough for them." He chuckled.

"Are you pleased with how the building is progressing?" Juliet politely changed the topic.

"Yes, very much so." Victor scanned around, raising his lips in a smile. "I'm still not 100 percent pleased with how our leader coerced all this from me, but I respect the balls it took for him to wrangle the building out of my hands and I agree with his vision..."

"Plus, you'll make a nice percentage from the construction cost." Juliet raised her eyebrows at him.

"Maybe." Victor flashed us a warm expression. "Did I tell you I'm in the market for a Keeper? I'm tired of this lone wolf business. I need the help, especially with all the changes Kirtus is implementing."

"Well, good—"

"May I have your attention please?" Kirtus clinked his wine glass. "I would..." He waited for everyone to quiet down. "I would like to thank you all for coming tonight. There is still much to discuss, but over the last two months a lot of progress has been made toward building our shared future. We have a solid foundation underway, and I'm excited to see what we are able to build."

Applause erupted from the gathered group.

"I want to thank Patricia and Deborah Carson for all their support and work." He skimmed the crowd, finding both women dressed much like the rest of us in casual clothes. "Without the two of you, I have no idea where we would be today." He offered them a slight bow of his head. "I'm so happy your coven and all the coven leaders are here tonight, and those unable to attend have agreed to share your knowledge and to not only hold an advisory seat and ambassadorial post at our council table, but to have nominated three amazing witches to be judges on our court of inquiry."

More polite applause from the group bounced around the room.

"Where is William?" Kirtus craned his neck to see around the group. "Ah, there he is." He pointed. "Thank you for agreeing to serve as the advisor and the ambassador for the covens as a whole—"

"I didn't have much of a choice," William stated, but his tone and body were relaxed.

There were a few chuckles from the crowd including Patty and Deb.

"Yes, well, the Carson women can be persuasive, but I am so honored you agreed." Kirtus beamed at him. "Your wisdom and your guidance is greatly needed and appreciated; plus, it doesn't hurt you are a retired lawyer and we can all use that expertise."

There were several more laughs from around the room.

Kirtus shined as he walked over to one of the images on the foam board. "This new home will welcome both our communities; we have a lot in common and we have much to figure out about true magic—"

"All three communities were welcome here," a woman's voice called out from the front entry of the building. She stood flanked by two members of the royal guard. They were decked out in suits and appeared more like Secret Service members or maybe men in black.

"Ashley." My mouth hung open before I remembered to close it again.

"She came after all." Juliet's reaction suggested she wasn't surprised, and her tone came across more relaxed.

Kirtus stepped toward her. "I didn't think you would be attending tonight." He waved off the guards next to her.

"If I'm honest, I wasn't sure I would, but given your gesture's in good faith, I didn't see the harm." She scanned the room. "Plus, it's good for me to meet all the players affecting our lives."

"You and your people are welcome," Kirtus added.

My shoulders relaxed at the exchange, and I was happy to see her and Kirtus making this effort.

"About that... Your Majesty?" She questioned. "We'll agree to keep all our shared secrets and to not engage in the affairs of either the Immortals or the witches, but we don't want any more involvement. Also, as a gesture of good faith, I would like to offer two members of my growing pack to serve on the royal guard, if you would like."

Several guests scrutinized the group. Everyone watched in polite silence, and I had to wonder if this interchange had been scripted on the part of Kirtus and Ashley. The topic seemed a bit odd for them to have here, in front of everyone, but at the same time Kirtus did want as much transparency as possible. Another item to ask him about later in private.

"That is kind of you and I accept your offer. Thank you." He offered a slight bow of his head. "Your involvement or lack thereof is up to you, but this court's offer stands."

She walked closer to Kirtus. "Thank you, and for my part, I will serve as something akin to a local consulate for you all. If something happens or if one of my pack gets out of line, you can address your concerns with me."

There were several nods from the witches and Immortals present.

"Depending on what will come from this panel of judges," she continued, finding members of the Mystical Inquiry Panel of Judges, "their ability will dictate our level of trust and future participation." She spoke directly at him. "As you can imagine given recent events trust will take time."

"Understandable."

"In the meantime, I will ensure Gregor and William have my information."

"Thank you." Kirtus offered a polite nod. "Would you like a glass of wine?"

"I thought you would never ask." She scanned the room and the attendees, possibly assessing the level of sincerity or threat.

Kirtus walked to the table nearest him and brought her a glass. "Welcome, Ashley." He raised a glass to her, encouraging everyone else to do the same. We all took a drink. "I'm sure you can work out whatever other concerns you have with William, but you won't be dealing with only Gregor, I'm afraid."

"So, I'll work with you?"

"You are always welcome to contact me, but you'll be dealing with the Light and the Dark representatives of North America. I believe you've met Victor." He pointed our way.

Her eyes narrowed on him "Yes, indeed." Her expression faltered for only a moment, but she speedily regained her polished presentation.

Victor raised his glass to her.

Well, that's going to be one interesting partnership, the three of them working together. I'm sure there won't be a single issue. I tried not to laugh.

"I'm looking forward to working with both of you." Gregor's voice was loud enough for the room to hear.

"Excellent." Kirtus offered a polite bow of his head.

My palms started to sweat, and my hands clamped into fists. I found I wasn't enjoying surprises so much anymore.

"Now please everyone enjoy the bar and the food, and please get to know one another." Kirtus wrapped up his remarks. "This is a place and time to build bridges...so start building."

After some final applause, he made his way over to Juliet, Victor, and me. "Juliet, I wish you would reconsider."

She exhaled, her shoulders releasing with her breath. "Maybe one day, but not today. Gregor is a good man—"

"Hardly." Victor sniffed at his drink showing a small frown, but still drinking it.

Juliet pursed her lips at Victor but said nothing.

"What I mean to say is he isn't you. No one is." Victor raised his glass. "Working with Gregor isn't the same."

"I agree." Kirtus clicked his glace with Victor's. "I can't force you, but I do wish you would reconsider." He sipped his red.

"What?" Surprised again, twice in one night. "You could have your spot on the council back?" Yep, I definitely wasn't enjoying being surprised.

"Once all that business with Taqi finished, Gregor willingly offered to step down, but after thinking events over, I have served the Light for more years than I care to admit and I want to focus on other things." Juliet said.

"Well, you'll be missed." Victor extended his hands out and rested them on Juliet's hand.

"I'm not going away, I'm still going to be here, but I'm going to be working with Gabe and helping to research true magic. I think there is a lot to learn. Plus, working with Deb, Patty, and William over these last several months, I found I enjoyed the time spent and their friendship. There is something to solving these larger mysteries."

"Well, your expertise is going to be greatly appreciated. Gabe is excited and even Ashley is curious to work with you and learn more about the Lycan race," Kirtus added.

"As long as you're happy," I said to her. I sensed her sincerity. She really was at peace with her choice.

"Now if you don't mind, I would like to borrow my boyfriend and show him off. There are a lot of people for him to meet." Kirtus leaned in. "Especially if your king is ever going to need for you to check in on them," he whispered in my ear, then kissed my cheek.

"You're enjoying this," I said in not such a quiet tone.

He laughed and dragged me off.

Chapter Thirty-One

A solid knock came from the outside my office door. "Yes," I called out.

The door opened, and the sweet smell of strawberries greeted me, "Don't *yes* me. I'm not your servant."

"Aren't you though?" I dragged out the word "though" to tease without looking up from the monitor. I would pay for my remark later, but our banter was all in jest.

"Hey! I work for the king, not some low-life flunky like you." Cindy hugged me around the shoulders. "Thank you." She kissed my cheek.

Every part of me tingled; I couldn't be happier at this moment, well, this moment without Kirtus. "I'm glad you agreed and that events worked out." I stopped and held her arms, which were draped over my shoulders.

Once things had settled down with the council and everyone had found a happy medium in working with Kirtus, he was able to focus on finding a much-needed Keeper. I didn't think he would honestly remember my suggestion of Cindy, but he did, and after asking me about it for months, I promised him offering her the post would be okay. However, I had two rules: first, the choice had to be hers, and second, she would have to agree without being influenced by anyone, including me. He promised, and now, not only did he have an amazing Keeper, but I had my best friend.

Juliet had continued her gracious offer to work with the crown and allowed both Kirtus and Cindy to work out of our offices at the foundation. Kirtus insisted on paying for and renting the space he and Cindy used. He told Juliet he would need to rent an office anyway since he didn't think running the Immortal community, as well as his business, from his home office was appropriate.

She agreed.

As for me, I personally liked the separation from office and home. How he ran his consulting business from home would have driven me nuts.

Cindy pulled away. "Kirtus asked me to triple-check you were still planning on dinner with him tonight."

I laughed.

"I'm going to assume that means yes."

"Who is this Kirtus you speak of?"

Cindy pursed her lips. "Oh, you are too funny."

"I try."

"And you fail."

"Ouch."

Her turn. She laughed.

I swiveled in my office chair and met her gaze. "How has your mentorship with Amanda been?"

"Good. She's funny as hell and she's turning into a great friend." Cindy leaned against my desk. "And Margo and Dan are nice."

"Good." Happy, seeing her so happy made my life so much brighter. "I'm glad Victor agreed to have his new Keepers work with the two of you."

"I don't think he had much of a choice." Cindy checked her nails.

"Seriously."

"Kirtus might have suggested the training."

I chuckled. "Well, considering Victor is the only Immortal with two Keepers, I can see why Kirtus put his foot down."

"From what I can see, he treats them both well."

I remembered Daniel and how much he had enjoyed working for Victor. Victor may have done many things, but treating people poorly wasn't one of them.

"How goes your research for Juliet? Are you liking the archive projects and all that other magic, Lycan, witch, stuff?"

"Honestly the assignment isn't too bad. I prefer the foundation work more, and Juliet knows it, so luckily she only pulls me in when she really needs something." I closed out the files on my computer, knowing I wasn't going to get any more work done with Cindy here. I didn't mind. "What I have enjoyed is getting to work with and learn more about William and the Ohlone Nation. Before the Spanish arrived, they were all over the San Francisco Bay, Monterey Bay, and the Salinas Valley area." I paused. "He introduced me to several of them at a meeting last week; they were some great folks. A couple weren't impressed with me, but that didn't matter; I enjoyed meeting them and hanging out."

"Seriously? I'm assuming you went as a representative from the foundation and not from the king."

"Yep." I tugged down my sleeves. "I got to meet some of the Mohawk ironworkers who work on some of the skyscrapers all over the Bay Area and the country. Those guys are crazy brave. I'm Immortal, and you wouldn't catch me doing any of the stuff they do."

"Chicken."

"Have you seen some of the images of them on these building? No thanks." My phone buzzed, and I glanced at the caller ID. "Ugh...the county. I have to take this."

Cindy waved. "Have fun at dinner tonight." She made her way to my office door.

"Thanks." I waved and picked up the phone. "Hello, this is Chris."

*

I walked through the double glass doors and stepped into the club. A lot had changed since the first council reception held here. The space still wasn't fully completed. A lot of the interior work needed to be done, but making out what the space would eventually be was easy especially with some of the larger finish pieces installed. No furniture or anything like that had been installed at this point, and the heavy scent of dust and sweat hung in the air.

Still, I could picture it. As with the original club there would be a bar in the center of the room with seating around the edges, and there would be the private VIP spaces for guests to watch the stage when there were live performances, accessible by the stairs now on the right and the left of the entry.

"Are you going to have a crow's nest like Sahin?" I peeked up to where the perch used to be.

"Yup." Kirtus pointed to where Sahin's private office had once lorded down on the dance floor. "I'll use that space to entertain guests, but there'll be a staircase in the back leading to the third floor and above so we won't have to use the elevators or the stairs to the VIP lounge upstairs."

"A way to bypass the rabble."

"Hey now." Kirtus shook his head. "This is a safe location for everyone to come to enjoy." His chest puffed up with pride. "We're going to have witches, Lycan, humans, and Immortals here, but that doesn't mean I'm not going to need my private moments." He squeezed my hand. "Do you want to see the rest of the building? How about the subbasements? They are creepy as hell right now, but they are going to be huge, bigger than I imagined, but worth the cost and the outfitting."

"I'll pass."

"Okay, well, you need to see the meeting space and the conference rooms. I think they finished the painting."

Kirtus bounced around, excited to show off his building and new offices. This location would be a special place with a lot of functionality, so I was happy for him. He had accomplished a lot, and my own chest swelled with pride for him.

We made our way to the private lobby with the elevators that would take us to the upper levels by passing the second and third floors. He pulled out his fob from the pocket of his perfectly fitted gray slacks and pushed the button.

"We're not going to break down in that thing, are we?" I asked as the doors opened.

"We better not or Victor's going to have a lot to answer for, especially for what this is all costing."

The elevator's floor, ceiling and walls were covered with protective cardboard so nothing got messed up, so I wasn't sure what they were going to look like when finished, but I would assume they would be nicely appointed. With a ding, the doors opened and we stepped out onto the fourth floor, which would have the conference rooms and council chamber and the courtroom. Kirtus led me down the hall and opened the double doors; the chamber was massive, especially with the high ceilings. Everything in here was about finished. A whiff of drying pant assaulted my nose. The huge picture windows that would have a view of the patio below were covered with plastic so I couldn't see out, but the painting was nice—neutral, but nice—and the room had a tray ceiling adding to the height.

There were no stone sculptures or wall-mounted torches. No engraved stone walls either. Again, my imagination had skewed the reality.

"Do you like it?" Kirtus let go of my hand. "I wanted to keep the space functional and not overly formal. The AV system hasn't been installed yet, but there will be all the latest and greatest tech." His grin and wide eyes reminded me of a boy showing off his favorite toy. "Cindy picked out these versatile conference room tables that can be moved out of the way and set up in any configuration." He laughed. "She's amazing."

"That she is." I walked around.

"The space isn't what you were expecting, is it?" He frowned.

I laughed.

"I chose against a throne and marble columns, but the royal court will look more like a judge's chamber or a city council chamber, if that is more your style."

"Everything here is beautiful and well thought out," I assured him and rubbed my nose, trying to get the wet paint smell out. "This space reminds me of the conference room at the foundation."

"It should. I kind of barrowed the overall feel from there." He dusted off his light green sweater, then adjusted it over his gray dress slacks, again a picture of perfection.

"I like the chamber. The openness of the space is functional and will be a good neutral location for everyone, and considering you're not an over-the-top kind of person, I can see a lot of you here."

He beamed at me, the single dimple in his left cheek popping for me to enjoy. "Come on." He took my hand, and we rushed out of the chamber, passed the bathrooms, and made our way to the elevator. Another quick ride and we were on the top floor. The doors opened. This space wasn't as finished as the chamber.

More dust and sweat and less paint hit my nose.

He pulled me along, pointing out some of the offices. There would be space for the head of the royal guard, and other support staff, as well as office space for the Lycan consulate and visiting members of the witches' covens. There were going to be a lot of open and empty offices for now. He came to a stop in front of a closed door.

"What's this?"

Kirtus only continued to grin and opened the door. We were greeted by a small reception area and a door off to the right. "This is the office for the royal Seer." He stepped aside, granting me access.

"What?"

"Well, I figured you should have a space here." He pointed. "This area will be for Cindy or Amanda or for when you get your own Keeper someday." He walked over to the door to the right and opened it.

I strolled over and peeked inside. "A closet?"

Kirtus frowned. "No." He flipped on the lights. The walls were painted like stone, and in each of the corners were columns extending from floor to ceiling. "Fire code won't allow torches..."

I laughed.

"You kind of have this image in your mind about all this, so I designed this space for your office."

The space appeared so open, and hidden lights in the columns gave the sense of daylight. On the ceiling much to my amusement a painted sky.

Kirtus dimmed the lights, and points of light appeared in the ceiling like stars.

"Cool."

"I figured when you do your thing you needed a nice quiet space, one you felt safe in and that had the quiet you require."

"I love it."

"When you're not doing your Seer thing, you can use the office space out there for your work, or you can play video games."

"Well, I appreciate the offer, but do I really need a dedicated space?"

"My building, my offices, my call," Kirtus reminded me. "Plus, my office is next door. I like having you close."

"Ah...that's sweet."

He smiled. He walked over and took my hands. "You ready to eat?" He kissed my hands. "I have a surprise downstairs for us."

"Another surprise, hmm." I pulled him close to me, kissing him. "You realize how much I *love* your surprises."

He winked at me.

We made our way down to the VIP patio. The outdoor space impressed me with how nice everything turned out. Everything was put together, soft lights, black patio furniture with bright blue cushions, and soft music played from an unknown location. Around the edges were planters filled with hedges, trees, and flowers blocking out most of the noises of the city below. Oddly, an intentional cut out of plants showcased the building that had seemed to always be in the shadow of Victor's glass and steel tower.

I had learned from Amanda that the building was the old Bank of Italy building. I came to realize how it could be seen from various parts of the city, even from William's house in the East Hills. The structure was always there, no matter what grew up around it. The building had a

Mediterranean Revival feel to it. But what always struck me was its uniqueness and the oddly scaled cupola on top, that didn't altogether fit the style or size of the skyscraper.

"What's the deal with the cutout?" I pointed to the plants and the building just beyond.

Kirtus glanced to where I indicated. "Oh," He smirked. "That's where I got my first job in finance. If it wasn't for working there, who knows where I would be today. One of the many choices that led me to you."

My cheeks flushed with warmth.

"You know, when it was built it was the tallest building between San Francisco and Los Angeles." His eyes sparkled in the light as he spoke. "Watching them build it was incredible."

"Huh.'"

"Anyway, I thought it was only fitting to highlight the skyscraper, especially from here."

It took a moment, but when I glanced back at the tower I could see that it represented Kirtus; the building was unique, maybe not the shiniest and often overshadowed, by the likes of Victor's building, but still the skyscraper was sturdy and had its own grace and power, not to be taken for granted.

Exactly like Kirtus.

I continued examining the courtyard. In the middle of the patio a table had been set for the two of us. The entire space was filled with flowers and candles. Several bottles were on the table and glasses but nothing else. Well, nothing else, but his sandalwood scent that I loved so much.

"This looks beautiful."

"I had the builders stop work everywhere else so this spot would be ready for tonight. The construction supervisor wasn't happy, but since it's my building and I'm paying the bills, I didn't care about his schedule."

"You did this all for tonight."

"Why wouldn't I? You're worth all of it." He pulled me over to the table. "We'll have to protect the plants, and they'll need to move all the furniture into storage so nothing gets jacked up, but for tonight this is the final product."

"You did an amazing job."

"None of this would have been possible without you." He let go of my hand. "Your faith in me and in all of this. In fact, if I hadn't met you or gotten to know you, where would I be? One thing is certain: I wouldn't be this happy." He got down on one knee and pulled out a small box from his suit jacket pocket. "Chris, I can't do this without you by my side and I wouldn't want to, so please will you do me the honor of marrying me?"

I couldn't believe I didn't see any of this coming, with all the practice and all the training with Deb, Patty, and William. But until this moment I had no idea he had planned this; he never talked about marriage or even moving in.

My heart beat a mile a minute, and my cheeks ached from the biggest, dumbest expression I must have had on my face. Any air in my lungs vanished. Hell, I couldn't even be sure air existed around us. I couldn't even smell his scent of sandalwood, which I had no doubt lingered all around us, but hell if I noticed it. About the only thing I sensed for sure was my mental wall and the sudden swarm of butterflies in my stomach.

"So will you?" he asked again.

I thought I had answered, but he still remained on one knee, waiting for me with his adorable dimple in his left cheek and his perfect green and gray eyes, the eyes I had fallen in love with. "Yes!"

He pulled out the ring from the box and slipped it on my finger. He got up and kissed me. I don't remember the rest of the night, because nothing could outdo this moment. We had a future out there waiting for us, and we would face whatever came next together—Kirtus, Juliet, Amanda, Cindy, and even Victor and William, all of them. But right now, tonight, right in this moment, only Kirtus and I, nothing else mattered. Right here I found my home, I found my family, and I found my love all in this valley of heart's delight.

Acknowledgements

As with all my other novels, this book would not be possible without the support of my amazing publisher, editor, and incredible beta readers. And most importantly none of this would be possible without those of you who pick up the book and read it.

About the Author

M.D. Neu is an award-winning inclusive queer fiction writer with a love for writing and travel. Living in the heart of Silicon Valley (San Jose, California) and growing up around technology, he's always been fascinated with what could be. Specifically drawn to science fiction and paranormal television and novels, M.D. Neu was inspired by the great Gene Roddenberry, George Lucas, Stephen King, Alice Walker, Alfred Hitchcock, Harvey Fierstein, Anne Rice, and Kim Stanley Robinson. An odd combination, but one that has influenced his writing.

Growing up in an accepting family as a gay man, he always wondered why there were never stories reflecting who he was. Constantly surrounded by characters that only reflected heterosexual society, M.D. Neu decided he wanted to change that. So, he took to writing, wanting to tell good stories that reflected our diverse world.

When M.D. Neu isn't writing, he works for a nonprofit and travels with his biggest supporter and his harshest critic, Eric, his husband of twenty plus years.

Email
info@mdneu.com

Website
www.mdneu.com

Twitter
@Writer_MDNeu

Facebook
www.facebook.com/mdneuauthor

Instagram
www.instagram.com/authormdneu

YouTube
www.youtube.com/channel/UCfGxwoRBSgsTiyYkA_UGhCw

RSS
www./feeds.feedburner.com/Blog-MDNeu

Other books by this author

The Calling Series
The Calling

A New World Series
Contact

Conviction

Conspiracy (Coming Soon)

T.A.D.

The Reunion

A Dragon for Christmas

Also Available from NineStar Press

Connect with NineStar Press

Website: NineStarPress.com

Facebook: NineStarPress

Facebook Reader Group: NineStarNiche

Twitter: @ninestarpress

Tumblr: NineStarPress

www.ingramcontent.com/pod-product-compliance
Lightning Source LLC
Chambersburg PA
CBHW022033120726
47899CB00001BB/234